Why did he have to run into *her?*

He'd known Juliana was on TV, but he'd never watched her show. What shook him to the core was that he gave a damn. He should be able to meet her on the street anytime and not feel a muscle twitch.

Who was he kidding? After eleven years, that meeting had done a number on him. He was a wreck.

Why?

Their love hadn't been a normal love. What he'd felt for her had been an addiction. He saw her and fell in love, even before they so much as exchanged a word. After their first date he'd decided he couldn't live without her. Both his mind and his libido had been a mess.

Raw heat.

Those were the only words that could describe what they had shared. And even while their relationship had slowly crumbled around them, that heat had continued to simmer.

"Mary Lynn Baxter is an innovative and daring writer who has helped define the romance market."

—Affaire de Coeur

MARY LYNN BAXTER

LONE STAR
Heat

MIRA BOOKS

MIRA

ISBN 1-55166-289-2

LONE STAR HEAT

Copyright © 1997 by Mary Lynn Baxter.

All rights reserved. Except for use in any review, the reproduction or
utilization of this work in whole or in part in any form by any electronic,
mechanical or other means, now known or hereafter invented, including
xerography, photocopying and recording, or in any information storage or
retrieval system, is forbidden without the written permission of the publisher,
MIRA Books, 225 Duncan Mill Road, Don Mills, Ontario, Canada M3B 3K9.

All characters in this book have no existence outside the imagination of the
author and have no relation whatsoever to anyone bearing the same name
or names. They are not even distantly inspired by any individual known or
unknown to the author, and all incidents are pure invention.

MIRA and the star colophon are trademarks of MIRA Books.

Printed in U.S.A.

A special thanks to Texas Ranger
Sergeant Donald Morris whose expertise
was invaluable in writing this book.

Prologue

He hated his curly red hair and freckles.

Worse, he hated his turdy classmates who made fun of them. That was the main reason he had played hooky from school on this particular day. However, it didn't take much of an excuse for him to skip classes. School was a drag, especially when he knew more than his teachers.

A sigh filtered through him as he slapped at a mosquito buzzing around his head. If that critter thought it was going to suck on his blood, it had another thought coming. He waited until it lit on his arm before squashing it. A bright red spot stained his skin.

Ugh!

Even with the pesky mosquitoes, this outing was better than sitting in class or duking it out with fatso Fred, who ribbed him unmercifully. One more crack about the color of his hair and it was a sure bet he would've decked Fred, or tried to.

Another sure bet was that when he got home, his old man would have decked *him*. He'd probably get decked anyway for cutting out on his classes. Right now, he wasn't going to worry about that. He was exactly where he wanted to be and doing what he wanted to do. Besides girls, fishing was his favorite pastime. And he couldn't have asked for a better day to wet a line. The spring weather was perfect.

Walking off campus had been a piece of cake. The bicycle ride to Lake Houston had been more difficult. He figured his calves would smart in the morning, but the pain would be worth it.

Releasing another sigh of contentment, he munched on peanut butter and crackers, and smiled. Holed up in his private niche, nestled among the trees, he continued to lie on the grass and watch his cane pole, which he'd anchored in the dirt.

It remained motionless. Maybe the fish weren't going to bite today. That was all right, too. He looked up and watched as a jet plane skimmed the sky. He focused on it until it disappeared. His eyes fluttered shut. Hell, he'd just take a nap and think about Kelly.

He was a freshman in high school and, for the first time ever, had fallen in love. He'd taken her out twice, and the second time had been awesome. Not only had she let him kiss her, but he had touched her breasts, as well. He'd thought he was going to die on the spot. Her breasts were round and hot and fit his hand perfectly.

After hearing her moan, he'd gotten braver, moving his hand down between her thighs and rubbing there. But when he'd tried to meddle in her panties, she'd stopped him.

He'd been disappointed, but hopefully there would be a next time. Instead of the fish, he'd think about easing his finger...

It was then that he heard the roar of a boat's engine. His eyes popped open in time to see the boat smash into a tree stump clearly sticking out of the water.

The noise sounded like an explosion.

He jerked upright just as a kid, who looked to be about five years old, literally flew out of the back seat straight into the water.

"Holy shit!" he muttered, scrambling to reach inside his satchel for his binoculars.

With shaking hands, he focused on a man and watched as he dove into the water after the child.

One

She looked down into a bloody palm. Her long, red nails had done the damage. The physical pain didn't register. She ignored the wheezing sound coming from her throat. Her chronic asthma would have to take a back seat to her mental pain. It took precedence over everything.

She wasn't about to let him weasel out of marrying her. She *would* force him to keep his promise. And she was in the driver's seat. Or, to put it more strongly, she had the bastard by the short and curlies. If she remained strong, she would get her way.

Margie Bowers smiled outright, only to turn instantly sober. While the tide had definitely shifted in her favor, she still had another big hurdle to jump. She'd better not uncork the bottle of champagne yet.

The man she was dealing with in this risky game was not like any other man she'd ever known or slept with. Regardless, he couldn't be allowed to ride roughshod over her.

Rusk O'Brien, touted as the next governor of Texas, had suddenly switched from being her boss and lover into being her adversary, which upped the stakes considerably.

Even so, his growing fame didn't give him the right to treat her like she was trailer-park trash.

He had promised to divorce his wife and make her, Margie, the center of his life. At first she hadn't demanded that he marry her; she hadn't cared about a stupid piece of paper. Besides, she had figured that with her expertise in bed, marriage would follow.

Wrong.

He'd had no intention of making her the next Mrs. Rusk O'Brien, though he had masterfully dangled that carrot in front of her for the purpose of getting her to do things to his body that no one had ever done. Well, he wasn't about to have it all his way.

While she didn't love him, she sure as hell loved the glamour and the amenities associated with being his mistress. He had given her some awesome jewelry and fur jackets. But she craved more.

Margie cleared her throat, the bitter taste on her tongue threatening to make her sick. She wouldn't panic. She would get even. She had the means. This time her smile was genuine and lingering as her gaze fell on her purse sitting on the table. Inside was information that controlled Rusk's key to the governor's mansion, something he didn't know she had—his proverbial little black book.

Margie was so disappointed that so far she hadn't been able to taunt him in person with the evidence and see the actual look on his face when she told him she had it in her possession.

Thinking back on the incident, she still couldn't believe her blind luck. She and Rusk had had a luncheon date, supposedly to discuss campaign strategy.

When she had arrived at his office and he hadn't been there, she had plopped down behind his desk to wait. After the minutes stretched into an hour, her conscience hadn't twitched in the slightest when she decided to rifle through his desk. She'd opened one drawer after another, not searching for anything in particular.

After she spotted the book, her curiosity won out. She removed it and began turning the pages, disappointed at what she considered mumbo jumbo. Then it hit her what that mumbo jumbo meant. Her blood pressure rose, and her mouth turned cotton-dry, when she heard the doorknob turn.

Having already shut the drawer, she had one last option—her purse. It was open on the floor beside her. She dropped the book into it, stepped from behind the desk and eased the bag onto her shoulder.

Her lover had stared at her for a long moment, his blue eyes cold despite his camera-ready smile.

"What the hell were you doing behind my desk?" he had demanded, his tone sharp.

"My, my, you must've had a hard morning," she cooed, sidling up to his side and pressing her breasts insinuatingly against him. He didn't grab her as he usually did when she teased him with his favorite play toys. Instead he backed away as if burned.

She was too stunned to react.

"It's over," he said into the harsh silence.

Margie blinked. "What do you mean, over?"

"Just what I said. I don't intend to see you anymore. I've moved back into my wife's bedroom."

Margie's mouth gaped, then snapped shut.

"The campaign's reaching its peak, and I can't afford to have anything go wrong at this point. It's too risky. There's too much at stake."

When she would have interrupted, he plowed on. "Tamara suspects I'm screwing around, and she's threatening to make trouble."

"Why, you pompous asshole!" Margie's mouth twisted. "You can't toss me aside like a piece of garbage."

Rusk laughed, his eyes roving her body. "Whatever gave you the idea that you were anyone special? You aren't the first piece I've had on the side, and once this election's over and I'm in the governor's mansion, you won't be the last."

"We'll see about that!" Margie's eyes flashed fire.

"I don't think you're in any position to threaten me, my dear. And by the way, you're fired. It's unwise for you to remain on the campaign staff."

"We'll see about that, too," Margie countered, her fury threatening to cloud her judgment. She knew this man better than he knew himself. He wasn't a fighter; he was a yellow-bellied coward. Someone else had always fought his battles, mainly his parents.

The O'Brien name in Texas carried as much weight as the Kennedy name in Massachusetts.

"I know what your devious little mind's thinking," Rusk said. "And it won't work."

"You don't have a clue to what I'm thinking, you bastard."

"Regardless, my mind's made up. Nothing you can say or do will change it."

Margie's eyes held a steady glower. "We'll see—"

The door opened suddenly. Startled, they both swung around.

"What?" Rusk demanded, facing his aide, anger on his face and in his voice.

"Sorry to interrupt, sir, but the president's on line one."

Once the door closed behind the aide, Rusk leveled a pointed and contemptuous stare at Margie.

She knew she had no recourse but to leave. Rusk wasn't beyond having her tossed out by one of his flunkies. Her lips curled. "I'm going, but don't think you've seen or heard the last of me. Our relationship is far from over."

She had walked out and slammed the door behind her.

Now, several hours later, she was still seething with an inner rage that called for physical relief. But attacking Rusk was out of the question, though she would like nothing better than to claw his face in the same manner she clawed his back when he was deep inside her, pounding hard.

She would get him, but in her own way where he was the most vulnerable—emotionally. She certainly had the ammunition to mount that kind of attack. First, though, she had to think about her plan of action, which included hiding the "goods." When he found out what she had, he would stop at nothing to get it back.

Her gaze roamed the living room of her close friend's posh condo in West Houston. She had been bunking in temporarily with Juliana Reed, one of the city's most successful syndicated talk-show hosts. Juliana had come to her rescue when Margie's apartment had suffered flood damage during the last heavy rain and was being refurbished.

She had been staying there for a month and was soon to make an appearance on Juliana's show, highlighting the governor's race and its candidates.

Juliana had insisted that Margie, as a high-ranking staff member of the O'Brien campaign, would be the perfect one to represent him.

A downward curve suddenly altered Margie's thin lips. She wondered if Rusk remembered that upcoming TV show. Probably not, she told herself, her eyes scanning the premises for a hiding place.

She didn't like the thought of stashing the book in Juliana's condo, but what choice did she have? Eventually she planned to return it to Rusk, but only after he came to his senses concerning their relationship.

Her eyes spotted the perfect place; within seconds the task was done. Margie then crossed to the phone, lifted the receiver and dialed Rusk's private line. If he was in his office, she knew he would answer. She wasn't disappointed.

"It's me."

"Don't call here again."

Rusk's deep voice dripped with ice, and she could picture him clenching the capped teeth that had cost him thousands of dollars.

"Are you missing anything?" she asked in her usual cooing tone.

"Don't fuck with me. I'm no longer in the mood."

"You're always in the mood, honeypot. In bed we were sheer poetry."

"Not anymore, Margie. So I suggest you go find another life." This time Rusk's voice sounded thoroughly bored.

"I have your black book."

Dead silence.

Margie hadn't been sure what reaction her words would garner. She didn't have to wait long to find out. She heard him suck in his breath at the same time that he scratched around in the desk drawer.

"You little bitch, I'll—"

"Save it, Rusk. I'm on top now, both literally and figuratively."

"I want that God damn book back, you hear! Right now!"

"All in due time, sweetheart."

"Right now!"

Margie chuckled softly. "Perhaps we'll talk about it at *work* in the morning. You see, I have no intention of resigning or being replaced. Understood? I'll be at my desk just like always. Oh, and don't plan anything for tomorrow night. It belongs to me."

"You listen—"

"No, *you* listen. Just remember that the word is mightier than the sword. And I've got your words, baby, in writing."

Margie dropped the receiver back on its hook, ignoring the curses ringing in her ear.

"Bitch!"

She had slam-dunked him, and for the moment, there wasn't a damn thing he could do about it. Calm down, he told himself. He had to keep his head on straight or he was doomed.

He needed a drink. Bad. Crossing to the bar, he grabbed a glass and filled it with straight bourbon. Leaning back, he poured it down his throat. But the huge lump of fear lodged there congealed instead of dissolving.

Stalking back to his desk, he sat down. How the hell could he have been so careless? He usually kept the book locked in the safe that only he had the combination to. That morning, however, he'd been adding notes to it, and because he hadn't finished, he'd slipped it into one of the drawers.

Rusk pounded his fist on the desk, barely noticing the pain that shot through his arm to his shoulder. If anyone else saw the contents...

Sweat drenched his scalp underneath the plastered-down gray hair. He couldn't think about that or he would go off the deep end. Tamara had warned him that his screwing around was going to come back to bite him where it hurt. She'd been right. Margie Bowers had just taken a big chunk out of his ass.

What if she showed the book to her friend Juliana Reed?

His stomach turned upside down. He didn't know which he needed worse—another drink or a piss. Neither one would solve his problem, though. For that he needed advice.

He punched out a number on his private line and while it rang, he mopped the sweat from his brow with the back of his hand. When his party finally answered, he didn't even identify himself, just explained what had happened.

"What do you want me to do about it?" The voice stung like a whiplash.

"I thought maybe you'd—"

"You thought wrong. It's your mess. You clean it up." The dial tone assaulted Rusk's ear.

Two

Juliana Reed had difficulty containing her excitement. She had been looking forward to hosting this particular show for a long time. Finally the day had arrived.

In a matter of hours, two women would sit on the posh TV set and each would offer reasons why her particular boss and candidate of choice should be the next governor of Texas.

Talk shows, Juliana's included, had started to gain new respect when they turned into an informal stage where both the political candidates and the audience became one. This bonding was further enhanced by viewers who phoned in.

While the method might irk journalists who were used to being first on the scene and poking a microphone in the candidate's face, it played much better with the average voter.

Under the auspices of the talk-show setting, those voters seemed to get a better feel for the candidates.

Harry Folsom and Rusk O'Brien were the two leading contenders for the coveted governor's office. To date, Rusk had the edge, much to Juliana's disgust.

She went cold all over at the thought of Rusk O'Brien, her *ex*-brother-in-law, occupying the mansion and directing her beloved state. But she had to keep her true feelings a secret and pretend she was neutral on the subject. That was not going to be easy, especially when she detested the man to the degree that she did.

She would love to walk onstage and expose him for what he was—a lowlife. The desire was so strong she had even played out the scenario in her head. Of course, nothing would come of that particular head game.

Still, she had hopes that a hint of the truth would leak out, and that she would be instrumental in a subtle way in bringing that about.

She had to tread carefully, however. Her loathing of Rusk must in no way compromise her integrity or the integrity of the show. What she hoped the hour would do was boost her ratings considerably and help her remain atop her profession, a feat that required every ounce of intelligence, energy and savvy she could muster.

"Hell, you worry too much," Benson Garner, the show's producer, had said time and again. "With your brain, you're a natural for this job, not to mention having the perfect face and figure for it."

"Flattery will get you anything."

"Damn it, that's not flattery, and you know it. Facts, ma'am, just facts."

"Being successful nowadays requires more than having great body parts."

"Okay, so forget your lovely face and figure. You're warm, open and dignified. Those are dynamite qualities that also come across great on camera."

While Juliana agreed that she came over well on-screen, she knew that wasn't enough. It wasn't her nature or her personality to settle for being the average, garden-variety talk-show host—hot one day and lukewarm the next.

She also refused to be one of the "gang." Her counterparts seemed to be content with grabbing the most sensational and off-the-wall topics and running with them. To make matters worse, they were content to parade guests before the audience who might or might not be remotely connected to the subject. With that came stupid questions and inane observations, which had the deadly potential of either boring or insulting the audience.

A microphone did *not* a talk show make.

She wanted "Juliana Live" to be a cut above even the "Oprah Winfrey Show," the one every host nationwide tried to emulate.

Benson agreed with her—a good thing, since he had a lot to do with how the show was perceived.

In Benson, she had one of the best producers, if not *the* best, in the business. When she'd first gone on the air, she hadn't been able to take any of the credit for her success. That had all gone to Benson. He had taken care of everything from finding and booking the guests to holding up cue cards prompting her with what questions to ask.

Now, for the most part, she was in charge. She selected the guests, researched the topic, chose the questions, sometimes even shocking Benson with her shrewdness and intuitiveness, despite his continued affirmation that she was a natural for the job.

While appearing before the camera seemed to be Juliana's calling, all right, it hadn't been easy. Her trek upward to this syndicated show had been long and steep.

She had stepped in more than her share of potholes, which had resulted in disappointments and heartaches. Her first encounter with the harsh world of television had been when she worked the weather on another channel and was fired suddenly and without cause.

She hadn't let that setback stop her. By then, she had become addicted to the glaring lights and the camera and was determined to look elsewhere. Her break had come a few months later, after her agent sent her to interview for a cosmetics infomercial. She'd been an instant success, which eventually led to her present position.

Juliana was far from content, though.

She wanted to be the best at what she did. Her reason was simple: her work was her life. She had nothing except that. She labeled herself first and foremost a career woman. While she was fine for now with her present status, she was driven by the desire to do better, to take her show national. She wanted "Juliana Live" to have the earmark of gritty news combined with the human side of life.

That wouldn't be an easy task, either. The competition was cutthroat and only the strong survived.

But *she* was strong, too, and she *would* survive. She'd been in the belly of the whale more times than she cared to admit and had managed to climb out. She never intended to get that low again, nor would she allow anyone to break through the barrier she had built around her soul. That solid construction was her guarantee that she would never be hurt again.

Hating herself for her maudlin thoughts, Juliana shook herself mentally. She refused to dwell on that sector of her life. She had chosen to put her tragic past exactly there—in the past.

Now, as she gazed about the set in anticipation of the upcoming show, she nodded her approval. Everything was in place, from the brightly cushioned and comfortable furniture to the vases of fresh flowers that not only added class to the backdrop but also made it smell heavenly.

She glanced at her watch. Patty Neuberg, the guest representing the Harry Folsom campaign, should be here any moment. So should Margie. Actually, she had expected her friend and houseguest long before now. Having once been in TV herself, Margie loved to hang around the set when she could spare the time.

After giving the room another cursory glance, Juliana walked into the hall at the same instant that Margie stepped out of Benson's office. Juliana noticed the perturbed look on Margie's face and felt a stab of uneasiness. Hopefully, today wasn't going to be one of Margie's "temperamental" days.

"Hey, I was just wondering if you were here," Juliana said, taking in the fact that her friend looked great, dressed in a short magenta skirt, blouse and jacket that not only enhanced her dark hair but her overendowed figure, as well.

Margie's sudden smile did little to remove the pinched look from her features, which was more apparent now that she stood in front of Juliana.

"What's going on? Did Benson tick you off?"

"No," Margie said, shifting her gaze.

"Couldn't prove that by the scowl on your face."

Margie pawed the air with a hand. "Oh, don't mind me." Then, switching the subject, she asked, "I'm not late or anything, am I?"

"No, you're early." Juliana motioned her toward the taping room. "It's just that I'm really anxious to get this show on the road." She grinned. "No pun intended."

Margie didn't respond, which again triggered that same sense of uneasiness inside Juliana. She held her tongue, however, until Margie had eased into one of the chairs.

"Do you by chance need a shoulder?"

"Excuse me?"

Juliana smiled. "Don't play innocent with me. Something or someone has you upset."

Margie sighed. "Is it that obvious?"

"Yes," Juliana said. "Usually it's a man who puts that look on a woman's face. So if it's not Benson…" She let her voice trail off, hoping Margie would rise to the bait.

Margie didn't, but she didn't voice a denial, either. Juliana's curiosity gained momentum. She knew her friend was seeing someone, at least, she suspected it. Margie was rarely home, and when she was, she wore a certain "satisfied, taken care of" look.

"Did you and your boss by chance have a tête-à-tête?" Juliana asked, deciding to jerk the line a little, especially since the show involved Rusk O'Brien.

Margie looked disconcerted. "What made you ask that?"

"Just a guess, really."

"Well, you guessed wrong. Everything's fine."

She's lying, Juliana thought. But if her friend didn't want to voice what was troubling her, then Juliana wouldn't push—unless her friend's mood threatened to put a damper on the show.

Although Margie shared her home, they didn't encroach on one another's personal lives, and Juliana aimed to keep it that way. She shuddered inwardly; bringing her own secrets to light was unthinkable. She surmised Margie felt the same way.

"So, then, are you ready for some nitty-gritty questions concerning Rusk?" Juliana asked with a forced lightness in her tone.

"As long as you play by the rules."

Juliana's eyebrows shot up. "Rules? There are no rules, and you know that."

"Right. Forget I said anything."

"You still want to do this, don't you? I mean, you're not having second thoughts?"

"Yes and no."

Juliana curbed her mounting frustration with difficulty. "Then for heaven's sake, show some enthusiasm. You're about to get the chance to sing Rusk O'Brien's praises for all of Houston to hear."

"You still hate him, don't you?"

Juliana didn't so much as flinch at the direct question. "My personal feelings don't and won't come into play here. You know that. This is about doing my job to the best of my ability."

"You're right, and I'm sorry. It's just that—" Margie broke off midsentence.

"Just what?" Juliana prompted.

"Nothing. It's just something I have to work out." A surge of color returned to Margie's cheeks. "It's no big deal. Actually, I'm looking forward to this. I miss the excitement of working in TV."

"Ah, so you do miss it?"

"More than you'll ever know."

Juliana gave her an incredulous look. "I had no idea you felt that way."

"It's something I'm just now admitting."

"So why did you desert TV for politics? Benson and I both were both upset when you left."

Margie shrugged. "Working as Benson's assistant behind the scenes suddenly stopped being fun."

Juliana had first met Margie right after she had gone to work for the station. Margie had been an old hand backstage, and she had made Juliana feel welcome from the get-go. Soon a friendship had developed. That was why Juliana hadn't hesitated to invite Margie to bunk in until her apartment was ready. So far, she hadn't been sorry.

"You could've done something else," Juliana remarked into the silence. "What I'm doing, for instance."

Margie scoffed. "No way. I don't have the looks or the class to get in front of the camera."

"That's ridiculous," Juliana snapped.

"No, it's not. It's facing reality. With that glorious red hair, those big brown eyes, not to mention that husky 'turn-on' voice—"

"And ghastly freckles splattered across my nose," Juliana cut in with a grimace.

"I think they make you more human."

Juliana rolled her eyes. "You're full of it. You and Benson both."

"Maybe," Margie said, smiling briefly. "Anyway, it was time for me to move on. My heart's always been in politics." Her chin rose a notch. "With Rusk a shoo-in for the governorship, my career change is finally going to pay off."

"We'll see. The election isn't over yet."

"Oh, yes, it is," Margie said with resounding confidence.

"I beg to differ with that."

At the sound of the unexpected voice, they both turned and watched as the other guest stepped across the threshold. Juliana moved to greet her, her hand outstretched.

Patty Neuberg was attractive enough, with a decent figure and short brown hair that hugged her head. Her voice, however, was the problem. She sounded nasal, as if she needed a steady stream of decongestant nosedrops.

"I have a feeling this is going to be one show to remember," Juliana said, her enthusiasm mounting again. "But let's leave the fireworks for the show," she added, peering at her watch.

"Fine by me," Margie replied, shaking Patty's hand.

Juliana's gaze swept from one to the other. "Then I

suggest you ladies take your seats, the show's about to begin.''

She stared at the clock on the set. Five more minutes was all they had left. Juliana had no complaints. In fact, she was giddy inside. The show had gone better than even she had anticipated. The audience had been as aggressive with their questions as she had been with hers.

Patty had just finished defending—or trying to defend—her candidate's known penchant for love of big government.

''Thank you, Ms. Neuberg,'' Juliana said, turning her attention back to Margie. ''Now, before we run out of time, I'd like to touch on the personal lives of both candidates.''

The audience clapped.

''Ms. Bowers, please tell us what makes your candidate human. We all want to know about the man behind the political facade.''

Juliana faced the audience for a second, smiled, then turned back to Margie. ''We're aware that all men, even the President, put their pants on one leg at a time.''

Laughter rippled through the audience, and for a second silenced Juliana, during which her adrenaline kicked in that much more. ''So what makes Rusk O'Brien different? What sets him apart, makes him more deserving of the governorship than Senator Folsom?''

Margie's eyes narrowed, and she smiled a cool, confident smile. ''For starters, he's—''

She got no further. Her voice constricted. Her eyes widened. Her features turned deathly pale.

''Ms. Bowers, what—'' Juliana began, only to have her own words come to a halt as Margie grabbed her throat and began to make a strange choking sound.

A murmur went through the audience, followed by a stunned silence. For a breathless moment, Juliana was as horrified as everyone else. Her limbs refused to move. Only after it dawned on her what was happening, that her friend was apparently having one of her debilitating attacks of asthma, did she move toward Margie.

She never made it.

Still holding on to her throat, and now making an inhuman noise, Margie toppled out of her chair onto the floor.

Pandemonium broke out.

Juliana heard gasps and muted screams from those around her. But she was oblivious to them. Her friend's pain was all she could think about. She dashed to her side.

"Margie! Margie!" Juliana whispered, kneeling and cradling her friend's head on her lap.

No response.

Margie's eyes fluttered, then closed.

Three

She despised waiting. Juliana must have glanced at her watch a hundred times already, which seemed to make time crawl that much slower. Why hadn't the doctor walked through those intimidating double doors and told them something? Margie had been in a cubbyhole in the emergency room for almost an hour and there had been nothing yet on her condition.

"You're going to wear a hole in that carpet if you don't stop pacing."

Juliana stopped and stared at Benson, who sat in a leather straight-back chair next to the window, the fingers of one hand drumming on the arm. "You're a fine one to be talking. Your hand is dancing a jig."

His fingers stilled instantly, and his mouth curved in a half smile. "Dammit, I'd give everything I had for a Camel."

Juliana frowned her distaste. "After all this time, you really still crave those nasty things?"

"I miss smoking every minute of every day of my life. In fact, right now I could eat a package of the damn things."

"You need help."

Benson chuckled, then turned sober and quiet, as if any kind of laughter was taboo.

Juliana didn't say anything else, either. She watched

Benson get up and stand in front of the window. He was a short man with a square jaw and an overabundance of wavy dark hair. Despite his lack of height, he didn't have that "little-man syndrome." On the contrary, with his keen intelligence and smile, he could be quite the charmer.

He was also a shrewd businessman who knew what he wanted and how to go about getting it. Those assets added to his charm. Too bad his private life wasn't as neatly packaged.

His wife of many years was institutionalized, with no chance of being released or recovering. She suffered from acute depression and had apparently had one too many shock treatments.

Benson seldom talked about her or their situation, and Juliana rarely asked, sensing the subject was too painful for him to discuss.

On rare occasions she had been tempted to encourage him to confide in her to a greater extent. But something always seemed to hold her back, even when she sensed he needed a listening ear. She suspected it was her penchant for guarding her own privacy.

She switched her gaze off Benson, but not before noticing the nervous tic that had begun in his jaw. The delay seemed to be playing havoc with both their psyches.

"The vultures are gathering," he said in the raspy voice that flagged him as an ex-smoker.

Juliana didn't pretend to misunderstand. He was referring to the media. "I can't believe they're still hanging around."

Benson snorted, turning from the window. "You know better than that, or at least you should, especially after you were just attacked yourself. Besides, the incident is news. The show is news. *You're* news."

"If that's the case, then it's a sad commentary on the human race," Juliana replied in a tight voice.

"You're learning. But in those guy's devious minds, they think *we've* sunk to their level. They're lapping this up like sharks at a bloody feeding frenzy."

"God forbid."

"My sentiments exactly, but what happened to Margie is just another tragedy to be exploited." Benson rubbed his chin. "Those folk are here to stay for the duration. If possible, they'll get up front and in your lovely face. Count on it."

Juliana didn't argue, because it was the truth. She had already been exposed to "those folks," as Benson had appropriately labeled them.

The instant after Margie had toppled onto the floor, the ghastly sounds continuing to erupt from her throat, the press had begun to load their guns and pounce.

Juliana had insisted on riding in the ambulance with her friend. Benson had followed in his car, leaving the other crew members behind. It was after she had climbed out of the ambulance that she'd been attacked. Microphones and cameras had been shoved in her face, and a barrage of questions had been fired at her like missiles.

"What do you think she was going to tell us about the Rusk O'Brien we never met?"

"Was she going to confirm the rumor that his success with women makes every other player look like a novice?"

"What do *you* think happened?"

"What's wrong with her?"

"Is she on drugs?"

"Could foul play be involved?"

That last question had robbed Juliana of her numbness and her cool. "That's absurd!" Her eyes had blazed.

"Why? It's happened before."

"Not on my show, it hasn't," she'd shot back.

"There's always a first time!"

Realizing she was playing into their hands—and fighting a losing battle, to boot—Juliana had shut her mouth and fought her way into the hospital. She'd sagged against the nearest wall, her heart hammering inside her chest. Thank God the emergency personnel had refused to let the cameras inside. That had been the only saving grace.

Now, as she stared at Benson once again, the reporters' menacing words played with her mind. "Something's terribly wrong, Benson. I just know it is. Margie...was so still, so..." Her voice faded into nothingness. "Of course, the paramedics wouldn't tell me a thing."

"Hey, don't go borrowing trouble."

"I'm not. But you know if it had been an asthma attack, we wouldn't still be waiting. It has to be something more serious."

"Adult asthma can be very serious," Benson said in a hollow tone. "Anyway, we'll know soon enough. In these damn emergency rooms, time moves like molasses running uphill."

Juliana felt a pinch of guilt for her own impatience and agitation. "I guess you're used to spending hours in these places, huh?"

"I've put in more than my share, that's for sure."

"I'm sorry, Benson," she responded, for lack of anything better to say. Her heart ached for him and his seemingly unchangeable situation.

"Me, too."

"With all the new medications, there's no hope?" she asked, brazeningly venturing into that heretofore forbidden territory.

His features turned gray. "Zilch. Her brain's been fried."

Juliana winced, refocusing her attention on her boss. At a young forty-eight, he was married, yet he wasn't married. How unfair, but how typical of life. He obviously didn't think divorce was the solution, and she had to admire him for that. Yet he had the markings of a lonely man with no social or sex life.

She could identify with that last thought. Sudden pity welled in her throat—for both of them. Her own social life was in the same sad shape—nonexistent. She hadn't had a date in two years. Or had it been longer?

"Have you ever considered—" she began, then stopped short of finishing her sentence, realizing that what she was about to ask was truly none of her business. Still, his plight got to her. Her circumstances were destined to remain unchanged from her own choosing. He didn't have the luxury of choice, which was too bad; he deserved better.

"Divorcing her?" Benson said into the silence. "Was that what you were about to ask?"

"Yes, but I shouldn't have."

"It's okay. I don't mind admitting that yes, I have, but..." This time his voice trailed off, and a shutter seemed to fall over his eyes.

"Well, you never did, and you're to be commended."

"Don't make me out to be a saint. I'm not."

"I know," she said softly, but with a teasing edge in her voice, hoping to relieve the jaw-biting tension in his face.

Her ploy worked. He smiled briefly, then changed the subject. "You know, this incident will succeed in sending our ratings skyrocketing."

"Surely not."

Benson leaned his head sideways, giving her an impatient look. "For someone who's on top of her job, you can still be awfully naive."

"I'll take that as a compliment."

"Well, you should. But mark my words, I'm right. You'll even get that national exposure you want."

"If it's at the expense of a friend, I'll pass."

Benson merely shrugged.

"I'll admit I want to make it to the top of my profession. I'd be a fool not to want that, but not this way. I want to make it on my ability."

"I wholeheartedly agree. However, the cold, hard facts remain, so you'd best be prepared." Benson paused. "Especially if Margie's problem turns out to be really serious."

"Like what?" Juliana asked, fear forcing a snap into her voice.

"I'm not going to speculate." His gaze was suddenly hard. "Let's just wait and see."

"Unfortunately, that's something I don't do very well. I'm going to the vending machine. You want anything?"

"Thanks, I'll pass."

Juliana made her way down the hall, determined to find a lounge that had a pot of brewed decaf. She wanted the real stuff, but her insides were already wired to the maximum, which gave her instant pause.

While this incident hadn't changed her love for what she did, it had clearly shaken her, forcing her to take a deeper look at her profession. No matter how much she stood to gain, surely she would never behave like those media vultures perched outside. The thought turned her stomach.

But now was not the time to wrestle with her inner demons and insecurities. She could do that later. For the time being, she needed to concentrate on Margie and how she could help her.

Finally stumbling upon the sought-after lounge, Juliana noticed that it was deserted. She crossed to the coffee bar and poured herself a generous cup. After taking a sip, she felt heat slide through her veins.

She didn't know what alerted her to the fact that someone was approaching. Twisting her head, she watched a man stride down the hall. Something fluttered inside her. A sense of recognition? So as not to be caught staring, she shifted her gaze.

No, it couldn't be.

Yet she whipped back around, curiosity getting the better of her.

He was close now, clearly within her vision. Without warning, the room spun and her hand jerked. "Ouch!" she muttered, staring at the dark liquid that stained the front of her suit at the same time that it burned the sensitive skin underneath.

"Are you okay?"

Words failed Juliana as she stared into the face of the one man she'd hoped never to see again—her ex-husband, Gates O'Brien. Her first frantic thought was that she was caught like a rat in a trap, with nowhere to go.

"Are you okay?" he asked again when she didn't answer. "Looks like you burned yourself."

This was no time to panic, Juliana told herself. As never before, she needed all her wits about her. "I'm fine," she said through stiff lips.

Gates' eyes dropped to the ugly stain on her chest, while hers remained on him. No signs of hair loss; the brown waves on his head appeared as thick and unruly as ever. No protruding waistline, either. If anything, he appeared bigger than she remembered. Maybe that was because he was no longer dressed in a trooper's uniform but rather western-cut slacks that highlighted his long legs, along with a white shirt, a Stetson and cowboy boots.

He chose that moment to turn his head. His face had changed. Deep lines were scored into the corners of his eyes and mouth, giving him a taut aura of danger that hadn't been there before. He could almost pass for the bad guy instead of the good one.

She suspected that guilt, combined with living on the edge, had left those marks. Still, at forty, he was none the worse for them. It galled her to admit it, but he looked better than ever.

What galled her even more was that she looked just the opposite; her appearance was appalling. Besides the ugly stain on her blouse, her hair was in disarray, her makeup was in need of repair, and she didn't have on a smidgen of lipstick.

She wondered if he still found her attractive. That inane thought almost buckled her knees, and droplets of sweat gathered between her breasts. She cursed as her anger mounted.

It didn't matter how she looked or what he thought about her.

Time crawled as she concentrated on a vein in his neck, watching it rise, beat, then fall.

Finally and impatiently, Gates adjusted the Stetson on his head and tipped its brim. A mocking smile broke across his lips before he said with passionate belligerence, "It's been a long time."

Four

Not nearly long enough, she wanted to say, but didn't. "Yes, it has."

Eleven years, to be exact. She didn't say that, either. She wouldn't dare give him the satisfaction of knowing that she was aware of exactly how much time had passed since their divorce.

Yet she was very much aware of *him.* She couldn't ignore that or make him disappear. All six foot two of him stood in front of her like an insurmountable roadblock that robbed her of her ability to think or function.

She had dreaded this moment for years, but it had never happened until now. Wham! Suddenly, out of the blue, she had encountered him, up close and personal.

When she had realized who he was, her energy seemed to have drained out of her. She felt as though she were standing in the middle of a railroad track, and even though she knew the train was coming, she couldn't move. It was a certainty the train would hit her; still, she was helpless.

And the pain he generated was as overpowering as his flesh-and-blood presence.

Juliana had sworn she would never feel this way again. Remembering that pledge brought on a surge of anger that gave her the power to meet his penetrating green eyes. That was when she noticed the tiny scar on his upper right cheekbone. Wonder when he got that?

She didn't care. She only cared about telling him to get out of her way and let her by. Instead, she continued to stand there while the silence mounted. She forced her legs to hold steady.

"You're looking good," he finally said, his deep voice crashing into the silence.

She looked like hell, and he knew it. He was merely making idle conversation, which was not only unnecessary but insincere. Even after all this time, this man knew which buttons to push.

Juliana opened her mouth to make what she hoped would be a suitable comeback, when a woman seemed to appear out of nowhere.

"Gates, darling, I've been waiting for you," she said. "I couldn't imagine what happened to you."

Juliana heard Gates swear before he swung around. The woman stopped at his side, her eyes darting between him and Juliana.

Was this wife number two? Juliana asked herself, though she hadn't noticed a ring on Gates' finger. But then, that didn't mean anything. He hadn't worn one when he was married to her, either.

"I told you I'd be right back," he was saying.

He spoke in a cool tone with his eyebrows arched, which Juliana knew to be a bad sign. He was unhappy at being chased down and forced to account for his actions. Ah, trouble in paradise, she thought snidely.

Juliana perused the woman. She was attractive enough—quite pretty, in fact. She had chestnut-colored hair sprinkled with gray and styled in a pageboy. She was short and small-boned, not thin, but not overweight, either. Voluptuous, that was the word that came to mind.

Under different circumstances, Juliana would have described her as having a sweet-looking face and nature. Not now. There was nothing sweet or good-natured about the way she was glaring at someone she apparently sensed was a rival. Protecting her property, Juliana thought with a bitter but hidden smile. Too bad she couldn't reassure the woman that she had nothing to fear from her. She was welcome to Gates with her blessings.

The last person she wanted back in her life was her ex-husband.

"Are you going to introduce me to your friend?" the woman asked.

"Nicole Rice, meet Juliana Reed."

"Pleased to meet you," Nicole said with a nod, then stepped closer to Gates' side, placing a possessive hand on his arm.

"Same here," Juliana lied. She could never have met this woman and done just fine.

"For some reason, you look familiar," Nicole said. "Have we met before?"

Though Nicole was smiling, Juliana picked up on the hint of nervousness in her voice as if she were picking up on the electric tension that crackled in the air.

"On TV," Gates cut in, his tone mocking. "Juliana has her own show."

"Oh," Nicole said, her eyebrows drawing together.

Juliana could almost see her confusion and frustration mounting. It was time to put her out of her misery. She forced a generic smile, then said, "I should go."

"What's your hurry?" Gates asked.

Juliana ignored his sarcasm. "If you'll excuse me..."

Gates made no effort to get out of her way.

"We'd best get back, too," Nicole said in a rushed tone before turning to Juliana, her chin slightly jutted. "I left my daughter in the other room alone."

Juliana didn't respond, but Gates did, after disengaging his arm. "You go on. I'll be there in a minute."

Nicole's eyes widened, her apprehension on display for all to see. "But—"

"I promise I won't be long," Gates said without looking at her.

"Fine," Nicole said, her tone flat. "But please hurry. You know how Amy depends on you." She then focused her eyes back on Juliana. "Nice to have met you."

"Same here." A lame smile accompanied Juliana's nod.

Once she and Gates were alone, the silence once again beat around them. To lessen its impact, along with that of his unsettling presence, Juliana said, "I hope you didn't stay here on my account."

"Actually, I came for some coffee."

She moved aside, gesturing toward the table. "Don't let me stop you."

He didn't miss her pointed rudeness; his lips curled in a nasty smile. "I see you still have a sharp tongue."

"Some things don't change," she said, though a shudder ran through her, and it was all she could do to hold her own against him.

"No, they don't."

She flinched against the striking force of his words, but again she refused to let him know his effect on her. If only he would move out of her way, but he showed no signs of going anywhere. Damn him and his newfound power to intimidate.

"Is Nicole your wife?" Juliana blurted out, then could have brained herself for asking.

Gates' gaze turned hard, like glinting metal, and he laughed. "Not no, *hell* no."

She didn't respond, unsurprised by his bitterness, first in his laugh, then in his tone.

"I'll never remarry." His eyes burned into hers. "You cured me of that malady."

That cruel, caustic statement was like a blow. She felt her face drain of blood. Before she could make a suitable retort, however, Gates changed the subject.

"You've apparently reached your goal in life. Congratulations. I've read about your success."

"I'm surprised you'd bother," she shot back, "considering how you feel about me."

"Dammit, how do you expect me to feel?" His words were hot and harsh, like a man battling a raging fire in his gut.

She backed up, her eyes becoming withdrawn and distant.

"You walked out on me, remember?"

"Only because—" Juliana's voice stopped in her throat when it hit her what was happening. For a moment it was as if they had stepped back in time, both furious, both hurting, both lashing out—their final heated showdown, which had led to her walking out and never going back.

"You were saying?"

"Nothing." She looked at him out of shadowed eyes. "I have absolutely nothing to say to you that hasn't already been said."

"Nothing? Hell, that's a first."

"Okay, why don't you do yourself a favor and give guilt a holiday?"

His face suddenly appeared to be carved out of stone; his eyes became dark holes, and his chest heaved. "That's what keeps me alive."

"No! That's what keeps you wallowing in misery."

"Damn you!" His features contorted with pain.

Suddenly the fight went out of her, and she wanted to cry, something she'd thought she would never do again. And though his nearness was tearing her to pieces, she couldn't end this nightmare conversation like this. For her own sake, she had to fix things.

Life had done a cruel number on both of them.

"I hope you've found what you're looking for, as well," she said in a hollow whisper.

"I'm getting there," he said, his tone now maddeningly calm, with no sign of the agony of a moment ago.

She concentrated on his shirt pocket, where a Texas Ranger badge in the shape of a star was pinned. Made from a Mexican peso, the badge was an impressive piece, signifying the elite in law enforcement.

If her gaze had traveled farther, she would have seen the thick bulge at his waist—a holster that contained his deadly Colt .45.

Her eyes jerked up to meet his. A mistake. Juliana suddenly felt her own vulnerability pitted against his dangerous energy. A shudder ran through her. She had to get away from him. Now. This farce had gone on long enough.

"So, what brings you here, to the hospital?"

Later she asked herself why she didn't ignore him and start walking. The door had long been closed on Gates and that part of her life. She had no intention of opening it again. Yet she answered him, explaining what had happened.

"The same Margie Bowers who works for my brother's campaign?" He sounded shocked.

"One and the same."

"I'll be damned. Is she going to be all right?"

"I don't know. That's why I need to get back to the emergency room and let you get back to your friend."

"You're right. I've kept *her* waiting long enough."

The emphasis on "her" didn't escape Juliana. The wonderful thing about that was she didn't give a damn.

Gates tipped the brim of his hat, then drawled, "Good luck."

Yeah, right, Juliana thought as she watched him turn and stride down the hall, out of her life for the second time. Feeling as if the breath had totally been sucked out of her, she collapsed against the wall like a rag doll and closed her eyes.

"I was getting worried about you."

"Why?"

"You were gone quite a while." Benson's eyes narrowed. "Are you all right?"

"I'm fine."

He was frowning. "You don't look it. You're kinda green, actually."

"I'll say something nice about you sometime."

His frown turned into an apologetic grin. "Sorry, I didn't mean to insult you."

"You didn't. Forget it. I'm just touchy."

"And well you should be, after what you've been through."

She didn't see the need to point out that Margie wasn't the only one who had upset her. Benson knew she was divorced, but that was all he knew. She meant to keep it that way.

"I take it there's been no word on Margie?"

"Nothing." Benson's features were grim.

"That's—" Juliana never finished her sentence. The double doors opened, and a doctor strode toward them.

"Someone here with Margie Bowers?" he asked.

Juliana and Benson stepped forward.

"I'm Dr. Michaels," he said, then went straight to the point. "Ms. Bowers is in a coma."

"A coma?" Juliana's heart lurched. "But why? I mean...I was hoping she'd just had a severe asthma attack."

The tall, lanky doctor scratched his head before shaking it. "I'm afraid her condition's much more serious than that."

"What happened, Doctor?" Benson asked.

"I...we don't know yet."

Benson's lips were stretched into a thin, white line. "But you'll find out."

"We're in the process of running tests right now."

"May we see her?"

The doctor's gaze swung to Juliana. "She's on her way to X ray for a CAT scan. Leave the number where you can be reached with the nurses' station, and we'll let you know if there's any change in her condition."

Once the doctor had left, Benson asked, "Can you handle this?"

"What choice do I have? But I'm scared."

"Me, too. But let's not borrow trouble." Benson craned his neck to see out the window. "It looks as if the vultures have finally flown the coop."

"Thank God for small favors."

"Come on, let's get out of here while we can."

Juliana didn't argue.

Five

"Are you sure I can't talk you into staying?"

Gates stood at the door of Nicole's house, staring down at her from underneath the brim of his hat. "Not tonight. I'm bushed." He made himself smile. "Besides that, I have a backlog of paperwork that would choke a horse. I've gotta take care of it."

"That's been your standard excuse for several weeks now."

He heard the mild rebuke in her soft tone, and it set his teeth on edge. "I didn't realize I needed an excuse to do my job."

Nicole flushed, and a hurt look appeared in her eyes, making him wish he could literally kick his own rear. She didn't deserve to bear the brunt of the sharp fear and anger that were churning inside him. She didn't have one damn thing to do with it.

Nicole did, however, have something to do with making him feel guilty. He hated that most of all. He already carried around enough guilt to last him a lifetime.

As if she sensed she had made an error in judgment by questioning him, she said, "Look, I don't know what's gotten into me. I didn't—"

Gates raised his hand and cut her off. "It's okay. You didn't say anything wrong."

"Yes, I did, now and back at the hospital. I have no right to make demands on you."

"Yeah, you do." He sighed. "I'm the one who's the jerk here."

Nicole smiled, then reached up and trailed a finger down one side of his stubbled cheek. "Forget it. Tomorrow's another day. It'll be better. I just get the feeling you've been really distracted lately, especially this evening."

"You're right. I'm working on a tough case."

"That's why I'll always be eternally grateful that you dropped everything and came when I called you. For me, a broken arm is traumatic stuff."

Gates captured her hand in his and squeezed before letting it go. "Glad I was in town. Amy's a great kid."

"For a seven-year-old, I guess she'll pass." Nicole's animation suddenly faded, and she was silent for a moment. "Can I ask you something?"

"Sure."

"Who was that woman at the hospital?" Before he could answer, she went on in a slightly breathless voice. "I mean, I know you introduced her and that she's famous, at least in my book, but—"

Gates felt a tightening in his gut. "But what?"

"I don't know," Nicole said, a troubled look marring her attractive features. "It's just that something's niggling in the back of my mind that won't let go."

"Maybe I ought to put you on the payroll."

"Excuse me?"

Gates smiled an empty smile. "Intuition. That's something all law officers should have but don't."

"Sorry, I'm still not following you."

"Which is probably a good thing."

"Gates!"

Her frustration had merit. It wasn't fair to toy with her psyche any longer. Yet he hated to say the words he knew had to be said. He blew out a harsh breath.

"Gates?" Obvious fear forced a crack in her voice.

"She's my ex-wife."

Nicole's mouth opened, then slammed shut. She leaned against the door frame, seeming to wilt right there in front of him. "She's...that woman's your ex-wife?"

"It's no big deal, Nicole. *She's* no big deal."

She lifted her eyes back to his, her chin quivering. "Are you sure? The whole time I was there with the two of you, the atmosphere was as explosive as a lighted stick of dynamite."

"That's a bit dramatic, don't you think?"

"Not at all. I—"

Gates placed a finger across her lips and forced another smile. "Rein in that overactive imagination of yours and give it a rest, okay?"

"It's not that easy."

"She's the past, you're the future."

Nicole's eyes were pleading. "I wish I could believe that."

Gates didn't answer. Instead, he leaned over and pecked her on the cheek. Then, lifting his head, he looked at her. "Believe it. I'll call you tomorrow."

She grabbed one of his callused hands and hung on to it. "Promise."

"Hey, you're okay with this, aren't you?"

"I...think so," Nicole said with a watery smile.

"Good girl."

Gates then turned and walked to his truck, knowing her eyes were troubled as they tracked him. By the time he started his truck, his own eyes were cold and his jaw was set.

This had *not* been a good day.

* * *

Gates didn't bother to switch on the light in his office. The moonlight streaming under the raised blinds bathed the room in a soft glow. He didn't want any harsh lights glaring at him. Existing in the dark had become a way of life for him. That was why he volunteered for the hardest and most dangerous jobs. His body was riddled with knife scars and even a bullet hole to prove it.

When he had started out in the law enforcement business, his job had been more mundane than anything. A cynical smile touched his lips. He would still put his record for issuing speeding citations up against anyone's and come out the clear winner.

While he had done what was required of him, he'd been much more ambitious. His goal had been to work his way up the ladder and become a Texas Ranger, the investigative arm of the Texas Department of Safety. After five years of trooper duty, he'd reached that goal.

He had no complaints about the job, either. It gave him a reason for getting up every morning. As a rule, facing tomorrow was a pain in the butt, so flirting with danger on a daily basis didn't bother him. He looked on it as an added incentive, something that had irked his family from the get-go and still did. Only Rusk, his brother, was the exception; he had backed his career choice one hundred percent.

Gates remembered the day he had sprung his plans on his family. He had just graduated from the University of Texas and had been back home only a few days. The family had gathered for dinner in his honor.

"I have something important to tell all of you," he'd said, breaking into the noisy chatter.

Norman O'Brien's fork paused in midair. "Let's hear it, son."

"I took a job today as a trooper for the Highway Patrol."

"What did you say?"

Like Gates, his daddy was a big man with a voice to match. It bounced off the walls.

His mother, Opal, raised a hand to her chest as if she were having a heart attack.

Rusk merely sat there with a smile on his face, as though enjoying the fireworks.

"You heard me, Dad, but I'll repeat it," Gates said, his own voice low and steady, "just so there's no misunderstanding. Starting next week, I'll be an official state employee, working as a state trooper."

"The hell you will!" Norman bellowed, his cheeks flushed. "Your job is the oil business. In fact, I just had your office in the corporate headquarters redone. It's ready for you to move in."

"That's not going to happen."

"You can't do this to your father, Gates," Opal said, her blue eyes swimming in tears. "Your place is in the family business, just as Rusk's is in politics. Besides, that's…that's dangerous work. You could be killed."

"Your mother's right," Norman snapped. "You'd best come to your senses and listen to her."

"Hey," Rusk put in. "Let him alone. A man has to do what he has to do."

"I don't remember asking for your opinion," Norman said coldly.

A scowl replaced Rusk's smile, but he didn't say anything else.

"But why law enforcement?" Opal asked, her face having lost its color.

Gates shrugged. "I've always been fascinated with the law. You know that." He turned his eyes on Norman. "You can take partial blame for my fixation. When I was only a kid, you taught me to shoot, and that got me thinking about a career where I could handle a gun. Anyway, you don't need me in the corporation. You're perfectly capable of handling the business."

"That's not the point," Norman snapped again. "I won't have a son of mine playing cop. You're an O'Brien, for God's sake. It's time you behaved like one." He faced Rusk. "Why, one of these days, your brother's going to be president of the United States."

"So?" Gates asked in a bored voice, growing steadily weary of the entire conversation.

Norman lunged to his feet, his mouth working. "Don't you dare take that attitude with me. You better get your head on straight, boy."

"Oh, please, you two, stop this," Opal wailed. "I can't stand to see you at each other's throats."

Gates stood and gave his mother a reassuring pat on the shoulder, though he didn't take his eyes off Norman. "My head's on straight, Dad. You know I'm lousy at the corporate gig. I'm also too damn restless. I refuse to be boxed in."

"That's absurd!" High color had invaded Norman's face.

Gates shrugged. "No matter. I've made up my mind, and nothing you can say is going to change it."

He had meant his words, and he hadn't backed down. A few days later he had delivered two additional blows. He'd told them that he was marrying Juliana Reed, whom they considered even further beneath him than the job, and that she was pregnant.

His parents had threatened to disown him. He hadn't cared. No matter what, he would have married her.

"Shit!" Gates muttered, shaking his mind free of the past.

He stomped to the makeshift coffee bar in one corner of the room, grabbed the pot and filled a cup full with the now-stale liquid. He sipped on what he likened to the taste of warm mud.

Although he grimaced, he kept on sipping as he eyed the open folder, but it wasn't the folder that suddenly filled his vision but rather a photo that used to dominate the desk—one of Juliana and...

The air in the room compressed. Breathing became impossible. Then the trembling set in, not from rage, or even anger, but from pain and pure anguish.

He gave his head a brutal shake. It worked. His locked-up breath escaped; and he grabbed the back of the chair. Now all he had to do was put his butt in that chair, dig in and wrap up the paperwork on the case he'd just closed, a murder in a neighboring county.

Gates sat down, but that was as far as he got. He couldn't work, not when his brain felt as if ants were crawling inside it.

"Shit," he said again, leaning back in his chair and propping the heels of his boots on the desk.

Why did he have to run into *her?*

He'd known she was on TV, but he'd never watched her show. What shook him to the core was that he gave a damn. He should be able to meet her on the street anytime and not feel a muscle twitch.

Who was he kidding? Even after eleven years, that accidental meeting had done a number on him. He was a wreck.

Why?

Their love hadn't been a normal love. What he'd felt for her had been an addiction. He saw her and fell in love, even before they had so much as exchanged a word. After their first date, he had decided he couldn't live without her. Both his mind and his libido had been in a mess.

Raw heat.

Those were the only words that could describe what they had shared. And even while their relationship had slowly crumbled around them, that heat had continued to simmer.

Stop thinking about her, Gates told himself. She was lost to him forever. Yet here he was letting thoughts of her eat away at his insides like the relentless hunger he'd always felt for her. He flinched visibly, then cursed.

He stared at his hands. Thank God they were steady, which meant his edge was still there. Underneath, though, the emotional pain was taking its toll. Seeing her today had delivered him one hell of a blow.

She had looked much the same. Gone, however, were the girlish red locks; in their place was a more sophisticated, grown-up style—short and tousled, like she'd just crawled out of the sack. The word *bedhead* came to mind, an aggressively sexy, disheveled look.

He cringed inwardly.

Every curve remained in its proper place, too, from her rounded breasts to her long lean legs. Her oval face, with its dainty nose dusted with freckles, high cheekbones and full bottom lip, was perfectly intact, as well.

The only significant change had been in her large brown eyes. They had reflected the sorrow and pain in his own.

Gates didn't realize he'd pounded the desk with his fists until he saw the blood on a knuckle. He didn't care. He'd had to do something to jerk himself out of that darkness sucking him under.

Only after he had met Nicole through a fellow ranger had he begun to see a hint of light. Now he knew that light had merely been a figment of his imagination. Today had shown him that. He could never love Nicole.

Was he still in love with Juliana? His flesh turned cold. No, love didn't enter into this. He'd sworn he would never feel that emotion again. Sex. That was what this was all about. Seeing Juliana had restoked that raw heat. She still had the power to give him an instant hard-on. So what? He would get over that, like he'd gotten over her walking out on him.

Then why couldn't he stop thinking about how she'd looked today? He knew why, but—

Gates raised his head. What was that noise? Someone whistling? No one else was supposed to be in the building. It didn't matter. The interruption was a godsend. He got up, moved quickly to his door and opened it. His immediate superior, James Ferguson, was striding down the hall.

He didn't stop until he was in front of Gates. "What's up? Man, you look like you just walked into a dark alley and met your worst nightmare."

Gates stared at his captain. "If that were the case, then the nightmare would definitely have come out on the short end of the stick."

Ferguson's bushy eyebrows shot up. "Huh-oh, something's put a bug up your butt."

"You could say that." Gates' chest heaved, his thoughts switching back to Juliana. But only for a moment. He'd wallowed in that pool of self-pity long enough.

"Anything I should know about?" Ferguson demanded in his brisk, no-nonsense voice.

"Nope."

"That's good, because I have something *you* should know about. Two things, actually."

Gates followed Ferguson into his office, plopped down in a chair in front of the captain's desk and watched as Ferguson rummaged through the clutter. He was tall, with thinning dark hair and thin glasses, which he habitually took off and cleaned.

Actually, his entire body was thin to the point of gauntness. Gates often wondered where Ferguson found the stamina to do what he did. His wife kept him on a strict diet due to a bad heart. He'd had two bypass surgeries within the last five years.

Though he grumbled about that diet, he rarely, if ever, strayed from it. Maybe that diet was what kept him going, what gave him the energy to keep up with the younger men. Lately, though, Gates thought he hadn't looked so good, which concerned him.

Ferguson was more than his immediate supervisor; he was his friend. Bosses within the Rangers didn't mean that much. Even though Gates was now a lieutenant and technically above the field sergeants, the unit worked as a team; people rarely pulled rank. When you were part of a group of only one hundred, that kind of cooperation was possible.

"So what brings you back to the old office at this time of the evening?" Gates finally asked.

"The same thing that has you here—work."

"Hell, Ferg, who you kiddin'? I'm down here practically every night, something you ain't."

Ferguson grinned. "You're right, but it sounded good."

"Something big must be brewing."

"It is. As a matter of fact, I was going to call and tell you to get up here ASAP."

This time it was Gates who raised his eyebrows. "What's so hot that it couldn't wait till morning?"

"Our unit's been called in on this prison contract debacle."

Gates straightened. "You've got my attention."

"The upshot's this—following a thorough review of the contracts awarded over the past two years, serious questions have been raised about the way the construction program was handled."

"It's about damn time, that's all I can say. From the beginning, those contractors have been taking the taxpayers to the cleaners."

Ferguson sat back in his chair. "You sound like your brother."

"Are you trying to tell me something, Cap?"

"If that were the case, would I be assigning you to head this investigation?"

Excitement leapt through Gates. "Is that what you're doing?"

"Yep. Headquarters said put my best man on the job. And that's you."

"Thanks for the confidence. Make no mistake, nothing my brother says or does will compromise my job in any way."

Rusk, a highly respected attorney at the time, had served on the Texas Board of Criminal Justice at the time that the prison boom had begun in the state. During his stint on the board, he'd suspected that all was not on the up-and-up with the contracts or the contractors. After his resignation from the board, he'd become a vocal critic of the way things were handled and promised to do something about it, which had led to his run for the governorship.

"I know that, Gates, or we wouldn't be having this conversation. Hell, it's going to take a lot of muscle to flush the corruption out of the system. If your brother gets elected and wants to stomp his share of ass, then so be it. Especially now that new contracts are about to go up for bid."

"You mean on the new high-security prisons that are about to get under way."

"Right. Billions are at stake there. Plus there will be commitments to purchase millions of dollars' worth of that damn soy-based meat substitute they use in the prison kitchens, not to forget more millions for security fencing, half of which you *know* is already stacked in somebody's construction supply yard."

Gates whistled. "Man, talk about 'sweetheart deals.'"

"Exactly."

"So when and where do I start?"

Ferguson shoved a folder toward him. "Read everything that's in here, then go from there."

Gates took the folder and rose. "You said there were two things we needed to discuss. What's the other one."

Ferguson cleared his throat. "I'm going to retire."

"You? Retire? No way. You're just blowin' smoke up my ass."

"I'm serious, and if you keep your shit together, I'm thinking about recommending you as my replacement."

Gates was dumbfounded, and it showed.

"I know what you're thinking, and you're probably right. I'm nuts on both accounts."

"I won't argue with you on that."

"Well, don't say anything, 'cause it hasn't happened yet. Meanwhile, you've got your work cut out for you."

"Looks that way," Gates replied, still reeling from the implications of what Ferguson had said.

"Won't give you much time to chase Nicole around the house, that's for sure." Ferguson grinned.

Or dwell on Juliana, Gates thought, then swore silently.

"Did I say something wrong?" Ferguson asked.

Gates shook his head.

"You *are* still seeing Nicole, aren't you?"

"Actually, I was thinking about asking her to marry me," Gates flung over his shoulder as he walked out the door.

Six

Thirty minutes later, Juliana inserted the key in the door of her condo and walked inside. Somehow the usual sense of welcome relief failed to embrace her. It wasn't because of the loneliness that accompanied her on this particular evening, either. She often coveted solitude.

Now, however, she fought the urge to swing around and walk back out. And go where? she asked herself, pitching her purse on the couch, then crossing deeper into the dimly lit living room, her favorite place in the house.

Though she'd hired an interior designer to advise her, most of the actual decorating had been her own handiwork. A high-beamed ceiling with skylights towered over an area filled with plants, bookcases and an eclectic assortment of furniture. The color scheme, magenta and forest green, dominated not only the couch and chairs, but was carried throughout the other rooms.

At the moment, though, it wasn't the effect of her efforts that claimed Juliana's attention but rather the fact that one of her most expensive and fanciest fish was floating belly-up in the aquarium.

"Oh, no!" she cried, racing to the far side of the room.

The fish was indeed dead. She sought the chair nearest her and sat down. That was when she felt the tightening in her chest, followed by the need to vent her building anger. After the day she'd had, maybe a good cry was what she needed.

That wouldn't help. She simply had to get through these difficult and latest crises. While Margie's condition and the dead fish had compounded her anger and depression, they weren't the underlying causes. The accidental meeting with her ex-husband was what had reduced her to this sorry state.

"Damn you, Gates O'Brien!"

Damn herself more, she thought, for letting him get to her. But she hadn't expected to see him, not out of the blue. Her defenses had been down, and she had paid for that.

After all the elapsed time and the unforgettable anguish she had endured, he could still tie her stomach in knots and make her heart beat faster. But then, he was that kind of man. When he walked into a room, he became the center of attention. He possessed the kind of energy that sparked his surroundings. He lived and worked on a short fuse.

That fact had always turned her on. But then, sexual incompatibility had never been one of their problems, which had been the reason she'd gotten pregnant before she married him.

Feeling her skin crawl at realizing where her mind was headed, Juliana tried to block out further thoughts of him. She couldn't.

She had met Gates her senior year in college; a mutual friend had introduced them at a weekend lake party. The instant she had seen him, she'd been intrigued. However, when he'd sought her out, she had been shy, almost tongue-tied, probably for the first time in her life.

He hadn't left her side the entire evening. She'd been flattered and a little in awe that Gates O'Brien, a senior at UT, and from a rich, influential family, to boot, would pay her any attention.

Her family was far on the other end of the financial spectrum. Her mother had died of cancer when Juliana was ten years old, leaving her in the care of her father, who was a preacher with a drained pocketbook. Burt Reed found solace in his church work, which left her by herself much of the time.

Despite her less than ideal home life, Juliana had no problems with her own identity; her mother had seen to that. She was popular in school because she was smart, outgoing and beautiful.

Still, when Gates first asked her out on a date, she was dumbfounded, but breathless with anticipation. That breathless anticipation had instantly turned into a deep, hot love that led to a proposal of marriage, an event that would have taken place whether she'd been pregnant or not.

His parents hadn't seen it that way. When told, they were vocally against the marriage. She and Gates hadn't cared; they were oblivious to anything except their feelings for one another and were determined that nothing would keep them apart.

After all, they didn't need anyone's permission. They were both of age and Gates had a job. Even so, Juliana had felt an urgency about marrying Gates. The O'Briens were a powerful foe. They were clearly embarrassed by their son's behavior and hell-bent on bringing him to heel. They had had plans for Gates that didn't include his marrying beneath himself, not to mention *having* to get married.

It had been on the eve of her wedding that Juliana's worst fears had become reality. She had been on her way out to meet Gates when she'd passed her father's study.

The door had been cracked, something she wouldn't ordinarily have noticed, except she heard another voice, a voice she recognized—Norman O'Brien.

Hovering in the shadows, she had watched and listened, a vein pulsing hard in her neck.

"What's on your mind, Mr. O'Brien?" Burt Reed asked, running his hand through his thinning copper hair.

"I think you know the answer to that, Reverend."

Reverend Reed sighed. "You're right, I do. But I can't stop—"

"I think you can," Norman interrupted, his tone as cold as a wet slab of concrete.

The reverend's head darted up. "Why should I? I mean, apparently they're in love, and Juliana is pregnant."

"Something you surely don't condone. My God, your daughter's barely eighteen. And pregnant *out* of wedlock, I might add."

Burt flushed, and his Adam's apple bobbed. "She's eighteen, Mr. O'Brien."

"All right, I'll put it to you straight. Neither my wife nor I wants this marriage to take place or this child to be born."

Juliana bit down on her lower lip to stifle her shriek of dismay. How dare he say such a thing? It was all she could do not to rush into the room and claw Norman O'Brien's eyes out.

"Juliana's always had a mind of her own," Burt said.

"Only because you've let her."

"Look—" the reverend began in a tired voice.

"No, you look. Here's the deal. I'll make a huge donation to your church. I'll also give you a tract of land to build a new church on—*if* you will first persuade your daughter to call off the marriage, then have an abortion."

Juliana grabbed her stomach and sagged against the

wall, her breath deserting her lungs. How dare he? Who did he think he was? God almighty? She needn't worry. Her daddy would set him straight, pitch him out on his rear. Burt Reed didn't believe in abortion under any circumstances.

"What about Juliana?" Burt asked.

"What about her?"

"If I do what you're asking, I want a guarantee she'll be taken care of."

"As in money?"

"Yes, for her college education and to get a start in whatever career she chooses."

"That's no problem, Reverend. So we have a deal?"

"We have a deal."

Juliana thought her heart would crack in two. How could her father, who was supposedly a man of God, so brutally betray her?

"Mind telling me how you plan to control that spitfire daughter of yours?" Norman asked coldly.

"That's my business," Burt said with equal coldness. "Now, if you don't mind, I have the Lord's work to see to."

"Yeah, right." Norman nodded. "I'll be in touch."

Juliana managed to flee the house and get inside her car before Norman O'Brien walked out the door. Only after he drove off did she follow.

Later, in Gates' arms, after having told him what she'd heard, he had held her close and insisted they not wait a second longer to get married.

"How 'bout we follow our hearts before our minds can blow the whistle?"

She hadn't argued.

The years that followed, while filled with their share of love, lust and laughter, had had their heartaches, as well.

Her father, whom she'd never forgiven for his duplicity, dropped dead from a heart attack while in the pulpit.

Gates' family, apparently feeling they had merely lost a battle, had been determined to win the war. They continually chipped away at their marriage. They had hounded Gates to leave Juliana and return to the family business.

Juliana had also suffered her share of abuse, especially from Gates' mother, who insulted her by telling her that she didn't know how to behave or dress like a lady.

For the longest time, Gates had refused to give in, distancing himself from them.

Finally, though, his family's meddling had taken its toll, and their marriage turned stormy. Still, Juliana had loved Gates and had been frantic to hold on, to make their marriage work.

Her efforts had failed, a fact that never stopped haunting her.

Suddenly pulling her thoughts out of the past, Juliana lunged out of the chair and raced into the bathroom.

A few minutes later, she was naked and eyeing the tub. She usually took a hot, leisurely bath with bubbles up to her neck. Not this time. She forced her exhausted body into the shower, where she stayed just long enough to let the sharp needles pound her skin, hoping to get the kinks out of her muscles.

However, when she climbed in bed, sleep eluded her. Too much had happened in one day. Though she hadn't expected to see Gates again, she had. And while she had to come to terms with that, she wasn't happy. That encounter had catastrophe written all over it. Her woman's instinct told her that.

Her heart was touched with despair as she asked herself that same old heartbreaking question.

Would she still be married to Gates if their son hadn't died?

"You think the show went all right?"

"Are you serious? It was great, and you were right on target, kiddo."

Juliana's mouth turned down. "I think that's a bit of an exaggeration, but it's music to my ears anyway."

She had just walked off the set into Benson's office. This afternoon's show had been the first one following the incident with Margie. She had been nervous about going back onstage, but what choice did she have? She had to put as good a spin on the situation as possible. Besides, she was certain Margie was going to get well.

"I've been wanting to do this segment for a long time," she told Benson.

"It showed, too." He cocked his head and gave her a thoughtful look. "I didn't know you felt that strongly about our legal system."

"Well, I do. I think the criminals have all the rights."

"You left no doubt about that, though without actually coming out and saying it. I think you would've made a hell of a lawyer."

"You do?"

"Yep. But don't get any ideas. I'm not about to let you quit this job and go back to school."

"Heaven forbid."

They both laughed, then turned serious.

"Have you been to the hospital?" Benson asked, motioning for her to sit down.

"I dropped by on the way here."

"And?"

Juliana frowned as she sat on the plush sofa adjacent to Benson's desk. "No change. I swear, Margie looks like she's just sleeping, and if you gave her a nudge, she'd open her eyes.''

"When I saw her, I felt the same way.''

"I talked to her,'' Juliana added, "hoping that she would respond. But she didn't.''

It had been two days since Margie had been rushed to the hospital, and her condition hadn't changed, something Juliana found hard to cope with. But then, she found almost everything hard to cope with, since she'd seen Gates. A sharp pain shot through her head. She massaged her right temple.

"You okay?''

"I've been better.''

"I—'' Benson's voice dried up when the door to his office opened. Juliana turned and faced his secretary, whose usually bright face was now solemn.

"Margie's mother just called and—''

"Is she still on the line?'' Juliana asked, standing.

"Uh, no. She said to give you the message.''

"Which is?'' Benson prompted.

"Margie…just died.''

Rusk peered down at his hands. Dammit, they were trembling. Grinding his teeth together, he smothered another curse. He stared at the phone while his mind ticked. Should he call back and tell them the whole truth? Or should he leave well enough alone for now?

A sick feeling, brought on by gut-wrenching fear, washed through him. If he failed to handle this debacle just right, the end result could be disastrous. At the moment, he didn't have a firm plan, but he would. Two could play this game. Rusk straightened as some of his old confidence returned.

Hell, he might be down, but he wasn't out. He was an

O'Brien. He had every confidence that his family wouldn't let anything happen to him, even if he got his balls in a vise.

So why couldn't he stop shaking? And why couldn't he stop the visions of someone stealing into his house, placing a pistol beside his head and pulling the trigger?

"Get a grip!" he muttered, trying to swallow around the wad of fear stuck in his throat.

He had to erase those terrifying thoughts or he wouldn't be able to function. After all, there was some good among the bad. One of his problems had been taken care of. Margie was dead, a fate she richly deserved. She could no longer physically torment him. If she hadn't become worm's food, she would have carried through on her threat to rat on him. And then his wife would definitely have pulled that imaginary trigger.

Sweat popped out on Rusk's face and under his arms. He lifted one arm, saw the wet spot on his white shirt and cursed again.

Right now, his wife wasn't his problem. The black book that Margie had swiped and hadn't returned was what was about to make him soil his underwear. What had the whore done with the damn thing? If only he hadn't been so cocksure he would get it back without any trouble, he wouldn't be in this god-awful predicament. She'd always been so gullible, so easily manipulated, that he hadn't worried.

After alerting him that she had his book, she had returned to campaign headquarters, then, later, he'd spent the evening with her.

Once he'd fucked her brains out, he again promised to divorce Tamara, thinking he had Margie right where he wanted her—putty in his hands. Wrong. The conniving little bitch had held out, wanting proof of his intention to leave his wife.

Then she'd turned that screw tighter. She reminded him that she was about to appear on "Juliana Live." That was when he'd warned her that if she did anything to damage him, his family, or his bid for the governorship, she would regret it.

That prediction had come true.

"What are you thinking about?"

He turned as his wife swept into the room, dressed in a Dior gown that he knew had probably set him back several thousand dollars. Maybe it would be worth it if that dress gained him some votes.

Tamara was an attractive woman with her black hair, fair skin, and silicone breasts spilling over the top of her dress. He stared at those breasts with his lips curled, knowing that display of flesh was not consistent with the real Tamara. She was cold, calculating and hated sex. Therefore, *he* hated *her*.

"Nothing that concerns you," he said, that hate bleeding into his voice.

"My, my, aren't we prickly this evening?" She smiled while fingering the chignon at her neck. "Wonder what your adoring public will think when you appear wearing that scowl."

"That doesn't concern you either."

"Damn you, it *does* concern me!" she flared. "Everything you do concerns me, especially now."

"I'm not in the mood for your threats."

"Of course you're not. All you ever think about is the campaign and who you're going to fuck next."

Rusk balled his fists, and when he spoke, his tone held a warning. "I wouldn't push it, if I were you."

"Just try and divorce me and see where it gets you."

"Believe me, I know. You'll do whatever it takes to become the First Lady of Texas."

"Let's say I've had a good teacher."

Rusk didn't bother to respond to her gouging sarcasm. Instead, he turned his back and said, "The car's here. You go ahead. I'll meet you downstairs."

"I'll be waiting, darling."

The second she was out the door, Rusk's mood soured even more as his mind switched back to the missing book. With that pressing on his mind, how was he going to get through the evening?

Not by soiling his pants, that was for sure. He had to take action before his backers found out about the book.

He reached for the phone. After his party answered, Rusk said, "I have a job for you. Meet me tomorrow at the usual place."

When he crawled into the limo beside Tamara, a smile had replaced the scowl.

Seven

"Do you suppose he's crapping in our backyard?"

Carl Mason, controlling stockholder in Worldwide Builders, refrained from answering. Instead, he swiveled his chair and stared out the long ceiling-to-floor window that overlooked downtown Houston.

A flash of lightning greeted him, followed by a growl of thunder. The weather was wreaking havoc outside, and Carl suspected the havoc would soon move inside to this corporate meeting room. He didn't mind. He was geared for whatever it would take to get what he wanted, which was money and power. He would take on the devil himself.

Mason was fair-complexioned, with a round face and rosy cheeks. His body also had that same round shape, though he never thought of himself as overweight, just sort of slack in places, mostly in the gut. But his baby face had its advantages; it made him appear younger than his sixty years, and much softer than he actually was. Both were useful tools in his business dealings.

At present, he was determined that the company would build the next round of prisons in the Lone Star State. If they didn't get the contract, he would be in deep shit. Without anyone's knowledge, he had borrowed from the company so that he could continue to feed his fetish for antique cars. Somehow, though, he'd gotten in over his head. Not to worry. This prison contract would bail him out.

"Carl, answer me," Ben Potter demanded.

Carl shifted his eyes toward the man who sat across the table, one of his two partners. Ben Potter was tall and lean and in his late fifties. He wore thick, black-rimmed glasses that matched a thick mustache draped heavily above thin lips. At the moment, those lips were stretched even thinner.

"Yeah, Carl, I'd like to know the answer to that question myself."

Carl transferred his gaze to the other partner, Lyle Stovall, who was the youngest and perhaps the most intelligent. He was in his early forties and had prematurely gray hair that was on the decline. His once-slender waistline was on that same decline, having been exposed to too much rich food and booze.

"Suppose *you* tell *me* if Rusk is crapping on our turf," Carl said.

He watched as they both looked at each other, then back at him. Lyle was the first to speak. "Yeah, I think he is. Hell, if what he told you a couple of days ago is the truth, then I *know* he is."

"Oh, it's the truth, all right. He sounded like someone who was so scared he was pissing in his drawers."

"Better his pants than ours," Ben Potter chimed in, tugging on one end of his mustache.

Lyle rubbed his swollen eyes. "So what do we do?"

"Nothing," Carl said. "At least, not until we see which way he jumps."

"Jumps on *what* is something I'd like to know." Ben's tone was sullen.

"Why?" Carl asked. "I sure don't want to. It's not our

problem. When Rusk called, I told him to take care of it.''

"What if he doesn't?" Lyle asked.

Carl's eyes narrowed into slits. "He has no choice."

"But what if he doesn't?" Lyle persisted, fidgeting in his seat.

"Look, do you think Rusk O'Brien's going to let the governorship slip through his fingers?" Carl shook his head. "Hell no, he isn't. He'll do whatever it takes to occupy the state house."

"That's great," Ben said, "as long as he cleans up his mess and doesn't forget who got him there. With the amount of money we've invested in his campaign, he ought to win by a landslide."

Carl took a sip of his iced coffee. "He will, and when he does, we'll get that prison contract. Voila! We'll be billionaires."

"It sounds so simple," Lyle said, "but—"

"But what?" Ben interrupted, staring at him with impatient disgust on his face.

"Call me paranoid, if you want to," Lyle said, "but I'd still feel better if I knew who or what was cracking O'Brien's nuts."

"As long as he takes care of it, who cares?" Carl injected.

"I do," Lyle stressed. "Even if his old man is a wheeler-dealer and a powerhouse in the state, he won't always be able to cover his son's butt. And we all know Rusk is playing both ends against the middle with the prison board."

"Actually, I think it's a brilliant move on his part," Carl said. "He's a vocal critic of how things have been handled so far, and he's made a verbal commitment to fix it."

"As long as we come out on the long end of that brilliant stick," Ben said, "it's A-okay. I don't think I'd fare very well behind bars, even if it's in one of those federal country clubs."

"Gentlemen, gentlemen," Carl scolded. "What's happened to your balls? Nothing has changed. When we *all* agreed to give Rusk the money to get elected in exchange for the prison contract, the deal was just as illegal then as it is now. Why the hell are you suddenly running scared?"

"Because of that phone call to you," Ben said. "I don't like glitches in a well-oiled machine."

Lyle rubbed a hand over his sparse hair. "Me, either, though we all knew going into this that Rusk was a risk, a loose cannon with his penchant for the opposite sex and booze."

"Who the hell cares, as long as our secret agreement remains just that? And I have no reason to think otherwise." Carl suddenly belched, tasting the garlic bread he'd eaten for lunch, and frowned. This conversation was responsible for his indigestion.

"Trust me," he continued. "Rusk *will* take care of his problem. Besides, he's leading in the polls, and as long as that's the case, he'll continue to have our loyalty and undivided support." Carl paused to let that last statement soak in. "Understood?"

Both men muttered their consent at the same time that the private line jangled. Carl lifted the receiver. Few people had that number, which meant it had to be important.

"Mason," he said in a sharp, businesslike clip.

A few minutes later he replaced the receiver, a smile on his face.

"Who was that?" Lyle asked.

"Rusk O'Brien."

Lyle's eyebrows rose a notch.

"I can't believe he called," Ben said. "Hell, that's mental telepathy."

"It's good news. Rusk said the sticky problem's been eliminated."

"Did he say how?" Lyle asked.

"As a matter of fact, he did." Carl's tone was gruff.

"Well?" Lyle prodded.

Carl hesitated. "The problem's dead. *She's* dead."

He hadn't come here, not since the day Patrick was buried. If he had any sense, he wouldn't be here now, Gates told himself. He stared at the intricately carved gravestone, but he couldn't bring himself to read the words inscribed there.

He turned his gaze and stared into the distance, feeling as if his nerves were crawling under his skin. He took several deep breaths; that didn't help. Under the most dangerous of circumstances, he never lost his control, even when someone pointed a gun to his head, which had happened more times than he cared to admit.

But he was out of control now, standing at the foot of his son's grave.

He couldn't even curse; his throat was swollen shut. He couldn't cry; the tears had frozen inside long ago. So why was he here? Patrick certainly wasn't. Hopefully, he was in a much better place than this sorry world.

Gates struggled to regain control of his emotions. Soon the folks from Margie Bowers' funeral service would be arriving at the cemetery. He hadn't wanted to come, but Rusk had pleaded with both him and their parents to make an appearance.

According to his brother, the young woman had been one of his best and most dedicated workers. Rusk had thought it important that his family gather around him. And what his brother wanted, he usually got.

Gates knew he couldn't hold Rusk responsible for his own actions. On lots of occasions, he'd told Rusk no. He could have told him no today. He blamed Juliana. Seeing her again had messed with his mind, which had in turn driven him to come here, something he'd sworn he wouldn't do.

He pawed the ground with the toe of his boot, and that was when he saw the tiny wildflower in the middle of the grave. It swayed on its flimsy stalk to the rhythm of the breeze. He remembered the time Patrick had picked such a flower and brought it to his mother, a smile on his face.

How could such a smile die?

His head pounded, his throat ached, and his eyes burned. Still, he couldn't stop his gaze from locking on the mental picture of his son.

Gates squeezed his dry eyes shut and reeled against the onslaught of pain and remorse that pounded him with the force of a sledgehammer. His sorrow was so deep, so complete, that he couldn't move.

"Why, God?" The words were a terrible plea, his voice surrounded by iron.

If he had lived, Patrick would have been fifteen and the image of Juliana. He had always favored his mother, from the day he was born. God, how he missed him and thought about him every day of his life.

If only he and Rusk hadn't taken Patrick fishing that day. If only he'd had better control of the boat and had missed that stump.

But the brutal fact was that he *had* hit that stump, and his five-year-old son had received a deadly blow to the head before being thrown overboard. He had received a similar blow himself and hadn't regained consciousness until hours later at the hospital. There he had learned that the trauma had robbed him of his son and part of his own memory.

To this day, he remembered nothing concerning the accident. Rusk, uninjured, had filled him in on the details, explaining that he had jumped overboard and tried to save Patrick. But his attempt had been too little, too late.

Even though Juliana had never blamed him, Gates blamed himself. The loss of Patrick, combined with his own guilt, had nearly destroyed him. Though he had managed to survive, their marriage had not.

Suddenly Gates uttered a cry from deep within as images of his son flashed before his eyes: Patrick's tiny mouth suckling Juliana's breast; taking his first steps on chubby legs; his bright laughter; his soggy kisses....

"No!" Gates cried, feeling the earth shift. Once it finally righted, he ignored the sweat that soaked his body. Feeling like a zombie and hating what he had to face, he slowly trudged down the hill.

Juliana chose that moment to get out of her car.

He wanted to turn away, to pretend he hadn't seen her. He couldn't. Even though he'd known she would be there, her appearance stopped him dead in his tracks. He clamped his teeth together as though he had the shakes.

Damn you, Juliana, he roared silently. *Damn you!*

"May we all take comfort in the knowledge that Margie Bowers, a loved one and friend, is in a better place...."

Following the pastor's words, the service mercifully ended. Juliana wasn't sure how much more she could have stood. She didn't think she had moved the entire ceremony, especially after she had seen Gates coming from their son's grave.

Every muscle in her body had turned so rigid that they felt like pieces of steel. She hadn't wanted to look at him, but she couldn't stop herself; it was as if her eyes had a will of their own. But it had been a mistake. He had looked like someone had just taken an ax and gutted him.

Guilt was still ripping him to shreds. Perhaps that helped mask the pain.

Attending Margie's funeral had not been easy, though she often came to the cemetery to Patrick's grave. The difference was that she came on her own timetable. Since she had seen Gates, her emotions had been too fragile to make that trek up the hill.

"You're trembling," Benson said.

He was standing next to her. Thank God for his presence, she told herself, in case she collapsed in a heap on the ground. At least he would be there to pick her up, although he didn't look much better off than she was.

He appeared preoccupied, or maybe uncomfortable was a better word. But she couldn't worry about him, not when she was in such turmoil. She felt a hot sting behind her eyes and fought it savagely. She need not concern herself. Inconsolable grief generated no tears.

"You're right, I am trembling," she whispered, keeping her head down.

Benson tightened his hold on her upper arm. "Come on, I'll walk you to your car."

"Thanks, but I'm okay. I have to speak to Margie's parents."

"Are you sure you're up to that?"

"I'm…fine," she lied. "Want to come with me?"

"Nah, I'll pass," Benson said gruffly. "Funerals aren't my thing."

"Mine, neither."

Benson cut her a look. "Sorry, didn't mean it like that."

She gave him a lame smile. "I'll talk to you later."

Once Benson was no longer at her side, Juliana searched the crowd for Mr. and Mrs. Bowers, only to suddenly settle on her ex-in-laws—Norman and Opal O'Brien.

It was uncanny how time seemed to have stood still, she thought bitterly, especially for the rich and famous. Though Opal's hair was grayer, she was still lovely. Her clear blue eyes and peaches-and-cream complexion were still intact.

Norman O'Brien had held his own, as well. Tall and well-built like his sons, he had a thatch of black hair barely dusted with silver, which added to his mature good looks.

If she dared move her gaze another fraction, it would probably have landed on Rusk, who she suspected was nearby. She couldn't bear the thought of that. In fact, seeing the elder O'Briens was like having tiny harpoons thrown at her body.

Unable to bear the sight of the two people who had used every dirty trick in the book to turn their son against her long before the death of their child, Juliana turned away.

Another mistake.

Her eyes landed on Gates. She stared at him, helpless. He stared back at her, his features deranged, like a madman's.

That look knocked the air from Juliana's lungs before his scorn-filled gaze had the chance.

"Juliana."

At the sound of her name, she struggled to rebound, having recognized the voice. She swung around to stare into the ravaged faces of Margie's parents, Perry and Ethel. She fought for composure so she could extend her condolences.

"I...hate to ask you," Ethel stammered, "but would you mind cleaning out Margie's desk at her office, along with her room at your place?"

"Not at all," Juliana said, a shudder running through her, though for a reason she couldn't share.

The thought of seeing Rusk O'Brien again filled her with utter revulsion.

Eight

Juliana paused inside the doorway to the guest room. The scent hit her in the face, and she fought the urge to turn and run. Margie loved the smell of roses, which had surprised Juliana. She had associated roses with someone who was extremely feminine and delicate. While feminine enough, Margie was definitely not delicate.

On the contrary, there had been something about her friend that Juliana hadn't been able to put her finger on, a coarseness, maybe even a slight mean streak. Thinking of Margie in those terms only a day after her funeral sent a dart of guilt through Juliana. She ought to be ashamed of herself, and she was.

The morning had been hectic. The show on street people had been okay, nothing to brag about, at least from her perspective. Benson, however, had told her it had gone extremely well.

Juliana frowned, thinking about the vultures from the media, who continued to flood around her like June bugs around a porch light after Margie's death. She wanted to bust them in the chops, though that unladylike thought was never carried out. Though her tone was often terse, she kept her smile intact and gave them her pat answer.

"I don't know anything more about Margie's death than you all do."

However, it was damn time someone knew, Juliana told

herself, taking the plunge into Margie's room. Although the open cottage blinds let the sunlight in, the room appeared uncomfortably eerie. Juliana rubbed her arms as if chilly.

Ridiculing herself for such foolishness, she sized up the situation. She didn't figure there would be much to do, as Margie had brought only the barest necessities with her. Still, she'd given her word to the Bowers that she would pack what was there and deliver it to them.

The other promise she had made would have to wait.

Juliana couldn't face any more of the O'Brien clan, at least not now. Suddenly her thoughts brightened. Maybe she would get lucky and miss Rusk. Chances were good that he would be on the road campaigning.

He wouldn't be overjoyed to see her, either. The bad feelings between them were mutual. Pushing unwanted thoughts of Rusk aside, she flipped on the light and forced herself to take care of the dreaded task. Even though Margie was gone, Juliana felt as though she were invading her friend's privacy.

The cause of Margie's death had not yet been determined. That in itself was unnerving, especially combined with the brutal fact that foul play could be a possibility, though Juliana found that hard to believe or to accept.

Apparently she wasn't the only one who'd made that assumption. The employees on the set seemed skittish and were inclined to gather in small groups and whisper. Juliana could just imagine the scene at O'Brien headquarters. She would bet the gossip mill was working overtime there for sure.

Since Margie had been heavily involved in Rusk's bid for the state house, her expertise was bound to be missed. That was another reason why Juliana hated the thought of going anywhere near the place. Margie's co-workers would most likely pound her with questions.

Perhaps she could just have someone who worked with Margie box her personal items. That would be the sensible thing to do. *Chicken.* She was that, all right. Her aversion to Rusk, however, went much deeper than that. But then, it wasn't just Rusk, per se. She had an aversion to the entire O'Brien clan, which irked her, because it showed she was still vulnerable.

After eleven years, she should be free of them, for crying out loud. A laugh erupted from her, but it held no mirth. Her accidental run-in with Gates at the hospital and later at the cemetery had proved she wasn't as tough as she'd thought. The past had come crashing back down on top of her like a huge boulder, followed by pain as fresh and clear as the morning dew on a flower petal.

Her baby boy was dead.

Juliana closed her eyes, slumped against the door frame and allowed a wave of nausea to sweep through her. Then, just as suddenly as the self-pity had crippled her, she jerked herself upright.

Some days the heartache was so intense, so harsh, she couldn't deal with it. Today was one of those days. Her saving grace was that once she retrieved Margie's things from Rusk's campaign headquarters, she would be through this dark period, hopefully with her newfound peace intact.

She wouldn't have to see the O'Briens again, unless Rusk was elected governor, a thought she didn't want to entertain. Even though he was leading in the polls, that didn't mean he would necessarily win. Surely the voting public would soon see Rusk for what he was: a lazy, pompous blowhard who had an outhouse for a soul.

As for Gates—well, she couldn't think about him, either. He had a more paralyzing effect on her. Why, after all this time, did he have to reappear in her life? She guessed she wasn't supposed to understand life's crazy quirks.

"Don't!" Juliana scolded herself before reaching for the two empty boxes behind her and pulling them to the middle of the room. The top one she filled with items from the dresser. Next she tackled the closet. Ignoring the sparse amount of clothing that was hanging from the rod, she packed the purses and shoes strewn across the carpet.

Only after she had finished and the box was taped shut did Juliana notice what looked like several small pieces of paper clipped together and stuck in a corner.

For a moment she contemplated ripping open the box and inserting the notes. "Ah, to heck with that," she muttered. They certainly weren't something Margie's parents would want to keep. Before the maid came and gave the room a thorough cleaning, she would get them and throw them away.

Thirty minutes later, Juliana was sitting in the living room at the Bowers' home, sipping a glass of iced tea. Margie's father had removed the boxes from her car first thing and put them in their daughter's room.

Once he joined them, tears covered his face. When Margie's mother looked at him, tears began to stream down hers, as well.

Juliana glanced away, swallowed hard, then took another sip of tea. These two elderly people didn't deserve this tragedy in their lives. They would never get over losing their only daughter. But then, she hadn't deserved to lose her child, either.

"Thank you again for bringing my baby's things," Ethel said, clearing her throat.

This time Juliana's heart constricted. Ethel was a mess.

It was evident that she hadn't bothered to comb her hair or put on makeup. Despair and suffering seemed to have dug the lines deeper in her face. Within the span of one day, at age sixty, she had become a shrunken old woman.

Perry Bowers was equally broken. Tall and already stoop-shouldered, he hadn't bothered to straighten. He kept rubbing the same spot on his bald head.

"You know how sorry I am," Juliana said, setting her glass on the coffee table and clenching her hands in her lap to hold them steady. "I wish there was something more I could do or say, but—"

"We know," Perry put in, then sniffed loudly. "And we appreciate everything you did for her."

"I didn't do anything, really."

"Why would anyone want to deliberately hurt our baby?" Ethel wailed suddenly.

Juliana's spine stiffened. "Have you gotten the coroner's report back yet?"

"No, but you know the doctors suspect that someone—" Her voice broke, and she couldn't go on.

"Now, Ethel," Perry said, reaching over and patting her hand. "You're going to make yourself sick if you don't stop torturing yourself like this."

"I can't help it." Ethel's tone was fierce now. "If someone did deliberately hurt our...Margie—" Again her voice played out, as if she didn't have the stamina to go on.

"Did Margie have any enemies that you know of?" Juliana asked in a soft but cautious tone.

"No," Ethel said, then went on with a note of hesitation. "But Margie never talked to us about her personal life. We tried not to interfere. She wanted it that way, you know. Perry and I respected that."

"What about you, Juliana?" Perry asked. "Did she ever confide in you?"

Juliana shook her head. "No. Like you, I found Margie to be a very private person." She didn't add that she suspected Margie had been seeing a married man, which might come to light later if Margie had indeed been murdered.

Murder.

Juliana forced herself not to visibly shiver. She still refused to believe that her friend had met that fate. It was just too mind-boggling to dwell on. There had to be a logical, medical reason for Margie's untimely death. There just *had* to be.

"You will come see us again, won't you?" Ethel asked, a desperate note in her voice as she reached for Juliana's hand and clung to it.

"That goes without saying." Juliana stood. "And much sooner than you think, too. I haven't been to her office yet."

"Maybe you shouldn't even bother," Perry said, rising to his feet. "Everything there will probably be business-related and should probably remain there."

"You don't know that." Ethel was almost glaring at her husband.

"That's right, we don't," Juliana responded. "I'll take a look-see and bring what's there, if anything."

She hugged them both, then walked to her car, where her chest felt like it was going to burst. While the chapter wasn't closed on Margie's death, once she left Rusk's campaign office, the chapter on the O'Briens would be closed.

She wouldn't have to see Gates again. Thank God.

"What do *you* think happened to Margie?"

At the sound of the unexpected voice, Juliana lifted her

head. A young blonde stood in the doorway of Margie's office, giving her the once-over while chomping on a piece of gum.

"Excuse me?" Juliana said in a chilly voice, though she'd heard the question. Hopefully her tone would send the intruder scurrying. No such luck.

"Everyone around here thinks there was more to Margie than met the eye, if you know what I mean."

Juliana's patience came to an end. "Look, I'm sorry, but I'm only here to clear out her personal things."

The woman lifted heavy brows. "She was on your show when she bought it, right?"

Juliana didn't say a word. Instead, she stood and slammed the drawer shut.

The woman flinched, then moved away from the door. "I guess I'd better get back to work."

Smart move.

Finally alone, Juliana breathed a sigh of relief. When she had arrived at the headquarters, an older man had let her into Margie's office. She had asked Rusk's whereabouts and was told that he was out.

Curbing her desire to shout her thanks, she had gone about her business, finding that Margie's daddy had been on target. Personal items had been scarce. Juliana peered down into the box at her feet. It consisted of a picture of Margie's parents, several books and a potted silk plant.

There had been no signs of any business relating to the campaign. It looked as if Margie had been easily, if not eagerly, replaced.

Juliana bent down and was about to lift the box when she heard the door open again. She rose to her full height and stared into Rusk O'Brien's cold features.

Her stomach bottomed out.

Nine

"What the hell do you think you're doing?"

Juliana stood rigidly erect and met Rusk's eyes while fighting against the urge to punch him in the mouth, sending those perfectly capped teeth down his throat. To show he'd riled her to that extent would make him the clear victor in this game of emotional chess. That wasn't going to happen. But, like Gates, he knew which buttons to push.

"What does it look like I'm doing?" she taunted.

"Meddling, dammit."

Juliana didn't say a word. Her gaze traveled over Rusk, and for a moment she thought she saw a flicker of uneasiness pass over his face. Good. For once she would like to have him on the hot seat, knowing that she'd put him there. She hid a smile. This untimely encounter could turn out to be a blessing in disguise. Maybe now she could flush away her anger toward him once and for all. He wasn't worth her time or energy.

After eleven years and added maturity on her part, her ex-brother-in-law didn't look nearly as formidable or intimidating. Instead, he appeared rather ragged around the edges, despite being dressed to the hilt in an aggressively starched monogrammed shirt with paisley suspenders under a Brooks Brothers suit.

And he was trying to appeal to the common people of

the state? Juliana wanted to burst into laughter. What a joke. *He* was a joke, only he was too full of himself to see that. Another joke was that no one in his family saw that, either, not even Gates, who had more than his share of intelligence. If ever any brothers were different, it was those two. Gates wouldn't be caught dead in this garb. But then, Rusk wouldn't be caught dead in boots, jeans or a Stetson.

Suddenly tired of trying to stare down such an egomaniac, Juliana yanked her thoughts back to the moment at hand and answered his question. "Actually, I was getting Margie's personal items."

"Who gave you permission?" Rusk's eyes were slits.

"Her parents. I figured that was all I needed."

"I want to see what you're taking."

Juliana moved from behind the desk, then, standing aside, gestured toward the box. "There it is. Help yourself."

Rusk's lips tipped into more of a condescending snarl than a smile. It was all she could do not to slap him. Hopefully, one of these days, she would get that chance.

No. What she hoped was never to see this man or any of his family again. On the spot, Juliana pledged to find time to work for his opponent—Harry Folsom. He *had* to stomp Rusk in the election that was still eight months away.

Rusk bent and shuffled through the contents. Juliana stared at the tiny thinning spot on the top of his head, though he had taken pains to cover it with plastered-down strands lapped from the right side. She hid another smile.

He straightened and stared at her.

"Satisfied?" she asked, her tone condescending.

His eyes became deeper slits. "You think you're smart, don't you?"

"I don't have the slightest idea what you're talking about."

"You know exactly what I'm talking about." His voice was cutting.

She cut right back. "Suppose you tell me?"

"Stay out of my way, Juliana." He inched closer.

She wouldn't have moved one fraction, even if she'd felt his spittle on her face. "Or what?"

"You don't want to know."

"You don't scare me, Rusk, not anymore. And you're not infallible, either." Her eyes sparked. "In fact, you're priming yourself for a fall."

Rusk laughed an ugly laugh. "Is that right? Since when did you become an authority on politics?"

"I'm not. I'm just an authority on *you*. And the public won't be far behind. It's apparent you've been kissing mothers and patting babies on the head, or else you wouldn't be leading in the polls."

This time his features turned ugly. "Take Margie's things and get out."

"I'll leave, but only because I want to, not because you're ordering me to." Juliana paused. "And if I were you, I'd be careful how I talked to me. Having my own TV show gives me a lot of power."

"Are you threatening me?"

"That depends."

Rusk's face turned red, then went white. "You little bitch. Your problem is that you can't let go of the past. You're still making me and my parents the scapegoat for the breakup of your marriage."

"That's because you're partly to blame."

"That's your sick mind at work. Even if Patrick—"

"Shut up, you bastard! You're not fit to even say my son's name."

Rusk closed what little distance was left between them, his features now a distorted blur. "It was your husband who was drunk, who plowed into that stump, remember? I was the one who tried to save the little brat!"

Now she *could* feel his spittle. "Stop it!" she cried, backing up, despite her earlier vow.

"I won't stop it. You started this shit, and I'm going to finish it. The biggest mistake Gates ever made was marrying you. Why, you're so far beneath the O'Brien family, you'd have to climb a skyscraper, then still jump up to reach us. You—"

The sound of her palm connecting with his cheek sounded like a muffled gunshot. Rusk's head bounced back, and for a moment, he was too stunned to speak. So was Juliana. She stared at him and the glaring red splotch on his right cheek, horrified that he'd succeeded in goading her down to his low-life level.

"You little bitch!" he said again, raising his hand. "No one slaps me and gets—"

"Rusk!"

The explosive burst stilled Rusk's hand in midair. They both whipped around and stared toward the door.

Gates. Juliana cringed.

Two against one.

"What the bloody hell's going on here?" Gates' fierce gaze was centered on his brother.

Silence met his loaded question, while icicles seemed to literally drip from the fixtures as that silence spread through the room like a malignancy.

Finally Rusk shrugged and backed away, the tenseness and the anger having visibly drained from him. "I was about to give your ex tit for tat."

"Have you lost your mind?" Gates bellowed, striding

deeper into the room. "If I ever see you raise your hand to any woman again, I'll—"

"Save it, Gates!" Juliana cut in. "I don't need you to defend my honor."

Gates swore.

"Still the same old Juliana, huh, brother?" Rusk said, dark humor lowering his voice.

A barrage of colorful obscenities flew from Gates' mouth.

Juliana flushed at the crude language. She'd had enough. Besides, this was just another replay of the past, which had no purpose. She lifted the box against her chest.

"Juliana, wait," Gates said. "Please."

She paused. Had she heard a slight break in his voice? Of course not. That was her emotions playing tricks on her. She spun around and said, "I don't think so. I'm not in the mood for a verbal gang rape."

Gates winced.

Rusk smiled, winked at Gates, then shook his head. "Bro, you don't look as if you've made a sale."

Gates threw him a murderous glance.

"This is ridiculous." Juliana headed toward the door.

"Would you just get down off that high horse—"

"Bro, you're wasting your time," Rusk interrupted, slumped against the desk, obviously enjoying the round of fireworks.

"Rusk, shut the fuck up!"

"I have a better idea," Juliana said, her gaze bouncing from one brother to the other. "Both of you go to hell!"

Gates watched Juliana's rigid posture as she walked out of the room, shoulders back, chin jutted and hips strutting. He tried not to look, but he couldn't help it. When she was in that mode, she exuded sex appeal and heads turned, especially in that getup—silk slacks with a silk shirt thrown over a tank top.

If the situation hadn't been so serious, and he hadn't been itching to knock the hell out of his brother, Gates might have enjoyed the spectacle. Instead, he endured the tightening in his crotch, then called himself every foul name in the book for that weakness.

When she was furious, as she was now, Juliana was every bit the spitfire he remembered. That was one of the aspects of her personality that had made him notice her— a streak of wildness she tried to hide behind the guise of self-assurance.

Underneath that facade was someone life had kicked in the teeth more than once. Unlike him, she had somehow managed to let go of her bitterness, her anger at God, and truly build a new life for herself. He had to admire her for that.

"Well, little brother, looks like you walked into a hornets' nest," Rusk remarked, filling the silence. "I'm not surprised you got stung along with me."

Gates squared his attention on Rusk. "So are you going to tell me what caused that blowup?"

"It's simple. She's not welcome here, and I told her so."

"That's not what I'm talking about, and you damn well know it." Gates was in Rusk's face now, both fists locked in hard knots.

Rusk backed up, recoiling as if Gates were a tarantula. "Hey, what's with you? I—"

"Don't you ever raise your hand to her again. Is that clear?"

Rusk straightened, as if working out a glitch in his spine. "I was just returning the favor."

"You mean she slapped you?" Gates' lips twitched, almost sorry he hadn't seen her take on his brother.

"She sure as hell did." Venom spilled into Rusk's voice.

"Well, I don't give a shit if she broke your damn nose."

"Why are you defending her, of all people?" Rusk's cheeks were purple now. "If anyone deserved to be popped, it was her."

"No woman deserves to be hit, you idiot! I don't give a damn who she is. How the hell long has that been going on? Have you knocked Tamara around?"

The cords in Rusk's neck jumped. "That's none of your business."

"I'm making it my business," Gates said in a dangerously low voice, not liking the gist of this conversation at all.

"Of course I haven't."

"You'd better not be lying to me."

"For chrissake, Gates! Have you forgotten who you're talking to here?" Rusk pounded his chest. "I'm your brother, your flesh and blood."

"I don't give a damn who you are. Just don't raise your hand to a woman again."

Rusk shook his head. "Man, what's with you, anyway? You're blowing this all out of proportion. I thought you didn't give a damn about Juliana, that you wouldn't piss on her if she were on fire. Now here you are, defending her."

"I'm not defending just her! I'm defending any woman you might take a notion to hit."

"Okay, okay," Rusk said in a suddenly smooth and controlled tone. "I was out of line, I'll admit. And it won't happen again, so get hold of that crummy temper of yours.'' There was an uncomfortable pause, then Rusk when on. ''What I'd really like to know is what's going on between you two.''

Gates bristled. ''Absolutely nothing, I can assure you.''

''Sorry, I'm not buying. I believe the bottom line here has everything to do with Juliana. I'd say you rode to her rescue like a knight in shining armor.''

''That's bullshit.''

And it was. He would have done the same thing if the woman had been a street whore or worse. Still, Rusk's accusation had merit. The idea of Rusk hitting Juliana had made him want to jerk his brother's heart out of his chest and stomp it, which was ridiculous. Granted, Rusk should have been taken to task for his behavior. But the fact that Rusk's target had been Juliana had sent his rage over the top.

Seeing her three times in a matter of days had him in a dither. Her vibrant beauty and pillow-talk voice had slammed *him* where it hurt the worst—in the groin. But he wasn't about to let Rusk know how he felt.

''You're still missing the point,'' Gates muttered darkly. ''I'm no one's knight in shining armor, certainly not Juliana's.''

Rusk harrumphed. ''You couldn't have proved that by me.''

''Don't push it.''

''Whoa, down, boy. I told you, it won't happen again. There's just something about your ex that makes me see red.''

''Forget her.''

''It looks like you're the one with that problem, not me. I hope you haven't forgotten that she fucked—''

''You just don't know when to put a lid on it, do you?'' Gates' voice had turned to steel.

"Okay, okay, you win. I'm sorry. I don't know what came over me. Like I said, it won't happen again."

"Good. Your conduct's certainly not becoming to the soon-to-be governor of Texas."

That comment drew a smile from Rusk and succeeded in dissolving the tension slightly.

"But she had no right to show up at my headquarters and rummage through Margie's desk." Rusk's tone had turned whiney.

Gates swallowed an impatient sigh. "Maybe not. I don't know. They were friends. Maybe that gave her the right."

"Nothing gives her the right to trespass on my property."

"Well, it's a done deal," Gates said flatly. "So put it behind you before you get your dander up again. Besides, you won't have to see her anymore."

"That goes for both of us."

"Right," Gates said, wishing he had a drink, but knowing he couldn't have one.

A silence fell between them for a long moment. Then Rusk said, "I'm glad you stopped by."

"From the message you left at my office, I thought it was something urgent."

"Take a load off," Rusk invited, gesturing toward the chair in front of the desk. "I'll get us some coffee."

"I don't have time, but thanks, anyway. I should already be long gone."

Rusk sat down, then picked up a pen and fiddled with it before adding, "I was hoping you'd tell me about your new assignment, fill me in on the details."

Gates gave him a startled look. "You talking about the prisons?"

"Yep."

"Pray tell, how did you know about that?"

Gates had toyed with the idea of discussing that assignment with his family at dinner the evening before. But he hadn't, even though he'd been aware that Rusk remained solidly committed to stopping the waste of taxpayers' money. Still, he'd decided to hold off until he knew more about the debacle himself.

Rusk puffed his chest out, and his tone was full of arrogance. "In my position, it's easy, especially when my constituents know how determined I am to get to the bottom of this prison mess."

"Which means you know a hell of a lot more than I do. I haven't even gotten my feet wet yet. When I do, I'll want your input."

"I realize that, but surely Ferguson gave you a jumping-off place—names and so on."

"Particular targets? Is that what you're asking?"

"Right."

"Even if I had names, I couldn't tell you."

"That's a crock," Rusk said in a huffy tone. "You want my help, but you're not willing to return the favor."

"You know the reason for that. You deal with politics, and I deal with law enforcement."

"You know you can trust me."

"Trust has nothing to do with it."

"I don't see it that way," Rusk countered.

"Look," Gates said, "I've barely had time to look over the info Ferguson gave me. But I'm going to go the whole nine yards, starting with the board members, the contractors and the senators who had a hand in the deals."

"Ah, so you're going after politicians, huh?"

"If they stink, I'm going to find out."

"I served on that board. Does that include me?"

"It might. But you were clean then, same as now, right?"

Rusk chuckled. "Right, little brother."

"Then you don't have anything to worry about. Uh-oh," Gates added suddenly, his beeper going off. "Gotta go. I'll be in touch."

Ten

Though she left the campaign headquarters immediately, Juliana didn't go home. She stopped by the station to pick up her notes on the next day's show, notes that she'd forgotten in her haste to get the visit to Rusk's headquarters behind her.

By the time she left the station and reached her car, the sunlight had turned into twilight. It was past time to go home. Even so, after she climbed behind the wheel, Juliana didn't start the motor. She couldn't. Not only was her head still splitting, but her heart was turning cartwheels.

In a nutshell, she was spent, an emotional wreck.

Juliana took deep, gulping breaths and looked outside the window. No one was around. Yet for some creepy reason, she felt as if she was being watched, which was ridiculous, though she had to admit Margie's death had her spooked. She pushed the Lock button.

Gates' unexpected appearance also had her spooked. That, combined with the fiasco with Rusk, was enough to send her frayed nerves straight into paranoia.

Juliana tightened her lips. She had to remain strong, to keep her focus. She had managed to restructure her life, had even reached a point where Patrick's face wasn't the first thing she saw each morning before she opened her eyes.

Biting down on her lower lip, Juliana managed to stifle her agonized cry. She had meant it when she'd told them to go to hell. Things weren't supposed to have happened this way. Rusk shouldn't have shown up and most certainly not Gates.

Fate had played another dirty trick on her. But the damage had been done, and she had to deal with it. Gates and Rusk together had bulldozed through that part of her heart she kept behind lock and key. Now she felt the poison of the past course through her.

Only days before she had left Gates, a verbal skirmish similar to the one she'd just endured had taken place in the living room of the O'Brien mansion.

She had gone there looking for Gates, who hadn't been home in two nights. But then, that behavior on his part had become the norm rather than the exception. Since the death of Patrick, he had turned into a person she no longer recognized. She hadn't been able to talk to him, much less reason with him. He had shunned her every effort.

He'd stopped making love to her, too, had even moved out of their bedroom. Guilt had become his new mistress, his new passion.

Not only had she lost a son, but a husband, as well. To counteract her own grief and loss, she had sought help through a counselor. Gates had spurned that idea, flatly refusing to join her.

Additional help had come from sessions with one of Gates' lifelong friends, Josh Philmore, who was an attorney. Josh had been deeply concerned about Gates and had spent hours trying to verbally knock some sense into him. Like Juliana's, Josh's efforts had failed. Gates had become a brick wall, impenetrable. It was as though they were trying to revive a dead man.

Eventually guilt had driven Gates to the bottle.

On that particular evening, Juliana had held fast to the hope that instead of finding Gates in a bar, she would find him at his parents' house. Although she'd loathed the thought of going there, she had, but it had taken all the courage she could muster to ring that doorbell, her own emotions in tatters.

Rusk and Norman had been the only ones present. Once she'd learned that Gates wasn't there, she'd turned to leave, only to have Rusk's mocking words stop her.

"We know what you're up to," he said.

"I don't know what you're talking about."

His lips twisted into a sneer. "Ah, so you're going to play the innocent all the way."

Juliana turned around, her eyes concentrating on her father-in-law. "What's he talking about, Norman?"

"My son can speak for himself."

Juliana saw red. "I didn't come here for a lecture from the favorite son. I came here looking for my husband."

"Now why would you do that?"

Rusk's tone was insulting, which heightened her anger, something she figured out later he had intended to do. She'd played right into his hands.

"Because he's my husband, and he needs me."

"Apparently you don't need him."

"What's that supposed to mean?"

Norman cleared his throat, which drew her attention back to him. He was looking at his oldest son, a question in his eyes. "Are you sure we—"

Rusk held up his hand, stopping his daddy. "Trust me on this. I know what I'm doing."

"What are you talking about?" Juliana demanded, fire in her tone.

"I hired a private detective," Rusk said.

Bands of fury seemed to squeeze her, and she could barely speak. *"What?"*

Rusk ignored her question. "So you see, you've been caught."

"Caught doing what, for God's sake?"

Rusk chuckled, averting his gaze and giving his daddy a knowing look. "I guess she's going to play hardball."

"How dare you hire someone to follow me!"

"How dare you fuck around on my brother!"

"So that's what you've been up to?"

At the sound of Gates' slurred voice, Juliana turned slowly around. She hardly recognized the man she had married. His eyes were trapped in a bloodshot net in a gaunt face that sported several days' growth of beard. His shirt was unbuttoned and only half tucked in his jeans. His hat was pushed back on hair that needed cutting. He was a mess, and staring at his slovenly appearance took another chunk out of her heart.

Still, she stood her ground. "Of course that's not what I've been doing."

"We've had her followed, Gates," Norman said. "She's lying. We've caught her several times with Philmore."

"In his bed?" Gates asked, swaggering toward Juliana, his eyeballs glaring.

"Surely you don't believe—" Juliana whispered, aghast at the way she'd been blindsided.

"Dammit!" Gates grabbed her and pulled her against him. "Have you been balling my best friend?"

"Let go of me!" Juliana screamed into his face.

"You'd better believe us," Rusk said. "Josh has been dipping in *your* hot tub. I'd bet my life on it."

Gates' head snapped back as if Rusk had socked him in the gut.

"If you believe him," Juliana cried, "then you're a fool. Can't you see what they're trying to do? What they've always tried to do? Break us up. They used Patrick, and now they're using your best friend—"

Juliana couldn't go on. With both her voice and spirit broken, she turned and ran out of the room. She didn't look back. Thirty minutes later she was at home, her bags packed. She'd been loading them in the car when Gates drove up beside her, then bounded out of his truck.

"Juliana."

She held up her hand. "Don't say anything. It's too late. I'm through talking. I'm through begging. I'm doing what I should have done months ago. I'm leaving you."

"Please—"

"No! For once I'm going to have my say, and you're going to listen. I never blamed you for Patrick's death. But I can see now that you'll always blame yourself. Well, go for it. Apparently you get off on wallowing in your guilt. I don't give a damn anymore."

"You don't mean that." Two red spots appeared on Gates' cheeks.

"And I don't love you anymore, either."

"Juliana, don't!" he roared, going white.

"Go back to that hole you crawled out of, back to your bottle and to your sick family. I'll admit it—they've won. They've finally succeeded in destroying our marriage." She looked him up and down. "I don't want to see you again."

And she hadn't, until that fateful day in the hospital.

"Oh, God," Juliana moaned, dry-eyed, yanking her thoughts out of the past and back to the present. Rehashing that dark period and torturing herself with it would serve no purpose.

Ten minutes later, she was at home in the foyer, where

she stopped, a strange feeling enveloping her. Brushing aside her unfounded apprehension, she ventured farther, then stopped again.

Her mouth opened, but nothing came out. Afraid her knees would buckle under her, she balanced herself against the wall and closed her eyes.

Surely she'd made a mistake, she told herself after a moment. She was imagining things. She eased her eyes back open. Nothing had changed. She screamed, then covered her face with her hands.

"Why?" she whispered, her voice so fragile it cracked. Who would do such a thing?

"What you got, Will?"

Will Conrad, the sheriff from a nearby county, swatted a fly that buzzed around his head before saying in a harsh tone, "Something you ain't gonna like. Something as bad as I've ever seen around these parts."

"Show me," Gates said, his face grim as he followed Will to a clearing surrounded by woods not far from a metal-framed building known as Andy's Beer Joint. The second Gates reached the actual crime site, he pulled up short and swore.

Three people lay in a crumpled heap on the ground. Three *dead* people. Gates' eyes studied the bodies. All had been shot in the head, their hands tied behind them, gangland-style.

Blood stained the grass under and around them.

"Has forensics been called?" Gates asked.

"They're on the way."

"Do we have anything to go on? Any witnesses?"

The sheriff removed his hat and fanned his face. "Not so far, but I have some men canvasing the area."

"Who are they? Do you know that?"

"Yep. It's Andy Nelson who owns the beer joint and two of his employees. They've been missing for days now."

"This is a professional hit," Gates said, studying the bodies, noticing that two of the victims, one male and the other one a female, were hardly more than teenagers. The owner was older, in his thirties, Gates guessed.

"We've had an all-points bulletin out on them ever since the cleaning lady showed up for work and no one was there, even though the door was open."

"So some bastard or bastards just walked in, took three people off and blew their brains out. And no one saw a thing?"

"So far that's the way it's coming down."

"Fuck that. Someone saw something. And I want that someone ASAP."

"I hear you. I suspect this happened long after the joint closed down."

"What time was that?" Gates asked, still kneeling, but looking up at the sheriff. He couldn't see the man's face. The spare tire around his stomach prevented that.

"Somewhere around eleven or twelve," Will said.

Gates rose. "As soon as you have anything else, I want to know." He turned then and walked to his truck. He sat there unmoving for a long moment, letting a slow breath out of his lungs.

What a day, he thought, wondering what else would go wrong. Nothing, he hoped. The scene he'd just left had shaken him. Three lives snuffed out. Three grieving families. Cursing, Gates pounded on the steering wheel.

What kind of sick bastard would do such a thing? He ought to be used to the violence he dealt with on a daily basis. But cases like this, which were rare, thank God, had the power to bring him to his knees. It wouldn't do for him to come face-to-face with the culprit or culprits in a dark alley. He would be tempted to take justice in his own hands and enjoy every minute of it.

Right now, his insides felt ready to explode. Not a great day overall, he told himself again, slumping back against the seat. He couldn't block out of his mind the episode with Juliana and Rusk and his reaction to it. But he had no choice. Now was not the time to reopen that can of worms. Anyway, Juliana was perfectly capable of taking care of herself.

Gates had just started the engine when he heard the call come through on the Houston Police Department's frequency. At first he wasn't sure he'd heard correctly.

He grabbed the microphone. "Ranger O'Brien here. Please repeat."

His blood curdled as he downshifted the Ford and headed in the direction of Juliana's house, all the while calling himself every choice name in the book, beginning with fool.

He couldn't afford to get involved with her again. After she'd left him, he'd nearly lost it. He couldn't let that happen again. This wasn't his responsibility. HPD was capable of handling the call.

Yet his vehicle never veered off course.

Eleven

People were crawling all over her home. Juliana wanted to scream at them to get out, to leave her alone and let her curl into a ball of misery. Neither one was an option. She needed the police there; she also needed to keep her wits about her, though the latter was becoming more difficult by the minute, especially when her gaze was fixed on the living room.

Rough, dry sobs stuck in her throat.

Whoever had broken in and torn her place apart had done it with a fierce devotion to the job. She had racked her brain for an answer to this maliciousness, but she remained clueless. Nothing on the entire premises was worth the effort that had gone into this perverse invasion of her privacy.

The two officers who had responded to her 911 call had immediately cordoned off the area, then begun questioning her.

"Ms. Reed, as far as you can tell, is there anything of value missing?"

Her response had been no, though she didn't really have anything of value, except her wedding-ring set, and that was in a safe-deposit box at the bank. Still, the officers, along with a forensics team, were milling about the entire house, checking out every room, looking for leads.

As Juliana sat on the couch while the "good guys"

further invaded her privacy, she sank deeper into herself. A funk was what she called it. If only she could rant and rave, throw things to release her frustration, she would be better off. She couldn't. She could only nurse the shock that had set like concrete in the pit of her stomach.

She closed her eyes, only to open them suddenly when she heard a noise. That noise was Gates striding across the threshold as if he had every right to be there.

Juliana lunged to her feet and for a moment felt the room spin. She closed her eyes again.

"Juliana?"

She knew he was close, within touching distance. She could feel his minty breath caress her face. Still, she kept her eyes closed until her head stopped spinning.

"Juliana," he said again.

Her mind was filled with fear, not a disabling fear, but helpless fear that rendered her speechless, as though she'd been gagged in the midst of this crisis.

Feeling him move, her eyes opened. She sensed he was about to touch her. "Don't...please," she said in a sharp but raspy voice.

His arms fell to his sides, while his eyes were hard and intense. "You looked like you were about to fall."

She ignored his explanation and rubbed her arms, trying to remove the coldness. "What are you doing here?"

"I thought I could help."

"Why would you think that?" she asked inanely, growing steadily uncomfortable under his piercing scrutiny. Dear Lord, the last thing she needed or wanted was Gates. Rather than an asset, he was another danger—and a greater one.

He seemed to sense that, and frowned. "I don't want to cause you any more trouble, but..." His voice faded as he continued to hold her gaze.

As always, he cut quite a striking and intimidating figure. He was dressed in gray Levi's slacks, a white shirt,
boots, and had that ever-present bulge on his belt. He was
indeed the consummate Texas Ranger. Big man, big hat,
big boots, big gun.

Big *everything*.

Or did he just seem that way because she felt smaller
and more vulnerable than usual? No. He was just as he
seemed—big and tough. Staring at him now, she found it
hard to believe that he'd ever had a soft, tender side, that
he'd held her in love, driven her mad with his touches
and kisses....

Making a strangling sound, she turned away.

"I obviously made a mistake," he said.

She shifted her eyes back to him in time to see his pulse
beat hard in his throat. Their eyes didn't waver. Before
she could say anything, he muttered tersely, "I shouldn't
have come here."

He pivoted on the heel of one boot and started toward
the door.

"Don't." The tiny word barely escaped Juliana's lips,
but it was loud enough that he heard it.

Gates stopped midstride and whipped back around. She
tried to read the expression in his eyes, but his hat prevented that.

"Don't what?" he asked, his voice sounding as if it
had been scraped raw.

She licked her bottom lip. "You...know what. Don't
go."

His rigid stance seemed to wilt in front of her. When
he spoke, however, his tone was hesitant. "Are you sure?
I mean—"

"No, I'm not sure about anything." She snapped out
the words, but she hadn't meant to. Or had she? Her feel-

ings were mixed. Someone had violated her home, and Gates, with his aura of toughness, did make her feel secure. The downside was that he was so intense that he also frightened her. She had to fight the impulse to run.

She stood motionless and continued to look at him, instantly aware of the heat that flared in his eyes. Suddenly she couldn't breathe as the room turned into a hotbed of tension. She steeled herself against responding to that heat. Damn him.

"Hey, Ranger O'Brien, when did you get here?"

Juliana quelled the urge to hug the young policeman who was walking down the stairs, smiling at Gates, his hand outstretched.

"Hello, Winston, it's nice to see you again."

"Same here, sir," the younger man said, awe in his voice. "Are you here officially or—"

"No, actually I'm an...acquaintance of Ms. Reed's."

"Oh, I see."

"How's it going?" Gates asked, his tone suddenly brisk and all-business.

Winston shook his head. "Not good. We haven't found one damn print. Whoever did this knew exactly what he was doing."

"Well, don't let up. Keep your nose to the grindstone."

"Plan to, sir."

Once the officer had stepped into another room, Gates faced Juliana again. "You look like you've about had it. What you need is some fresh air."

She didn't respond. She couldn't. Her gaze had drifted from Gates to the floor, where a picture frame lay, the glass crushed and broken. "Oh, no!" she cried, squatting and picking up the photograph of Patrick's smiling face.

Holding it to her chest, she peered up at Gates, then caught her breath. His face was white. His green eyes, now black holes in their sockets, were filled with a wild, murderous rage.

She struggled upright. By then his features had contorted into a tragic expression of pain.

"Damn them to hell!" he roared.

"Gates—" She couldn't go on, not when her own voice was cracking with tears.

For another moment his mouth worked, and she thought he was going to cry, something she'd never seen him do and something she knew she couldn't handle. Not now, not when the awful past was pounding her even as she cradled her dead baby's picture in her arms.

"Go outside while I make us some coffee." Gates spoke like a zombie.

"I don't think—"

"For God's sake, don't argue."

She nodded, incapable of making any decisions at the moment, anyway. She watched as he seemed to stumble drunkenly from the room; then, moving as if on automatic pilot herself, she placed the picture on the couch, stroked it a time or two, then ran onto the deck.

Once there, she sat down, immediately kicking off her sandals and pulling her legs under her. In light of what had happened and for her own sanity's sake, she had to regroup. She pulled the fresh air deep into her lungs, realizing it smelled heavenly, though she couldn't pinpoint the odor.

Spring. That was it, her favorite time of the year. Her small yard bore testimony to that. Her eyes settled on a row of salmon-colored azaleas next to the house, breathtaking in their beauty. Farther out were several dogwood trees in full bloom. In the fading sunlight, it was a toss-up as to which were the loveliest.

However, nature's soothing effects were short-lived.

Her mind continued its unraveling. What else was going to happen? The bullets were coming so fast she didn't have time to dodge.

Gates was the one bullet she hoped wouldn't hit her and prove to be fatal. She could withstand the ransacking of her house. It could be put back in order and broken things replaced. Gates was another matter. She had been without a man, without love, for so long that both her heart and her thighs were empty.

Panic, along with sheer terror, seized her. She had to stop this. Gates had smashed her soul once. She...

"Here you go."

He was coming toward her with two cups in hand, having completely regained his composure. If she hadn't known better, she could have sworn that distressing scene inside hadn't taken place.

But then, Gates had a knack for turning his emotions on and off like a faucet, she reminded herself bitterly.

When she took the cup from him, she was extra careful not to touch him. As if he was aware of that, a tiny smirk flirted with his lips, then disappeared. But the cords in his neck remained tight, and his face hadn't quite regained all its color. He wasn't as immune to this nightmare as he would like her to think, though he was doing his best to hide that fact.

"Apparently you didn't have any trouble," she remarked to cover the awkward silence.

"In the kitchen, you mean?"

"Yes." Her voice was strained.

"Nope. You're in a rut. The coffee was stashed in exactly the same cabinet as it was in our house."

His eyes burned into hers, while her body turned clammy at the slight emphasis on *our*, which did nothing but create a false intimacy. She purposely averted her gaze, though she felt the color steal into her face.

He sat down in the chair opposite hers and set his cup on the glass table. Then, crossing one leg over the other, he asked, "Do you have any idea who would do this?"

"None whatsoever." Her voice was flat, distant, as she continued to avoid eye contact by peering down and blowing on the steaming liquid.

"Nothing of value is missing."

"I don't have anything except—" She broke off, not about to mention her rings.

"Except what?" he pressed.

"A few pieces of jewelry," she said in a rushed tone. "But they're at the bank."

"That's smart."

Juliana took another sip of coffee and watched him over the rim. He had removed his Stetson, and the lingering sunlight was on his hair, highlighting the silver streaks nestled in the dark strands.

"I've earned them all, and more."

Her color deepened. She'd forgotten that he had the uncanny ability to know what she was thinking before she did.

"It seems rather odd that your friend Margie dies, under mysterious circumstances, to boot, and then your house is broken into."

"What could one possibly have to do with the other?" she snapped.

He shrugged as he eased back in the chair. He filled it to capacity, which she found oddly comforting, a fact that made no sense, as his presence was unnerving. Still, she was uneasy over what had happened. She would be a fool to deny that.

"I'm not sure," he said, "but at this point nothing should be ruled out, no questions left unasked."

She frowned. "Margie was living here, you know."

Gates didn't so much as move, but she saw every muscle in his body tense as if an alarm had gone off in his head. "Permanently?"

"No. Her condo flooded, and she needed a place to stay while it was being redone. I offered my guest room."

"How well did you know her?"

"Well enough, but if you're asking if we were best friends, the answer is no."

"There could be a connection, given that she lived here."

Juliana stood, not liking where this conversation was heading. When she spoke, her voice was stern. "I doubt that."

"At this juncture, it's not wise to doubt anything. If this were my case, I'd—"

"But it's *not* your case, right?" When he didn't say anything, she hammered on. "You shouldn't even be here."

He still didn't respond, but rather rose and walked over to the bench that ran along the deck, propping one foot on it. He stared into the distance. Maybe he'd gotten the message, she thought. Regardless of his take-charge mindset, she didn't have to answer his questions, not now, not ever.

"What did you do after you left me?"

The silence that followed that question was absolute. Even the birds seemed to have stopped chirping. Juliana blinked against the spasm in her chest.

He turned and looked at her, his green eyes once again dark holes in his head.

"Don't, Gates, don't do this."

"Answer me."

"I don't know how to answer you."

"Yes, you do. How did you take care of yourself?"

"I worked night and day, that's how."

"You didn't have to. I was more than willing to help."

"I didn't want your help."

"That was obvious when you returned my checks."

"I didn't need your money," she said fiercely. "I was making my own, modeling and selling cosmetics." She lifted her head in a defiant gesture. "If your conscience is bothering you on that score, then give it a rest."

"That money you returned is still in an account in your name."

Juliana tried to smother the sudden, explosive anger that rocked her, but she couldn't contain it. "Money! God, who cared about that? I sure as hell didn't. But then, you and your family think that's the answer to everything. Well, let me assure you, it couldn't have made up for your carousing and betrayal."

"Betrayal!"

Two long steps put Gates in front of her. "Dammit, I was never unfaithful to you." His nostrils flared. "I just wish I could say the same—" His voice broke off.

"Go on," she spat. "Finish your sentence."

"I didn't mean to open that can of worms."

"The hell you didn't!" Her voice was thin, and she could feel herself continuing to unravel on the inside. She had to get rid of him. She couldn't allow him to dig up any more buried bones. There was already enough pain between them to fill an ocean.

"I don't have to explain myself to you anymore," she finally said, her voice now under control. "I just want you to leave."

"No."

"Damn you, I don't want you here."

"You asked me to stay, remember?"

"Which was a big mistake."

"Aren't you the least bit curious at to why the intruder went to such lengths to tear things up yet didn't take anything?"

She forced a blasé attitude that she was far from feeling. "They didn't find anything to take, which made them mad, so they trashed my place."

"You're wrong. Whoever did this was looking for something. And if they didn't find it, they'll be back."

"Always the cop." Her tone was snide.

"Dammit, Juliana, stop making light of this."

She slapped at a loose strand of hair that blew in her mouth. "I'm not, but it's none of your business."

"I'm not leaving you alone. Either you go somewhere and spend the night—"

"No!"

"Then an officer will remain on guard here."

"Not if I don't want him to, which I don't."

"Yes, you do."

"I'll get an alarm system."

"You'll be wasting your money. They're as useless as tits on a boar hog."

"It's *my* call."

"Stop being so damn stubborn!"

"You stop meddling!"

They were practically shouting at one another, but Juliana was past caring. She cared only about getting him out of her house.

"Why are you doing this?" she asked, a searing pain ripping through her temple. "I don't have to answer any of your questions. You're—"

It happened then, what her subconscious had most

feared. He reached for her. Hot and fast, he reached for her and yanked her against his chest. The second their limbs made contact, she felt it.

Heat.

That raw heat of old that never failed to burn took control.

Then came the onslaught of his lips. They crushed hers with a hunger that she was unprepared for and unable to stop. She dug her hands into his shoulders and matched his hunger as their moist mouths clung in desperation.

"Shit," he muttered, finally jerking away.

Without taking her eyes off him, she dragged her hand across her lips. "You had no right to do that!"

"Right or not, it was the only surefire way I knew how to shut you up."

Juliana ached to slap his face, but she didn't have the strength. She was shaking all over, and her mouth was as parched as a desert. Bracing herself against the table, she looked at him.

He wasn't faring much better. His face was gray, and his breath was coming in angry bursts.

They stared at one another for a long moment; then he turned and stalked toward the French doors. Once there, he whirled, reached in his pocket and pulled out a card. He pitched it on the nearest table.

"My home number. If you need me, use it."

Twelve

The private club was empty. Rusk couldn't have been happier, although the newest bimbette would be joining him shortly.

He needed to get laid. Maybe that would work the kinks out of his mind and his body. He was certainly counting on it. The broad wasn't cheap. One of his aides had found her, vowing she was famous for her blow jobs.

Thinking about the pleasure that would bring him, Rusk squirmed in his seat.

"Ready for another drink, sir?" the bartender asked.

"Yeah, Freddy, hit me another lick."

The club atop one of the high-rise offices in downtown Houston was Rusk's favorite hangout. He felt secure and protected here, because the clientele were rich and prominent men like himself who coveted their privacy and could be assured of getting it.

Downing the whiskey in one gulp, Rusk swung around and watched the door, then glanced at his watch. The hooker wasn't late, but she was pushing it. He was growing impatient. He didn't want to get drunk and miss out on the fun. Yet he didn't want a clear head that dwelled on the fear that had become his constant companion.

That fear covered him like a shit storm. Thoughts of the missing black book with its far-reaching consequences never left him. Perhaps even more frightening was that conversation with Gates.

Why, out of all the Texas Rangers, had his brother been put in charge of the prison investigation? When it came to doing what was right, Gates was like a dog chewing on a bone. He wouldn't let go. Not only that, but a challenge was what he lived for. Rusk's body shifted into high gear, the blood in his veins turning to Freon.

Rusk didn't know which one was more of a threat. The black book could end his life. Gates could end his career. Suddenly Rusk had the urge to vomit, only to look up and see the woman walk through the door.

His fear disappeared, especially when he saw those big breasts and thick cherry lips, then thought how they would feel sliding down his dick.

He stood and walked toward her.

Juliana smiled and acknowledged the exuberant round of applause before "Juliana Live" went off the air. Today's show had been extra special, she thought, hoping that as a result more people would consider donating their organs.

Lord knows, she felt the need to feel good about something. Yesterday's encounter with Gates had left her mentally and physically bruised. The first thing she had done when she'd awakened from a fretful night of turning and tossing was go to the window. An unmarked car had been parked across the street.

A man was leaning against the door, smoking a cigarette. When he had seen her, he'd dropped the cigarette, crushed it with the toe of his shoe, then nodded at her.

Sighing, Juliana had closed the blinds. Gates had been determined that she wasn't going to be alone, and he had made good on his promise—or threat, as she'd perceived it. However, a plainclothesman had been the least of her worries.

She'd had the task of putting her home back together, though she had managed to make some headway before she'd gone to bed. She had also called her maid, who was more than capable of restoring things to normal. Juliana had no doubt that when she returned home this evening, no signs of the chaos would be evident.

Now, as she remained on the empty set, her thoughts turned back to Gates. How could she have let him kiss her? She *hadn't*. As always, he had simply taken what he wanted. And that moment he'd wanted her. Pressed against him, she had felt that bulge through his slacks, hard and hot, digging into her stomach. She had revelled in the thought that no matter what, she could still make him hard, make him *ache*.

Revenge.

That had been what came to mind, thinking he deserved that particular brand of misery. In her heart she saw it as a taste of justice. But then the reverse had happened. She had gotten caught in her own trap. She had wanted him just as much as he'd wanted her.

Now, as she turned and fled the set toward Benson's office, she upped her pace, determined to outrun her thoughts. She didn't want anything to do with Gates; she didn't want him back in her life. It had taken every ounce of fortitude she had possessed to leave him in the first place, even though he had killed her love for him.

When Patrick had died, he hadn't been there for her; he'd only been concerned about his own sorrow and guilt, trying to drown both by swimming in the bottom of a bottle.

In the end, though, his lack of trust—the conviction that

she had found her solace in the arms of his best friend—
had been the blow that had destroyed their marriage.

Still, they had made a child together, a precious child
who for five years had brought her untold joy. Because
Gates had been a major player in those treasured memories, he would never be totally obliterated from her mind.

That didn't mean she still loved him or wanted him
back, though. Nor did she want him to touch her again.
Then why hadn't she been able to put out that fire he'd
restoked inside her?

A sexual jolt. That was all it had been. She would get
over that. She was no longer a starry-eyed young girl who
thought Gates could walk on the water. Instead, he continued to walk on the edge of a precipice, and if he
weren't careful, he would fall off.

Well, she wasn't about to hang around to pick up the
pieces. She had already trod that path. Anyway, that disastrous clash was a fluke. To think otherwise created a
crippling, mind-numbing terror inside her.

By the time Juliana reached Benson's door, she was
drained. Knowing her face was devoid of color, she
quickly pinched each cheek, convinced she looked bright
and calm, even if she wasn't.

"Great show," Benson said with enthusiasm.

Juliana sat down. "Thanks. I thought it went well myself."

Benson flicked a worried glance at her. "We have to
be careful that tomorrow's show doesn't pale in compari-
son."

"It's on adoption, so it has the potential for a lot of
emotional punch." Juliana paused. "Right now, I don't
know if *I'm* up to it."

"Something happen I ought to know about?" Benson's
gaze pinned her, and there was a slight tension in his tone.

"No," she lied. "It's just a combination of things—Margie's death, for one."

"I still can't believe we don't know the cause yet."

"Me neither. Why is it taking so long?"

Benson reached in his pocket for a cigarette, then, as if realizing he couldn't smoke with Juliana in the room, he put it back. "I'm wondering the same thing."

"You don't sound so chipper yourself."

"It's my wife. I should be with her."

"Do you want to postpone the meeting? It's not that important. I know what has to be done."

"No. Life has to go on, which includes waiting on the cause of Margie's death."

"Well, it's a sure thing that the press isn't going to let up until it's been made public. The vultures haven't lost interest."

"The ratings show that."

"Which I hate," Juliana stressed. "But then, you know how I feel on that subject."

"Right, so let's not belabor it. Let's go over what's on tap for tomorrow."

A short time later, Juliana walked into her office to hear the ringing of the phone. Her secretary was away from her desk, probably in the ladies' room, Juliana told herself, reaching for the receiver.

"Juliana Reed," she said in a distracted mode, her mind lingering on the next day's show.

"I know you have it."

She couldn't pinpoint what alerted her, what made a shiver dart through her. It didn't matter. She recognized a menacing tone when she heard one.

"I beg your pardon," she responded in a chilling tone of her own.

"Lady, this isn't a game."

"I agree."

"Just turn it over."

"Turn what over?"

"If you want to play rough, it's okay with me."

That shiver of a moment ago turned into icy rage. But before she could nail him, the caller went on, "We know Margie gave it to you. So where the fuck is it?"

"Margie didn't give me a damn thing!"

With that, Juliana slammed down the phone, hoping she had burst his eardrum. "Bastard," she muttered, though for all her bravado, she felt hollow inside and scared.

That had been no random call. Someone knew—or thought he did—far too much about her. Suddenly her legs felt as if they had turned to gelatin. Pawing for the chair behind her, she sat down.

What was going on? She didn't know, but whatever it was, it involved Margie, and it was ugly. *And Margie had been living with her.* Had Gates been right? Was that why her house had been broken into? Juliana felt her flesh crawl.

Gates had tried to warn her, but she had been sure his concern had no merit. She knew better now. A new surge of fear compressed her rib cage.

What should she do?

"What a fucking mess."

"Please, Norman," his wife said in a prim tone. "You know how I feel about that vulgar language."

"Oh, for God's sake, Opal, join the real world."

Opal glared at him.

"Careful, or you'll get a wrinkle in that forehead."

"You can be a real bastard when you want to."

"Ah, when the shoe's on the other foot, it's all right."

Opal's mouth tensed, and for a while there was silence

in the master suite in the O'Brien mansion as they both went about dressing for the day. The maid had delivered coffee to the sitting room. They both had yet to partake.

"Are you ready to tell me what's going on?" Opal asked at last, sitting down at her dressing table and reaching for a bottle of makeup.

Norman leaned against the bedpost behind her, his features pinched.

"She's causing trouble."

"Who?" Opal shook the bottle, then opened it.

"Juliana."

Opal's hand stilled, and she swung around, her eyes wide. "Juliana Reed?"

"None other."

"Oh, dear." Disgust altered her soft voice.

"Actually, she and Rusk got into it." Norman went on to explain what had happened, having been apprised of the situation by Rusk.

"You mean she slapped him? How dare she?"

"Don't misunderstand, I'm not making light of that," Norman said. "Not by a long shot. But what concerns me more is that Gates jumped on Rusk when he would have slapped her back."

"Oh, dear," Opal repeated, placing a hand across her chest. "Surely you're not implying that Gates still cares about her?"

"I don't know what's going on. That's why I said this is a fucking mess."

Though Opal blanched again at the use of the foul word, she didn't rebuke him.

"Juliana can hurt Rusk. That talk show of hers is a breeding ground for trouble."

"It's hard for me to believe that fate could play such a mean trick on us," Opal wailed. "It's unthinkable that one of Rusk's campaign workers could be good enough friends with Juliana to live with her.''

Norman's jaw quirked in wry humor. "Murphy's Law."

"So what happens next?" Opal asked.

"That depends on Juliana's modus operandi."

"Maybe this will all blow over." The makeup shook in Opal's hand. "I mean, I find it hard to believe that she'd want anything to do with us."

"God, you *are* out of touch."

"There's no need to insult me just because you're—"

"Spare me," Norman interrupted. "I'm not one of those addle-brained ladies you play bridge with. Credit me with having more sense."

He paused and squeezed the bedpost. Even when he felt his knuckles pop, he didn't let go. "Now that Rusk has crossed that bitch, she'll go for his jugular, you wait and see."

"She could hurt him."

"Hurt him, hell! She can bloody well ruin him."

"She…she knows too much."

"My point exactly."

"So what are you going to do?"

Norman rubbed his jaw, staring into the distance. "I'm going to stop her, that's what."

Thirteen

Gates rubbed the back of his neck. His head felt like a bowling ball sitting on top of his shoulders. He was dead tired, down to his bone marrow. He knew what it meant to burn the candle at both ends.

Hell, who was he kidding? He'd been doing that for years, only he hadn't stopped to think about it. But he was thinking about it now, and the conclusion came as a shock.

He had been convinced that once he'd stopped drinking and turned all his energy to his job, he would find a peace that had heretofore eluded him. Plus he'd had Nicole's company, which he'd hoped would help heal him from within. He had even gone so far as to imagine he could one day look in the mirror without wanting to smash it.

Think again, Bubba.

His life remained a farce. He was merely existing. The last few days had proved that. *Kissing Juliana* had proved that. When it came to her, his head was still up his ass. Warding off a strong urge to vomit, Gates sprang to his feet.

He looked up at the ceiling and breathed deeply, then stared down at the open folder on his desk. He swore and eased back into his chair. He couldn't afford the luxury of indulging himself with thoughts of his ex-wife.

His job had to take top priority. Until Juliana's reappearance, he had never lost sight of that goal or his obligations. Not so anymore. Suddenly he couldn't seem to control his mind and get it back on track; it was like a runaway train headed for a surefire collision. But then, collisions were a way of life for him.

As a rule he had no trouble handling them—as long as they were job-related. Actually, he enjoyed walking the edge of that proverbial cliff, felt it challenged his instincts, which in turn kept him sharp.

What he couldn't handle was the brewing fire in his gut, something he hadn't had to contend with since his marriage crumbled. When he touched Nicole, nothing out of the ordinary happened. A peaceful and secure sensation filled him. There was a lot to be said for that, he reminded himself frantically, trying to bring Nicole's sweet face and smile to mind.

He failed. The vision of Juliana consumed him. It was as if he could feel her warm, pliant body against him, their hearts pounding as one. And her lips—he could taste their clinging, moistness, so sweet, as if they had been coated with invisible honey.

Gates moaned, then lunged to his feet again, fearing his insides would explode. He wished he hadn't seen her. He wished he hadn't gone to her house. More than anything, he wished he hadn't kissed her.

His anger mounted as a powerless feeling stole over him.

Seeing her, touching her, had traumatized him. He would admit that. He was so traumatized, in fact, that he was afraid he would be knocked back into that emotional war zone where he had existed for so long.

He wouldn't let that happen, he vowed, feeling the clenching in his gut relax slightly. He would do the sane thing and stay the hell away from her. She had made it clear that she didn't want anything to do with him or his family. And while he couldn't deny that he wanted her, that he'd walked around with a hard-on since that kiss, she was not going to win the battle.

He had Nicole, who had the ability to put out that fire in his loins rather than start it. He was comfortable with that. His heart was not involved, his emotions untouched. And that was the way he preferred things.

While married to Juliana, he had never stopped aching for her. She had consumed his body, his head and his heart. No more. If the break-in at her home was something more than that, then the police would have to take care of it.

It was not his case or his concern.

He would listen to his brain and not screw up anymore. So what if the organ in his chest wasn't exactly cooperating at the moment? It would. *It had to.* He couldn't risk any more hits to the groin or to the heart.

Losing a child and a wife was enough loss to last him a lifetime. And just because that wife had jumped back into the picture didn't mean a damn thing.

He wouldn't have to see her again.

That thought gave him the peace and strength to clear his mind. He just wished the pounding in his head would cease.

After he had left Juliana's house, he hadn't closed his eyes. Then, this morning, after gulping down a pot of coffee, he had driven to Huntsville to the Texas Department of Corrections main office. For over two hours he had met and talked with the director, who was responsible for letting out the bids to the contracting firms that were now under investigation.

It had been a grueling session; the man hadn't been exactly cooperative, which hadn't surprised Gates. He had expected it, with the investigation threatening to turn ugly and everyone involved in the debacle determined to pass the buck.

Since his return from that meeting, he had been reviewing the contracts awarded in the last two years, which had holes in them big enough to drive a Mack truck through.

In addition to the ongoing investigation into the millions spent on the soybean meat substitute that had turned out to be inedible—rotten, in fact—and the millions' worth of security fencing, much of which was still unused and stacked in a construction supply yard, there was the glaring misuse of other funds.

Misuse was proving the rule rather than the exception.

Gates cursed as he returned to the contracts, which clearly showed that higher than average fees had been paid to several subcontracting companies. It also showed that computers and other office equipment had been purchased but remained unaccounted for.

Some contractors, he noted, had gone so far as to order birthday cakes and pizzas for the inmates, who were supposed to be punished and not praised, for God's sake.

Simply reading that made him furious.

"This stinks big time," he muttered.

"I hope you're not talking about me."

Gates lifted his head and watched as fellow Ranger Dwight Clark walked into the room. Along with Captain Ferguson, he and Dwight were the high-ranking Rangers who manned the Houston office. For the most part, each had his own assignments.

Although Dwight was short, he looked shorter because of his bulging muscles, a reward from working out religiously in a nearby gym. He had a happy-go-lucky personality that complemented his sandy-colored hair and blue eyes.

Gates had found out quickly that Dwight was no push-over, however. In a second, that smile could turn lethal. Gates felt confident and secure with him at his back. When necessary, they made a good team.

"Only if the shoe fits," Gates said drolly.

"Well, I've never been accused of having smelly feet, but armpits—now that's a different story."

"Shit, Clark, give me a break." Gates scowled.

Dwight grinned, then his features turned sober. "So if it's not me that stinks, what is it?"

Gates brought him up to speed on what he'd learned on the prison front.

"Man, that's the pits."

"Tell me about it."

"So what's your next step?"

Gates leaned back in his chair. "Keep muddling through all these papers until I get a clearer sense of what I'm facing." He shrugged. "Then go from there."

"Who gave you the goods?"

"Well, it certainly wasn't the director. Talking to him was like looking through a steel blanket."

"So who came across?"

"Hector Gonzales, the board member who blew the lid off in the first place. But he kept stressing that he's not sure anything underhanded went on."

"Then what the hell is he saying?"

"That all this raises red flags, which isn't good for the prison board's image."

"He sounds like a politician."

"My thoughts exactly."

Dwight scratched his chin. "Ought to be interesting reading, anyway."

"What's interesting is the info on the contractors." Gates reached for a manila envelope under the folder, then patted it. "After I'm finished going through this with a fine-tooth comb, I plan to pay each of them a visit."

"When they open the door and find you standing there, it oughta make their day." Dwight chuckled.

"It'll sure as hell make mine. And would you believe that two of the same firms are in the hunt to build the next round of prisons—the maximum-security units?"

"Wouldn't surprise me."

"It sure as hell does me. After all the screwups, why would you even consider any of the same firms?"

"You know the answer to that. Hell, it's the oldest and dirtiest game in the business world—sweetheart deals."

"You kiss my ass and I'll kiss yours."

"You got it, pal."

"I hope this investigation will put *all* these sons of bitches out of business."

"I second that," Dwight said. "Hell, everyone in the state knows about the corruption. Since the taxpayers are fed up, maybe it'll happen. And if your brother's elected governor, I figure the prison board will definitely get a face-lift."

"Right, only Rusk might not get elected."

"He's leading in all the polls. Don't you ever see your family or read the papers?"

"Families tend to be prejudiced, and the media—well, you know how I feel about them."

Dwight rolled his eyes. "Don't we all. If they'd kept their noses out of our business, then we'd have a hell of a lot more criminals behind bars."

"Amen!"

Dwight grinned, then leaned over and added another folder to Gates' pile. "There's the info you wanted."

Gates frowned. "I could be way off base here, you know."

"Then deep-six it."

"I might just do that."

"Only after you look at it," Dwight said, cocking an eyebrow.

"Get outta here."

Dwight grinned again. "I'm going. For now. But when you get a chance, I need to go over what we've got so far on that Conroe murder."

"A suspect, I hope?"

"It's looking that way."

"But nothing on the beer joint murders?" Gates asked.

"Our boys from Austin are still crawling all over that crime scene. Maybe in a few days we'll have something concrete to sink our teeth into."

"Do you have the same feeling the whole fuckin' world's gone nuts?"

"Every day," Dwight drawled on his way out the door.

Once the other ranger had gone, Gates shoved the prison folder aside and stared out the window. He hadn't even realized that the sunshine had turned to rain.

Sighing, he reached for the folder that Dwight had brought him. This morning, before he'd left for Huntsville and the Texas Department of Corrections, generally referred to as TDC, he'd asked Dwight to run a check on Margie Bowers.

Now, after having faced the brutal fact that neither Juliana nor the break-in was his business, he wished that Dwight had turned down his request.

Gates cut a glance toward the folder, then, muttering violently, snatched it and flipped it open. A short time later he closed it. He couldn't hide his disappointment. The file had contained nothing out of the ordinary about Margie Bowers, and nothing that connected her with the break-in.

Still, there were too many factors that didn't add up: her mysterious death; her connection with Juliana; the break-in at Juliana's apartment shortly after Margie's death.

He had hoped that something in the report would jiggle his gut instinct, but it hadn't. Still, it didn't matter, because it was none of his concern. He had no business getting involved. As Juliana had so succinctly pointed out, this was *not* his investigation. And Juliana's welfare was not his responsibility, which meant he could stay out of the loop and not feel a damn thing.

Too bad it wasn't that simple.

Swearing, Gates shoved the Bowers folder aside, then reached for the envelope.

He opened it and begin reading, studying the pictures that had been included. Gonzales had been thorough, Gates was glad to see. Company heads had been photographed coming and going at their buildings, their homes, restaurants and various other places.

He didn't know what caused him to stop at a particular photograph and take a closer look. Maybe it was the gut instinct that never failed him. He didn't know and didn't care.

He only knew that the head of Worldwide Builders, Carl Mason, was walking out of the building in the company of a woman—and not just any woman, either.

Margie Bowers.

"How 'bout them apples?" he mused aloud.

Could there be a connection there, a common denominator? It would be interesting to know just how well Margie had known Carl Mason.

Then something unexpected kicked him in the gut. *Margie had worked for Rusk.* So what was she doing with

Mason? Had he been just an acquaintance—or something more?

He should tip off HPD, Gates told himself. But first he wanted to make sure he wasn't reading more into this than was actually there. Lifting the phone, he called the medical examiner at the police department.

When his party came on the line, Gates asked, "Hey, Ellis, you by any chance know the cause of the Bowers woman's death yet?"

He waited for what seemed an interminable length of time before he heard Ellis' voice.

"This is your lucky day. Got it right here."

"Shoot."

Gates listened, then hung up, but not before he felt his blood curdle.

Fourteen

The cell phone rang.

The conversation ceased as Oscar Maroney, the most lucrative sponsor of "Juliana Live," smiled apologetically before reaching into his coat pocket.

Juliana tried not to listen or watch, so she shifted her gaze to Benson, who looked as uncomfortable as she was. His eyes seemed focused on their surroundings.

She followed suit, thoroughly enjoying this upscale Italian restaurant. It was touted as one of Houston's finest. She hadn't been disappointed. The food and service had been impeccable.

However, the purpose of this night on the town had been business, though Maroney had called it a celebration. Juliana noted that the establishment's population of young movers and shakers had dwindled as it got close to eleven.

Still, a few remaining couples were either drinking heavily or digging into delicate helpings of rich French pastries, something that she had just enjoyed. She was stuffed, but it felt good. She had needed a good meal, since she hadn't taken the time to eat all day. She couldn't. Her stomach rebelled every time she thought about—

She must have made some kind of noise, because Benson gave her a strange look.

"What's the matter?" he asked.

Juliana forced an innocent smile. "Nothing. Why?"

"Whatever that noise was, it sounded like it came from your toes."

Juliana made a dismissive gesture.

"Tired?" Benson pressed, seemingly unsatisfied.

"Lately I'm always that way."

"Me, too."

His features bore that out. His eyes were sunk into his head, and the nervous tic in his right cheek was working overtime. He'd been drinking quite a bit, too. Juliana suspected that stress had contributed to his lack of focus tonight and the past few days. She had never considered Benson nervous, but now she wasn't so sure.

But then, who wasn't nervous? she asked herself, swallowing another sigh. The sudden and unexpected events had certainly flipped her life upside down.

Oscar Maroney finally clamped his phone shut and turned back to them. "Sorry about that."

"No problem," Benson said.

Maroney frowned. "Unfortunately, I'm afraid there is, and I'm going to have to leave."

"Please, don't apologize," Juliana responded, her gaze focused on the tall, thin, graying executive. "It's time I was leaving, as well. It's late and I...we do have a show to do tomorrow, you guys."

Broad smiles broke across both men's faces, and they lifted glasses filled with Dom Perignon.

"Amen to that!" Oscar said, his intense blue eyes scrutinizing her. "And you're doing a stupendous job, so don't get any ideas about leaving us. If New York knocks on your door, you tell 'em to knock elsewhere. We can make you as big a star right here in Big H."

While Juliana couldn't help but bask in the praise, she

knew that Margie's tragic death had contributed to the show's current popularity. She despised that.

On the other hand, she had worked hard and hoped that, regardless of the incident, her show would have come into its own. It was to that thought that she clung as she smiled at Oscar. "Thank you for the vote of confidence and a wonderful evening."

Maroney shook his head. "I'm the grateful one here. I should be thanking you and Benson."

"You just did," Benson said, taking a healthy sip of his drink. "With this marvelous dinner."

"The first of many—count on it. I want to stress how ecstatic my company is with the ratings. My God, it's phenomenal how they've skyrocketed, which is what's going to enable us to implement some of the things we've been discussing tonight."

Benson grinned. "The sky's the limit."

"Absolutely," Oscar said, rising, then glancing at his watch. "You two stay put and finish the champagne. I'll be in touch."

With that he strode off, having already taken care of the check. Benson used the ensuing silence to drain his glass. Juliana hid a tinge of concern, never having known him to hit the booze with such intensity.

"Do you think you can make it home?" she asked, forcing lightness into her tone.

He didn't take offense. "Probably not. Mind driving me?"

"Not at all."

"Thanks," he muttered, averting his gaze.

"So, are you ready?"

Benson eyed the remaining contents of the bottle, and an eyebrow quirked. "Do we have to?"

"Yes."

His mouth turned down. "Hell, you sound like—" He broke off, a flicker of something akin to both anger and pain changing his features.

Juliana turned away, certain he was about to refer to his wife. When she looked back at him, he seemed to have collected himself and was watching her.

"Don't," he said.

Juliana stared back, confused. "Don't what?"

"Keep beating up on yourself over why the show's a success."

"I'm trying not to."

"Don't try, just do it. Believe me, I hate what happened to Margie." For a moment he hesitated, clearing his throat. "She was my friend, too."

"Are you sure about that?"

Benson looked puzzled. "What does that mean?"

"I'm not sure, just that I realized afterward that I really didn't know much about her at all." She paused. "How 'bout you? How well did you know her?"

Benson averted his gaze and shrugged. "I'd say not even as well as you. Why?"

"I'm not sure. It's just that, since she died, strange things have been happening."

"Besides the break-in?"

"I received a crank call."

"Go on." His tone was brusque.

She told him what the caller had said.

Benson cursed. "What could Margie have had that was so damn important?"

"Beats me, but I intend to find out. So if you know anything that might shed some light on this, speak now."

"Oh, no, you don't. You have no business playing detective. You leave that to the police, you hear?"

"I haven't even told them."

"Now that's the craziest thing I've ever heard."

"I know. I intend to, though."

"Meanwhile, you'd best take care. I don't like the sound of all this."

Juliana shivered. "Me neither."

Later, after she was home in bed, her eyes slid to the phone. Would it ring? Or had the caller found what he'd been looking for? She prayed that he had.

As much as she feared that stranger's call, she feared another caller more. Gates. Something told her that she hadn't heard the last of her ex, which was ridiculous, of course. Why would Gates bother her again? He wouldn't.

It was that damn kiss. It had done a number on her, reawakened her body, *made her ache.*

God help her, if it came down to tangling with that threatening caller or Gates, she would choose the caller.

A tremor ran through her, and she yanked the covers up to her neck.

"Ah, baby, don't stop," Rusk muttered, then groaned.

The brunette, whose head was hanging over him, had his dick on fire. Her mouth and tongue had been teasing him for a long time—too long.

He snatched her by that long hair, then flipped her onto her back. Without so much as a word, he spread her thighs and entered her. After two hard thrusts and groans, he came.

Once he'd rolled off her and back onto his side of the bed, she propped her head on her palm and peered down at him. "That wasn't very nice," she said in a petulant tone.

"You had an orgasm, didn't you?" Rusk's tone bordered on boredom.

"Yes, but—"

"Then stop bitching. What more do you want?"

"More than just a fuck, that's for sure."

Rusk laughed, sat upright, then swung his legs off the bed and onto the floor. "Yeah, right."

Her mouth puckered even more, but when she spoke, her tone was conciliatory. "I mean it, Rusk. I—"

"It ain't gonna happen. We roll in the hay, then you go home or wherever. End of story."

She raked a long fingernail across his shoulders. "It doesn't have to be that way."

"Yes, it does." He stood.

"Where are you going?"

He turned around and gave her a hard stare. "That's none of your business."

Her mouth curled in displeasure. "You're really being an ass."

"You're really pushing your luck. Get dressed and get out."

"Will you call me?"

"Maybe."

She flounced off the bed, her eyes bright with tears. "I thought we—"

"Shit," Rusk interrupted in an ugly tone. "Don't think. Just get the fuck out. I have an appointment."

He leaned over, picked her clothes up off the motel-room floor and pitched them at her. "You've got five minutes."

In twenty minutes, not only was he alone but dressed in his finest, as though he were going to a fund-raiser, though that wasn't the case. He was to meet Tamara at his parents' house for drinks and dinner.

Without some pussy first, he couldn't have gone. Since Margie had croaked, he hadn't found anyone who could satisfy his sexual appetite. He needed that release on a steady basis or he would go off the deep end.

The bimbette he'd just booted out had been okay. She had taken the kinks out of his body so he could endure the evening ahead, but that was as far as it went.

She couldn't get him off like Margie. But then, she hadn't stolen something of value from him, either, something that he hadn't yet recovered.

Stinging sweat that felt like needles pierced his skin as he walked out into the evening air and straight into his waiting limo. A short time later, he was in his family's formal living room, a glass of Chivas in his hand.

"So how was your day, darling?"

Rusk glanced at Tamara, who was also in formal attire. Always the lady, he thought, swallowing a sour belch. Her cocktail dress was a soft pink, complementing her fair skin and dark hair, which was swept up on top of her head rather than in its usual chignon.

He supposed many men would find her attractive, though he didn't. But then, he knew the cold and clinical side of her. He had only married her because his parents thought her fitting. So far, she had been the asset he'd hoped for in his bid for public office. He had to make sure that didn't change.

"Actually, I had a good day," he lied, peering at her over the top of his glass.

"Any word on Margie Bowers?"

Her question startled him so that his whiskey hit his stomach with a thud. Careful, Rusk reminded himself. Keep your cool. Tamara suspected he'd had an affair with Margie, but she had no proof. He aimed to keep it that way. "I'm not following you."

"Don't play dumb with me. I'm talking about the cause of death."

Tamara's tone was cool, as if she was just making polite conversation. Rusk wasn't so sure, and that bothered him.

"If it's been determined, I'm not aware of it."

"Then you should find out."

His daddy's gruff voice brought him around to face the door. Both Norman and Opal were standing just inside the room. They were also dressed in their finery, which didn't surprise him. Dinners at the O'Brien home were formal, and those who put their feet under Norman's table were expected to adhere to certain rules.

Only Gates bucked those rules and got by with it.

"What's that smirk about?" Norman added, striding toward the bar and pouring himself and his wife a drink.

"I was just thinking about Gates and how he always thumbs his nose at all this."

Opal looked pained. "If he didn't look so much like an O'Brien, I'd swear that hospital gave me the wrong baby."

Everyone smiled, but only fleetingly, especially Rusk. Even though he loved his brother, Gates could be a royal pain in the butt. The more he thought about his brother sticking his nose and perhaps his gun where it didn't belong, the more he wanted to snatch that full bottle of Chivas and chug it down.

"So let's talk some more about that campaign worker," Norman said, sitting down next to Tamara.

Rusk ran his finger under the collar of his shirt. "That's not a very pleasant before dinner topic."

"Death never is," Norman said in a matter-of-fact tone.

Opal glanced at her husband, her eyebrows raised. "What are you getting at?"

Norman never looked at her. Instead, he kept his eyes on his son. "The media's still having a high old time with the way she died."

"So?" Rusk asked with controlled indifference.

Norman's eyes crinkled. "So, if there was foul play involved, *you* can't afford to be linked with her."

"It's too late for that. She worked for me." Rusk hated talking about Margie; where she was concerned, he was much too vulnerable. But that was his secret; his family must never know.

"Then it's your responsibility to find out how and why she died. Hell, man, there's a lot of sympathy you can milk from that situation."

"If there wasn't any foul play involved, that is," Opal put in softly.

"Hell, she probably had a heart attack," Rusk declared.

"At her age?" Tamara said in a flat tone. "Get real."

Rusk glared at her, though his voice was nonchalant. "It happens every day."

"Maybe she owed someone some money," Norman said, smiling coldly, "and he bumped her off."

"Maybe it was a scorned lover," Tamara chimed in, also smiling.

Rusk didn't smile. He couldn't, not when his lips felt like bloodless worms. Damn them for tormenting him this way.

As if his mother sensed his distress, Opal crossed to where he stood and linked her arm through his. "All we're saying, son, is that we don't want you involved in anything shady."

"Your mother's right," Norman said. "Nothing must soil your name, or that of this family, if you want to be governor of this state."

"I'm well aware of that," Rusk snapped.

"Then clear the matter up and move on."

Rusk belched again as his gaze met and locked with the elder O'Brien's. "Yes, sir."

"You'd best not just give lip service to your daddy, Rusk, dear. We're too close to victory to let anything stop us now. And you know what even the merest hint of impropriety can do," Tamara said silkily.

He would like nothing better than to slap that cool but taunting smile off his wife's lips. Perhaps she did know he'd been sleeping with Margie. He fingered his collar again, then muttered, "Rest easy, all of you." His tone was testy, at best. "I, more than any of you, know what's at stake."

"Fine, then you'll act accordingly." Norman rose and smiled. "Now that we've settled that matter, let's go in to dinner."

Rusk brought up the rear, dreading the thought of putting anything in his stomach. He felt certain it wouldn't stay, thanks to Margie Bowers.

The idea that she might be burning in hell brought him little comfort.

Fifteen

Bullets whizzed by Gates' head.

"That sumbitch is really pissin' me off."

Gates cut a quick glance at Sheriff Weaver, who was squatting beside him and dodging those same bullets. The two deputies weren't immune, either.

Gates wanted to say amen to Weaver's words, only he didn't. Now was not the time to be flippant. Besides, he was too busy assessing the situation. His mind raced, as did his adrenaline.

The arrest of the man inside the small, secluded building should have been a piece of cake. The perp had supposedly mugged, then stabbed, a man under a bridge in this county. Several weeks before he'd been assigned the prison case, Gates had been called in to help investigate the murder at the request of the sheriff's department.

DNA testing on two items found at the crime scene had led them to suspect the man inside, Simon Landry. Finally they had gathered enough evidence to issue a warrant for his arrest. Apparently Landry had other ideas. He wasn't going down without a fight.

Another round of bullets zipped by their heads.

"Shit!" Weaver snapped. "When I git my hands on that old scrawny sumbitch, I'm gonna—"

"Hold your horses, Sheriff," Gates interrupted in a terse tone, his eyes darting to the lean-to that was a few yards from the house. "We've got to get him first, then you can have your say."

Gates had been on his way to interview the first contractor on his list, Carl Mason, the one Margie Bowers had been photographed with, when he'd gotten the call from Weaver, saying the suspect was finally in his house.

What they had hoped would be a surprise visit had turned out to be anything but. Landry had obviously been watching and had seen them drive up the long road. Before they reached the house, he'd barricaded himself inside what looked to Gates like an old outhouse.

Gates had wondered why the man hadn't hidden in the woods, but now Gates knew—Landry figured as long as he had guns and ammunition, he was all right.

Wrong.

Like Weaver, Gates wasn't keen on getting shot at. In fact, his piss factor was also rising by the moment, especially when more rounds kept on coming, pinging all around them. Enough was enough.

"Can you see the sumbitch?" Weaver asked while lifting his own head slightly above the hood of the car.

"No, and I don't think we will, either."

"Hell, the way them bullets are flying, that sumbitch can use us for target practice for forty forevers."

"I don't think so." Gates' tone was deadly.

"You gonna try and take him?" Weaver asked, looking at him through faded blue eyes. "Say, from the rear?"

"You got it."

"We'll cover you."

"Only until I get through that clearing. Afterward, I'm home free. I know these woods just about as well as our boy does. Used to hunt in these parts." Gates checked, then reloaded, his .45. "You just keep him busy by returning his fire."

"How 'bout I go with you and leave my boys here to fire the rounds?"

Gates didn't miss the wistful note in the sheriff's voice, and though he understood the man's position, he couldn't indulge him. This was probably the only time Weaver and his deputies had ever been involved in this kind of danger. In fact, he would bet the deputies had never even drawn their guns outside the pistol range. Still, the guy firing at them knew what he was doing and had to be stopped.

Landry's records showed that he had fought in Nam and wasn't to be taken lightly. At this point, Gates felt secure in his own ability to take him down.

"It'll be better if only one of us goes in."

"Whatever you say." Weaver sounded disappointed, but resigned.

Gates crawled between the cars, then paused and glanced back over his shoulder. "Just keep the bastard busy."

Weaver spat a stream of juice from the wad of tobacco lodged in his jaw; the thick brown liquid landed a few yards from Gates. He flinched, thinking he would almost rather be struck by a bullet than the shit that came out of Weaver's mouth.

"Will do," he said before spitting again.

Gates swallowed a curse, then, crouching lower, ran into the woods to the sound of rapid gunfire.

So far, so good, he thought a few minutes later when he arrived at the precise spot where he wanted to be, the rear of the cabin. It proved to be his lucky day. The back door was open, and from where he stood, he had a clear view of Landry's slender frame.

With the hammer back on his pistol, Gates dashed from tree to tree until he reached the entrance to the shack itself. Pressing against one side of the rotten wood, he sucked in air and raised his gun.

Gates peered around the corner and watched as the man reloaded and fired off another round.

He made his move, tiptoeing into the room. Luck was with him; the surface was dirt and muffled his booted steps. Gates didn't stop until he was directly behind Landry. That was when he positioned the barrel of his gun against the back of Landry's head.

"Grab some sky, asshole!"

Why didn't his cell phone ring? Any other time, it would have been driving him nuts. He was hoping for a call from his secretary confirming an appointment with Carl Mason.

As soon as Simon Landry had been taken into custody and the property cordoned off, Gates had bade his farewell, leaving Sheriff Weaver in charge.

He had felt good about arresting Landry, a loner whose motive for killing the man under the bridge was still unknown. Gates almost smiled. If Sheriff Weaver had his way, it wouldn't be that way for long. The man had been itching to interrogate the war veteran turned criminal.

Gates pulled his mind off that investigation and glared at the phone again. Miraculously, it rang. Placing it against his ear, he said, "Talk to me, Gretchen."

"Sorry, it's not Gretchen."

Hiding his irritation, Gates asked, "What's up, Nicole?"

"I shouldn't have called. I can hear it in your voice."

"It's okay."

"No, it's not."

Gates wasn't about to argue. "Is something wrong?"

"No."

She paused then, and Gates could picture the confusion on her face and the twist of pain. He didn't need this aggravation, not when his body was already coiled into one big, hard knot for more reasons than the incident he'd just gone through.

"I just wanted to know if I should cook dinner for you. I'd planned..." Her voice faded, and he cursed silently.

"Not tonight, I'm afraid. I'm swamped with work. I'll call you, okay?"

"All...right."

She didn't sound convinced, but Gates couldn't do anything to reassure her. Spending time with Nicole was far down on his agenda. Soon, though, he would have to deal with her and their relationship. She deserved better than his present conduct.

The second after he hit the Off button, the phone jangled again. This time it was Gretchen, but with news he didn't want to hear. Carl Mason was out of town for the next two days.

Grim-faced, Gates considered trying to see another of the contractors, but only for a moment.

"Screw it," he muttered before heading in a direction that he had declared off limits. He'd only gone a few yards when he slammed on the brakes.

He'd made a pact with himself to stay away from her. Yet he had to do this, or so he told himself. Even if his actions were grounds to commit him, he wanted Juliana to hear this particular bit of news from him.

A few minutes later, Gates nosed his car into a spot marked for visitors only, then got out, but not before reaching for the Stetson and plopping it on his head.

The sunlight was waning as he strode into the TV station. Since he had no idea where to find Juliana, he wound his way down the hall until he came to a reception area.

A young lady was on her feet and reaching for her purse. When she saw Gates, she paused, her eyes widening. He didn't have to follow her gaze to know that it had drifted from the badge pinned to his shirt down to the pistol attached to his belt.

"Uh, can I help you?" she asked, curiosity warming her voice.

"Hope so. I'm looking for Juliana Reed."

"She's not—"

"I'll handle this, Gwyn. You go ahead and leave."

The woman nodded, then hurried out the door. Gates turned toward the man who had spoken and waited for him to speak again.

"I'm Benson Garner."

Gates didn't have the slightest idea who he was, and he didn't give a damn, either. He didn't have time for pleasantries.

As if Benson picked up on that, he added, "I'm the producer of Juliana's show."

He held out his hand. "Gates O'Brien."

Instant recognition flashed in the man's eyes as he took Gates' hand in a brief shake. "Juliana's ex-husband." It wasn't a question but rather a flat statement of fact.

Gates ignored the man's instant hostility. "Is she here?"

"No, she's gone on a preinterview."

Gates swore under his breath, his feelings so mixed that he felt like a grenade ready to detonate. He didn't want to be here, yet he did. He had to see her, yet he didn't want to see her.

"Is there something I can help you with?" Benson asked.

Gates got his emotions under control. "No, but thanks anyway."

Benson gave him an odd look but didn't respond until Gates was halfway down the hall.

"Wait up."

Gates turned and watched as the man came toward him. When Benson reached him, it was obvious he was uneasy. Gates tried to hold his eyes, but he couldn't. The man kept shifting his gaze away. His sixth sense kicking in, he simply waited as if he had all the patience in the world.

"Juliana's my friend," Benson began.

"That's nice."

Benson flushed, and his chin jutted. "Maybe you're too busy to hear what I have to say."

"Does it concern Juliana?"

"Yes."

"Then I'm not too busy."

Benson cleared his raspy throat. "I don't figure Juliana will tell you this, so I'm going to." He paused. "I'm worried about her."

Gates' body tensed. "Has something happened?"

"Yes. Some idiot called her on the phone."

"And?" His tone was chilling.

"He…he threatened her."

A few minutes later, when Gates walked back outside, after hearing the whole sorry story, that grenade inside him had blown.

He was about to do some serious ass kicking.

Juliana's eyes scanned her living room. Her belongings had been put back in their proper places, yet she no longer felt at home here. It wasn't because her furniture was different, either, though the couch and two chairs were new, the intruder having shredded both beyond repair.

New plants also occupied old positions, which added

to the change. The only thing that hadn't been touched was the aquarium.

While those visible changes were acceptable, the hidden ones weren't. The break-in seemed to have reawakened her old vulnerabilities, her insecurities, especially when she dwelled on how her son's picture had been shattered.

Her heart and her space had been violated, and she couldn't get past that. Now, each time she walked inside, she paused, her heart lodged in her throat.

Part of the irrational feeling stemmed from that phone call, though it hadn't been repeated, which had kept her from going to the police. The media hype had dwindled, and she had no intention of setting them off again.

Besides, she didn't feel in danger. Not really. The emotion festering inside her was more akin to anger. Plus she was feeling sorry for herself, unable to find peace where Gates was concerned.

Suddenly Juliana's head began to spin, but she fought off the wave of dizziness. She refused to dredge up any more emotions she was ill-equipped to deal with. Before that dizziness moved her into the panic zone, she made her way toward the bedroom. What she needed was a bath and a long night's sleep.

She was halfway there when the doorbell chimed.

"Damn," she muttered. If that was someone peddling aluminum siding or inviting her to join the Mormon Church, they were going to be sorry they'd picked her doorbell to ring.

She opened the door, only to let out a gasp, fighting off another bout of light-headedness.

"What do you want?" she bit out.

Gates was equally blunt. "To know why you didn't tell me about the phone call."

She glared at him at the same time that she grabbed the door, prepared to slam it in his face.

"Oh, no, you don't." He stuck his booted foot across the threshold.

For a moment their gazes tangled, both breathing hard.

"Go away." She heard both the pleading and the breathlessness in her voice. She couldn't deal with him, not when he looked so mad, so tough, *so safe.* God, what was she thinking? Safe was the last thing he was.

"I'm not going anywhere until I talk to you."

"Dammit, Gates."

"You can curse me all you want, but I'm not leaving."

Juliana stepped back, her face crimson with fury, knowing that he meant what he said. Even after he was inside and the door closed behind him, she couldn't bring herself to say a word. She could only stare at him, taking in how tired he looked, not to mention the way the warm, muggy air had dampened his white shirt, calling attention to the pulsing muscles in his jaw and across his shoulders.

Without his hat, she noticed for some crazy reason the way his hair clung to his neck just above his collar. But it was the way he looked at her, with that dangerous wildness of old, that sent a shaft of heat through her.

"Juliana, talk to me."

"Give me one good reason why I should."

His green eyes pinned her. "Because Margie was murdered."

She opened her mouth, but nothing came out.

"Someone poisoned her."

Sixteen

"Poisoned?" she whispered, finally able to force that vile word past her lips.

Something seemed to shift behind Gates' eyes, and when he spoke, his voice was surprisingly gentle, as though he was trying his best to soften the blow. "I'm afraid so."

Juliana continued to stare at him, grappling to cope with this latest nightmare, her mind already on overload. "I...don't understand."

"I don't either. Yet."

Now he was the Gates of old—the lawman, in charge and hard-edged, steel running though his bloodstream. She could hear the repressed fury in his voice, even in his breathing.

"But how...I mean...?" Juliana couldn't go on. The words stuck in her throat. The thought of violent death so close shook her to the core. She hugged herself as if for protection—though from whom she would rather not think.

"I can't imagine who would do such a thing to Margie."

"Can't you?"

"What are you saying?"

"Forget it."

Juliana had enough wits about her to know that something was going on here, something she couldn't quite grasp, something not only disturbing and sick but something that involved *her*. Though she hated to ask and have that suspicion confirmed, she had no choice.

"How...do you think I fit into all this?"

"I'm not sure yet."

"But you have your theory, or what was it you used to say? Your gut instinct's kicking in?"

Gates arched an eyebrow, as if surprised she remembered. "You're right on both counts, only you've already heard what I have to say."

"Maybe I'd like to hear it again."

"Okay. I'm still of the opinion that the break-in wasn't random. Margie obviously has or had something someone wants. Since she lived here, it's also obvious that the scumbag thinks it's here." He paused. "To make this scenario even worse, he thinks you know where that something is, or possibly have it yourself."

Juliana wet her lips. "That's crazy!"

"To you, maybe."

A short silence followed before she asked, "So how do *you* fit into all this?"

He shifted his shoulders in a nonchalant manner and averted his gaze. "I'm a cop."

"What you are is a Ranger."

"Who goes where he's needed."

"And you're needed here?"

"As far as I'm concerned, I am."

She heard the belligerence in his tone. He didn't like to be questioned. Too bad. "Stop being evasive, Gates. And stop pretending you don't know what I'm talking about. The police are perfectly capable of handling this case. They haven't called you in."

His face grew distant.

"Have they?"

"Nope," he bit out.

"They won't, either."

"That remains to be seen. Margie's death might be related to a case we're...I'm already involved in."

"I don't believe you," she said flatly.

"Why else would I involve myself?" His voice turned raspy and bitter. "Surely you don't think it's because of you, that being around you is something I enjoy?"

She blanched, but her tone was hot. "You always did know how to go for the jugular!"

"You ain't bad at that yourself."

They glared at one another for a long moment; then Juliana turned away, appalled at her lack of control. Gates continued to possess an uncanny ability to get under her skin.

"Okay, so tell me exactly how her death relates to your case."

"I can't."

"Can't—or won't?"

"That's not the point."

"That's exactly the point."

"Look, you know me. I never shot a rattler that didn't bite me first."

She rolled her eyes. "Save the homespun gibberish for someone else, okay?"

His mouth turned sulky, but she didn't care. "So what *can* you tell me?" she pressed. While he might not be lying entirely, she held on to her suspicion that he was conducting his own outside, renegade investigation, though she had no idea why.

He had already made it clear that he would rather be anywhere than around her. That she believed. This kind of togetherness was an untenable situation for both of them.

"I know that everyone closely associated with Margie will be checked out," he was saying.

"Including me?"

"Including you."

"Surely no one will think I had anything to do with her...death?"

"At this juncture, HPD won't rule anyone out. Everyone will be in their line of fire."

Juliana noticed how quickly he sidestepped volunteering his opinion as to her innocence or guilt, which cut her slightly, only to reinforce her foolishness for trusting him.

"What about your dear brother?" Her tone was snide. "Does that include him, as well?"

Gates' features contorted with anger, then he seemed to regain a semblance of patience. "Damn straight it does."

"Oh, really? I thought Rusk was a sacred cow."

"This is not about Rusk."

"It might be. Margie worked for him."

"But she lived with you."

"Which doesn't mean that much. I've already told you I didn't know much about her personal life."

"Someone else apparently doesn't think so."

"Ah, so we're back to the break-in?"

"No, we've beaten that horse to death for the moment. I'd rather talk about the phone call."

Juliana felt a cold, metallic taste invade her mouth.

"Whoever called you came right out and accused you of having that certain something apparently belonging to Margie."

"Benson should've kept his mouth shut."

"Jesus, is that all you can say?"

Droplets of perspiration collected between her breasts. "Go on. I'm...listening."

"It all connects. She was murdered...and you were threatened, right?"

When she didn't answer, Gates moved closer and this time spat the word. "Right?"

She nodded.

"So are you finally getting the message that you're in danger yourself?"

Juliana placed her hand over her ears and shook her head. "No!"

He stepped toward her. "Yes! You can't ignore what's happening here!"

Their eyes locked for one terrible moment.

"Stop raising your voice to me!"

"Then stop being so pigheaded!"

Suddenly she felt herself go limp, frustration and terror clamoring inside her.

"Hey, it's going to be all right."

She hadn't expected the shift in his tone or the pinched agony mirrored on his face. It completely unnerved her.

"No, it's not," she whispered, blinking back the tears. Nothing was ever going to be all right again. The fear he had forced on her was like a fist, pounding her insides. "You're...you're scaring me."

"It's for your own good. You have to know that."

Before she could reply, he reached out and put a hand on her upper arm. To her dismay, she didn't pull away but basked in the safety it represented. Then, realizing how foolishly she was behaving, she fought to reclaim her senses. She didn't know if he was touching her out of concern or anger, but it didn't matter.

Both represented danger, that kiss flashing to mind. Still, she didn't pull away.

"Juliana, I won't let that bastard hurt you."

It was the heat from his body that was her first clue that, if left alone, things would get out of hand. The second clue was another change in his voice. She heard that unidentifiable something, a sound that had never failed to turn her into putty. No longer. She gave her arm a jerk.

That was when his fingertips made contact with her breast.

They both froze. Trembling, Juliana sucked in her breath and held it. Cursing, Gates backed away, his thick brows drawing together in a frown.

Their eyes met again, and the silence that followed was almost painful in its intensity.

"Sorry, I shouldn't have—"

"Forget it. I have."

He went rigid, and when he spoke, his voice was hard. "Let's get back to business."

"No, let's not." The stress was wearing on her.

"Look, we still have to talk. I need to hear in your own words exactly what that crank caller said."

"No, you don't. I've had it."

For a moment it appeared that he was determined to press the point. His eyes, like a laser, peered into her. Then, as if he realized she'd indeed had enough, he relented. "Okay, I'm going, but I'll be back."

"No."

"Hey, that's not your call. Whether you like it or not, I'm in this for the long haul. So let's do this with as little bloodletting as possible."

With that he turned and walked to the door, but before he left, he whipped around, announcing, "And when I'm not around, someone else will keep an eye on your place."

When she would have opened her mouth to argue, he

stalled her with an impatient gesture. "That's nonnegotiable, Juliana."

"I don't want you back in my life."

He winced as if she'd kicked him. "That's obvious, but you'll get over it."

"Look—"

He tipped his hat. "I'll be in touch."

"Gates!"

"That's also nonnegotiable."

This time he walked out and slammed the door behind him.

Juliana shook all over, and her tears spilled over. The idea that she had put her past behind her had proved a sham. She had thought she was through remembering, through crying, through blaming herself for what might have been. Now, because of an unexpected twist of events, her past was once again nipping at her heels.

While she grieved that someone had deliberately taken Margie's life, she grieved more, God help her, that Gates was back in hers.

Sweat highlighted Carl Mason's pink, flabby cheekbones, while his eyes squinted on Gates. "I'm sure you'll find everything in order."

Gates thumbed through the packet resting on his thigh but made no move to get out of the soft leather chair in the contractor's posh office. He didn't know what it was about this man that raised his hackles, but something did. Certainly his looks were off-putting, but that wasn't it. His voice was the same way; it was deep and thick, reminding Gates of mud stuck in a drainpipe.

Yet neither his looks nor his voice won the vote. It was something about his arrogance. His own father behaved in the same manner, as if he was just a tad better than most humans who walked the earth.

"I certainly hope so, Mr. Mason," Gates said at last. "I appreciate you having this info ready."

"You're welcome. Glad to help in any way I can."

Mason's cheeks turned pinker, yet Gates had to hand it to him; the contractor's voice was cool, even cold. He might be dealing with a crook, but he damn sure wasn't dealing with a dummy.

Carl Mason and his partners hadn't built an empire of this magnitude on luck alone. Gates suspected that this round man in front of him was the brains behind the operation.

"While I assume all the contractors who built prior prisons are being investigated, you'll find that, with us, you're barking up an empty tree." Mason paused and stood. "Our company is and always has been above reproach. Otherwise, we wouldn't be on the list to build more prisons."

"Then you won't have anything to worry about," Gates drawled, still making no move to get up, though he sensed Mason was eager for him to do just that. He wondered why. What, if anything, did the man have to hide?

Gates realized that if any dirt *did* exist, it wouldn't be overt. He would have to dig for it.

But that wasn't the only reason why he'd come here. It was Mason's connection to Margie that had put him at the top of Gates' prison hit list.

"I'll cooperate in any way I can," Mason said.

Before Gates could comment, his cell phone rang. "Excuse me."

Moments later, Gates stood and extended his hand to Mason. "I have to go. With any luck, we won't have to meet again."

"We won't, I'm sure of it," Mason responded, his voice curt and confident.

Gates reached the door, then turned. "By the way, how well did you know Margie Bowers?"

Mason didn't so much as blink. "I don't recall knowing her at all. Why?"

"Just wondering."

He'd thrown him the tainted bone, Gates told himself as he made his way to his truck and climbed inside. Now he would sit back and watch the arrogant bastard choke on it.

That thought was very much with him thirty minutes later when he turned onto the street where Margie's parents lived. He was responding to the call he'd gotten in Mason's office.

Perry and Ethel Bowers were sitting on the porch, looking dazed and traumatized. Forensics and a detective from HPD were inside, going over the entire premises. Like Juliana's, their home had been torn apart.

Gates introduced himself, then sat in a chair across from the swing. "Was anything taken?" he asked in a gentle tone.

Ethel clutched her husband's hand before focusing her watery gaze on Gates. "Not that we've found. But then, everything's such a mess." She bit down on her lower lip to stop it from trembling.

Perry squeezed her hand. "It's okay, honey."

"No, it's not okay," she said fiercely. "First someone murders our Margie, then someone destroys our house."

"That same someone did the same thing to Juliana's," Gates said bluntly.

Ethel threw her free hand over her lips to cover her gasp. Then, removing it, she said, "I'm so sorry."

"Is there anything you can tell me about your daughter that you haven't already told the police?"

"No," Perry said, his tone hardening.

"Did she perhaps ask you to take care of anything for her?"

Ethel spoke. "Absolutely not. She wouldn't do anything that might harm us."

"My wife's right," Perry put in. "She was a fine girl and didn't deserve what she got. And *we* don't deserve *this*."

Gates stood. "You're right, you don't." And neither did Juliana.

"I hope you get whoever did this to my girl and to us, Ranger."

"Count on it," Gates said, his jaw rigid. "And that's a promise."

Seventeen

Harold Lacy stepped out of his underwear.

"Mmm, not bad," the young woman behind him murmured, then patted the empty space beside her on the bed.

Harold saw her gesture, but instead of doing her bidding, he paused, catching a glimpse of himself in the mirror. He cringed and wanted to turn away, but he couldn't. He hated the fact that he was getting bald. It was bad enough to have been cursed with red hair all his life, but losing it was even more traumatic, especially as he was only in his late twenties, for heaven's sake!

"Come on, baby," the young lady wailed.

Ignoring her again, Harold leaned closer to the mirror, praying that the pale gleam of his scalp wouldn't be visible. It was. His features contorted before he turned and walked to the bed.

"What were you looking at?" she asked, smiling. "Checking for gray hair, I'll bet."

He didn't bother to answer as he crawled in next to his companion. Instead, he folded his arms across his chest and stared at the TV lodged in a cabinet in front of him.

"Surely you don't want to watch the tube." She scooted closer, nestled her fingers in his chest hair and tugged playfully.

He grabbed her hand, thrusting it aside. "Knock it off, Crystal."

The brunette's eyes clouded. "What's the matter with you? I thought you wanted me."

"I did. But hell, we've already screwed our brains out."

She giggled. "And wasn't it fun?"

"Yeah, but I'm tired now. Anyway, I have to think."

"About what?"

Money, or rather, the lack of it, he thought silently.

"I hope you're thinking about buying me that ring you've been promising me for ages. I went by the jewelry store and looked at it again yesterday." She punched him in the ribs. "It's still there."

Harold laughed outright, but with no humor. "And that's where it'll stay."

Crystal sat straight up in the bed, then turned and glared down at him. "What's that supposed to mean?"

"Exactly what you think it means."

"You promised I could have it," she said petulantly.

He shrugged his shoulders. "Some you win, some you lose."

"You're a bastard, Harold, and I don't know why I put up with you." She flounced down onto her back and turned her head sideways.

"No one's stopping you from hauling ass."

She flung her head back toward him and gave him a nasty look. "You talk a good game, but when you get horny and want a blow job, you'll come running back."

She was right, though he hated to admit it. Most of the time he couldn't get enough of her. But now that she had already satisfied him, he had come back down to the real world, a place where nightmares haunted him, and not only at night, either.

"So tell me what's going on in that head of yours."

"Nothing you need to know about," he said.

"Harold!"

"Okay, okay." He wanted to tell her, because he was scared. But he didn't know how.

"I'm waiting."

"I stole some money."

Her eyes widened in disbelief. "You *what?*"

"I stole some money," he repeated in a terse tone.

"From who?"

"My company."

"Oh, sweet heaven."

Harold worked as an accountant for a prestigious firm and had since he'd gotten his degree. He had a good job, though it was boring, like himself. In hopes of putting some spice in his life, as one cohort had put it, he'd begun going to dog races and betting on them.

Voila! He'd fallen in love with the greyhounds. Unfortunately, they hadn't returned his ardor, and all too soon, that love affair had soured.

"What on earth are you going to do? This is terrible, terrible."

"Stop babbling and calm down, will you?"

"But—"

"Look, I just got tight for some cash."

"For the races."

He didn't miss the censure, laced with fear and irritation, in her voice. That made him that much madder, made him feel that much guiltier. "Yes, for the races," he spat.

"When did you get caught?"

"A couple of days ago."

She played tug-of-war with the sheets. "Did…did they arrest you?"

"No, at least, not yet. If I pay it back, pronto-like, they promised to let me resign."

"That's great."

"Yeah."

"For heaven's sake, Harold, count your blessings. You could've gone to jail. In fact, you're damn lucky they didn't can your ass that day."

Harold's mouth turned down. "I guess."

"Maybe you'll win the lottery," Crystal quipped.

"In another lifetime."

"I have a little money."

"Forget that."

"Don't argue. I—"

"Shut up and listen," he interrupted, then, jerking upright, he locked his eyes on the TV screen.

A man was talking and grinning into the camera, declaring that he was going to be the next governor of Texas.

"Who is that?" Harold asked.

Crystal flashed him an incredulous look. "You mean you don't know?"

"Just answer the damn question."

"That's Rusk O'Brien, our next governor, according to the polls."

"Governor?"

"I can't believe you didn't know that."

"I never listen to that political shit."

"Well, you should."

"You mean that guy's actually going to get elected?"

"It sure looks that way, though I'm not going to vote for him."

"It doesn't matter. They're all crooked as a barrel of snakes, anyway. One politician's about as good as another."

"Then why the sudden interest?"

The wheels in Harold's head were turning. "I know that man from somewhere."

"Get real, Harold."

"No, I'm serious."

He was quiet, frantically searching through the archives of his mind. Something about that grinning idiot was familiar.

What?

Then it hit him—the boating accident he'd witnessed that day long ago, when he'd skipped school and gone fishing.

With that memory came a deep laugh.

Crystal stared at him as though he'd lost it. "Harold, are you all right?"

He grabbed her and yanked her tight against him. "Baby doll, I've never been better."

"What on earth are you talking about?" She scrambled out of his clutches. "You're not making any sense."

"Oh, yes, I am."

"Then tell me."

"Can't, not right now. Not to worry, though. My...our money problems are solved." He raised his eyes to the ceiling. "Hallelujah! Thank you, Jesus!"

He glared at the man, who looked more like a baby-faced priest than a lowly private detective. "Find it, dammit!"

"Okay, sure, I'll give it another shot."

"You do that," Rusk said, sarcasm thick in his tone.

"What if I—"

Rusk held up one hand, cutting him off. "If you want the rest of your money *and* if you want to stay in business, you'll do your job."

The man toyed with one curly end of his mustache. Watching him, Rusk almost laughed. If he only knew how absurd he looked, his baby-face loaded down with that fur on his lip. But who gave a fuck? He didn't. If the man did what he was hired to do, he could look however he damn well pleased.

"Are you threatening me?" The P.I. was staring at him through beady eyes.

"Sure am," Rusk said with confidence.

"One of these days you're going to get what's coming to you."

"You're right—the governorship of Texas. Now get the hell out of my face."

After glowering at Rusk, the private detective turned and stomped out of the room.

Rusk rubbed the back of his neck, feeling the bunched-up muscles. He needed a professional massage in the worst way. But until he had his black book back, he couldn't relax and enjoy it.

Hell, for that matter, he couldn't relax and enjoy anything. He was so close to having it all, too. Dots of sweat broke through his skin. Time was not in his favor.

If he didn't find that book before it got into the wrong hands, he was dead meat, literally. His stomach did a somersault, forcing him to sit down.

The phone rang, and he jumped, but he didn't answer right away. It was always a bit disconcerting when it was his private line, even though many times the news was good. Let us hope, he thought, reaching for it.

"O'Brien? Mason here."

Rusk knew from the tone of his backer's voice that it wasn't good news. He held his breath, waiting for the karate chop.

"Guess who came to see me?"

"How should I know? Why don't you just tell me."

"A certain Texas Ranger."

Rusk was puzzled by the suppressed fear he heard in

his cohort's tone. He'd never known Mason to hesitate, no matter the circumstances.

"Granted, it's not the ideal situation, but it's nothing to get bent out of shape over."

"Don't you dare lecture me!"

Rusk curbed his own temper. "The Rangers have been called in on the TDC scandal. Gates is one of the investigating officers, and since your company built several of the prisons..." His voice trailed off.

"I can handle that," Carl said with irritating force.

"Then what's your beef? You're clean on those contracts, aren't you?"

"Of course."

"So spit it out, Carl. I'm no God damn mind reader."

"On his way out, he asked how well I knew Margie Bowers."

Rusk's stomach dropped around his kneecaps. "Why the hell would he ask that?"

"Hell, I don't know, but Gates could connect us through her."

When Rusk remained silent, Mason went on. "That woman can connect *us*. She's your link to me."

"I'm well aware of that."

"So get your brother, that gun-toting Ranger, off my back. Now!"

"How can I do that? He won't back off this prison mess."

"I told you, that's not a problem. But the Bowers broad is. Need I remind you that she's been murdered, for chrissake?"

"Simmer down."

"Simmer down, hell! I want those new prison contracts, O'Brien, and you promised them to me, if I greased your greedy paws and got you elected. And that's exactly what me and my partners are doing.''

''I still plan to uphold my end of the bargain.''

''Then I suggest you use your influence to yank your brother back in line. No way can the two of us be connected, and certainly not through Margie Bowers.''

With that Mason slammed the phone down, leaving Rusk holding a humming receiver. He tried to swallow, but his mouth was too dry. A new fear held him in its icy grip.

Tamara was due at the office any moment now. She couldn't see him like this. He had to get control of himself. How had he gotten himself into such an ungodly mess? The answer was easy. Because Margie had been a trusted employee, she had often been his go-between with Carl Mason. He knew now that that had been another big mistake.

Even bigger had been his ongoing sexual appetite for Margie.

He should never have gotten personally involved. But she'd been hot, and he had never been one to turn down a good lay. The problem was, she'd been smarter than he'd thought.

Although he was still glad she was dead, it had come about too soon.

His God damn book was still missing. If he thought Carl Mason was pissed over Gates' visit, then wait until he found out about the book. He couldn't let him find out. The underpinnings of his career, his life, depended on that.

He just might have to go another route. That brainless detective he'd hired was turning out to be as worthless as a whore in church.

Simmer down, Rusk warned himself. The book would

surface. Luck had always been on his side. While there was a lull in his good fortune, it wouldn't last long. The tide would turn, and he would prevail.

Rusk swore, then got up and trudged to the bar. Once he'd downed a healthy slug of whiskey, which took the edge off his nausea, he felt much better. Things *would* work out; they had to. Smiling, he took another swig, which made him feel even better.

The bottle was half-empty when his private phone rang again. Tamara. He smirked; Her Highness was waiting. They were due at a fund-raiser and rally, which would most likely bring in a lot of money.

He lifted the receiver and said, "I'm on my way."

Someone chuckled—a maniacal chuckle from a man's voice he didn't recognize. Rusk's hair stood up on the back of his neck. "Who is this?"

"A friend."

"You're no friend of mine."

"Consider this your lucky day, 'cause that's about to change."

"Who the hell are you?" Rusk demanded again, wondering why he didn't slam the receiver down.

"Now, now, don't go gettin' your dander up."

"How did you get this number?"

"That's not important. What is important is that you listen to what I have to say."

"Go to hell! I don't have to—"

"I wouldn't hang up, either. I think you'd rather talk to me on the phone than have me show up at your rally."

Silence.

The caller chuckled again. "Now that I have your attention, here's the deal."

A few minutes later Rusk slammed the phone down, but only after his face had turned purple with rage.

* * *

Juliana couldn't wait to get home. It had been a grueling day, though a very productive one. In fact, over the last few days her show had hovered near the top of the local ratings.

Benson was dancing in the aisles of the studio, along with their sponsors. Oscar Maroney had sent her a dozen long-stemmed yellow roses. She'd even had a couple of calls from cities such as Saint Louis and Dallas. But still no offer from a New York station, promising to take her show national. That would come; she was sure of it.

So why wasn't she on top of the world?

At the moment, Margie's murder and the backlash it had produced were the most obvious reasons. Poisoned. Juliana couldn't yet come to grips with that or wipe it from her mind. She was also finding it difficult to accept that she, among many others, was a suspect.

The police had questioned her twice, though not with a heavy hand. She sensed that because her house had been broken into and she'd received that terrifying call, she had been placed at the bottom of the suspect list.

They had also questioned Margie's parents, whose house had taken the same abuse as hers. It was after they told her that Gates had been there, asking questions, that her depression had deepened. She hadn't seen him since the night he'd pushed his way inside her condo, telling her how Margie had met her fate.

She had begun to think he'd finally backed off. But after she learned that he'd shown up at the Bowers' house, she knew better.

Damn him and his snooping. What possible interest could he have in Margie's case? Although he had hinted at one, she didn't believe him. So what was it going to take to convince him that she didn't want him back in her life?

Liar.

She wanted him, all right, and that was the problem. He had aroused her physically to the extent that she was miserable, but she refused to give in to her base needs. He was the last person she would ever sleep with.

She was convinced he wouldn't sleep with her, either. Besides, he had someone else in his life. Why didn't he just go screw her?

Juliana winced at that crude thought, though she wasn't about to pursue the reason why. Not now, not when she was dead tired.

Having reached her house, she forced Gates and his meddling out of her mind and maneuvered her car into the garage. She grabbed her purse and her small sack of groceries, and went inside.

After everything was in place, Juliana didn't leave the kitchen. She leaned against the cabinet, her body turning rigid as she fought to stifle her desolate feelings.

Loneliness.

Where once her home had been filled with a child's laughter, cookies baking in the oven, a man's strong arm's around her.

Gates' strong arms.

She had to stop beating up on herself, had to stop reverting to the past when the present turned dark. Her child was dead. Her husband was gone. Those two things would never change.

What had to change was her maudlin attitude. Margie's death had spooked her; she wouldn't be human if it hadn't. Still, she tried to talk herself out of that mood as she made her way down the hall.

Once she had undressed and gotten comfy, she would return to the kitchen and make herself a cup of flavored coffee. With that in mind, she stepped into the bedroom and was about to unbutton her slacks when she froze. Something was wrong.

Someone was in her room.

For a moment paralyzing fear kept Juliana immobile. When she would have turned, an arm crossed her breast, holding her in a deadly vise. When she would have cried out, she was jerked violently back against a hard chest.

"Stay cool, you hear?" a man rasped.

It was then that she felt the knife, its razor-thin edge pressed against her throat.

Eighteen

"Now, where is it?"

Juliana still couldn't say a word; she was almost choking on the scream that was frozen in the back of her throat.

"If you think I won't slice this beautiful neck of yours, you're dead wrong."

He left no doubt that he spoke the truth. If nothing else, his chilling, raspy voice convinced her of that, shooting her terror factor even higher.

"Talk to me!"

As if he realized she couldn't meet his demand with the knife pressing against her larynx, he removed it, though he didn't let her go. His arm remained around her upper body, feeling as heavy as a band of concrete.

"I...don't know what you want." Juliana failed to recognize her own voice. It sounded frail and barely audible, like someone who was dying.

Perhaps she *was* going to die.

She wouldn't think about that now. If only she knew what this maniac wanted, she might have a chance. But she had no idea, and that in itself could end her life. God, she wasn't ready to die. She squeezed her eyes shut to hold in the tears. If there was an upside to going to heaven early, it was that she would get to hold her baby again.

"Stop jerking me around," he snapped.

She could hear his heart pounding and his breathing

deepen. It was a toss-up as to who was actually breathing the loudest. If he hadn't had the upper hand, she would have sworn he was as frightened as she was.

"I'm not…not jerking you around. Tell me what it is you want." Her tone was begging.

"The book, goddammit! I want the book your friend took."

"Book?" Juliana croaked. "I—"

"I've already warned you to stop playing fucking games with me."

"I'm not—"

The knife returned to her throat, once again shutting down her voice.

"No more excuses, y'hear?"

"Please…" She swallowed around the pressure of the blade. "Please…you have to understand that Margie didn't give me anything."

"You're lying!"

Tears brought on by anger and rising terror poured from Juliana's eyes, soaking her cheeks. What to do? Apparently, he wasn't going to take no for an answer.

"Stalling's only going to make it worse."

Juliana's mind wrestled to come up with something that would convince him that she spoke the truth and at the same time defuse this ticking bomb, who had his wiry mustache against her cheek and his stinking breath in her ear. If only she could see his face. If only she recognized his voice. *If only* she had listened to Gates and his gut instinct, she might have headed this off.

Gates! Her panic reached a new level. She couldn't think about him now.

"Who…are you?" she asked, hoping to buy time, for what she didn't know. Perhaps if she kept him talking, she could figure out if he was the same man who had called her. She would bet anything that he was. "Why are you doing this?"

"Don't matter, lady. I was told to get the book, and I'm not leaving without it."

"Who...told you?" If she was going to die under this man's knife, she wouldn't give in without a fight, albeit a verbal one.

He laughed a guttural laugh, and another pang of fear suddenly stabbed Juliana in the stomach. Even if she knew where the so-called book was and gave it to him, he would probably kill her anyway, taking delight in the act.

"Time's up, lady. My patience is at an end."

"I—"

The doorbell rang.

For a fraction of a second they were both stunned by the unexpected interruption. He rallied first. "Keep your mouth shut!" he spat.

"Yo, Juliana!"

The loud, shrill voice carried through the front door and into the bedroom. "It's me, Mary."

Thank you, Lord, Juliana thought, looking up. Mary Turner was her neighbor.

"I need to borrow some butter."

Silence.

"Juliana!" Mary called again.

"I'm warning you," the man ground out, so close to her ear that Juliana now felt the tip of his tongue. A shudder rippled through her.

The pressure of the knife increased. The scream that remained lodged in her throat begged to be released, but that was impossible.

"Yoo-hoo! I know you're in there. I'm not leaving till you let me in."

More silence.

"Are you all right, dear?"

A string of expletives broke through the intruder's lips while time seemed to drag. What was he going to do? Juliana asked herself. The answer didn't bear thinking about. But she figured she wouldn't have to wait long. She didn't.

"Consider this a reprieve," he hissed. "But just so you'll know I mean business, I'm leaving my calling card."

His cold, hollow voice recharged the crippling, mind-numbing terror that held her captive. That was when it happened, when he nicked the blade into her tender flesh.

No! Her cry was as pitiful as it was soundless.

She must have moved, because his hold on her tightened.

"Oh, no, you don't! Hold still. I'm not through with you yet."

The knife went deeper into her flesh, before slowly cutting a trail across her throat. Juliana's knees buckled, and blind pain seared through her. She knew she was about to faint.

That was when he shoved her to the floor.

"Till next time, bitch."

Reeling from shock and fear, Juliana fought to remain conscious, to keep from drifting off into a place where she wouldn't feel the pain. She reached up and touched her neck.

Blood.

Don't pass out, she begged herself. She could get through this. She had survived Patrick's death, and that was worse. Still, she struggled for even the tiniest breath when she heard her neighbor holler again.

"All right," Mary said in a huff. "I'll let you off the hook this time. I'm going!"

Oh, please, don't go!

Juliana knew that Mary couldn't hear her broken, silent plea. By now her neighbor's hyper, wrenlike body would be back in her own yard.

The phone.

That was her only chance. Juliana crawled to the bedside table. Later, she wondered why she didn't simply call 911. That would have been the logical thing to do but at this point, all rational thought had long gone. She fumbled in the drawer for the card.

The taste of salty tears in her mouth and her shaking limbs made punching out the numbers difficult. But she did it, then prayed.

Gates, for once, please be home.

"Don't stop!" he pleaded.

Her smile, as hot and seductive as the water that cascaded around them, widened. "Now, why would I do a thing like that? Especially when I'm having so much fun."

"Tormenting me, you little imp," he said, swallowing hard, then staring down at her through glazed-over eyes.

"That's my kind of fun," she said in a teasing but breathless voice.

Gates' body was on fire. And she hadn't even touched him with her hands or her lips. The erotic way she was using the soapy sponge, combined with the *spots* where she placed it, was all it took to feed his starving libido.

But he wanted more. He wanted her to touch him. As if she could read his eyes, she tossed the sponge aside.

He groaned as her hands, also soapy, tugged at his pointed nipples before trailing down his flat stomach. He was already so hard and ready, he feared that when her slippery fingers circled him, he would lose all control.

"Oh, darling," he whispered, his gaze now centered on her full breasts, which glistened like rain on a flower petal. "You're making me crazy!"

"Good."

She sank to her knees then and surrounded him with her lips, taking as much of him in her mouth as possible. He slammed his hands against the wet fiberglass and let the sweet agony pound him along with the water.

It was only after he felt himself about to come that he dug his fingers into her hair and pulled her up.

"Don't you—" she began, her eyes questioning.

His response was to grab her under each cheek of her buttocks, then ease her down on him. Instantly, he was buried high inside her.

She clutched his shoulders, and mewing sounds erupted as flesh pounded against flesh....

Gates shook his head and lunged out of his chair. "Hellfire!"

For a moment he wasn't sure where he was or what was happening, besides the fact that he'd been making love to Juliana.

But only in his dreams.

He swore again as a helpless feeling came over him. Juliana. Would she ever stop haunting him? he asked himself, continuing to feel dizzy and disoriented while sweat gushed out of his pores like a severed waterline.

He'd fallen asleep in his chair—at work, no less—something he hadn't done in a long time, not since he quit getting commode-hugging drunk. He looked toward the window and saw that night had fallen. He peered at his watch. Eight-thirty. He'd been asleep for over an hour.

Cursing again, Gates reached for the lamp on his desk and flipped it on, blinking against the instant brightness.

He focused his eyes on his laptop computer, flanked by the papers spread across his desk.

He'd been working on the computer, getting his report ready on the man he and Sheriff Weaver had arrested. He'd also been checking the evidence on the beer-joint murders through the crime lab in Austin.

But when he'd actually drifted off, he'd been delving through Mason's records, where he'd found nothing out of order. The records could account for every penny spent and on the exact item. And as far as anything relating to Margie Bowers—zilch.

Gates stared at the massive folder again, sat down and rocked back in his chair. Placing his hand on the back of his neck, which was still wet with sweat, he kneaded the cramped muscles.

His guts were a tangled mass. That dream had more than resurrected thoughts of Juliana. It had shoved their sex life to the forefront of his mind with all the color and flash of a neon sign in Vegas.

But then, that was how it had always been between them. Hot. Heavy. And *daily*. They couldn't seem to get their fill of one another. While there had been tender moments, they were rare. Most of the time, they had made love like there would be no tomorrow.

Gates paused in his thoughts and leaned his head in his hands, rubbing his eyes. But the vision of her wouldn't disappear. He had to get a handle on himself and the situation.

Yet here he was, slashing open old wounds. For what?

She was in danger, and for some insane reason, he felt responsible. Was it because he'd been married to her? Was it because she'd had his child? Was it because he'd been a drunken asshole who'd driven her into another man's arms? Or was it because he'd gone off the friggin' deep end?

"Shit!" Gates pounded the desk, his face twisted. But the thought of someone else having the same carte blanche with Juliana's body as he'd had still pinched hard. Could that be the reason why, whenever he got the chance to pinch *her* emotionally, he took it?

His libido aside, he couldn't ignore the danger she was in. His Ranger mind-set couldn't let that go. On the other side of that coin remained the indisputable fact that this case was not his.

Yet he'd taken the liberty of calling the investigating detective, Dave Bishop, at HPD, telling him about Juliana's crank caller, which he hadn't known about. They had also discussed the two break-ins.

Bishop had told him that they were in the process of checking out anyone who'd had any association with Margie. Gates had almost told him about the photograph of Margie and Carl Mason, but he hadn't.

Why?

He wanted to check on that himself. Chalk his interest up to curiosity or whatever. Until he learned where and how Mason fit into Margie's life, he would continue to nibble around the edges of the case.

Even though he didn't expect it to tie in with his investigation of the prison scandal, he wasn't totally ruling it out, either. Hell, stranger things had happened.

Wouldn't it be something if Mason turned out to be a prime suspect in Margie's murder? he asked himself, warming to the idea. If that did prove to be the case, then he could step into the investigation legitimately. By doing that, he could make Juliana take precautions.

Ha! He'd never been able to control her strong will.

She didn't have red hair for nothing, silky hair that he had loved to bury his face in and...

His heart jolted. Juliana had his dick in a knot that only she could untie, which made him one walking, sick son of a bitch.

Gates sucked in a harsh breath, forcing his mind back on the case. He hadn't been totally up-front with Detective Bishop on another matter. He'd wanted to talk to his brother first.

He'd called Rusk and asked him to drop by his office, which as yet his brother hadn't done. Then, as if on cue, Gates heard a tap on the door, looked up and watched as Rusk walked in.

"Well, I'll be damned. I was just thinking about you."

Rusk didn't mince any words. "What's up?"

"You look like hell."

"No shit."

The cowlick on the back of Rusk's head, which was usually plastered down, was sticking up. His face had an unnatural-looking tint to it. Gates' gut alarm sounded. "You been drinking?"

"I wish to hell I had."

"That wouldn't be smart."

"Don't patronize me, little brother."

Gates shrugged. "All right. So, has your campaign hit a snag?"

"You might say that."

"Want to talk about it?"

"I'd rather talk about why I'm here." Rusk looked at his Rolex. "Tamara's having some people over for drinks. They're probably there by now, and she'll be having a spasm because I'm not."

"That's par for the course, isn't it?"

Rusk ran a hand through his hair, then sat down. "Yep."

"How well do you know Carl Mason?"

Rusk's eyes narrowed. "He's a contractor who built some of the first prisons. I know that from having served on the TDC Board."

"Then you know he's being investigated along with the others?"

"That figures. But what does that have to do with me?"

"Nothing, I hope."

"Then why the third degree?"

Gates' dark gaze pinned his brother. "There's a connection that's got me by the short and curlies and won't let go."

"Which is?"

"Margie Bowers."

He hadn't known what to expect from Rusk. What he got was nothing—no reaction of any kind. Rusk remained calm, then repeated his earlier question. "What does that have to do with me?"

"Margie Bowers knew Mason. And since she worked for you, I thought—"

"Whoa!" Rusk interrupted. "Wait a minute. What are you doing—"

"Hopefully, surfing where I don't belong. Or at least, that better be the case."

"It is." Rusk cocked his head. "What's this really all about?"

"Juliana."

"Why am I not surprised?"

"She's in danger."

"So?"

"I don't expect you to understand."

"Do *you* understand?"

Gates blew out a pent-up breath.

"Aw, hell, Gates, stay away from her. She's poison, but then, I shouldn't have to tell you that."

"Our personal relationship doesn't figure into this."

"Who the fuck are you trying to kid?"

Gates' face darkened. "Who the fuck do you think you're talking to?"

They glared at each other for a moment.

"My pecker-poisoned little brother, that's who."

Gates ignored the added insult, though he had to clench his fists to keep from popping Rusk in the jaw.

"Margie's death is not your problem, I know that much. HPD's running the investigation. Since the diagnosis was murder, cops have been crawling all over the place like maggots."

"You didn't answer my question," Gates said in an unruffled tone.

"That's because I don't know the answer."

"I don't buy that. Margie was your employee—a highly valued campaign worker who was photographed with Mason several times."

Gates plunked the pictures down in front of his brother. Rusk's only reaction was to grin, then say, "Maybe she was fucking him."

"Maybe she was."

"Look, don't try and make something out of nothing. As it is, her death has been an albatross around my neck. The fact that she was murdered is not playing well in my camp."

"I'm sure it's not."

"Mother and Daddy are having a hissy fit."

"That doesn't surprise me. They're living for the day you become governor."

"What about you?"

Gates lifted his shoulders in a half shrug. "I want what you want, and that's for you to be happy."

"Well, sticking your nose in where it doesn't belong isn't going to make me happy."

"Meaning what?"

"Involving yourself in something that's not your concern because of Juliana."

"You've made yourself clear on that," Gates said.

"But you don't intend to listen."

Gates didn't respond.

Rusk's expression turned ugly. "That God damn ex of yours—"

"That's enough." Gates' tone was clipped. "All I want from you is your word that Margie's relationship with Mason had nothing to do with you or your official business."

"It didn't," Rush said harshly, then stood. "Now, if you're through grilling me like a two-bit criminal, can I go?"

"Sure. Next time, I hope you're in a better mood."

"Don't count on it," Rusk muttered over his shoulder, then slammed the door behind him.

Something was still not quite right. Gates felt the urge to scratch, only he couldn't find the itch. His gut told him Rusk was sliding down a slippery slope, but if his brother wasn't willing to confide, there was nothing he could do about it.

Still, it bothered him. Gates just hoped that his itch had nothing to do with Margie's death. The phone rang.

"Yeah?"

"Gates?"

Cold moved down his body. "Juliana?"

"Yes," she said in a voice that sounded raw with suppressed sobs. "Please, I need your help."

Nineteen

He drove like a maniac. By the time he reached her house, his blood pressure was at stroke level. Gates refused to think about what had happened. His first response after hearing the sobs in Juliana's voice had been to call 911, but he knew he could get there before the cops could.

Since Juliana had reappeared on the scene, he had found a shortcut to her house. Of course, he'd had no valid reason for finding her place, other than the fact that he'd wanted to. Still, when he'd driven by, he'd felt like an idiot.

Come to find out, they didn't live all that far apart, especially now that Houston had added so many freeways.

Now it seemed like an interminable length of time before he reached her street and shot around the corner. His mind was churning faster than the wheels of his truck. What would he find?

Had someone broken in again?

If so, had that someone *hurt* her?

Gates increased his speed, thinking irrationally that she lived down the longest damn street in Houston. His stomach was on fire as though someone had poured acid in it. For a little of nothing, he could stop, open the door and throw up, but he couldn't allow himself that luxury.

Whatever had happened, Juliana would expect him to

have his head on straight and his grit intact. After all, that was what he got paid for.

Sounds good, he told himself, noticing that his knuckles were bloodless from his death grip on the steering wheel.

Since Patrick had died and Juliana had left him, he'd been aware that he'd functioned for the most part more like a robot than a human. He hadn't realized just how inhuman he'd become until he accidently bumped into Juliana at the hospital, a moment that had sent him hurtling down yet another road.

More than that, his mind and body had been jarred back to life, and he was having trouble coping. Not only had Juliana messed him up sexually, she had messed him up professionally, as well. He wasn't sleeping. He wasn't eating. He wasn't concentrating. In a nutshell, he wasn't as sharp as he should be.

Therein lay the danger.

But that was about to change. His eyes blazed with fury, and every nerve inside him was primed for confrontation. Finally reaching her drive, Gates roared into it, jumped out and bounded up to the door. He was prepared to beat on it, but when he placed his hand on the knob, it turned.

Moisture lined Gates' upper lip. The door shouldn't have been open. Not a good sign. He eased his way inside, his heart laboring hard in the silence that greeted him.

"Juliana?"

No answer.

A steel hand seemed to grab his guts and squeeze. She was still here. *She had to be.* He edged deeper into the foyer, and that was when he heard her soft, wrenching sobs. For an instant he couldn't seem to move; his legs felt as if lead weights were tied to them.

Someone had hurt her. When he got through with the

bastard, only God would be able to help him. For now, he gave himself a savage mental shake and felt his professional instincts kick in.

Drawing his gun, Gates ventured still farther inside. Was she alone? He had no clue. But she was alive, and that was what counted. The thought of finding her any other way was not an option.

He took comfort in the fact that only a few minutes had passed since she had called him.

"Juliana," he said again, only louder.

"Gates...in here."

Her voice was weak, but he had no trouble locating her. Still, his cop instincts kept him from barreling into the room, fearing she might not be alone. Getting himself blown away wouldn't do her any good.

He eased toward the door to her bedroom, where he lined his frame against the wall, then leaned his head just enough to see inside. She was sitting on the floor, bent over, rocking back and forth.

Icy rage shot though him, once again turning his limbs to mush. "My God!" he breathed, overcoming his body's sudden clumsiness and crossing to her, kneeling at her feet.

That was when he saw all the blood.

His entire body shuddered. "I'm taking you to the hospital."

"No, please," she whispered between shivers. "It's not as bad as it looks."

"It's bad enough," he said in a strangled tone.

She reached her hand up to her neck, where the blood had crusted. When she touched the raw wound, he saw her wince.

"When I catch the bastard who did this, his ass is

mine,'' he spat at the same time that he slipped his arms under her, lifting her against him.

Juliana didn't say anything, but he didn't expect her to. By the time he reached the bathroom and flipped on the light, her head was buried against his shoulder. He hated to turn her loose, even for a second, but he had no choice. He had to see how much damage had been done and whether he should take her to the hospital after all. He couldn't allow her to go into shock.

Gently, he eased her onto the commode seat, and without looking directly at her said, ''Let me take a look-see.''

Juliana lifted her head, and though it was steady, her lower lip wasn't. It continued to tremble.

''It's going to be all right,'' he said, trying to keep his voice from showing his own shattered emotions.

After checking the cut and realizing she'd been right, that it wasn't as bad as it had first appeared, Gates stood. Then, turning to the closet, he fetched a washcloth. After wetting it with warm water, he knelt back down and bathed the wound.

Moments later, he had a clear view of the damage. A razor-thin line had been cut with precision across her throat, though despite the blood, the cut was indeed only superficial.

''How...how bad is it?'' she whispered.

''Bad, but not life-threatening.''

''Thank goodness.''

''He didn't mean to kill you. He only meant to scare you.''

''He...he did that, all right.''

Another jolt of icy rage shot through Gates as his scrutiny deepened. ''You've lost a bit of blood, though.''

She was tissue-paper white, except for her brightly colored lips, lips that he had...

Suppressing a groan, he diverted his thoughts. "I'd feel better, though, if you'd let me take you to the ER."

Juliana shook her head. "I don't want to go anywhere. Please, don't make me."

Gates understood her reasoning. When you were frightened and helpless, home was where you wanted to be, your sanctuary. She wouldn't have been normal if she hadn't felt that way. But when she pleaded with *him* not to make her do something, he realized how truly traumatized she was by what this scumbag had done to her.

And she had phoned him, the one person she hated most in the world. Why? Now that he thought about it, he couldn't believe he was here, in her home, at her request. Yet he was glad that she had turned to him. Besides the underlying reasons he refused to explore, he had confidence in himself, in his ability to help her.

"It's your call, for now," he said, reining in his runaway thoughts. Now was not the time to speculate why she had done what she did. Hell, he was having enough trouble with the moment. "I'll doctor it, then we'll see how you feel."

"I'll...be fine."

"Not so fast. Like I said, you've lost some blood."

"I know."

"I bet you feel weak."

"I do, but not enough to go to the hospital."

"What about light-headed?"

"Sort of."

"If you can, move your head a little to one side so I can dress the wound. Do you have some antibiotic cream and some bandages?"

"In the cabinet behind you."

"I'll be as easy as I can," Gates said, kneeling again. By sheer force of will, he kept his hands steady. It was hard, especially when her warm breath struck his face with each breath she took.

Fighting a jolt of lust, he tried not to look at her. But he couldn't help it. Her eyes were closed, which proved his saving grace, though he knew she was aware of the tension their close proximity was creating. Her body was as rigid as a board.

"Relax," he whispered.

"I…I'm trying."

"I'm not going to hurt you."

"It's okay. Do what you have to do."

Her vulnerability, her pain, ripped at his gut, reminding him of when they had buried their son. She had reacted in much the same way—all broken inside. He couldn't think like that now or he would lose it for sure.

He focused his attention on doctoring the wound while trying to ignore the tears creeping down her cheeks.

"I'm sorry," he said thickly.

Her eyes fluttered open. "Don't be. It's not your fault."

"I know, but—" He couldn't go on, not when a strand of her hair was tickling his face like a cobweb, triggering a jolt of another kind—temptation. It gnawed at him, broke his concentration.

He could smell her, a delicate, sweet scent that had nothing to do with cologne and everything to do with her flesh, flesh that he'd tasted, savored….

Stamping out the urge to lunge to his feet and run like hell from his own misery, Gates clamped his teeth together and tried to finish the task. But with each passing second, his misery cut deeper.

The buttons on her blouse were open, allowing him access to the creamy slope of her breasts. He closed his own eyes, trying to pretend he couldn't see them. If not, he would soon be drooling like a horny teenager.

How could he think about sex at a time like this? And with his ex-wife, no less. Therein lay both the answer and the problem. He knew the delights of her body, knew how it felt to tongue those breasts, to take those nipples in his mouth and suck....

The saliva dried up in his mouth at the same time that he felt his zipper pinch him. He was nearly through and would soon have to stand. If she so much as looked down, she would see his arousal. It felt like a piece of hot iron wedged between his legs.

Once there was some distance between them, then maybe he could curb his raw, sexual frustration and concentrate on the professional side, which was why he was there.

"Done," he declared at last, though in a strangled tone.

"Thank you," she whispered, staring down at him, then suddenly weaving like someone who was drunk.

His heart accelerated as he reached out to steady her. "You've got a choice—the bed or the ER."

"Bed."

"Let's get these bloody clothes off you, then."

Ignoring the fever continuing to rage inside him, he began undoing the remaining buttons of her blouse.

She stilled his hand. "I...can undress myself."

"I don't think so."

"Gates," she murmured, shaking her head in protest.

He looked at her again, and for an intense moment, the air around them was electrified.

"Don't be ridiculous," he said in a forced, detached tone. "It's not like I haven't seen you naked before."

Twenty

His stark words left her speechless.

As if her silence gave him the green light, he went on, "So, first things first."

"Gates...don't...please, I don't need you. I can do this."

She might as well have kept quiet for all the good it did. He didn't hesitate. He reached for the next button on her blouse and, without looking at her, undid it.

For a moment Juliana held her breath and watched his fingers fumble with the flimsy fabric, praying hard that those fingers wouldn't make contact with her skin. Fearing the inevitable, she let out her breath and shifted her eyes toward the ceiling, concentrating on the shadows flickering across it.

Even with that distraction, she could see the top of his head and literally had to grip the sides of the commode to keep from sinking her hands into that coarse hair.

She wanted to scream at him to stop, not to take further advantage of her. The harrowing experience she had just gone through, combined with her utter exhaustion, should have been torment enough. The thought of him touching her bare skin deepened that torment.

So why didn't she slap his hands away and be done with it? Perhaps it was because Gates was acting as if it was no big deal to undress her.

"Are you cold?" he asked, his voice low but surprisingly even.

Looking down, she noticed that the bloody blouse was completely off and on the floor. She stared at it for a second, then shuddered.

"I know," Gates said, reading her mind. "I'll deep-six that."

"Please...I couldn't bear the thought of wearing it again."

"That's understandable."

She thought she was home free now and could relax. He had removed the soiled blouse, and she had actually survived the ordeal.

Then it happened. Staring at her with hooded eyes, Gates reached for the front clasp on her bra. Her eyes widened, and panic kicked in. No! He had gone too far. Juliana's hand shot up, only to find she was too late.

Those dreaded fingers hit their mark—her soft flesh. She reacted as if she'd been shocked; her heart clamored, and she couldn't find her next breath.

"You don't have to be afraid of me," he said in a taut voice.

Dear Lord, it wasn't him she was afraid of; it was herself. His touch was re-creating sensations she didn't want to feel, yet she seemed powerless to halt his actions. Was it because she really didn't want to? Was it because she longed to have him look at her breasts, touch them again?

"Gates—"

"It's...all right."

It wasn't all right, and they both knew it. She could see the fine sheen of moisture on his upper lip and forehead. And while his fingers were anything but steady, he continued his task with determined accuracy, unclasping the wispy piece of nylon.

All too soon the bra had joined the blouse, and her full breasts were exposed. She thought she might pass out. Yet in the midst of her dizziness, she couldn't take her eyes off him.

Time seemed to crawl.

"Your breasts are more beautiful than I remembered," he said in a thick voice.

"Don't, Gates," she whispered tightly, covering herself with her arms.

His face was set in an expression of profound agony. "Sorry," he muttered, then straightened to his full height.

That was when she noticed the bulge behind the zipper of his jeans. She wanted to turn away, but she couldn't. Her gaze lingered on that bulge for seconds before she felt the pull of his eyes.

They held on to hers as a hot awareness leapt between them. The only sound in the room was the loud ticking of the wall clock, which mimicked the beating of her heart.

"If you're wanting another apology," he said in a sudden raspy voice, "you can forget it."

She didn't know what he would be apologizing for. She was just as much to blame for the static tension that surrounded them as he was.

Quickly lowering her head, Juliana felt something suddenly turn loose. She began to shake inside, desperate to pretend none of this had happened. No murdered friend. No trashing of her home. No intruder with a knife.

Most of all, no Gates.

"You can step out now."

Juliana blinked, then looked down. Her linen slacks were settled around her ankles. How much more was she going to have to endure? Still, she did as she was told and reached for his outstretched hand. He pulled her to her feet, and though slightly dazed, she stood as he grabbed the robe hanging on the back of the door and slipped it around her.

For a second, his eyes settled on her panties. She stiffened. No way was she going to let him take those off. Besides, there was no reason.

"Don't worry, I'm not that brave."

His mouth curved into the barest hint of a smile. She wished he hadn't done that. His smile was his most lethal weapon, more so than the gun he wore.

When he looked like that—boyish and unsure of himself—she thought he was the most compellingly attractive man she'd ever seen. And the most dangerous.

She had to fight down another surge of panic brought on by her own burgeoning sense of helplessness. "It's…it's a good thing."

"Oh?"

Her head jerked. "I'm not past hiring a hit man."

Again he smiled, and again she felt that raw heat.

Then the smile fled, and the darkness returned. "Hold that thought, only not for me."

She didn't pretend to misunderstand his meaning, which brought reality crashing back down.

"This isn't all a dream, is it?" she asked, her eyes wide and stricken.

"I wish to hell it was." Anger coarsened his voice.

"What next?" she asked, as if she were speaking to herself.

"The police. We call them."

She nodded.

"But not until I've gotten you something hot to drink."

"I'm not thirsty."

"But you're nervous."

She couldn't argue with that.

"I'll fix some coffee."

"That does sound good."

He nodded, then strode toward the kitchen.

While he slammed a cabinet door and turned on the water faucet, Juliana stared out the window into the inky blackness. Evil seemed to lurk there, and for the first time ever, she was afraid of what she couldn't see. Now that the incident was over, she had trouble believing what had happened.

She touched her bandaged neck. The dull throb there made it impossible to deny. Were her attacker and her caller one and the same? Most likely. Since he had come up empty-handed, would he try again? If so, the third time might be the charm. He might succeed in killing her.

No! She wouldn't let her mind do this to her, not when Gates was rattling around in her kitchen. At the moment he was more of a threat, since she had let him undress her. God.

What must he be thinking now? She didn't want to know. What she *did* want to know was how she was going to get herself out of this jam, Gates notwithstanding.

Calling him had been a knee-jerk reaction. He had responded, and she was grateful for that. But she'd made a mistake. Her body, as well as her emotions, had taken a beating.

When Gates had freed her breasts, she had wanted to feel his tongue....

Juliana shook her head, feeling like a child who had pulled a prank and watched it turn into a nightmare. She couldn't do this to herself, not when she was already hanging on to her sanity by a mere thread.

Gates had to go. She couldn't let herself depend on him. He still had too much sexual power over her, something that both irked her and excited her. No matter. She couldn't afford to indulge herself. As soon as he finished with the coffee, she would insist he notify Detective Bishop, then leave.

Suddenly Gates strode back into the room, two half-filled cups in his hands. He gave one to her, then sat down in the chair across from her and immediately took a sip.

Juliana watched his upper lip curl over the rim, then turned away. "I didn't think you liked coffee." Why did she have to say that? It added another personal dimension that was both unnecessary and risky.

"I don't."

"Then why are you drinking it?"

He smiled, but without humor. "Old habits die hard. I was under the misconception that it would sober me up."

"Only to find out that was just a myth."

"Yep," he said in a bleak tone, shifting his gaze. "I was still a drunk, just one who was full of coffee."

She didn't want to feel sorry for him, but she did. She wanted to curse him, to tell him to go away and leave her alone. She was too intensely aware of everything about him. Though his white shirt was stained with her blood, it didn't stop her from noticing how perfectly it fit his chest and broad shoulders.

The V in the neck allowed her access to the mat of dark hair underneath, hair that she had clung to when she'd been on top....

Juliana dug her nails into her palms in a vain attempt to halt the self-inflicted punishment. Still, she couldn't turn away, her eyes continuing their pilgrimage, taking in his jeans and the way they hugged his hips and sinewy thighs.

His body hadn't changed, except maybe for the better. It was hard and fit and had suffered no ill effect from all that alcohol he'd consumed.

"Are you up to telling me what happened?"

Red-faced, Juliana swung away from him. If he knew what she'd been thinking, he showed no signs of it. Instead, his tone was brisk and detached.

"I thought you were going to call Detective Bishop," she replied sharply.

"All in due time."

"Gates—"

"Juliana, don't start. For the time being, you're stuck with me. Don't you think I deserve the full story?"

"He...he grabbed me from behind," she said in a dull tone. "Then demanded I give it to him."

"Give him what?"

"A book. Margie's book."

"So *that's* what the threatening call, the break-in, and now this attack, have been all about."

"What?"

"Blackmail."

Juliana's eyes widened. "You think Margie was blackmailing someone? That doesn't make sense."

"It might not make sense, but I betcha I hit the proverbial nail on the head. Go on. What happened next?"

Juliana told him about her neighbor and how she'd scared the attacker off.

"Thank God for nosy neighbors."

Juliana tried to summon a smile, but she couldn't. "I'll never complain about her again, that's for sure."

Gates didn't say anything. He stared beyond her shoulder, his expression grim.

"Whoever Margie was blackmailing thinks I'm involved, right?"

"Up to your armpits."

Juliana fought off a wave of nausea. "I told him I

didn't know what he was talking about, that I didn't have it.''

"Of course the sub-maggot didn't believe you."

"He'll be back, won't he?"

"More than likely."

"But I don't have any book," Juliana stressed.

"Her parents don't, either."

Juliana flinched. "Do you think he'll hurt them, too?"

"I doubt it. For some unknown reason, whoever's involved has made you their prime target. They're convinced you have what they want."

"They're wasting their time."

"I know how the bastard got in."

"You do?"

"Through the French doors off the kitchen. I looked around while I was waiting for the coffee to brew."

"Doesn't sound as if you had far to look."

"Can you tell me anything about him?"

"I told you, I never got a look at his face."

"I know, but was there anything that maybe struck you as different? His voice, for instance."

Juliana stood, too antsy to remain seated. Gates followed suit. They faced one another in the middle of the room.

"It was sort of raspy, like he was either a heavy smoker or drinker."

"What about his hands? Could you see them?"

"Yes, but he was wearing gloves."

Gates cursed. "I was afraid of that."

"He had soft cheeks, a mustache and gross breath."

"Which could fit thousands of men in this town."

"That's the best I can do." Juliana's tone was flat.

"Under the circumstances, that's not bad."

"But it's no help, either."

"'Fraid not."

"What about the lab boys?" Juliana asked. "Do you think they'll come up with something?"

"I doubt it, but we'll just have to wait and see."

Unwittingly, Juliana lifted her hand to her throat, which was throbbing. She began to shake, recalling the terror of the moment when he'd first placed the edge of that cold knife against her tender skin.

"Don't," Gates urged in a disjointed voice, closing the distance between them. "Don't think about it."

"I…can't help it," she gulped.

"I promise you, he's not going to hurt you again."

Juliana couldn't respond; she couldn't do anything except stare at him through eyes brimming with unshed tears.

He muttered under his breath, and before she realized his intentions, he pulled her into his arms and held her close, like he used to long ago, before…

She tensed.

"I only want to hold you. You have my word."

For a moment Juliana reveled in his strength, in the comfort of his arms, feeling the fear drain out of her. It was only after she felt his erection against her stomach that she jerked out of his embrace.

His face went white, and his mouth turned down. "Despite my condition, I wouldn't have taken advantage of you."

"How was I to know that? I don't know you anymore."

"Dammit, Juliana—" Then, as if he realized where this conversation would lead, he shoved a hand through his already disheveled hair and abruptly changed the subject. "Before I call HPD, what about Margie? Is there anything about her you've failed to tell me?"

"Did I tell you that she had a lover?"

Gates squinted. "A married man?"

"I think so."

"Go on."

"There's nowhere else to go. Margie and everything that belonged to her are long gone."

He muttered several expletives, then began pacing the floor.

"Call Detective Bishop, okay?" She didn't know how much longer she could remain on her feet.

"If you're sure there's nothing else about Margie—"

She frowned. "Now, that you've jogged my brain—"

"What?" he demanded.

"I'm sure they're of no consequence."

"Let me be the judge of that," he snapped. "What are we talking about?"

"Motel receipts."

Twenty-One

"Motel receipts?"

"See for yourself."

Frowning, Gates glanced down at the clipped pieces of paper in his hand, then back up at Juliana. "Where did you find these?"

"After I had packed her things to take to her parents, I noticed them stuck in the corner of the closet. Later, when I vacuumed, I tossed them in a drawer."

"It's a wonder you didn't just throw them away."

"If Margie hadn't been...poisoned, I probably would have."

"Good thinking."

The compliment was offhand and absently given. Nonetheless, she noticed it and was taken aback, not so much by the praise—she didn't need or want that from him. But the fact that they were having a discussion like normal people was what was mind-boggling.

Since Margie's murder and the following chain of events, Gates had been like a hot needle jabbing her emotionally and physically at the most unexpected times, which had kept her on edge. Thinking about how he'd used his pushy high-handedness to take charge, then undress her, made her crazy.

And mad. At herself.

"Look, you've had enough for one night," he was saying. "I suggest you take something stronger than aspirin and crawl into bed."

His gruff voice brought Juliana back to the moment at hand. She massaged her temples, hoping to stave off the headache that was toying with her. "That's the best idea you've had yet."

His mouth quirked into another smile. "Want me to tuck you in?"

"In your dreams," she snapped.

He gave her an odd but pained look. "I've already done that." His voice had dropped to a husky pitch, and his eyes were aimed at her breasts.

Juliana swallowed with difficulty, aware of how little she was wearing under the robe and of the intimacy between them only moments ago. "You're not making any sense." Her tone was terse.

"I dreamed we were in the shower together, like we—" His voice broke off, and he turned ashen.

"God, I don't believe this."

"There's still that raging fire between us. You do believe that." His features were gaunt. "Why did you throw water on it?"

"Because I don't intend to get burned again, damn you!"

Two red spots replaced the pallor on Gates' face, and his eyes blazed. "You're right. I must be out of my fucking mind."

He swung around and strode out of the room.

Juliana grabbed her churning stomach. Had he left? She listened, hoping she would hear the door slam. Nothing. After that spectacle, surely he wouldn't stay. Something had to give. Their situation was steadily growing more explosive.

She knew he wanted her, and that she still had the

power to arouse him. If she had shifted her gaze lower, she would have seen that ridge in his jeans. She wasn't any better off. His hands on her body had created a moist ache between her legs that wouldn't go away.

He knew that, too, and had called her bluff on it. That was what smarted. But she wouldn't give in to those needs no matter how much she wanted him physically. Emotionally, they were no good for one another.

Granted, he had gotten his head out of the bottle and buried himself in his work, becoming the ultimate Texas Ranger he'd always wanted to be. But that was all that was different.

He continued to blame himself for the death of their son and her for being unfaithful to him. She winced at the path her mind had taken. The fact that he could even think she would sleep with his best friend had lost none of its punch. Juliana pressed her hand harder against her stomach.

The sound of Gates' booted footsteps returning to the room pulled her upright. So much for his having left. She made it a point not to look at him.

"I called Bishop," he said in an abrupt tone. "They'll be here shortly."

"Good."

"I told them you weren't up to answering any questions tonight."

"Oh?"

"You were headed for bed, remember?"

"What if I want to talk to Detective Bishop?"

"No need. I'll take care of things."

"That's not your place. You're not my keeper."

"So what do you suggest?"

She rubbed her temples again. "I don't know."

"Look—"

She held up her hand, cutting him off. "I want to be involved in this investigation."

"That's not going to happen."

"You can't stop me."

They glared at one another before Gates broke loose with a string of expletives. "If anything, you've become more hardheaded than ever."

"That's called survival."

"It doesn't have to be that way," Gates countered fiercely.

"Yes, it does."

A frown rearranged his lips. "So just what do you plan to do?"

"Go to the motel."

"That's bullshit!"

He was furious; his voice was barely under control, and she could see his Adam's apple pulsing. Too bad. He would get over his tantrum. Besides, she didn't care.

"No, that's a fact. I don't intend to sit back and do nothing. That pervert's not going to get away with terrorizing me."

"You're right, he's not. But you're not going to have anything to do with him."

Juliana's chin jutted while her eyes challenged. "You can't stop me."

"Hell, you're not thinking straight. You're already in enough danger without snooping on your own."

"This is something I have to do."

"We'll see about that!"

It happened so fast, she couldn't have headed it off even if she'd wanted to. He moved like he was in pursuit of a criminal—fast and deadly—attacking from behind. He circled his fingers around her upper arms.

"*What*—"

"Shut up!"

She almost strangled on the fury that raged up the back of her throat as he marched her to a decorative wall mirror in the room, then pointed to the bandage on her neck.

"Whoever did this to you meant business."

Tears filled her eyes. She didn't know if they were from anger or from fear. "Don't you think I know that!" she lashed back, her breathing ragged.

He swung her around to face him. "Then leave things be."

"When are you going to get it through that thick head that you don't have the right to order me around, personally or professionally?"

"I—"

Juliana poked him hard in the chest with her middle finger. "So back off!"

Gates latched on to her hand and held it in midair. "I'm trying to help you. Don't you see that?"

"No! Besides, I don't want your help. I don't want you in my life, period."

Before he could make a suitable comeback, she went on, knowing that she was fast reaching the stage of hysteria. "Just go back to your lady friend. I'm sure she's—"

His lips were on hers even before her pliant body made contact with his rigid one. For a moment she was caught so off guard she didn't resist. But when she felt him, hot and hard, nestle between her legs, she struggled against the onslaught. That was when he upped the ante; his mouth and tongue drove against hers, hot and hungry.

Desperate to break his hold on her before she capitulated and let him take her on the spot, Juliana wedged her arms between them and was about to push with all her might, when he suddenly let her go.

For what seemed like minutes, they stared at each other, their breathing harsh and their features pinched.

"God, Juliana, I'm—"

"Sorry? Is that what you were about to say?"

"I—"

"Don't bother."

Their eyes stayed locked for another disturbing instant.

"Your neck? Did I hurt you?"

"No," she said in a quivering voice.

"You remember when we used to fight and Patrick would cry?"

"Don't, Gates," she pleaded, feeling tears clog her throat. "That's a low blow."

His eyes were glazed over with the look of a wounded animal. "You're right, it was."

Still holding that terrible gaze, Juliana deliberately took the back of her hand and drew it across her lips. "Will you please...just go."

"No."

"*No?*" This time her voice *had* reached hysteria level.

"I'll go, but only as far as that couch over there."

Juliana was so flabbergasted at his audacity that she couldn't reply. Finally she found her voice. "You can't stay here."

"That's exactly where I'm going to stay, being the hands-on kinda guy I am." He turned and walked to the door. "Right now, though, I'm headed outside to wait for Bishop."

"I'd rather you went to hell."

He stopped short and whirled around, his features distorted with pain. "I've been there since the day our son died." His voice was a tightly coiled whisper.

Juliana opened her mouth, but nothing came out. What

was the use, anyway? When he continued to pound her with that brutal ammunition, there was nothing to say.

She sank wearily onto the couch.

Rusk looked at his Rolex. Again. Where was the little fag? He was supposed to have been here twenty minutes ago. Hell, he would just leave, Rusk told himself. No one left Rusk O'Brien flapping in the wind and got by with it, certainly not some two-bit blackmailer.

He stomped to his car, only to suddenly halt, his sound judgment coming to his rescue. He couldn't leave; that would be an unwise move. So he had to eat some shit? Happened every day, just not to him. But no one had to know—at least, no one he couldn't trust or who wasn't on his side.

Using the door for support, Rusk sagged against it. This jaunt was an added pain in the ass he didn't need. Yet he had no choice except to wait like some lackey for his master.

The taste of bile was so heavy in Rusk's mouth that he almost gagged.

How and when this latest calamity had come about remained a mystery. It had hit out of nowhere, beginning with that blasted phone call. Now, rocks were coming at him from so many different directions, he didn't know which way to dodge. Maybe he should have seen this one coming, but rationally, he knew that hadn't been possible.

The people he dealt with were the kind who shot you in the back of the head without warning. Margie, with snakes in her pussy, had taken the first shot.

Even though she was dead and no longer a personal threat, she still had her fangs in him, having stolen his book, which could cause Carl Mason to take the second shot.

Then there was his brother, a fucking Ranger, who had been assigned to investigate Mason, thus sniffing where he didn't belong. If Gates ever made the connection between himself and Mason, then it was all over but the slamming of the prison doors behind them.

That wasn't going to happen, Rusk vowed. Besides, after their talk, Gates seemed satisfied. He wouldn't try to force the issue. His brother had always been in his corner, and that wouldn't change. Mason could forget about Gates causing trouble—*unless* Mason had his own agenda, something to hide, like maybe a personal involvement with Margie. If so, that would automatically qualify him as a suspect in her murder.

When Gates had shown him the pictures of Margie and Carl Mason coming out of that office building, all smiles, Rusk had lost ten years off his life.

Margie had been balling *him*, so why not Mason, too? When he'd first suggested that to Gates, he hadn't been serious. Now he was. He almost grinned at the thought. Fact was almost always stranger than fiction. Looking back, it had been a stupid mistake for him to have sent Margie to Mason's office. But who would ever have guessed that such an innocent move would come back to haunt him?

He should never have trusted Margie, either. But she had seemed so smitten with him that it had never occurred to him that she might double-cross him, that she had the moxie to do it.

Well, he'd been wrong, and until he found that book, he was a prime target for Mason's bullet.

Now, though, he had another bullet to dodge, one that had the same deadly potential, but that had nothing to do with Mason and their under-the-table prison deal.

Rusk shoved himself away from the vehicle, trying to

ignore the itchy line of sweat that trickled down his face. He ran a finger under and around his collar, loosening it. Damn, but this Texas sun beat all. Deciding he'd best get out of it before he had a heat stroke, Rusk hurried to a huge oak tree and leaned against it.

A new poll had come out yesterday showing him way ahead of Harry Folsom, his closest opponent. His family was jubilant; his campaign staff was ecstatic. And Carl Mason was orgasmic.

But for how long? If anyone got wind of this latest debacle, everything would come to a disastrous end.

Fear ballooned from Rusk's gut up to his throat and lodged there.

That was when he saw a redheaded man step out of the thicket into the clearing. Rusk was reminded of one of those disjointed oddballs in the sixties who preferred pot to food.

This creature sauntering toward him had chosen this rendezvous site. Meeting in the God damn woods certainly hadn't been Rusk's idea, but he'd had no choice. Not at the moment, anyway.

Soon all the choices would be his. This guy and Mason might think they were going to de-nut him, but he had news for them. He would protect his crown jewels at all costs. This was just another temporary setback.

"You got the money?"

Rusk's eyes, filled with contempt, toured the long, skinny frame of the man who stopped a few feet from him.

"What's your hurry?" Rusk demanded in an even tone. "You owe me an explanation. I want to know what I'm paying for."

"Hey, I'm calling the shots, old man. When I see the cash, I'll talk."

"Look, you little shit, I've about had it with you."

The young man laughed. "You got that wrong. *You've* been had."

Rusk quelled the desire to flatten the scumbag's nose. "You're bluffing. I don't think you have anything on me."

"Can you take a chance on that?" the younger man drawled. "Like I told you on the phone, I was there the afternoon that kid flipped out of the boat."

Rusk went white with terror.

"So you'd best climb down off that high horse."

"I—"

"The money, Governor." The redhead's tone dropped below freezing. "Hand it over."

It wasn't so much what he said but the taunting way he said *governor* that popped like a firecracker in Rusk's gut. He had no recourse but to walk over to his car and get the bag.

The man grabbed it, dropped to his knees, opened it and began counting. Moments later, he looked up with a scowl on his face. "You're short."

"That's all I had on hand."

The man stood up. "Don't fuck with me."

"If you want any more money from me, you'll have to keep your end of the bargain. I want to hear your story."

The man gave him a lazy smile, then started talking in a slow, precise tone. When he finished, he said, "Now, about the rest of my money?"

Rusk's blood pressure was in the stoke zone. Still, he held on to his cool. "You'll get it."

"When?"

"Soon."

"Forty-eight hours. That's all the time you got."

"Or else…?"

The man grinned. "Oh, I expect I'll go to your ex-sister-in-law, who I believe has a talk show. Need I say more?"

"And if I comply?"

"You won't be hearing from me again," the redhead said. "I'm outta your life, man."

And pigs fly, Rusk thought, knowing the end would never come. Blackmailers never knew when to quit. They were like dogs with a bone; they kept chewing until there was no bone left.

"I'll be expecting that call."

Without waiting for an answer, the man turned and disappeared into the woods.

Rusk remained where he was, too livid to move.

"I got several good photographs of him," his companion said, tinkering with one end of his mustache, when he walked over a few minutes later.

Rusk didn't bother to turn around. His hate-filled eyes were still squinted toward the other side of the woods.

"Good, now find out who that son of a bitch is and everything about him, down to the number of freckles on his skinny ass."

Twenty-Two

"How's the old ticker behaving?" Gates' tone was light, but he wasn't smiling. "Is it keeping correct time?"

"Damn straight it is," James Ferguson said, staring at him over a huge Texas Ranger cup filled with coffee. "My wife sees to that."

"I betcha she doesn't know you're mainlining that caffeine," Gates added pointedly.

It was early, and they were in Ferguson's office. Gates had a lot of business to go over with his boss. However, when he'd walked in, Ferguson hadn't looked so good.

"Ah, hell, Gates, gimme me a break. She's got me off of everything."

Gates' lips quirked. "Everything?"

"Well, she does give me a little occasionally," Ferguson said with a chuckle. "But outside of that, I'm here to tell you, it's grim."

"How's that?"

"She's starving me to death. Food with fat is out. She won't let me near any booze, not even a beer, for chrissake. Next thing you know, she'll be picking out my eyeglass frames."

"Might help your ugly mug."

"Go to hell."

"That's the second time I've been told that within twenty-four hours."

Ferguson lifted an eyebrow. "Oh?"

"Forget that for now. I'll tell you later."

"Suit yourself."

Gates was quiet for a moment, grappling to collect his unwieldy thoughts. Juliana was the last person he should be thinking about now.

"Speaking of looking like hell, I could say the same for you, my friend. In fact, you look strung out to the max."

"My caseload's getting a bit heavy."

"So fill me in," Ferguson said, his manner brisk.

Gates tossed his Stetson on the second chair, then crossed one leg over the other. "Actually, I'm not sure where to start."

"What about the mugging and murder under the bridge?"

"That's about to be history," Gates said. "I'm due in court this morning."

"It's an airtight case?"

Gates' expression twisted. "You bet it's airtight. That asshole tried to blow us away. Besides that, we found the weapon in his pigsty cabin, with the victim's blood all over it."

"Chalk one up for the good guys."

"I wish I could say the same for the beer-joint murders. I got the crime report from Austin last night. It ain't good news. So far, nothing points to a suspect."

"Damn," Ferguson grumbled. "Stay on top of that one. I want an indictment."

"Will do."

"Outside of the beer-joint investigation, I want your time focused on the prison case. The governor's office is starting to get antsy."

"Because there's been so much publicity?"

Ferguson tinkered with the right earpiece on his glasses. "You got it."

"I wish they'd butt out of our business."

"You can forget that."

"Well, I have made some headway," Gates admitted. "I've waded through several of the contractors' construction reports."

"And?"

"There's no doubt that laws have been violated. Besides the soy-based meat and the fencing, there's a sizable and glaring amount of other misuse, mainly items improperly billed to the state."

"Even if we nail their asses, wanna bet they won't be prosecuted?"

"That's one bet I'm going to hedge on." Gates' jaw hardened. "I'm thinking TDC will try to get the money back. And if the companies are smart and want to continue to do business in the state, they'll comply."

"Which amounts to a slap on the wrist," Ferguson said angrily. "Which is a crock of crap."

"I agree. That's why I'm going to do my best to make 'em pay." Gates paused. "At least most of the companies have been axed from the list. That keeps them from building the next round of high-security units."

"Hell, I hope so. Next thing you know, they'll be using faulty material and those bastards inside'll knock down the walls and walk out."

"I hear you."

Ferguson drank some more coffee, then stared down into the half-empty cup. "Let's back up a bit. You said *most* of the contractors. You mean they haven't all been axed?"

"Nope. Two companies are still in the race for bids. Brown and Root, and Worldwide Builders."

"So they must not have any dirt under their fingernails."

Gates hooted.

"Okay, let's have it," Ferguson said in a disgusted tone. "You obviously know something I don't."

"You're probably going to have my ass."

"It won't be the first time you've been called on the carpet, and I'm sure it won't be the last. I reckon you'd best fess up."

Gates sighed. "You know who Margie Bowers is. Or was."

"The young woman who was murdered. Poisoned, if I remember correctly."

"Right." Gates fell silent, trying to figure out the best way to explain without sounding like an irrational idiot.

"So?"

"So that incident sorta hits close to home."

"In what way?"

"Margie was not only a friend of Juliana's, but she lived with her, as well. She also worked for my brother's campaign."

Ferguson whistled. "Ouch."

"You don't know the half of it."

Before Ferguson could respond, Gates told him what had taken place since Margie collapsed on Juliana's TV show.

By the time he finished, Ferguson was wearing an incredulous expression. "Is Juliana going to be all right?"

"Physically, yes. Emotionally, who knows?"

"Shit, man. She's not involved in any of this, is she? I mean, she doesn't know anything, does she?"

"My gut says no to both questions."

"Too bad whoever murdered Margie can't accept that."

"Carl Mason knew Margie."

Ferguson's thinning eyebrows shot up. "Oh? How do you know?"

Gates explained about the photographs in his possession, then asked, "What's your read on the situation?"

"It's odd, I have to say. But that doesn't mean the Bowers woman's death and the prison case are in any way related."

"I know, but—"

"No buts, just facts, and you don't have them."

"Not yet."

"Hell, Gates, Mason could've just been an acquaintance, or maybe a friend or her lover, none of which make him suspect in a murder case."

"He could've killed her, too."

Ferguson made a gesture of impatience. "What's the bottom line here, Gates? I'm getting a bad feeling in my gut."

Gates' mouth tightened.

"Is it Juliana? Are you that worried about her?"

"Yes."

"Still, you're fishing in someone's pond. This is HPD's case. *She's* HPD's responsibility."

"Hell, I know that."

"But you're interfering anyway, nibbling around the outer edges."

Gates fidgeted under Ferguson's scrutiny, then stood, feeling as if he was on the hot seat. "Actually, I'm bunking in at her place."

He might as well have dropped a grenade in the middle of the room and pulled the pin. The silence that followed was just that explosive.

"Are you out of your mind?" Ferguson demanded at last.

"Probably."

"What does Juliana think?"

"Do you really have to ask that?" Gates said grimly.

Ferguson chuckled, then sobered. "No. Right after you were hired as a trooper and I met her, I knew you had your hands full."

"That never changed, either," Gates said, his voice hollowing.

An awkward silence followed his words. Then Ferguson asked in a low voice, "What about Nicole? The way you talked the other day, I thought y'all were about to walk down the aisle."

"I was just talking to hear my head rattle."

"Ah, I get it." Ferguson's smile didn't come anywhere near his eyes. "Juliana's not only messing with your sound judgment, but she's messing with your pecker, as well."

Gates was about to vehemently deny that, but he didn't. What would be the use? Ferguson had his number. Fury at himself threatened to boil over.

"Watch your step is my advice to you. Where you live and who you live with isn't my concern, but the way you do your job is."

"So what are you saying, Cap?"

"I'm saying don't go too far afield here. I'll cut you a little slack, but not much."

"Even if I know I'm onto something?"

"That's the problem, you *don't* know that. The way I see it, you're trying to make a connection so that you'll have an excuse to keep sniffing around your ex."

"Damn, Ferg, that's a low blow."

"It's the truth. And the problem with it is your promotion." There was a lengthy pause. "You want my job, don't you?"

"Hell, yes."

"Then think with your brain instead of your dick. If this rogue-cop jag you're on backfires, then you can forget about occupying my chair. As it is, you're already a hard sell. You're not exactly loved and understood in the upper ranks."

"I still feel I'm onto something," Gates muttered darkly. "But I hear you loud and clear."

Ferguson snorted. "That'll be the first time. But for now, get out of here and get back to work."

When Gates reached his office, he felt like he'd been in a fight and lost, though there were no visible marks on him. Ferg was right; he *had* lost his mind—and a night's sleep, to boot.

Shortly after he'd announced his intention of occupying her couch, Juliana had stopped speaking to him, even when HPD arrived and went over the place from top to bottom. Afterward, she had gone into her room and slammed the door.

He'd made sure he was out of her house this morning before she awakened. He should have gone home and left a policeman on duty. Detective Bishop had offered to put a man on stakeout. Gates had declined the offer without consulting Juliana. At the time he'd convinced himself that he was the best one to deal with the pervert, should he return.

He had longed for the opportunity to wrap his bare hands around that son of a bitch's neck, especially after seeing how her beautiful skin had been violated.

That wasn't the only reason he'd stayed, though. After he'd tended to her wound, then undressed her...

Gates suddenly blew out a breath, then lifted his head, feeling as if he were drowning in his own need and lust. Once he'd unclasped that wispy piece of lace that held her breasts, he'd been spellbound, aching to touch them just one more time.

But he had known it wouldn't have stopped there. He would have wanted to keep on touching until he was buried inside her. Groaning, he moved in his chair, trying to relieve the pressure building behind his zipper. Thank God he hadn't taken advantage of her weakness and her pain. She'd been so terrified, so fragile, he'd feared she would shatter.

What next? Gates asked himself. He knew what it should be—leave her alone. This time *he* should walk out of *her* life and never look back. That was the only way to keep from opening any more old wounds and stop any more blood from splattering on both of them.

While that sounded great in theory, he didn't know if he could do it.

Benson's eyes were serious. "I hope we didn't go too far."

"You mean *me*, don't you?"

Benson crinkled his forehead. "Well, you were insistent, and, as usual, I capitulated."

"You're a good boy." Juliana smiled, then patted his hand. "Keep it up."

Benson scowled. "I'm not sure I did you any favors."

"Look, it's obvious that something's happened to me. I'm no good at hiding that. So I think the show on random violence, with me being the focal point, was brilliant, actually."

"Maybe. But the verdict's still out."

They were silent while the waiter placed their lunch in front of them. Both stared at it as if it were something foreign; then Benson began eating. After a moment, he peered at Juliana.

"What's wrong? I thought you were hungry."

"I thought so, too, only I guess I'm not."

Benson put down his fork, then wiped his mouth. "You've been through a tough time lately, but you have to eat. You look like a scarecrow as it is."

"I'm aware of that, but so do you."

And he did. Benson had lost weight, along with some of his patience and enthusiasm. Juliana suspected something other than his wife's condition was bothering him. Yet he hadn't confided in her. Perhaps that was because he sensed she'd been too wrapped up in her own misery.

"We'll both eat, okay?"

Juliana moved the Mexican food around her plate, then took a small bite. She made a face, then pushed it away. Benson did likewise and reached for his drink.

Juliana watched him drain the glass of Scotch and tried not to flinch. He was also drinking more than usual. She had smelled it on his breath this morning, which disturbed her.

"I'm worried about you, Juliana."

"And I'm worried about you."

He looked put out. "Hell, I'm the last person you need to worry about. I'm a survivor."

"That's what I've always said, only now—" Juliana broke off and swallowed painfully.

"All this is a bit much to digest. Margie dies, then your life's threatened." He motioned for the waiter, holding up his empty glass. "They seem connected, but how is beyond me. I'd like to think your danger stems from a kooky guest or crazed fan."

"Neither scenario appeals to me."

"No, I suppose not." Benson's tone was bleak. "So, have you ever figured out what Margie had that's causing all this grief?"

Juliana met his troubled gaze. "We're...the cops are still working on that."

She hadn't out and out lied to him. But Detective Bishop had told her not to discuss the case with anyone. While she trusted Benson, she decided for the time being to follow Bishop's advice and not tell him about the book.

"I hope you didn't stay alone last night."

She gave a harsh, strained laugh. "Unfortunately, I had company."

"Who?" Benson asked bluntly.

"My ex-husband. He spent the night on my sofa."

Benson looked shocked. "I'm sorry, Juliana. You don't need that."

"You're right, I don't."

"I guess I shouldn't have told him about that call."

"It's not your fault."

"Is he directly involved in the case?"

"I'm not sure."

"What do you mean?" Benson asked.

Juliana gritted her teeth. "I mean either way, he's *not* getting back in my house."

Twenty-Three

"Thanks for coming."

"All I can say is, this better be important," Carl Mason said, his heavy jowls bunching.

Rusk hid his anger. "Believe me, it is. I wouldn't have called you, otherwise. My time's just as valuable as yours."

"This is your party, Senator, so get on with it. Although one-on-one meetings shouldn't become a habit. The less we're together, the better off we are."

"I agree, but this was...*is* a matter of great urgency."

"I hope that doesn't mean you're in trouble again."

"What if I am?" Rusk couldn't keep the defensive edge out of his voice.

"Damn, Rusk, your whining's beginning to get on my nerves. You really should get hold of yourself."

For a moment Rusk was so taken aback by Carl Mason's in-your-face comment that he couldn't respond. How dare that bastard talk to him in such a condescending manner? Just who did he think he was?

The person with megabucks who's going to get you elected governor of Texas, Rusk reminded himself, his overinflated temper suddenly deflating. Besides, he had known when he asked for this meeting that the ice beneath him was thin, for more reasons than Mason could begin to know.

But Mason didn't know about the missing book yet, which was in Rusk's favor. He suddenly severed those thoughts, unable to think about Mason's reaction to that book. Nor could he think about his own fate, figuring it might be worse than death. Men like Mason and his cronies didn't mess around. They had more money than they could ever spend. Now, they wanted power.

Bored men with too much money and too much power were dangerous; Rusk also reminded himself of that. It was too late to cry foul. He had joined hands with the devil in the guise of Carl Mason. And Mason wasn't about to let him go now.

While it stuck in his craw to have to ask for help, Rusk had no choice. Desperation had overtaken pride.

The sounds of singing birds relieved the silence in the woods, the same woods where he'd met with that black-mailing scumbag. When he'd decided he had to bring Mason up to speed on the latest crisis, Rusk had tried to think of someplace where they wouldn't be seen together. This ungodly spot had jumped to mind.

"So stop stalling and let's get on with it," Mason said in a bored tone, then slapped a mosquito dead center, which left a bloody spot on his arm. "Shit."

Rusk forced himself out of his mental funk and faced the man who was once an ally but at the moment seemed more of an adversary.

"I also have an important golf game in thirty minutes," Carl said, not even bothering to check his watch again.

Rusk turned red but hung on to his temper. When he won the election, he just might renege on his part of the bargain, if this bastard didn't learn his place—and soon, too. Rusk almost laughed out loud at that thought. Men like this one didn't have a place.

Rusk cleared his throat. "I've got another problem."

"What's with you, O'Brien? Hell, for someone who's supposedly a smart man and a smart politician, you can get your tail in more cracks than anyone I've ever seen."

"When you're in the limelight," Rusk lashed back, "everyone wants a piece of that tail, which creates trouble."

"I disagree."

"Look, you want those prison contracts, right?"

Mason nibbled on the corner of his bottom lip. "If we didn't, I sure as hell wouldn't be here."

"So, as per our agreement, you scratch my back and I'll scratch yours."

"Only problem with that is me and my partners are the ones doing all the scratching."

Rusk decided not to let that additional slap in the face pass. One of these days this man was bound to get his comeuppance. It might as well be today. No one had a hassle-free ride forever. "That's a crock of crap. You asked me to get Gates off your ass." He paused. "Have you heard from my brother anymore?"

"All right, you've made your point," Carl said in a grudging tone, seeming to back off his high horse a bit.

"You spoke of 'we' a moment ago. So where are Potter and Stovall?" Rusk asked, convinced the other men were much more tolerant of his shortcomings and, if need be, would side with him against Carl.

"Busy. So you're stuck with me, but then, what I say goes anyhow, pretty much."

God, the arrogance of this man, Rusk thought, his breath faltering.

"When I hear what's on your mind, and if I think it's necessary," Mason went on, his tone both cold and impatient, "I'll see that the others are informed."

"I'm being blackmailed."

Carl's eyes narrowed at the same time that he rubbed his forehead, which left a big red spot on his fair skin. "Tell me I didn't hear that right."

"You heard it right," Rusk said in an agitated tone.

"Does it have to do with Margie Bowers? You didn't murder her, did you?"

"No, did you?" Rusk shot back.

Mason laughed. "No. But then, if either one of us had knocked her off, we wouldn't admit it, would we?"

They glared at each other for a long moment. Then Mason said, "I just hope the hell it doesn't have anything to do with me and our deal. If you think—"

"It doesn't," Rusk said in what he hoped was a strong, convincing tone, though his conscience on that issue was far from clear. The little black book Margie had stolen, then hidden, had *everything* to do with them. Mason could never know about that. Only his rigid self-control kept Rusk from wincing visibly.

He was faced with two terrible problems, and both were like screws forever turning in his back, causing him mental and physical pain.

"So who's blackmailing you, for chrissake?"

"Some faggy little pervert."

Carl appeared stunned for a second, then laughed again. "Don't tell me *that's* your problem."

Rusk blinked in confusion. "What?"

"That you're gay?"

"Of course I'm not gay."

"That's a relief," Carl said. "I'm not sure the Bible Belt's ready for a homosexual in the governor's mansion."

Rusk wiped beads of sweat off his upper lip, though for spring, it wasn't all that hot. But then, it was only eight o'clock in the morning. By noon the temperature would be unbearable, especially in these woods.

"Well, this problem has nothing to do with sexual orientation."

"Okay, I'm listening, though my patience is waning by the second."

Rusk took a deep breath and started talking, not stopping until he'd told Carl everything the young man had told him.

Following his confession, the silence was deadly. But not as deadly as the look on Carl Mason's face.

"You're something else, O'Brien."

"Insulting me won't solve a friggin' thing," Rusk snapped. "Anyway, it's too late for that. We've both made our beds and we have to lie in them."

"That's what you think. You're *not* governor yet."

"And you don't have those contracts you want, either, and no chance of getting them unless I do become governor."

Following that second heated outburst, they were quiet.

"Does anyone else know about this?" Carl asked at length, rubbing his jaw.

"No."

"Are you sure?"

"I'm sure!"

"Then it's not too late for damage control. You can count on us."

"I knew I could."

"I wouldn't be too cocky, if I were you. This is a highly explosive situation that could shit-can your career before a cat can lick its ass."

"Why the hell do you think we're having this conversation?"

"All right, just keep your cool. Who is this guy?"

"Harold Lacy." Rusk handed him a sealed manila folder. "Everything you need to know about him is in there."

Carl took it, then said, "Here's what you do. Set up another meeting with him, only you don't show up."

"I don't understand."

"You will. Just do it."

"Consider it done."

Rusk didn't know how long he stood there after Carl's Lincoln disappeared, wondering how much longer he could keep dodging the whizzing bullets.

Gates decided to stop pussyfooting around. The only way to do something was to just do it, like that commercial said. Gates tried to smile at that thought, but there were no smiles inside him. They seemed to have dried up.

There wouldn't be any smiles from Juliana, either, when she learned what he had in mind, not that there would have been to start with. Taking his eyes off the road for a second, he glanced at the seat next to him and grimaced.

Suddenly a horn honked, and his grimace turned into an expletive, especially when he realized he'd veered into the other car's lane. Thanks to Juliana, he couldn't do anything right anymore, even drive.

Still, he wouldn't be put off. He had made up his mind, and he wasn't going to change it. However, his immediate destination was not Juliana's condo but the TV station. He knew she would be leaving shortly, and he wanted to make sure she wasn't followed by anyone other than himself.

What happened when they reached 1510 Shadybrook Lane—well, Gates refused to dwell on that now, knowing there would be hell to pay, at least for him. Shrugging that thought aside, he pulled into the parking lot at the studio and killed the engine. He was about to climb out of his truck when he happened to glance in the rearview mirror.

Juliana was walking out of the building, heading toward her car. He waited and watched.

The second she reached the street and took a right turn, he knew she wasn't heading straight home. Giving in to his heightened curiosity, he hung far enough behind so that she wouldn't guess she was being tailed.

Only after he realized her intentions did red-hot fury rip through him, shutting off his breath.

Talk about stubborn! That woman had invented the word.

Gates parked a short distance from her, and when she got out, he followed suit. He never knew what alerted her to his presence. All he knew was that she whipped around and watched him walk toward her.

"How dare you follow me?" Her voice sounded thin and high-pitched.

He shrugged, then lied. "It just so happens this was where I was heading."

"I don't believe you."

"I don't care what you believe as long as you skedaddle."

"I'm not going anywhere, except inside."

"That's not your job. I thought we had agreed on that last night."

"That was your agreement, not mine."

"Dammit, you could mess up the investigation by interfering. You don't have the foggiest idea what questions to ask."

"Then you ask them."

"And you'll stay out here?"

"I didn't say that."

"Would you stop trying to get my goat and think about yourself? Prancing in there might make you more of a sitting duck than you already are. Do you want a replay of last night?"

Juliana blanched, but her steely determination didn't waver. Her words confirmed that. "I'm going inside, with or without you."

"You always did know how to make me madder than a junkyard dog."

Juliana turned, then proceeded to prance her butt up the sidewalk. For a moment Gates simply stood there trying to collect himself, though he had to admit, he was enjoying watching the sway of her hips in that short black shirt.

Unwillingly, his loins tightened. If only he didn't know what was under that skirt, then maybe this would be easier. Muttering an expletive, he followed her inside.

Without hesitation, she stepped up to the front desk and introduced herself to a tall, good-looking young man with blue eyes and blond hair.

"Bill Honeycutt," he replied, dropping her hand, albeit a tad reluctantly, Gates thought, striding forward and introducing himself.

"What can I do for you, Ranger?" Honeycutt asked in a soft drawl.

Gates reached into his shirt pocket, took out a picture of Margie and handed it to him. If the desk clerk denied having seen her, then Gates had the receipts for backup.

"Do you recognize that woman?"

Honeycutt was silent for just a second while he studied the photograph. "As a matter of fact I do." He smiled. "She's a real looker, too."

"Was," Juliana put in. "She's dead."

Honeycutt's fair skin lost what little color it had.

Gates cut her a hard look before switching back to the clerk and saying, "I'm assuming she didn't come here alone."

"Righto."

"Could you by chance describe the man or men she was with?"

"Man," Honeycutt said. "And the last time they were here, they either had one hell of a fight or a damn good time. I'm not sure which."

"What makes you say that?"

"Because they broke a lamp and busted a coffee table in our most expensive suite."

Juliana's eyes widened, but she didn't say anything, for which Gates was grateful.

"So would you know this man if you saw him again."

"Sure. In fact, I see him all the time."

"You mean he still comes here?"

"Nah, not that I've seen."

"So where do you see him all the time?" Gates pressed.

"On TV. He's one of those guys running for governor."

"Are you sure?" Juliana asked in a breathless voice.

Gates could feel her eyes on him, but he couldn't look at her. Fear was too busy hammering a hole in his own stomach.

Still, Gates forced himself to ask the next question. "Which candidate are you referring to?"

"The one with the same last name as you, Ranger. Rusk O'Brien."

Twenty-Four

Juliana's breath was fast deserting her. Yet she wouldn't quit; she simply dug deeper, despite the thousand-pound weight she seemed to be carrying on her chest.

Only after she rounded the corner of her street and saw her condo did she slow her run to a walk, all the while sucking air into her lungs and out.

She had hoped this late-evening jog would clear some of the cobwebs from her overloaded brain. She had been wrong. It had added to her fatigue, both in mind and spirit. When her Nikes had pounded the sidewalk, her thoughts had been on the pain shooting through her joints; she hadn't gone running since Margie's death.

Too, her entire body was covered with sweat, and the drops that ran down her neck stung the cut place like crazy. Her friend and doctor, Clarence Lattimer, had warned her that she should be careful, especially since part of the wound hadn't yet healed. But she'd needed to do something to release her restless energy.

Someday her stubbornness and hardheadedness were going to get her into trouble she couldn't get out of. While she wouldn't take Gates' advice, maybe she should heed the doctor's warning. Juliana sighed as she recalled her visit just this morning.

"You're one lucky lady," Clarence had said, after first

hearing her story, then reproaching her for not coming to see him before today.

"I know," she'd said quietly.

Clarence frowned, making his wrenlike features more pinched. "If that knife had gone just a tad deeper, it could have cut an artery."

"And I would have bled to death."

"Unless you'd gotten help immediately, which you didn't."

She shifted uncomfortably. "You're right, I didn't. But I did have help, sort of, after the fact," she added lamely, not looking at him.

"I can see that. Whoever patched you up did a fine job."

She didn't respond.

"As your friend, appease my curiosity. Just why didn't you call 911?"

"I think I was in such shock that I didn't know what to do."

"So what *did* you do?"

"I called Gates."

A silence followed that statement.

"Gates? But—"

"It's a long story," Juliana interrupted. "Over lunch sometime, I'll tell you all about it."

"I don't want to wait for lunch."

"I was afraid you'd say that."

Clarence had been the doctor who had pronounced her son dead. He had been to hell and back with her. Even now, after all this time, she didn't know what she would have done without him. Gates, on the other hand, had refused Clarence's offer of help, too grief-stricken to reach out to anyone.

"Don't."

Juliana met his direct gaze, then licked her dry lips. "Don't what?"

"Think about that day."

"How could you tell?"

"Your face."

"Never a day goes by that I don't think about the accident and my son."

Clarence patted her arm. "You're a strong woman, Juliana, and I've always admired you for that. I just wish Gates had pulled from your strength, but..." His voice faded; then he cleared his throat.

"He didn't and never will."

"So why call him?" Clarence pressed in a gentle tone.

"I told you, it's a long story."

"Sure you don't want to talk? You know I have big shoulders."

Juliana forced a smile. "How well I know. I've cried bucketfuls on them."

A silence followed, and when she didn't elaborate, Clarence said, "Okay, back to business. I want you to promise you'll be extra careful. Whoever did this to you, for whatever reason, could come back to finish the job."

Juliana shivered. "You don't need to remind me of that. Besides, I'm being well looked after."

"I assume by Gates."

"HPD, actually," she said hastily, tempted to confide in Clarence, yet unable to do so. She simply wasn't up to the ordeal. Her last skirmish with Gates had left her raw inside.

"What about Gates?"

"He's...he's out of the picture."

"Oh?"

"This isn't his case."

"Juliana, you're not making sense."

"Please, Clarence, I just can't talk about it now. Okay?"

"Okay. But I trust Gates, at least when it comes to his work. Despite that humongous chip on his shoulder, he's the best at what he does."

Her chin jutted. "So is HPD."

"All right, I give up," Clarence said, tossing up his hand. "Go home and rest. You look like you could use it."

She *had* gone home, only to run instead of rest. Now, as she walked into her yard, dusk settling around her, she smiled at the officer on duty.

"Detective Bishop wants you to call him, ma'am."

"Thanks."

Even though she felt protected, she nevertheless flinched when she walked inside her house. She hated that feeling and told herself she had to get over it or move.

Wiping the sweat off her face with the towel around her shoulders, she went to phone. Moments later, Detective Bishop came on the line and didn't mince any words.

"So far, we're batting zero. The perp's a professional who's left nothing behind to incriminate him."

"Figures."

"Still no idea where Margie Bowers might have hidden that book?"

"This house has been torn apart, Detective, and if the intruder didn't find it, then it's not here."

As if he heard the frustration in her voice, Bishop expelled a breath, then softened his tone. "Don't hold it against me for hoping."

"Sorry. It's been a long day."

"And getting longer."

"Right."

"You be careful, and if anything does come to mind, let me or Ranger O'Brien know."

"I will, and thank you again for the protection."

"You're welcome, only I can't spare my men much longer."

"I understand."

After she hung up, Juliana made her way into the bathroom, undressed and climbed into the shower. Twenty minutes later she was in her robe, back in the living room and on the couch, a glass of iced tea in her hand.

For the first time since the incident involving Margie, she had a free evening. Tomorrow's show, hitting on cancer treatment and the big business it had become, was planned to the last detail, which supposedly left her this evening for relaxation.

Ha!

Some joke that was. A friend had been murdered. Her house had been trashed. Her body had been abused. Her privacy had been invaded. How much more of a relaxing time could a person want?

The entire hour she'd been running, Juliana had expected a reporter to jump out of the bushes and bombard her with questions, despite the cop who jogged several yards behind her. She had kept her eyes peeled for anyone who looked as if he didn't belong in the neighborhood.

She despised living like that, but to do otherwise would be insane. Yet she refused to let that creep force her into becoming a shrinking violet. If she went down, it would be fighting. That was her nature, and she couldn't change at this late date. She just wished her outing had accomplished what she'd hoped. It hadn't. It had merely zapped what little mental and physical energy she'd had left.

Perhaps that stemmed from the scene at the motel. She couldn't get it—or Gates—off her mind. It had sucker-punched her in the gut, and she continued to reel from the impact.

But it was Gates who had taken the fatal slam dunk. When that clerk nonchalantly identified Rusk O'Brien as Margie's lover, Gates had looked as if he'd been rapped upside the head with a bowling ball. The tan had visibly leached out of his face in front of her eyes.

"Are you sure about that?" he'd asked in a voice that was low and unwavering, showing none of his inner turmoil.

Juliana had known better. Despite the fact that he cut quite a figure and looked the part of the consummate Texas Ranger—big man, big hat, big gun, big *everything*—he was staggering from the blow.

His lack of emotion had been a sham.

"I'm positive, Ranger," Honeycutt had said. "In fact, I'd swear to it."

Moments later, back out in the waning afternoon sunlight, Gates had turned to her and said, "There's something I have to do."

"Gates—" Her voice had frozen even before he interrupted.

"Not now, Juliana," he'd snapped.

She hadn't bothered to argue, knowing she would lose. Besides, what he did wasn't her business. They had both gotten in their cars and parted. She had gone home. As to where he'd headed, she wouldn't place any bets against him going to see his brother.

Now, as she reached for her glass of tea and took a swallow, Juliana wished she could have been a fly on the wall. Gates had been so quietly furious that for a moment she had almost pitied Rusk. Then that thought had fled. That pompous bastard deserved whatever he got from Gates.

Rusk and Margie…lovers.

What a mind-boggling turn of events. She'd suspected that Margie had been seeing a married man—she'd even told Gates that—but Rusk? Who would have thought he could be that stupid, that careless, when so much was at stake?

If he'd been making whoopee with Margie, could he have been involved in her death? That thought had probably stampeded through Gates' mind, as well. Suddenly a chill darted through Juliana that had nothing to do with the iced tea.

According to Detective Bishop, everyone who had been close to Margie was suspect. But no one, not even Bishop, had considered Rusk a serious suspect. Now, that would change. She was sure of it.

Poor Gates.

To hell with that! she told herself brutally. She couldn't afford to feel so much as a twinge of pity. In many ways she held Gates responsible for the shambles her life was in. And she had meant it when she'd told Benson that Gates wasn't getting back in her house.

Juliana rubbed her head, feeling a mega-headache coming on. From the moment he'd walked up to her in the hospital, nothing had been the same. But she'd consoled herself that as soon as he walked right back out of her life, those uneasy feelings inside her would disappear. Now something told her that wasn't so.

He was trouble, and nothing that had happened since had reversed that conviction.

"I don't want them to know I'm here."

Evelyn, the O'Briens' housekeeper, smiled, then stood on her tiptoes to give Gates a kiss on the cheek.

"You don't come around here near enough." Her smile disappeared. "You oughta be ashamed."

"Hey, someone's gotta chase the bad guys."

She snorted, which shook her more than ample frame. Looking at her stomach, Gates was reminded of a bowl of Jell-O. But even if Evelyn was overweight and sometimes a bit dizzy, she was still the best friend he had in this house.

"Well at least there aren't any of those bad guys here."

Gates didn't respond to that. Instead, he winked, then said, "You take care of yourself, you hear?"

"I baked your favorite pie," Evelyn added in a conspiring voice and with a twinkle in her eyes. "Even if it is your brother's birthday."

Gates was taken aback. He'd forgotten what today was, though his mother had left a message on his machine to that effect. Unfortunately, this special day didn't change a thing. He intended to do what he had to, even if the president of the United States had been there celebrating.

No one played him for a fool and got away with it, least of all his own brother. The fact that Juliana was involved in it made it that much worse.

"I'll have a piece before I leave," he lied, unwilling to hurt her feelings. He patted her on the shoulder, then made his way back toward the den that ran the entire length of the house.

Gates paused in the shadows, waiting for the right moment to make his entrance, giving in to the rage that was building inside him.

Norman, his daddy, was standing in the middle of the room, dressed to perfection, watching Rusk, who was at the bar.

"Hell, son, I know this is your birthday and that we

have a lot to celebrate, but don't you think you're hitting that sauce a bit heavy?"

"Too heavy," Tamara put in, her lips curling into a sneer, which managed to detract somewhat from her cold beauty.

Rusk didn't so much as falter. He continued about his business. Only after the glass was filled with Chivas did he turn around. "Give it a rest, all of you." He took a gulp, raised his glass, then grinned. "Cheers."

Opal stepped up to her son and placed a hand on his arm. "Rusk, honey, I think you'd best listen to your daddy and wife." A frown furrowed the space above her perfectly arched brows. "You're well on your way to getting drunk."

"Aw, Mama," Rusk responded, placing his arm around her. "I thought for sure I could count on you for support. Hell, if a man can't get a little soused on his birthday, then when can he?" He paused and hugged her closer to his side.

Opal kissed him on the cheek. "We want you to celebrate, but you have to control your drinking."

"Surely not here," Rusk slurred.

"Here as well as everywhere else," Opal chided. "Nothing must interfere with you becoming governor."

Gates strode into the room, his heart in his throat. "Unfortunately, something already has."

Twenty-Five

Gates' cold statement garnered everyone's attention. They faced the doorway and stared at him.

"Gates," Norman said, "we're glad you're here, of course, but if you came to start trouble—"

Gates strode deeper into the room, his eyes focused only on Rusk. But he spoke to his daddy. "In other words, don't spoil the party."

"Especially with a remark like you just made."

"Oh, do be quiet, Norman," Opal chided, smiling at her other son. "I'm so glad you came. I left a message on your answering machine. I knew you wouldn't want to miss your brother's birthday celebration. And it has been a while since we've seen you."

Gates heard the soft censure in his mother's tone, but he couldn't deal with her slighted feelings right now. He was a man with one mission at a time.

"That's right, it has," Tamara put in, her tone mocking. "Not only are you in time to celebrate his birthday but his lead in the polls, as well."

Gates barely acknowledged his sister-in-law.

Rusk swayed toward Gates, nursing his drink. "Hello, little brother. Glad you could make it." He held out his glass. "Wanna join me?"

"I want to talk to you," Gates said in a tone that brooked no argument. "Alone."

Rusk raised his eyebrows, then smiled. "Whoa! Down boy. Surely a heart-to-heart can wait. Hell, have a drink and get the kink out of your colon."

"Now, Rusk." Gates never raised his voice. He didn't have to. The cold authority in it was enough to bring a stunned silence to the room.

"Gates, please—" Opal began.

"This won't take long, Mother." Gates' gaze never wavered from Rusk. "I promise. Then you can all get back to having a high old time."

"I hope that includes you," Norman said, his tone much less gruff.

"I don't think so," Gates said, motioning with his head.

Rusk's mouth twisted as he sloshed the remainder of his liquor around in his glass. "Mind if I take this with me?"

"In the study. Now!"

"Gates!"

His mother's plea fell on deaf ears as his boots nipped at his brother's heels. After they were inside the room, Gates slammed the heavy door, determined to have complete privacy.

Rusk whipped around, his eyes squinted, but not so narrowly that Gates couldn't see the red streaks.

"As usual, little brother, you managed to make an ass out of yourself."

"Save it!"

Already flushed from too much booze, Rusk began to shake like a drunk. "Now, see here. I don't have to take this crap—"

"The hell you don't!" Two strides, and both men were nose to nose.

Rusk swallowed and backed up, his eyes turning into

those of a trapped animal. "What in the devil's the matter with you?"

"Tell me about Margie Bowers and room number nine."

"I don't know what you're talking about."

"Then maybe I can help refresh your memory." Gates grabbed Rusk by the front of his shirt and slammed him back against the wall, the first time he'd ever put his hands on his brother in anger. It wasn't a good feeling, either.

"The truth. I've had it with your lies!"

"Stop—please. I'm…not…lying."

When Gates saw that Rusk's face was turning purple and that he was having difficulty speaking, he relaxed his hold, but he didn't move back an inch. "I'm waiting."

"Okay, okay, so I slept with her," Rusk whined, placing a hand on Gates' shoulder. "But it wasn't serious. She just caught me in a weak moment."

"Bullshit!"

"Please, Gates, you've got to believe me," he pleaded in a sniveling tone.

"It doesn't matter what I believe, you idiot! It's what your constituents believe. Your sacred career's at stake. Does anyone else know about the affair?"

"No. At least, not that I know of." Rusk's voice was shaking like he had the palsy.

Gates cursed. "I thought you would have known better. But then, this isn't the first time you've screwed around, is it?"

"No."

"Did you kill her?"

Rusk bristled, then shrieked, "How can you even ask that?"

"Easily. So don't jerk me around. I want to know everything about this particular dirty little tryst."

"She was a good worker and a good lay; that's all. I swear to God."

"Was she blackmailing you?"

Rusk's mouth trembled, and his breath was coming out in sour spurts. It was all Gates could do to remain in his face. But he couldn't afford to back down, not for a second.

"No, dammit!"

"But she did think you were going to marry her, didn't she?"

Rusk hesitated. Too long. Gates tightened his grip again. "The truth!"

"Okay, maybe she did."

"So was she threatening to blackmail you as in threatening to go to Tamara, or was it cold cash she wanted?"

"Neither. You've got to believe me."

"What about Tamara? Did she know?"

"She suspected I was seeing someone, but she didn't know who."

"Are you sure?"

"No, but—"

"If Tamara had known, does she have the stomach to kill someone?"

"What the hell's the matter with you, Gates? Can't you stop being a Ranger for one God damn minute of your life? If you could just hear yourself, you'd wanna puke."

"Shut the fuck up! You're the one who's in trouble here, not me. Now answer my question."

"All right. Tamara…has her faults, but killing someone wouldn't ever occur to her."

"She wants to be the first lady of the state awfully bad."

"That's still not possible."

"For your sake, I hope to hell you're right."

"I know I'm right about both of us. Now get out of my face."

"Not yet. Margie Bowers apparently had sticky fingers. Did you know that? She stole a book from someone who wants it back."

"I don't know anything about Margie's business," Rusk panted. "And I sure as hell don't know anything about a book."

"Are you sure?"

"After hours, we just fucked."

"Well, if Detective Bishop finds out about those fucks, I don't have to tell you it could put you at the *top* of the suspect list. If you think HPD's on you now, just wait. Bishop himself'll be on your ass like ants on honey."

"Back off, please," Rusk pleaded in a hoarse whisper. "I'm not going anywhere, so give me some air."

Gates stepped back, but not far.

"I know I shouldn't have slept with Margie, that I made a mistake. But I didn't kill her."

Gates wanted to believe Rusk, *had* to believe him. Besides, he had no concrete evidence to the contrary. God help them both if he ever did.

"What about Carl Mason? Could that have been his handiwork?"

Rusk shifted his gaze. "Why the hell are you asking me that? I've already told you I don't know that much about Mason, especially his personal business."

"If Margie was doing him, too, then maybe he was the one she was blackmailing."

"I wouldn't know."

"What *I* know is that Juliana's in danger. Because of that book, someone damn near slit her throat."

"God, Gates, you care more about that whore—"

"Enough, already! That is, if you don't want me to

knock those pearly white teeth of yours down your throat."

"Okay, okay, you've made your point."

"Fine. So if you know anything, then you'd best tell me now. As it is, it's going to be hard to cover your butt."

"You're not going to tell Bishop about Margie and me, are you?"

"No, I won't tell him, but I wouldn't count on him not finding out on his own. He's a sharp cookie."

Rusk's eyes bulged with fear. "Oh, God, that could ruin me."

"Not nearly as much as having killed her."

"I told you, I didn't kill her. So back off and don't cross me on this."

"Don't make me have to cross you."

Sweat gleamed on Rusk's face, and for an instant Gates saw something flicker in his eyes. Hatred? Was that it?

Suddenly disgusted and sickened and aching to belt Rusk in the mouth, Gates turned his back. "Get out of my sight before I forget you're my brother and do something we'll both regret."

"Gates—"

"Get out!"

Juliana gnashed her teeth.

"What's with you?"

"It's not me. It's that jerk."

"Who?" Benson asked, following Juliana into her office.

"That jerk from the *Chronicle*."

"He get in your face again?"

"Yes, but for the last time."

"I take it you nailed his ass."

"With more than one nail."

"Atta girl."

Juliana shoved her windblown hair back out of her eyes. "If one more person sticks a microphone in my face and asks me who killed Margie, I'm going to—"

"Even if it's Paul Jeffery?"

Juliana blinked. "What did you say?"

"I thought that would get your attention."

"That got my attention, all right, but—"

"No buts. Paul Jeffery's office called and wants you to be a guest on his show."

"I—" Juliana opened her mouth, but she was too stunned to say anything. This was national exposure, exactly what she'd been hoping for. But to get it this way...

"You've made it, my dear." Benson smiled. "How does that feel?"

"Does his asking have anything to do with Margie?"

"Of course."

"Then I won't do it."

"Have you lost your mind?"

"Probably, but you know how I feel about using a tragedy as a stepping stone."

"I respect that, but this is the chance of a lifetime. Besides, you could turn the tables and use this for Margie's benefit. After all, her killer's still out there."

"Good try, Benson," Juliana said drolly. "Only it won't work."

"Don't give me an answer now. You have a few days to think about the offer. Put that time to good use."

"My mind's made up. Unless I can name the topic, I'm not interested."

Benson sighed. "I'll just be glad when all this is behind us—Margie's death, the media frenzy, those threats against you."

"I'm beginning to think it's never going to end."

He leaned over and squeezed her hand. "It will. Have faith."

"You're a good friend, Benson. I don't know how I'd get along without you."

"Fine, I imagine. But I'm glad I'm here for you."

"The same goes for me." She paused. "I know how lonely you must be. I wish I could do more."

"Unfortunately, there's not anything anyone can do," he said in a surprisingly hard tone.

Juliana was quiet for a moment.

"Has anything developed on the case that I should know about?" He gave her a close look. "You haven't been threatened anymore, have you?"

"No, thank goodness. Maybe the pervert's finally gotten it through his head that I don't have what he wants."

"Let us pray."

"Anyway, Detective Bishop's on top of it."

"What about your ex? Is he still in the picture?"

"Not in my personal picture," Juliana responded in what she hoped was a matter-of-fact tone.

"Good deal. So how 'bout dinner tonight?"

"If it's to try and make me change my mind about the Jeffery show, the answer is no."

"I promise I won't mention it."

"You're on, then."

He told her where to meet him, then left her alone.

Juliana looked down at the blank paper on her desk, knowing that she should be filling it with questions for tomorrow's show on gang violence. Houston was becoming famous for its Hispanic gangs, and she thought it was time someone in the media acknowledged that. She expected the show to be gritty and highly volatile.

Fifteen minutes later, the page was still blank, much to

her disgust. She found her thoughts wandering back to Gates and yesterday's happenings.

Without a doubt, Rusk was probably still wiggling like the cornered bug that he was. Gates' tongue-lashings weren't fun. But after learning that Rusk had had an affair with Margie, Gates would step back from the investigation.

The O'Briens stuck together, through thick and thin. She could testify to that, having been shunned by all of them.

Blowing out a breath and refusing to dredge up those bitter thoughts, Juliana hugged herself and grinned.

Paul Jeffery.

It was finally soaking in that he wanted her to appear on his show. And even though she intended to stick by her convictions, the idea was nevertheless heady stuff and cause for celebration. She wouldn't let further reflections on Gates or his family usurp her attention, not when she wouldn't be seeing Gates anymore.

She picked up her pen just as the phone rang. "Juliana Reed."

"How's the neck?"

That voice sent a cold knot of fear streaking though her stomach. "Leave me alone!" she cried.

"When I get what I want." He laughed. "I'll be seeing you."

Juliana slammed down the receiver, then sat there, too furious and scared to move. Finally, when the shaking stopped, she stood, grabbed her purse and fled her office. She met Benson in the hall.

"What on earth? You look like you've seen a ghost."

"Worse. Can I have a rain check on dinner?"

"Of course, but—"

"I'll call you."

Thirty minutes later, when she turned into her driveway, the first thing Juliana noticed was the absence of the plainclothesman. Her heart plummeted. Maybe she shouldn't go inside. Maybe she should keep on driving.

No!

She wasn't going to let that bastard rule her life. If she could survive burying her child, she could survive him. Yet she was perilously close to tears when she unlocked the door and walked inside, only to suddenly stumble on something foreign.

"What the—" she muttered, struggling to regain her balance. When she was again steady, she looked down and saw a duffel bag.

Juliana stiffened, then wrinkled her nose. She smelled food. Cooking. What was going on? She charged into the kitchen, where she pulled up short.

Gates was standing in front of the stove.

"What do you think you're doing?"

"Cooking your dinner," he drawled.

"The hell you are."

"You're welcome."

"Gates—"

"I know about the phone call. Your lines are tapped."

She blanched, but managed to ask, "Where's the plainclothesman?"

"I told him he wasn't needed."

"What?"

He ignored her question and said in a tone that was as calm as hers was hysterical, "You needn't worry. I'm moving in."

"The hell you are." Juliana emitted a feral cry. "Get out of my house. Now!"

His eyes toured her body. "By chance, should I put my bag in your room?"

Twenty-Six

He had ripped it for sure. Juliana was royally pissed, but there wasn't anything he could do about it. It was for her own good—or at least he kept telling himself that, though he had to admit his conscience pricked him a bit.

But he *could* take care of her better than anyone. Logic was on his side. Boy, was he ever reaching. HPD was more than up to the task; he just didn't want them on the premises. With him, it was personal.

He would have liked to lock Juliana in a room and guard her with his gun. He knew why. He wanted her; he wanted to make love to her so badly he could taste it—taste *her*.

Even now, lying on the couch, long after she'd whirled around and marched out of kitchen and into her bedroom, he still had that ache between his legs. Hell, all she had to do was come anywhere near him and bingo, he got a hard-on.

When she was mad, it seemed to make it worse. And had she ever been mad! She'd slammed the door to her room with such force it had rocked the entire house. And though he was on the couch, that didn't mean he'd won the war. Far from it. He'd only won a battle.

Though for a moment there, after he'd tried to inject some humor into the situation by making that comment about dumping his things in her bedroom, he'd had his doubts even about that battle.

Juliana's eyes had blazed with fury, and he'd known she was so outraged that she couldn't say a word.

"Look, forget I said that," he'd told her, turning off the stove and removing the pan of bacon.

"I don't want you here," she'd said again, sounding as though she were having trouble breathing.

"I know that, but it's for your own protection. Whoever is after you isn't going to let up, not as long as he thinks *you* have the goods. But then, we've been over this before."

"But I don't have that damn book," she said tersely. "If I did, I would have given it to him."

"I doubt that, even though it would have been the smart thing to do."

She gave him an obstinate look, and he changed the subject. "Bishop tried to trace the call, but he didn't get it. The bastard knows exactly how long to talk."

Juliana's shoulders suddenly sagged, and she crossed her arms over her chest. She looked so fragile standing there, so defenseless, it was all he could do not to walk over and take her in his arms.

As if she knew exactly what he was thinking, she took another deep breath while their eyes met and held. Though they never spoke of those hot kisses they had exchanged, the memory nevertheless hovered between them, beckoning and titillating and taunting.

Gates pulled his gaze off her, ruthlessly reminding himself that it was "hands off, Bubba," for both their sakes. So far, they had been to the river a couple of times, but they had not gotten wet. If he ever slept with her again, he would be in deep shit.

When this fiasco was over, he wouldn't see her again.

He wondered if the bulge in his pants would disappear along with her. He doubted that, especially when the rise and fall of her full breasts was up front and in his face.

Suddenly he saw her flush. She was on to him. No wonder she didn't want him hanging around. In his own way, he was as much a threat to her as that pervert who had attacked her.

"So how much longer is this going to go on?" she asked, her voice quivering.

"Don't know."

"Has Bishop come up with anything?"

"Not so far."

"What about you?" Her voice sounded desperate, as if she had to talk. "You've never told me yet how you figure into all this, or even *if* you do."

"You're right, I haven't."

"And you still aren't going to."

He hesitated, but not for long. She deserved an explanation, and he was damn well going to give her one. "Actually, I'm swimming in some bureaucratic sewage."

"What does that have to do with all this?" Her tone was impatient.

"I'm looking into the prison scandal. Are you familiar with that brouhaha?"

"Isn't everyone?"

"Well, one of the contractors I'm investigating, Carl Mason, might have been more than just a friend to Margie."

Juliana fixed him with a hard stare. "Are you saying he could have killed her?"

"Maybe, maybe not. Right now, everyone involved in this case is pretty much sucking air."

"That's just great."

"Margie was killed with a slow-acting poison, which

could have been administered by anyone she came into contact with on a daily basis.''

Juliana shivered. "I can't imagine someone hating her that much."

"If their livelihood or career was threatened, I can."

"Such as your brother's?"

Gates had been expecting that torpedo; he was surprised it hadn't come sooner. If she thought he was going to punt instead of play, then she was mistaken. "He didn't kill her, Juliana."

"Are you sure of that?"

"Damn straight."

She didn't say anything, which shot *his* piss factor up.

"He was having an affair with her, that's all."

"Whatever you say." Her tone was mocking, which rankled that much more.

"Rusk may be a lot of things, but a killer he ain't."

"How can you be so sure?"

"For one thing, he doesn't have the stomach for it. For another, he wouldn't give Margie or anyone else any ammunition to shoot at him with, not at this juncture in his life. He wants to be governor too much."

"I'm not going to argue with you about Rusk," she said, her tone weary. "In fact, I'm not going to argue with you at all."

"Good. Truce?"

"No."

He rubbed the back of his neck in frustration. "You're going to fight me all the way, huh?"

Again, she didn't answer him right off, and the tortured minutes seemed to crawl by.

"The couch is as far as you go," she snapped. "Then, tomorrow, I want you out of here."

"Yes, ma'am." The minute he said that, he knew he'd made another mistake in a long line of them.

"Why are you doing this, Gates? Why are you torturing us both this way? We can never go back, and you know that. Patrick—"

"Knock it off." He heard the crack in his voice, despising his own weakness. "Now's not the time to shove another A-bomb up my ass."

She looked him up and down with scorn. "That's par for the course. You still think only about yourself. Well, in case you're interested, not one day goes by that I don't hurt, too." This time there was a crack in *her* voice, and tears shimmering in her eyes.

"Juliana—"

"Don't bother! It's wasted breath, anyway."

She fled then. After the door to her room had slammed, he didn't know how long he stood there like an idiot, holding that pan of bacon, both his heart and his head thudding. Finally he'd cleaned up his mess and headed for the couch.

Now, as the moonlight streamed through the open blinds, he hadn't even closed his eyes. His body was bathed in a cold, clammy sweat. He should have kept his mouth shut. More than that, he shouldn't have come here.

No matter what happened on the surface, underneath was Patrick. His death would always be between them, a deep and painful wound that neither time nor medicine could heal.

He pressed his hand over his eyes. They were moist. When had he begun to cry?

Lunging off the couch, he paced the floor, only to suddenly find himself tiptoeing down the hall to her bedroom. To his surprise, the door was ajar, not locked as he'd expected.

Temptation outweighing his sound judgment, he nudged it open a little more, telling himself he just wanted to make sure she was all right.

Right, as if someone could have gotten past him and his .45.

Yet he didn't move. He stood in the doorway and stared at her while trying to dodge the memories that flew at him. When they had been married, he had often come in late and simply stood and watched her sleep, as he was doing now.

Her lashes were long and curved delicately against her fair skin; her lips were parted slightly; her glorious red hair fanned against the white pillow. But what drew his gaze and held it were the tops of her bare breasts. Apparently she still slept nude.

He actually stood there and salivated over the need to touch them, to suckle them, as he'd seen their son do so often.

That need strengthened to such a degree that he almost did the unthinkable. But he didn't. His common sense came to his rescue and fastened his feet to the floor with steel bolts. Finally he rebounded, pulling himself together enough to step back and lean against the wall.

Why did he punish himself like this? She was right, nothing good could come of their being together. They truly had no tomorrows. So why couldn't he do the right thing? Why couldn't he let go, knowing that she'd cheated on him?

His breath congealed in his lungs even as another bout of queasiness buckled his knees, forcing him to stumble back into the living room and onto the couch. Pushing aside his total exhaustion, he squeezed the bridge of his nose and forced his eyes shut.

Would the time ever come when she didn't have the

power to shake loose the monsters inside him? He prayed for that day.

Juliana pressed her eyes together and literally held her breath. Would he come farther into the room? If he did, what would she do? Would she let him crawl in beside her and make love to her?

No way, she screamed silently, only to know that she was lying to herself. She had been very aware of his erection; from the onset the image had toyed with her. Even now, her body felt like a furnace, especially with him standing in her doorway, tempting her with his hard body, his talented hands, his seeking lips....

Please, dear Lord, she had to trample those thoughts. She had to shut them down. Lights pulsed in her brain as she opened her eyes.

He was gone.

Instead of rejoicing, a feeling of helplessness swamped her. While she didn't want him back in her life, she wanted him in her bed, which was the worst part of all. Despite the hot and exciting sex they'd enjoyed, their child had been the glue that held their marriage together. When Patrick drowned and Gates could not stop blaming himself, that glue came *un*glued, along with their relationship.

Or so she had thought. Now his presence in her home forced her to admit that he was again threatening to become an obsession, taking hold of her like a poisonous vine. She couldn't let that happen.

Flipping onto her side, Juliana stared into the darkness. That was when the phone rang. Her blood ran cold even as she reached for it on the first ring. If it was *him*, maybe she could keep her cool and get him to talk long enough to trace the call.

"Hello," she whispered.

"Is this Juliana Reed?"

She didn't recognize the voice. It wasn't the same man. "Yes." Her tone was low and guarded.

"I have something you want."

The first thought that came to mind was Margie's book. She forced herself to keep her cool. "What?" she asked.

"Information."

She frowned her disappointment, deciding this was probably related to her TV show. Some out-of-booze drunk was probably hoping to get money for a story he'd made up.

"Are you there?"

"Call the office tomorrow," she responded in a weary tone. "We'll talk then."

"No. Meet me tonight. In the parking lot of Shanghai Red's in a half hour."

"You're crazy."

"It has to do with Rusk O'Brien."

Her heart kicked in her chest.

"How does that grab you?"

"By the jugular, but I still won't meet you now."

"Not even if it's about the boating accident that killed your son?"

Shock choked Juliana, and her body turned cold. What could this stranger know about that fateful day? Whatever it was, she had to find out. Still, she put him off. "What's in this for you?"

"Let's just say I'm appeasing my conscience."

Juliana didn't even try to figure that one out. "How will I know you?"

"My red hair."

"I'll be there."

She had just replaced the receiver and was still shaking

when she looked up and saw Gates standing once again in her doorway. Her startled look met his.

"Who was that?"

"Wrong number," she lied through dry lips.

His eyes held hers while her heart pumped in her throat. If he came to her now, to hell with the rendezvous. She wouldn't turn him away.

He released a harsh breath, then said in a voice brittle with old pain, "Go back to sleep."

Right.

An hour later, Juliana was in the parking lot at Shanghai Red's Restaurant, still waiting for her caller to show, her anxiety at having been duped by a cruel hoax building to a slow boil.

That was what she got for coming here alone. That in itself was crazy. She should have been honest with Gates; he should be with her. But when the caller had told her the information concerned Rusk, confiding in Gates had lost its appeal.

Where his brother was concerned, Gates didn't think clearly. Anything the stranger might have told her had to reach her ears first. But apparently that wasn't going to happen.

Unable to sit in the car any longer, Juliana got out and walked toward the ship channel. Even though it was only ten o'clock, and the restaurant was still open and the area well lit, she felt uneasy.

She'd paused by the water's edge, her thoughts buzzing, when she felt the hand on her shoulder.

Her heart dropped to her toes.

Twenty-Seven

"**Y**ou lied to me."

Juliana clutched her chest as if that gesture would prevent her from having a heart attack, then swung around and stared into Gates' stormy features. She couldn't utter a word. Both fear and fury had a lock on her throat.

"Have you lost your mind, or what?"

"How dare you follow me?" she snapped, finding her voice, though she didn't recognize it.

"Ah, shit, Juliana, give me a break."

"Give you a break? You're the one who scared the living daylights out of me."

"And for a damn good cause, too. This is about the most asinine stunt you've ever pulled."

"That's still no excuse for you sneaking up behind me."

"Maybe it'll teach you a lesson. Hell, you haven't changed a bit."

"So what?"

"It's going to get you in trouble, that's so what." Gates removed his Stetson and shoved his fingers through his hair, then slapped the hat back on. "You're still as wild and reckless and daring as you ever were, which in this case is *not* a compliment."

Juliana tried desperately to regroup, to realize that she was safe, that Gates was here after all. Still, her heart hadn't settled yet. It remained somewhere in the vicinity of her ankles.

She knew he was experiencing the same difficulty. His voice was low and unsteady, and she could see his heart thundering in his chest, but for a different reason.

Gates wasn't afraid. He was livid.

"Jumping on a roller coaster and to hell with the risks could buy you the same fate as Margie."

"Why should you care?" she asked before she thought, knowing this was not the time or the place for indulging in a verbal slinging match.

"Under the circumstances, that's a good question. And I wish the fuck I knew the answer."

His directness cut. He always did have the power to drive a stake deep into her heart with words.

"After all you've been through, if anyone had told me this would happen, I'd have told them they were nuts," he was saying. "I gave you credit for having better sense."

Juliana lifted her head and stared at a sky filled with twinkling stars and a moon that was almost full. The beauty of the night did little to comfort her, not with her ex-husband looming over, his features pinched in a scowl and his own breathing heavy. Yet for a reason she refused to explore, she was tempted to throw herself in his arms and beg him to hold her.

Perhaps it was because he was right. Even with her rare combination of self-assurance and bravado, having come here alone to meet a stranger was no doubt another of her low points. Still, she wasn't about to admit that to him.

When she held her silence, he muttered, "Anyway, you should know better than to try to con a con."

"I thought you had gone back to sleep," she said through tight lips.

He spat out an expletive. "On that hard couch? You've got to be kidding."

"You're lucky you got that, which, by the way, is as good as it's going to get."

His nostrils flared. "I'm aware of that."

She averted her gaze. He was in a reckless mood, barely hanging on to his control, which further unnerved her. She stepped back, putting some much-needed distance between them, hoping to regroup, to put her emotions back on an even keel. As she did, her eyes scanned the area. She didn't see anyone who appeared interested in her.

"How 'bout we stop snapping and cut to the chase?"

Juliana's chin jutted, and she suddenly felt the urge to inform him that there was no "we," that she was the lone player in this game. But she didn't have the gumption. Even if she did, she would just be wasting good energy. He wasn't going anywhere, and if she was truthful with herself, she didn't want him to.

"First off, who was that on the phone?"

"I don't know."

"Dammit, Juliana!"

They were standing on the walkway that led from the restaurant's deck down to the lake. The wind picked up suddenly and whipped around them, flinging the smell of fish in their faces.

Juliana winced, the foul odor robbing her of her breath. Just as quickly, the wind shifted and, with it, the smell. "That's the truth, I swear it. He never gave me his name."

"So what *did* he give you?"

When she hesitated, he made a choking sound. "Don't make me pull it out of you, for heaven's sake."

His gaze was scanning the area, and she knew those trained eyes and sharp instincts missed nothing.

"It's not that easy," she said in a quivering voice.

"You'd try the patience of a saint!"

She ignored his insult and said, "Actually, our conversation was short. He just said he had some information that I'd want."

"That's all? He didn't give you a hint?"

"No," she lied, still unable and unwilling to tell him the truth, knowing how he would react.

"No? With nothing but a lure from a lunatic, you came down here?"

Her pulse rate inched up a notch. "That's right."

He cursed again, then passed his tongue across his lower lip, staring down into her upturned face. "Right now, I'm fighting the urge to throttle you."

"He said he had something on Rusk."

Her softly spoken words fell into the night air with a hard thud.

As she suspected, he was taken aback. He looked as if she'd picked up a rock and hit him between the eyes. "Rusk?"

Suddenly the fun of tormenting him lost its appeal. She would rather have a tooth pulled without Novocain than to tell him the gist of the conversation with the caller.

"Yes, Rusk. Your brother."

"Did it have to do with his campaign?" Gates' voice held irritation and impatience.

"No, or at least, not directly."

"What does that mean?"

"If you'll just give me time, I'll explain."

"Rusk, huh?" he muttered, peering into the distance.

She saw his jaw bunch and knew that she'd hit a nerve. Did Gates know more about his brother's business than he was letting on? More to the point, was Rusk involved in Margie's murder, after all? Was Gates covering for his brother the way he'd always done?

No. Rusk might be party to something outside the law, but Gates wouldn't protect him. When it came to upholding the law, her ex-husband was a straight shooter.

"Juliana, if you don't—"

"He told me it involved the boating accident...and Patrick's death."

The lights surrounding them allowed her to see Gates' face clearly. It turned the color of wet concrete. "Oookaaay, so you've taken your shot, hit me where it hurts the most."

"That's exactly why I didn't want to tell you. But you just kept on."

"So I did." Gates' tone was flat, but cutting as a whiplash.

"It was then that I agreed to meet him, only it looks like I've been had."

"Did he mention money?"

"No. He said he wanted to appease his conscience."

"His conscience? That doesn't make any sense."

Juliana shrugged, then shivered, the wind coming off the water a tad chilly. "That's what I thought, too."

"Still, he sounds like a man with a definite mission."

"So why didn't he show?" Juliana asked.

"How the hell would I know?" Gates' reply came in a strained growl.

"Look, if it's any consolation, his words cut me, too, like another knife to my throat. The last thing I wanted was to rehash that accident." Juliana shivered again, her flesh tingling. "I'm going. This place is giving me the creeps."

"I'll follow you."

"Then do what?" she demanded, suspicious of his easy capitulation.

"Come back, take a look around."

"I don't think that's—"

"Hold it!" Gates whispered in a voice that sounded as if he'd just stepped into a confessional. He was staring beyond her shoulder toward the wharf.

Turning, she followed his gaze, then gasped in horror. "Oh, my God!"

A body, facedown, was floating near the edge of the water.

He belched, then rubbed his distended stomach.

Though he would pay for the rich food and the expensive booze the rest of the night, he had no regrets. Man, but he'd enjoyed that dinner. Those oysters on the half shell had been the cat's meow. In fact, he didn't know when he'd enjoyed anything as much, except maybe a good lay.

Now that was another delicious thought, one to which he should give serious consideration. What more could a man want than good food, followed by a good woman? Especially after he'd just blown a man's brains out.

But then that was all in a day's work.

He was about to get into his car when he saw them. Dammit, what were they doing there? He recognized them both—the talk-show lady and the Texas Ranger. Sweat popped out on his upper lip. He knew enough about this assignment to realize their presence was a bad sign.

The killer's thoughts raced. Rusk O'Brien had been told to set up this meeting, then renege on his end of the bargain. Instead of O'Brien, he'd shown up and done what he'd been paid a shitload of money to do—kill the skinny-ass redhead.

But had the kid not trusted O'Brien and pulled a fast one? Had he set up a prior meeting with those two? Or was their presence here just a coincidence?

He knew for a fact the redhead hadn't met with them in person. Since his target's arrival at the waterfront, he'd watched the man's every move—right up until the time he'd pulled the trigger. Still, if the redhead had engineered this meeting, he'd apparently smelled a setup. If so, what had he said on the phone to Juliana Reed and the Ranger that had lured them here? Too damn much, he would bet. His boss wasn't going to like this one bit.

"Shit fire and save the matches!" he muttered, belching again. The second time around, the food wasn't so appetizing. He dug in his pocket for a peppermint.

This job was supposed to have been a piece of cake. And it had been. Granted, his target had been early, but he hadn't thought anything about that—until now. He'd taken him out, just as he'd been told.

No muss, no fuss. And no mess to clean up afterward, either. According to the guy's background, he certainly wasn't a candidate for the American Legion Award. No one would miss him or care that he was dead.

By anyone's standards, he was a loser.

Still, his client would not be happy if he thought the kid had talked to that broad before he'd gotten his just due. And the Ranger? God, that was even worse; the Ranger had found the body.

Now he was walking back up the embankment after having gone down to the water to examine it. Next he would be making a call on his cell phone, and then the place would be crawling with cops. Noticing that the restaurant had finally closed and that clouds had blocked out the moon, he strode to his car and got inside.

Using *his* cell phone, he punched out a number.

"We might have a problem."

"How's that?"

His boss listened without interrupting.

"You know what to do."

"Hey, man, we're talking about a cop here."

"So?"

"So I'm not killing a cop."

"Then scare the shit out of him."

"That's going to cost you more."

"Just do it!"

The shooter eyed the rifle next to him on the seat.

"Get in."

Gates had parked beside her, and now he was standing beside her car, holding the door open. Juliana paused and peered up at him. His eyes were shadowed but alert. He was tense, as well; inside, he was coiled about as tight as she'd ever seen him.

Bishop and his crew were on the way.

"I should stay. Detective Bishop will want my statement."

"He can get it later. I want you out of here ASAP."

Juliana had to admit that seeing that body had taken its toll on her. She couldn't seem to stop shaking, inside or out.

"Take a hot bath, then go to bed. A plainclothesman will be there waiting for you. I'll follow."

"I don't want you coming back to my house."

"For God's sake, don't start—"

He never finished his sentence. A bullet whizzed by his head, barely missing it. Juliana screamed. Gates cursed, then jerked her down beside him, drawing his gun.

"Gates!"

Ping. Another bullet bounced off the top of her car.

"Get into the car!" He gave her a shove. "And stay down!"

She grabbed his hand and stammered, "Wh-where are...you going?"

"After him."

Before she could plead with him not to go, he crouched low, then moved into the darkness. She bit her lower lip to keep from crying out, wondering if she would ever see him again. She didn't have to wonder long. Although it seemed like an eternity as she sat there, shaking.

"Juliana?"

Relief washed through her, rendering her so weak that she could barely sit up. She rose and looked at him through wide, frightened eyes. "What...happened?"

"It's okay."

If his hard features were a barometer, it was anything but okay. Even though her teeth were banging together, she managed to ask, "Did...you get him?"

"No. The son of a bitch got away."

Twenty-Eight

"Hang in there," Gates ordered her.

"I'm...okay."

He took his eyes off the road and cut her a quick glance. Like hell she was okay. The clouds were covering the moon now which made it hard to see her face. But she'd spoken in a hoarse whisper, and she was sitting so stiffly that she looked as if her body had been wired together.

After the ordeal, he was surprised she was still upright.

But then, she had more guts and grit than any woman he'd ever known, though she now appeared so thin and vulnerable that a hard puff of wind could blow her away.

"What...about my car?"

Compared to the ordeal she'd been through, he didn't think she was all that concerned about her vehicle. Yet it was something sane to talk about among all the insanity. At least she hadn't given him any more grief about going home with her.

"I'll have someone get it in the morning."

She didn't reply. Instead, she continued to sit in that rigid stance and stare straight ahead with her arms folded together in her lap.

He had the urge to pull his truck off the road and take her into his arms. He ached to comfort her, to somehow reassure her, but he didn't have the words. Guns and getting shot at were a normal part of his life. He flirted with death every day; to him it was no big deal.

Not so for Juliana. He was afraid she wasn't far from going into shock. After the bastard who'd shot at them got away, HPD had arrived, Detective Bishop leading the pack. Gates had given him the details from the bottom up, then whisked Juliana into his truck.

Now, as they turned into her driveway, her head was back against the seat. "Hey, kid, we're here."

Juliana's eyes fluttered open, and she groped for the door handle.

"Hold your horses. I'll get the door."

Before she could answer him, he climbed out and came around the truck. When he opened her door, he reached for her hand, certain she would rebuff him.

She didn't. Her hand slipped into his, and for a moment its unsteady coldness almost made him shiver. "Come on, let's get inside," he said with brusque softness.

The instant they reached the living room, she took her hand back and stood in the middle of the room. The house was dark except for a lamp burning in one corner. In the stark quietness he stared at her. She looked so weary, so breakable, that it frightened him. If he were to touch her now, she might shatter into a zillion pieces.

Ignoring his own palpitating heart, Gates took off his hat and pitched it onto the nearest chair. "Sit down before you fall down. I'll get you something hot to drink."

"No."

The tiny word stopped him in his tracks and sent a shot of dread through him. So much for positive thinking. Apparently she wasn't so out of it that she was going to let him take over. She intended to fight him. He shouldn't try to stop her, either.

This thing gnawing at him was going to end up biting

him in the ass nineteen different ways. Still, he couldn't just walk out.

"No?" he asked.

"I...I'm all right."

"You're *not* all right, and we both know it."

"I will be."

"I agree, after you've had something to drink and a hot bath."

Juliana shook her head.

"Humor me one more time, okay?" He tried to keep his voice emotion free, but that was hard, especially when that stubborn streak was rearing its ugly head, and at the worst possible time.

"I told you, I don't want you here."

He lost it. "You're shell-shocked, for chrissake! You need me."

"No, I don't."

He moved toward her, and before he thought, Gates placed both his hands on her upper arms. They were icy to the touch. He tried again, desperate to make her see reason.

"You don't have to pretend with me, you know? What you've been through was a slice of hell on earth. Believe me, it's okay if you want to cry and even pitch a hissy fit. You've earned it."

She tightened her lips; Gates suspected the motive behind that gesture was to keep him from seeing them quiver, possibly because he had his hands on her. When she finally peered up at him, her eyes seemed haunted, though they were still beautiful, reminding him again of Patrick's.

Pain ripped through his gut like a tiny tornado. He dropped his hands to his sides. "I don't think now's the time for one of our pissing contests," he said thickly. "Do you?"

"I just want you to leave."

Gates lifted his head and counted to ten, trying to control his battered senses. "Juliana, I can't leave you, not like this."

Her breathing was shallow. "You have to. Don't you see, this constant pain we keep inflicting on each other has to stop. We've been there, done that. It didn't work then, and it won't work now."

"I can't—I *won't*—leave you."

"What about Nicole?"

He hadn't been expecting that again, especially not now. It socked him where it hurt—in the gut. "What about her?"

"Does she know where you've been spending your nights lately?"

Charming. He couldn't believe they were having this conversation after all they had been through. In spite of her efforts not to let it show, he did hear a tremor in her voice. She was suffering, too, just as much as he was.

But when Patrick had died, they hadn't been able to comfort one another. Not that time.

He would be there for her, no matter how high the price to his body or his peace of mind. Regrets could be dealt with later. No matter what, he wasn't leaving unless she pitched him out. And that wasn't going to happen.

"Answer my question, Gates."

"Then will you go to bed?"

"Yes."

"Fair enough," he said, feeling at that point as if he were flying blind and heading straight into a mountain. Nicole was the last person he wanted to talk about.

"She...Nicole and I have an understanding." Shit! He was already handling this badly.

She didn't respond.

"I don't love her, Juliana," he said in a raspy, intense voice. "I never have. She's just a friend." He paused and pinned her gaze. "I haven't been with her since I ran into you at the hospital."

"Gates—" Her voice broke, and she began to tremble in earnest.

"I haven't wanted her since I saw you."

"Oh, Gates," Juliana whispered. "What are *we* doing?"

He put his hands back on her upper arms, but he was afraid to pull her close to him, even though he thought his heart might rupture if he didn't. First he had to make her understand. Understand what? That he wanted her and no one else—ever? Hell, he couldn't tell her that; he couldn't deal with that himself.

Gently, and without warning, he eased her backward toward the couch. When she was seated, he looked down into her upturned face. Tears filled her eyes.

He groaned inwardly and knew that he had to put some distance between them. "I'll be right back," he said, striding into the kitchen.

Five minutes later the coffeepot was gurgling, but Gates barely heard it. He was gripping the counter so hard, he feared he might pop his knuckles. His head was throbbing so badly that he shut his eyes.

Run.

That was what the detector in his gut was telling him. If not, he was bound to unearth old bones that were better left buried. She was right; they had been there, done that. Neither of them was equipped to survive a second time around, which was why he had to be the strong one.

By the time the coffee was ready, he'd made his decision. Carrying two cups, he strode back into the living room. Juliana was standing now, giving him a start. He hadn't expected her to have the strength to exert that much energy. But then, he wasn't dealing with just any woman, he reminded himself. This one had more gumption than even he did.

"It's hot," he said inanely, holding out the cup to her.

She shook her head. "Sorry, I can't drink it after all."

"You don't have to apologize." His tone was soft but impatient. Now they were behaving like two strangers who had never shared a life, much less a bed and a child.

Suddenly he felt that old quicksand of a moment ago tugging at him again. He turned and placed both cups on the coffee table, then looked back at her.

"I can't stop seeing…that man's body."

Gates' throat went dry, too dry to say a word.

"And all the blood." Juliana bent her head and rubbed her eyes.

When she looked back up at him, tears, mixed with her makeup, had left smudge marks on her delicate skin.

"The water around him was…all red."

"Juliana—" His voice shook. "Don't do this to yourself. Don't think about that."

"How do I *not* think about it?"

For a moment he was at a loss for words, there were no easy answers to that question. She'd seen a man who'd been brutally murdered.

"Why?" she whispered. "Why is all this happening?"

"I wish I knew, but now's not the time to worry about that. Right now, you need to think about yourself and get some rest. You can't take much more."

"You're right, I can't."

To keep from hauling her into his arms and to hell with

the consequences, he balled his fingers into a fist and said in a harsh voice, "Look, if you still want me to go, I will. Outside, that is. I won't leave the premises, but I won't stay on the couch, either."

Silence.

"So, is that something you can live with?" He prayed silently that his reflexes would deaden, that *he* could live up to his promise.

"Hold me, please."

Gates snapped his head up, certain he'd heard her wrong. After all, her voice had sounded as flimsy as a piece of gauze.

"Hold me, please," she said again.

He blinked, then felt a tremble start in his neck and end up in his groin. "I can do that, but I don't know for how long." He expelled his breath in a rush. "Just hold you, I mean."

"I know, and that's okay." Juliana lifted her hand and placed it against his cheek.

His pulse jumped off the chart as he covered that soft hand and brought it to his mouth. Without removing his eyes, he tongued her palm and each finger.

He felt her shiver, a shiver that was as hard as his own. What was she saying to him? That she wanted him as much as he wanted her? If so, should he give in? She was a wounded, vulnerable soul who needed to escape from her pain, from her fear. But in him? Would he be taking advantage of her in a weak, traumatic moment?

Yes, but God help him, he didn't care. He wanted her, wanted to be inside her, to fill her with himself one more time. Still, he hesitated, and his eyes fastened on her face, his belly on fire.

"What are you saying?" he whispered. "Tell me."

I want you.

Though those powerful words were unspoken, Juliana knew he heard them. They shared that special gift; time had not altered that.

She also knew that what she was doing was wrong. But she didn't care. Gates was here, in the flesh, and she couldn't let him go.

Logic had ceased when he'd touched her palm with his lips and tongue, igniting her, reviving that primal need that came from deep within, that only he could assuage. She'd thought she would never feel that again, nor had she wanted to.

Pain.

For so long that word had been synonymous with Gates. Now that pain seemed to have disintegrated along with the fear she'd felt a moment ago. Only pleasure coursed through her.

"Make love to me," she pleaded, delving deep into his eyes.

His mouth worked. "No ghosts, no regrets?"

"No ghosts, no regrets."

Gates groaned, and they came together in a need so mutual, so inflammatory, so out of control, that when he urged her against the wall, she offered no protest.

With her back pressed against the hard surface, his hands were all over her, while his mouth, hot and arousing, sank onto hers. She tried to clutch his chest, but he stopped her, clasping her hands together and anchoring them against the wall high above her head.

She moaned under his mouth's assault as it devoured and inflamed. Using his free hand, he ripped open the front of her blouse. One button pinged off the wall before it hit the carpet.

Because her chest was heaving so hard, her breasts

were almost out of her bra. He leaned over and licked the creamy top of each.

A wrenching cry erupted from her lips, and Juliana shook her head from side to side. *Don't!* she wanted to scream. But how could she possibly think that when she was melting and aching for more?

Gates lifted his head. His eyes had fire in them. They burned into hers. She knew he was asking if he should go on, if this was *really* what she wanted. She also knew that if she indicated in any way that it was not, he would pull back.

No way could she tell him no, not when she felt the blood pumping through his veins with a force that matched hers. Since he had reappeared in her life, this moment had been inevitable.

She heard his guttural moan as he unclasped the flimsy piece of material. When her breasts were exposed, he ducked his head, encircled a nipple and began to suck.

In a frantic gesture, Juliana loosened her hands, clutched at his shoulders and dug her nails into them, reveling in the shots of heat her body was taking.

When both nipples were swollen and pulsing, he dropped to his knees, taking her shorts and her panties with him.

"Gates!" she cried, transferring her hands to his hair, watching as his lips and tongue caressed her skin.

Only after she cried out did he stand and unzip his pants. Then, in one quick move, he reached for the cheeks of her buttocks, lifted her, then thrust hard and high.

Her legs circled him, and her eyes glazed over as heat met heat and flesh pounded flesh in sweet, savage perfection.

Twenty-Nine

She stretched, then moved her arm. That was when she felt him. Her breath caught as she eased her eyes to the right. Gates was on his side, facing her, his eyes closed.

Juliana stared at him, taking in his strong features, the dark stubble on his jaw and chin. But it was the long sweep of those thick eyelashes that held her attention. They were much too pretty to be on a man.

Then, realizing how senseless that thought was, she whipped her gaze off him, her emotions wildly chaotic. Her life was already in an uproar. She didn't dare speculate just how much this latest development would up the ante, though she'd known it was only a matter of time until it happened.

When he was near, anything pertaining to rational thinking seemed to fly out the window. It was all she could do not to reach out and touch him, touch the man with whom she'd shared so much—passionate love, a home, the pure, unsullied laughter from a little boy.

And sorrow. Because of that dark blight, they could no longer be a family. The death of their precious son had planted a bomb inside each of them. After the funeral, that bomb had exploded, shattering them and their life together.

They were destined to go their own ways. They had changed. But the circumstances that had driven them apart had not. His guilt and her pride stood between them like a boulder.

But to her dismay, she still wanted him and had allowed him to chip away at that boulder. What she couldn't afford to do was love him again. Nor could he continue to intrude in her life.

Suddenly Juliana's heart contracted. What if…? She wouldn't think about that possibility. Yet the thought wouldn't go away. They had made love without protection. Then she calmed down. She wouldn't get pregnant, not again, not under the same circumstances. Lightning never struck twice.

Still, she had played a dangerous game of Russian roulette. She couldn't blame it on the situation, either, though that could certainly qualify as a factor in absolving her conscience.

So the unthinkable had happened. Gates had stormed back into her life and into her bed. And while he could protect her body, what about her soul? Who would protect that?

She felt that heat, that same *intense* heat. She moaned, then opened her eyes. Had she fallen back asleep? She must have, but what a glorious way to wake up.

Gates' head was buried against her chest, lips tugging on a nipple, bringing it to full peak. Shuddering at the familiar yet exquisite sensation it created deep within her, Juliana laced her fingers through his hair.

After a moment of laving both nipples, he lifted his head and said in a thick voice, "I wasn't sure you were really here."

"I'm here."

"Are you sorry?"

Her eyes darkened. "I should be, but I'm not. Are you?"

"What do you think?" His tongue teased a nipple again while his gazed fixed on her. "I've wanted you since I saw you at the hospital." He paused and cleared his voice. "And before. Actually, I've never stopped wanting you."

The fact that he failed to say he'd never stopped loving her didn't go unnoticed. "Oh, Gates," she whispered, "I know I'm cracked in the skull, but so are you."

"What we *are* is starving for one another."

She couldn't refute that, especially when he rolled her over onto her stomach. Immediately, his mouth began nipping its way down the middle of her spine, stopping only after it reached the cleavage at the top of her buttocks.

"Gates, please."

"Please what?" he murmured against her skin.

"I...don't know."

She could imagine a smile of sorts on his lips before she felt him lightly insert a finger in the indention and trail slowly up and down. Her breath halted under the heated assault. She ached to brush his hand away, only she didn't have the will.

Only after her groans rose in volume did he turn her back over. But he didn't stop the pleasure, lowering his head between her thighs and stroking. She held him tightly, whispering incoherently and giving in to the added sweetness that his mouth and tongue were bringing her.

Then he rose and stood over her, his eyes glistening with passion. Without saying a word, Juliana touched his aroused flesh, first with her hand, then with her lips, tasting herself on him.

He threw his head back and gasped.

Knowing when he'd reached the limit of his endurance, she surrounded his erection and pulled him toward her.

Wordlessly, he leaned over and kissed her, his mouth a hot testimony of his need and desire. But he didn't stop there. Nudging her legs apart, he eased a finger inside her. She pitched against the bed, barely able to hold off an orgasm.

"Please," she cried. "I want to wait for you."

His answer was to reach for her legs, place them against his chest and ease into her.

Their eyes locked as he moved, hard and fast. They cried out simultaneously, their bodies writhing in spasms of impossible pleasure.

Afterward, he held her close to his heart long into the night. Only when the rays of dawn peeped through the window did she feel him move, realizing that he was still inside her.

She opened her eyes to find him staring at her at the same time that he cupped her buttocks and swung her on top of him.

"Gates!"

"Shh, just let it happen," he ground out. "Just one more time."

She did, once again feeling him hot and full inside her. Finally spent, she collapsed on top of him. When their breathing evened out and her strength returned, she rolled off him.

They were quiet for a while. During that silence, reality came crashing down around her, leaving her at a loss as to how to cope.

"I wish I didn't have to leave," Gates said at last, propping one side of his head in his palm and staring down at her. His features were twisted in agony.

She avoided meeting his gaze. "We both have to go."

"I'll be back."

His statement, though softly spoken, had punch. She

swung her eyes up and met his gaze head-on. "I don't think that's a good idea."

For a moment he looked green. "How can you say that?"

"This was about sex, nothing else."

He winced, and it took him a few seconds to respond. "You sure about that? What about need?"

"Okay, so I needed you, but..." Her voice faltered.

"But what?"

"Our romp in the hay hasn't changed anything, Gates."

"Only because you don't want it to."

"It's not that simple," she said hotly. "And you know it."

"We can make it that simple."

"No, we can't."

He lunged upright and sat on the side of the bed, his shoulders bunched in anger. Angry or not, she couldn't keep herself from saying, "All right, then, tell me things have changed. Tell me *you've* changed."

"What the hell are you getting at?"

"You know what I'm getting at. Have you stopped wallowing in your own guilt about Patrick?" She was practically shouting now, but she didn't care. "Can you tell me you've dropped that baggage?"

He faced her again, his eyes dark with pain and fury. "You know that'll never happen. I'll take the blame for Patrick's death to the grave."

"And do you still think I was unfaithful to you?"

He didn't respond, which was her answer.

"I rest my case," she said in a flat, dull tone.

He cursed, got up, reached for his jeans and put them on. "If you don't want me back in your bed, I'll have to live with that. But I'm *not* leaving you alone, not with some gun-wielding son of a bitch running loose out there.''

"So…you think whoever shot at me…us will try again?''

"Who knows? But I'm not taking any chances.''

"What if those bullets were meant for you?'' she asked out of the blue, shocking herself.

If he was shocked, he disguised it. "It's possible, but not probable, given the circumstances.''

"God, I can't believe this is happening.''

"Me either, but it is, and we have to deal with it.''

"I told you, I won't let all this disrupt my life.''

"If you don't stop being so pigheaded, it just might *cost* you your life.''

"I'll take my chances.''

"Like hell you will.''

"I'll be careful.''

He snorted. "Careful like the man who was killed?''

"That was a low blow,'' she whispered, the picture of the redhead floating in red water jumping back to mind.

"It was meant to hit low.''

She pursed her lips. "Why do you think he was killed?''

"That's the million-dollar question, especially since his information concerned the boating…accident.''

To this day, Gates seemed unable to say that word without stumbling. Unexpectedly, Juliana's heart went out to him, and she wanted to fold him in her arms the way she used to do to Patrick when he was hurt and in need of comfort.

But Gates was not a child, and to touch him again would be a lethal mistake. Already she had committed the unpardonable.

"That's what I find so bizarre. Do you think any of

this could be connected? Margie's and Patrick's deaths, that is?''

"Because he mentioned Rusk? Is that what you're getting at?''

"What if I am? If you think about it, Rusk is the common denominator—the *only* common denominator.''

"You've lost your mind if—''

"If what? If I think the redhead had some incriminating dirt on Rusk?''

He kept a brooding silence.

"Apparently he knew something," Juliana stressed. "Now that he's...dead, we won't ever know what that something was.''

"My call is that he was full of shit.''

Gates' flagrant disregard of the idea that his brother was anything other than lily white made her crazy. "I think it was much more than that. Why is it that you can't see your brother's faults?''

"I see them every day.''

"Baloney.''

Gates' face suffused with color.

"It's even occurred to me that the book Margie took might have belonged to Rusk.''

"Oh, come on. You're stretching it, big time. Besides, the guy who called you last night didn't even mention the book. The two have no connection whatsoever, and you know it.''

"Do I?''

"Yes, you do. Will you do me a favor and get off Rusk's case? Margie was just a fling to him. Nothing more, nothing less.''

"Whatever you say." Her response was taut.

"As for the book, my gut says it belongs to Carl Mason.''

"That contractor you're investigating?"

"Yep. I think it contains something illegal that has to do with the prisons he built."

"How would Margie have had access to that?"

"She was screwing him, along with Rusk."

"You have proof of that?"

"Nope, but I'll get it. I'm hoping that if I give Mason enough rope, he'll hang himself."

"Then Rusk will come out smelling like a rose?"

Gates gave a harsh, strained laugh. "You just don't give up, do you?"

"Not when I know that rose has thorns."

"Cute."

"It wasn't meant to be."

"You can honestly say that you believe my brother, the next governor of Texas, is a murderer?"

Juliana didn't flinch. "I'm withholding my judgment till *all* the facts are in."

"You're dead wrong, but I'm not going to argue with you any longer. You're never going to change your opinion of Rusk."

"That's because I'm not blind."

"That's because you've got your stinger out for Rusk," he countered.

"And for a damn good reason, only you can't—or won't—see that."

"Drop it, okay?"

"Fine."

Gates stared at her for a long moment; then, like a shutter closing, his face suddenly lost all his expression, and his eyes iced over. "I'll see you later." He grabbed the rest of his clothes and stomped out.

When she heard the door slam, Juliana staggered mentally under the heavy weight crushing her chest.

Thirty

Her performance could easily have garnered her an Academy Award. Juliana could still hear the thunderous applause in her ears. She had tackled the subject of teenage mothers on welfare with what she thought had been both dignity and grit. The audience had apparently agreed with her.

Yet the entire time she had been in front of the camera, smiling, she'd had to fight to concentrate, to zero in on those hard questions that demanded hard answers. Her mind had wanted to splinter into a thousand different directions. That lack of focus and ability to concentrate frightened her. Her work had been her mainstay, her reason for getting out of bed every morning and facing the day.

Now, with her life falling apart in front of her, that mainstay was being threatened, something she couldn't allow to happen. It had been three days since she'd taken that ill-fated trip to the docks, where she'd encountered a dead body and bullets whizzing past her head.

For the past three nights, Gates had slept on the couch.

"I hope I'm not interrupting a brilliant thought turning in that head of yours."

Juliana looked up from the work on her desk and gave Benson a cursory smile. "Hardly. In fact, I'm glad of the interruption. What's up?"

"Congratulations, that's what."

"Thanks."

He didn't bother to answer. Instead, he practically fell into the nearest chair.

Juliana thumped her pencil on the folder and gave him the once-over. "You look as bad as I feel." There were dark circles under his eyes that she'd never seen before. His skin looked drawn and sallow. He had an overall disheveled appearance that was not in keeping with him.

"I've been better, I'll admit," he said, sounding slightly out of breath.

He'd started smoking again, she knew, though not in front of her. She had smelled it on his clothes.

"Is it your wife?"

A bitter expression darkened his features, and his hands shook, though he tried hard to hide that by gripping the arms of the chair. "Always."

"I'm sorry," Juliana said, for lack of anything better.

"Well, it's a sorry world."

His voice was as blunt as it was angry.

"What's going on, Benson?" she asked quietly. "I agree your wife's a tragic problem, but I sense there's more here. Is the network giving you a fit about something?"

He fidgeted in his chair, then averted his eyes as though he didn't want to face her. "I'm worried about losing you."

Juliana raised her eyebrows. "I hope you don't mean that literally." Humor lurked around her mouth, hoping to lighten his mood.

"Of course I don't," he snapped.

She had told him about the incident outside the restaurant. He had blinked in disbelief, then anger had taken over. That was when he'd insisted the studio hire someone to protect her.

She had explained that that wouldn't be necessary, that HPD was providing that. She hadn't mentioned Gates and the fact that he'd moved in with her, not when she was still choking on that herself.

Now Benson was smiling a lame smile. "Poor choice of words, huh?"

"Nah, I was just picking at you."

"I know, but the thought of losing you *is* what's giving me chronic heartburn."

Even as he spoke, Benson reached inside his coat pocket, pulled out a package of antacids and popped one in his mouth.

Despite what he said, Juliana didn't believe for one minute that she was responsible for Benson's distraction. Still, it was nice to know that she was a valued employee.

"Anyway, I feel bad about complaining," Benson added. "My troubles are nothing compared to yours."

"No, they're not."

"I've been meaning to ask, how's the throat?"

"Much better." Juliana loosened the scarf around her neck and showed him the wound.

"You're right. It's barely noticeable."

"I doubt I'll be scarred."

"You're damn lucky."

"I know, and I'm thankful. I'm also thankful that at least for now things are pretty quiet. I've even managed to convince Detective Bishop to remove my bodyguard."

"Is that smart?"

"Only time will tell. But they're shorthanded, and I'm tired of living under someone's shadow. So I figured it was worth a try."

She hadn't told Gates about her conversation with the detective. But then, she'd only just talked to Bishop.

"But aren't you frightened?"

"I'd be a fool if I weren't. But I also don't want to let these people rule my life. That frightens me, as well."

"What about your ex?" Benson asked. "Is he still in the picture?"

"That's another story I don't want to go into."

"Do you honestly think you're out of danger?"

"God, I hope so."

"And you're one hundred percent sure you don't have what that sicko wants?"

"Absolutely. Anyway, if something had been in my house, whoever trashed it would have found it. I've even looked here in the office, turned it upside down."

"Did I tell you that you were smashing this morning?" Benson said, suddenly switching the subject.

Juliana smiled. "Not in those words, but I appreciate that. This was one of the hardest shows I've ever done."

"I assume you still don't want to appear on the Jeffery show?"

She shook her head. "Until my life's truly back on track, that's the last thing I want."

"That's your choice, and I can't say I'm sorry. I know that if you do, I'll lose you."

"We'll see."

Benson stood. "If you don't need to go over anything for tomorrow, I'm outta here."

"Take off."

"Why don't you leave, as well?"

"Are you serious?"

"I don't kid about time off."

"Where are you suggesting I go?"

Benson shrugged. "Home. Shopping. Buy something

new to wear.'' He grinned. ''That's what—'' His voice dropped off, along with his grin. When he seemed to have regained his composure, he added, ''Just get out of here.''

''I might take you up on that.''

Benson nodded, then strode out, leaving Juliana feeling more confused than ever. It seemed as if Benson, who had always been so reliable, so steady, was truly unraveling. He'd been about to mention a name, someone who thought shopping was a woman's cure-all.

He hadn't been referring to his wife, obviously. Maybe he was seeing someone. If so, it was none of her business. If she had a husband in that condition, she didn't know what she would do. Besides, she was in no position to judge. Look at the emotional mess she'd gotten herself into.

Dismissing Benson and her own screwups from her mind, Juliana got up and walked to the window. Though warm, the morning was gorgeous, not a cloud in the sky. Maybe she should get out for a while, only she wouldn't go shopping.

However, there was something else she could do, something she *needed* to do.

Thirty minutes later Juliana parked at the cemetery, got out and wound her way to Patrick's grave. She had the place to herself, for which she was grateful. Without worrying about getting grass stains on the knees of her slacks, she knelt and smiled at Patrick's picture framed in the headstone, tears instantly forming a lump in her throat.

She had promised herself she wouldn't cry. Yeah, right.

After Patrick died, she had come here on a regular basis, only to return home wrung-out and feeling as if she'd been stomped on, her grief rendering her useless.

Time.

It had done what everyone had told her it would do. It

had saved her sanity and lessened the mind-numbing sorrow, which had allowed her to pick up the pieces that were broken inside her and glue them back together.

While she would never again be the whole person she'd once been, having lost the part of her heart that had been Patrick, she had been able to go on with her life.

She wished Gates had been as fortunate.

Gates.

Thinking about him unnerved her. To counteract that, Juliana lovingly brushed off the leaves that clung to Patrick's headstone. She fought off a renewed feeling of hopelessness and self-pity, peering into the distance.

A fence nearby was covered with morning-glory vines that lent a quiet reverence. Another of God's miracles in blue, she thought. A robin perched on one of the blooms, proudly belting out its glad doxology.

Juliana smiled through her tears, then returned her gaze to Patrick's picture, a big grin showing his row of white baby teeth. What a beautiful child he'd been. What a happy child. What joy he had brought both her and Gates.

One such joyous occasion sprang to mind—the time Patrick had made mud pies and taken them inside the house to Gates. She had walked in from the store, only to stop dead in her tracks, the sack of groceries sliding out of her hands to the floor.

"What on earth is going on?" she'd gasped.

"Hi, Mommy. Want some?"

Gates' lips had twitched at the same time that desire had sprung into his eyes, as it always did when he looked at her. "Sure, Mommy wants some mud pies." His grin widened as he patted her chair at the table. "Don't you, honey?"

"You're both nuts!" she'd cried, though she'd laughed at the picture they made, their mouths smeared with mud.

"Ah, a little wet dirt never hurt anyone," Gates responded, again patting the chair. "In fact, it's dee-licious."

They had all giggled uncontrollably then, especially when she'd sat down and Patrick had served her.

Shaking herself mentally, Juliana suddenly pulled her thoughts back to the moment at hand and wiped the tears that trickled down her face.

"I miss you, sweetheart. I wish I could hold you."

Reaching for a tissue in her pocket, she dabbed at her eyes. Making love to Gates had driven her here. Being with him had awakened the past and its sadness. Damn him. She'd worked eleven hard years at getting this far.

Grief work, her counselor had called it. And as arduous as the process was, she had put in her time. It had been her only chance for emotional healing and a hope for the future.

At first she'd been determined to fast-forward through the process, only to realize there were no shortcuts. She'd had to grovel on her belly before finally getting back on her feet.

But there were scars; she couldn't deny that. Just as a deep wound left a scar on the physical body, emotional scar tissue was just as permanent, even when one had moved on.

From time to time, that scar would ache. Like now. Juliana rubbed her hand across his picture and gave in to the cleansing tears.

She had put on a brave front to Benson, but the horror of what she'd been through had brought her to a standstill. Yet she refused to let that fear control her.

Since there hadn't been any calls or attempts on her life during these past few days, maybe the book *had* been found and she was indeed off the hook.

However, she mustn't get too complacent. Margie's killer remained at large. Until the murderer was apprehended, she not only had her emotional stability to think about, but her physical well-being as well.

She had to get Gates out of her life. First, though, she had to get him out of her house.

Out of her bed.

Juliana's stomach roiled, and she leaned over and rocked for a moment as her agony deepened on another front. Now that the hot passion of that night had evaporated and stark reality had returned, she realized just how foolish she'd been.

Fear.

That word again. In the light of day, she had decided it had definitely been the culprit, the reason for her irrational behavior, for her loss of control.

Nevertheless, while she had been in Gates' arms, his lips and tongue working their old magic, she'd relished the moment, lost herself in the desire raging inside. They had even managed to pretend the world and its problems didn't exist, that *their* problems didn't exist.

Perfection, as always.

Those few precious hours, while they had lasted, had been as perfect as ever. But now she felt gutted and shamed that she had allowed Gates carte blanche with her body and her mind.

Thank God it hadn't happened again. Still, his presence was wearing on her, though she rarely saw him. When she did, he kept his distance. Yet she knew he was in the house, on the couch.

Too close.

That closeness was telling on him, as well. He was bleary-eyed, and his features were strained. She dared not think about his disposition. She pitied the poor criminals he apprehended.

It would have been different if there had been a second chance for them in the offing, but there wasn't. Even if he were to stop beating up on himself for Patrick's death, which he wouldn't, she could never overcome his family and his allegiance to them.

That didn't matter. What did matter was that she was left alone. Her gaze returned to the morning glories, which once again soothed her troubled spirits.

Pushing herself upright, Juliana stood still and stared at her son's grave. Before another bout of tears could take over, she leaned down, rubbed her hand gently across the picture again, then touched her fingers to her lips and placed them on the smiling face.

"Patrick, my darling," she whispered, "peace be with you in heaven. You certainly had the right stuff on earth."

Juliana was halfway back to the office when it dawned on her that she was being followed—and not by an officer, either. The guy she saw in her rearview mirror appeared too sleazy for that.

Her expression turned glacial. What to do?

She rammed down on the accelerator; he did the same.

A new fear chilled her blood, though she kept herself in check. She would be at the office soon. Once there, she would be safe; she could barricade herself inside.

A short time later, that was exactly what she did. After nodding to her secretary, Juliana locked the office door behind her, then crossed straight to the window. Trembling, she scrutinized the surrounding area. No sign of the car or the man who had appeared to tail her. Since she couldn't be sure her imagination wasn't being over-active, she wouldn't call the police. Still, she had made another mistake. She should have kept her protection. Who had followed her, and why? She had to think.

Rusk hadn't been the culprit. She had seen enough of the man to know that. But was Rusk behind that latest escapade?

Thinking about him made Juliana's blood boil. She still believed he was capable of killing Margie, God help her. And what about the death of that young man? Was that perhaps another sin Rusk could add to his tally?

The redhead had known something about Rusk, something so terrible that it had cost him his life.

Even if Gates was right and there was no connection between Margie's death and that of the young man, Rusk still had a lot to atone for. Beneath that smooth, charismatic facade was a rotten individual who would stop at nothing to get what he wanted.

While she trusted her instincts, she had no proof of Rusk's guilt, which meant she could be wrong. What if she was? What if Rusk was guilty simply of infidelity and stupidity?

Maybe Carl Mason had been involved, as Gates had suggested. When it came to money and power, Mason was on the same level as the O'Briens, which would have appealed to Margie. Maybe she and Mason had played more than footsie, and it had been his book that Margie had stolen.

Suddenly an idea came to her. Juliana rose and snatched her purse. If someone was determined to hurt her, then she might as well give them a reason.

Anyway, wasn't prying into people's lives what she did best?

Juliana got out of the car. Grimacing against the slap of the now-hot sun, she walked into the motel's cool lobby.

Luck was indeed with her. Honeycutt was behind the desk.

Right off, she saw the recognition in his eyes. "Hello, Ms. Reed," he said.

She held out her hand; he took it.

"You here to sign me up?" he quipped with a smile.

"Excuse me?"

"You know." His grin grew. "For your show."

Juliana forced herself to answer his grin. "Well…"

He laughed outright. "Just kiddin', of course. What can I do for you?"

"You didn't happen to see Margie Bowers with anyone else, someone you might have forgotten about?" Even as she asked, Juliana knew she was grasping for straws. She wished she hadn't come.

"Can't help you there, I'm afraid. Like I told you and the Ranger, I only saw her with that O'Brien fellow." Honeycutt paused and leaned closer, then spoke out of the side of his mouth. "Think we oughta elect another guy who runs around on his wife?"

"I don't—"

He went on as if she hadn't said a word. "What if he has AIDS?"

Ignoring his comment, Juliana said, "Thanks anyway."

"No problem."

She was halfway to her car when she heard someone from behind say, "Ma'am. Er…Ms. Reed, hold up a second."

Stopping, Juliana swung around and stared at a tall, lanky young man sporting a buzz haircut and glasses. "Yes?"

"I work here and overheard your conversation."

"And?"

"I saw Ms. Bowers with someone else."

Juliana's pulse kicked in, but she tried to contain her excitement. "Do you know who he is?"

"No. But then, they never use their real names."

"Can you describe him?"

He rubbed his face while scrunching his forehead. "I can't remember. Sorry."

Moments later, back in the car, Juliana sat still, frustration gnawing at her. Okay, Margie had indeed been screwing someone else. So did that exonerate Rusk? No.

He remained *her* prime suspect.

Thirty-One

Gates needed hip boots to wade through the crap he'd gotten himself into. Slamming his pencil down on the desk, he leaned back and massaged his temples, hoping to head off an oncoming headache. He rarely had one, but when he did, it was a dilly.

Actually, he ached all over. Sleeping on that damn couch was like lying on a slab of concrete. So why hadn't he gone into the guest room? Easy answer. Juliana's room was next door, and frankly, he couldn't take the pressure, especially after he'd slept with her.

Bad move. Bad idea.

Gates rubbed harder, which didn't help. Until he got out of Juliana's house, he was going to have a permanent headache and a permanent hard-on.

However, as long as she was in danger from unknown sources, he wasn't budging. He would just have to suck it up and endure. He deserved to be miserable for making love to her, though he told himself it wouldn't happen again.

"Keep telling yourself that, Bubba," he muttered, feeling that old darkness knocking at the door of his soul.

Being with her again had reawakened his explosive desire for her, and now he wasn't sure he could stay away and survive.

His mind had let her go, but his body hadn't. He would

never want another woman in the way he wanted Juliana.
His sexual craving for her was tantamount to someone
who was addicted to cocaine. The years had not tempered
that. The more he touched her, the more he wanted her.
But he couldn't have her.

They were traveling two different roads. She was a
mover and a shaker, no longer the same person she'd been
when he married her. Losing Patrick had changed her,
changed her goals.

He'd changed, too, only not for the better.

The phone rang, bringing instant relief. He had beaten
up on himself long enough.

"Gates O'Brien."

"Hello, son."

"What's up, Daddy?"

Norman chuckled. "Does something have to be up for
me to call you?"

"You really want me to answer that?"

A sigh filtered through the line. "All right. I do have
something on my mind."

"Let me guess. My brother." Gates didn't bother to
keep the censure out of his voice. Always Rusk. Would
the day ever come when his parents didn't feel responsible
for their eldest child?

"Look, if I'm disturbing you, I'll call back later."

"No, it's okay."

"I'm worried about Rusk," Norman said in his blunt
fashion. "Something's wrong, only he won't confide in
us." He paused. "And he's drinking again."

"But he's still leading in the polls." Gates tried hard
to keep the sarcasm out of his voice, but knew he hadn't
pulled it off.

"That's not the point."

"Yes, it is."

"Okay, it is. Because if he stays on this road to self-destruction, he won't be leading for long."

"Maybe he should withdraw."

Gates braced himself for his father's reaction.

"What the hell kind of talk is that?" Norman demanded coldly.

Gates knew he was wasting good breath trying to reason with the elder O'Brien when it came to furthering his son's career. Anyway, it wasn't worth it.

"I'm worried about him, too, but I don't know exactly what's going on."

"But you know something."

"Not really."

"Hell, Gates, now's not the time to be coy with me."

"Hey, my silence has nothing to do with being coy. But it has everything to do with being an officer of the law with access to privileged information."

"Sorry, I forgot Texas Rangers walk on the water." Before Gates could respond to that sarcasm, Norman went on, "Is he a suspect in that girl's murder?"

"That I can tell you. Yes, he is."

Norman cursed. "He didn't do it."

"Look, Dad, I'm not in charge of that case. I've just been nibbling around the edges."

"Because of Juliana, right?"

Gates didn't respond to the scorn in his daddy's tone. They had fought this battle too many times already.

"Why don't you talk to Rusk yourself? Ask *him* what's going on?"

"Daddy, I—"

"He'll listen to you. He always has."

"Rusk is his own man."

"In other words, you won't try."

"I didn't say that."

"The hell you didn't. When it comes to choosing between family and Juliana, she wins hands down. She's got you by the balls again and—"

Gates calmly dropped the receiver in its cradle.

He had never hung up on his daddy, but there was a first time for everything. Juliana aside, he was tired of fighting Rusk's battles. It was time his brother learned he couldn't run with dogs and not get fleas.

Margie had been a flea. Though he loved his brother and had always been his champion—still was—this was one tight corner he was going to have to get himself out of.

Rusk was no killer, but Norman was right, something was going down. That young redhead had known something about Rusk and had gotten killed. His mind backtracking to the incident at the docks, Gates grimaced.

If he ever got his hands on the bastard who'd fired those shots at Juliana, he would yank his balls off and stuff them in his mouth.

He wouldn't think about Juliana in terms of danger. HPD was looking out for her during the day, and he was with her at night. Once HPD found out who the floater was, then maybe that mystery would get cleared up, which would mean one less thing to worry about.

Since there had been no more fireworks concerning the missing book, he was hoping it had been found. But he wasn't ready to disappear from the picture just yet, even though he should.

Margie's murder was still not his problem, unless he could pin it on Carl Mason, which was unlikely, unless it was Mason's book that Margie had stolen. He hadn't ruled that out.

He had tried to shake something loose on Carl Mason, but so far he'd struck out. Questions without answers continued to hopscotch through his mind, working on his psyche.

Had Mason misused prison funds?

Had he documented the facts?

Had Margie gotten her hands on those records?

Had Margie and Carl's relationship involved his brother?

Had Margie been a pawn or a major player?

Whose book had she stolen?

That was the kicker, the question that Gates most wanted an answer to. That information would provide him with the killer and permanently remove Juliana from harm's way.

While he wanted justice served, wanted that son of a bitch to pay for taking Margie's life, he had to be honest with himself and admit that Juliana's safety took precedence.

Still, he hadn't let that stop him from concentrating on the prison investigation. Already he'd found several discrepancies in the contractors' books. He was close to proving that Mason was dirty, if not the dirtiest kid on the block.

The other case that had required his attention was the beer-joint murders. Just this morning, he, along with the sheriff and his deputies, had made an arrest.

"Glad I caught you."

Gates' head jerked up. His boss, James Ferguson, stood on the threshold. He'd been so lost in thought, he hadn't heard him. "Yo, Cap, come on in."

Ferguson sat down, crossed one booted leg over the other one, then squinted at Gates through his glasses.

"This is perfect timing," Gates said. "I needed to talk, to bring you up to speed."

"Congratulations on the arrest this morning."

"Thanks. I just hope we can make it stick."

"Hell, I thought it was an open-and-shut case."

Gates let out a sigh. "Should be, but you know a high-profile case like this brings those 'do-good' attorneys crawling out from under every rock. When an honor student who's black takes part in shooting four whites to death…" He let his voice trail off.

"I don't care what color he is. If he pulled the trigger, then he's gonna pay, especially for a brutal crime like that."

"You're right. I've never seen so much blood."

"We got a confession?"

"Yep. He admitted he fired six rounds into the owner."

"Shit, what's this world coming to?"

"You haven't heard the worst. The perp also admitted to walking up to another victim, putting his gun in his eye and pulling the trigger."

"Nail that son of a bitch." Ferguson's eyes were hard.

"Not to worry. If I have my way, that piece of shit's going away forever."

Ferguson was quiet for a moment, then he asked, "What about the TDC investigation?"

"My latest report's ready, and believe me, when you read it, you'll puke."

"I understand you met with the boys from Alcohol, Tobacco and Firearms yesterday."

"Right."

"What's ATF's take?"

"Same as everyone who's involved in this mess. Corruption is continuing to flourish, which leaves us with a sorry mess indeed."

"Well, just keep on shaking the tree. Sooner or later, the rotten apples will hit the ground and we'll bag 'em."

"I hope the hell one of those apples is Carl Mason."

"He's the one who was involved with that Bowers woman, right?"

"That's him."

"So how's that coming?" Ferguson asked. "Anyone arrested for her murder yet?"

"Nope. No suspect and no book."

"How 'bout the shooting episode at the wharf? Anything on that?"

"Actually, things have been pretty quiet on both fronts. But I'm looking to hear from Bishop on the floater's identity any time now."

"Maybe whoever owns that book found it, and Juliana's out of the woods."

"Let us pray. But I'll keep you posted, and thanks again for letting me keep a hand in on the case."

"Just as long as you come away from her with your body intact." Ferguson grinned. "Pun intended."

"Believe me, bunking in at my ex-wife's house is not fun."

"What about Nicole? Does she know?"

"She will. Shortly, in fact. Today's her birthday, and as soon as I leave the office, I'm going by there."

"Good fuckin' luck."

"Thanks, Ferg. You're lots of help."

Ferguson stood, then tipped his hat. "Anytime."

Long after he'd gone, Gates still had a scowl on his face.

His truck was parked in the driveway.

"Damn," Juliana muttered as she got out of her car, knowing it was too late to do anything about her appearance. Splotches of tears remained on her face, and she knew her makeup must be a mess. The fact that she cared what he thought added to her anger.

If he didn't hurry up and get out of her house, *she* might commit murder.

When she walked inside, the scent caught her attention. It smelled heavenly. She slipped her purse off her shoulder just as he strode into the living room.

He sort of smiled, then asked, "Hungry?"

"No. What I am is tired."

"You've been crying. What's wrong?"

She heard the concern in his voice, but right now, she couldn't confide in him. She hadn't expected him to be there yet; she needed time to regroup.

"I'd rather not talk about it, if you don't mind."

"What if I do mind?"

"That's too bad."

Gates thrust a hand through his over-long hair. "Look, let's not fight tonight, okay? I've cooked, and I want you to eat."

"I'm really not hungry."

"It's your favorite."

"Meat loaf?"

He grinned. "You got it."

"Give me time to change."

"No hurry."

She slipped out of her clothes immediately, all the while wanting to scream. She had capitulated too easily. This was not going to work. He had no right to be in her house, she fumed, much less act as if they were still married.

Frightened or not, he had to go.

That thought was very much on her mind throughout dinner, though surprisingly she ate quite a lot. She pushed her plate aside and looked at him. Unexpectedly, their eyes met and locked.

She averted her gaze, but not before she saw the glint of desire leap into his. Heat invaded her cheeks.

"Why the tears?"

His low, thick voice drew her back around.

"I went to the cemetery."

"I see."

She didn't respond.

"If you meant to kick me in the nuts, you succeeded."

"Gates..."

"Sorry, it's not your problem. It's mine."

She was quiet for another minute, swearing she could hear his heart beating over hers.

"After that, I went back to the motel."

He straightened. "Why?"

"That doesn't matter. What I found out does."

"Dammit, you don't—"

"Margie was sleeping with someone else besides Rusk."

Gates eyes sharpened. "Who?"

"Unfortunately, I don't know that." She told him what she had learned.

"I told you my brother was innocent."

She made a face. "That doesn't prove he's innocent. Only time will tell that."

"How 'bout we don't fight that battle again, okay? But what I will fight about is your snooping around."

"There's a chance I was followed to the station, which means someone may still think I have that book."

Gates let out a harsh breath. "Thank God HPD's keeping an eye on you."

Despite her effort to keep the color out of her face, she didn't succeed. The look on *his* told her that.

"You didn't?"

Juliana's color deepened, and her voice rose. "I didn't think I needed protecting anymore."

An expletive singed the air. "Until this matter's resolved, I don't want you going on the air."

Juliana lunged out of her chair. "That's not going to happen."

"I can have you put under house arrest."

She stared at him in disbelief. "On what grounds?"

His eyes sliced through her like razors. "You're a material witness."

"That'll be a cold day in hell. Besides, you don't have the authority."

"Juliana—"

She turned then and fled the room. She barely made it to the bathroom before she lost the contents of her stomach.

Thirty-Two

Juliana saw Gates standing at the back of the audience.

He knew that she was aware of him because he nodded, then tipped the brim of his hat in a mocking salute. Even though the show had cut to a commercial, she didn't respond.

What she did was fume inside while her heart did mini flip-flops. Propped against the wall, he radiated an aura of exactly what he was: the heart and soul of the Texas Rangers.

More than that, it was the effect he had on her personally. The raw energy he exuded drew her like a moth to a flame.

While his presence should have reassured her, it did not. He had planted himself firmly back in her life, which kept her in constant turmoil.

She despised having her ex-husband as her unauthorized guardian, even though she remained in danger. However, nothing had come of her suspicion that she was being followed from the cemetery. Maybe her vision *had* played a trick on her, she thought, and she'd imagined the sleazy-looking character. But in her heart she knew better, which was more reason to be thankful she was under HPD's and Gates' watchful eyes.

She wasn't thankful, though. A stranger she could handle—Gates she couldn't. As if he sensed what was going through her mind, he smiled and again touched the brim of his hat.

Juliana didn't know if it was that smile—a rarity and a turn-on—or his mere presence that had her in such a frenzy.

Did his determination to remain underfoot stem from revenge? Was that what this was about? Right now, she couldn't think about that possibility—or about him.

She had a show to finish.

Forty-five minutes later Juliana had accomplished that task and was on the way to her office, feeling as if she'd been run over and flattened by a truck. She paused at her door and looked around. Gates was nowhere in sight.

Had he gone? Yes, she told herself. A plainclothesman nodded at her from across the hall.

Once inside her office, she sat down, though she couldn't sit still. Her nerves had her jumping out of her skin. Good thing she'd decided her hormones were out of whack and had finally made an appointment with a gynecologist.

Or she was pregnant.

She had told herself lightning never struck twice. But after she'd counted the days and realized she'd been ovulating during that sexual romp, her self-confidence had been severely undermined.

There was only one thing to do. She would rather take a beating, but she had no choice.

"Got a moment?"

Juliana looked up and forced a smile for her secretary, Gwyn, a middle-aged woman with beautiful skin and hair. Juliana often wondered what she would do without her. "Sure."

"Good. I have the research on adoptions you wanted for tomorrow's show. I thought we'd go over it."

"If it can be done in an hour. Remember, I have a doctor's appointment."

"No problem. This won't take long."

Juliana forced another smile and some enthusiasm into her voice. "Then have a seat and let's get to it."

What was taking so long?

Juliana stared at her watch. Her waiting-room stay had been short, a miracle in itself. She hadn't had to linger in this cubbyhole, either, before Dr. Pierce made his appearance.

The stooped, gray-headed man, with his watered-down but kindly blue eyes, had listened to her symptoms, and because she hadn't had a physical in well over a year, he'd insisted on taking care of that immediately.

Once the exam had been completed, he'd left the room and now here she sat. She'd called the office the day before yesterday and told them she'd had unprotected sex and wanted a pregnancy test. They had sent her to a lab for a serum blood test, results guaranteed in two days.

As if the nurse sensed her impatience, she opened the door and stuck her head in.

"The doctor will see you in his office."

Once she was seated in front of Dr. Pierce's huge desk, he smiled. Juliana tried to return that smile, but her lips wouldn't budge. They seemed made out of plaster, though deep down she didn't think she was pregnant.

Stress was her problem. She was sure of it.

"So, am I a candidate for a light nerve pill?" she quipped, trying to lighten her mood.

His smile broadened. "There's no such thing."

"Well, then, maybe I just need some heavy-duty vitamins."

"You'll get those for sure."

"I was hoping for something stronger, of course. Like I told you earlier, I can't sleep. I'm sluggish. And I'm under a lot of pressure."

"Before we go any further, suppose you tell me about the pressure."

She hadn't intended to, but everything seemed to spill from her lips at once. By the time she'd finished, she'd told him everything, except the fact that she'd made love to Gates.

"Unfortunately, my dear, all that stress is the last thing you need." His gaze pinned her. "Especially in your condition."

Her breathing faltered, and she licked her dry lips. "Exactly what *is* my condition?"

"You're pregnant."

The entire house was dark.

Juliana sat huddled on the window seat in her bedroom, something she did only on rare occasions when she had something difficult to work through.

She listened to the thunder and watched the lightning zigzag across the sky. It seemed so close that she felt if she reached out she could actually touch it. An incident from her childhood came to mind. She'd had a window seat in her bedroom then, too. On just such a stormy day, she had climbed onto that ledge, lifted her head and struck a pose.

Her daddy had come into her room at that particular moment and demanded to know what she was doing. With the innocence that only a child could claim, she'd laughed out loud, then said, "Why, Daddy, it's God. He's taking my picture."

"Don't you dare say that, young lady. That's talking

ill of our Lord. You get out of that window right now before I blister your bottom.''

With her head drooping from his harsh chastisement, Juliana had done as she'd been told. But for the longest time thereafter, she had refused to go near the window seat.

Time, of course, had taken the sting out of that memory. When she had looked at this condo, she'd actually bought it because it had a window seat.

Often, she had imagined Patrick sitting here in this very spot, posed, for God to take his picture. But then, God didn't need a picture of her son; he had the real thing.

Feeling the lump in her throat burgeon to the size of a goose egg, Juliana lifted her head and took a deep breath. But she couldn't stave off the tears. How could she have been so careless, so stupid?

She had hoped someday to have another child, but not now, not like this, not when her career was just starting to take off. And most certainly *not* with Gates, she cried silently.

Shivering, she folded her arms over her body, then rested her head back against the wall. She didn't know how long she sat there, numb from shock. Finally she swung her legs around and stood. The bed suddenly looked more inviting than it had in a long time. If she could sleep, the terror building inside would disappear, at least for a while.

She discarded her robe, but though she lay down, she didn't close her eyes. It wouldn't do any good. She couldn't rest; her mind wouldn't stop punishing her. Pulling the sheet with her, she sat up, placed her forehead on her knees and sobbed.

''Juliana?''

Gates' harsh, unexpected voice brought her head upright. His almost-nude silhouette loomed large in the shadowed doorway.

Swallowing another sob, Juliana let her gaze roam his hard, beautiful body, the body that was responsible for her condition—no, she was responsible, too, she added violently.

A sudden flash of lightning, followed by a bark of thunder, bit another chunk out of her nerves. She still couldn't turn away. The illumination from the light allowed her to see his face twisted with anxiety and something else—longing.

Their eyes locked.

"Did something happen?" He could barely get the words past his lips. If someone had hurt her again, he would...

Juliana's lips quivered before she turned her face to the window. But he'd seen the anguish in them.

"Please...go away," she whispered.

"Not until you tell me what's wrong," Gates responded in a thick but firm tone. "Then I'll go."

He didn't know where or how he was going to get the strength to keep his word. The sheet had slipped, and from where he stood, he could see the curve of her breasts, smooth and rich as cream. He didn't have to imagine how they tasted—he knew.

He also knew she was naked.

He shifted from one foot to the other, fighting off the need to slide his hand under that sheet to the tender flesh between her thighs....

"I don't want to talk about it," she said at last, to the tune of more tears.

Dear God, he couldn't leave her, not like this, not when her condition reminded him of how she was the day Patrick died. He couldn't wipe the tears fast enough from her eyes for the tears in his own.

He wouldn't let her down now. No matter how much she rejected or berated him, he would hold steady.

"I won't leave you like this." He walked to the bed, but he didn't sit down. He couldn't, or he would be lost. The delicate scent of her body lightly flavored with perfume enveloped him, threatening to snap the choke hold he had on himself.

He didn't know how much longer he could hold out, though. He was already reeling against the pressure rising inside him and the hard arousal that strained against his underwear.

"Please—don't touch me."

It was that broken plea that did it, that inflamed his senses to such a degree that he couldn't keep from touching her, no matter how hard he tried.

He was drunk on lust and need. Too, he had to make sure no one had hurt her. Easing onto the side of the bed, Gates placed his hands on her shoulders, gently forcing her to face him.

"I'm not going to do anything you don't want me to," he whispered. His sanity, along with his control, was losing ground.

"Gates…"

The breathy use of his name was the catalyst, the deal breaker. He was touching her, but that wasn't enough. Her tears had broken something inside him. To appease his own selfish needs, he had to feel her against his heart.

"Juliana," he echoed, his voice breaking on her name. As he drew her to him, the sheet completely disappeared.

Though he felt her quiver, then stiffen, she didn't stop him. But when he moved his hand down her back to where her buttocks began, her breath escaped her lungs in jerky gulps.

"Please," she said breathlessly.

"Please what?"

"Please...stop."

He wouldn't have stopped, as God was his witness, if she had meant what she said. She might have had good intentions, wanting to resist him. But her body spoke louder than any words as she leaned into him, her sweet breath caressing his face.

"Oh, Juliana," he murmured against her lips, lips that felt like hot silk against the hungry sandpaper feel of his.

He laid her down, reveling in her tongue invading his mouth and sucking with a hunger she'd never shown before.

"I want you now," he ground out at the same time that he felt her hand capture his hardness.

"And I want you," she gasped.

He settled between her thighs, then straddled her. Only after that became unbearable for them both did he enter her.

"Yes!" she cried, riding with him.

His lungs almost collapsed as he spilled his seed into her.

For the first time in a long while, Juliana had been eager for a show to end. Nothing had gone right. Even the audience hadn't been as responsive as she thought they should have been.

She assumed full responsibility for that, too. The past few days, her mind seemed to have gone on a hiatus. She functioned, but more by rote than from conscious action.

Her stomach hadn't exactly been cooperative, either. Several times she'd had to fight off nausea, especially during working hours. She had caught Benson giving her more than one strange glance, but she'd ignored him.

Now that the day from hell had finally ended and she was home, Juliana tried hard to ignore *herself.* To offset her bad mood, she had done some chores, then followed those with a cup of mint iced tea. That was all she could hold in her stomach. Food was a turnoff.

That tea had tasted so good, she took another sip, eyeing the aquarium that had to be cleaned. She had often considered getting a maid to do the hard labor, but she liked to do her own chores; it was part of her stress-relief therapy.

Now, however, she was forced to rethink the situation.

Because of the baby.

She still found it hard to believe she was going to have a baby. Staring down at her flat stomach did little to confirm that fact, which was a good thing.

Her condition remained her secret, since she hadn't told Gates.

Realizing she was about to leap into forbidden territory, she rerouted her thoughts. Staring at the fish tank from her position on the sofa, she realized another fish was dead.

Within the past month or so, she'd lost two fish, which was peculiar.

The job of removing the fish could wait until after she'd savored the remainder of her tea. Unfortunately, her mind wouldn't let her relax while she drank. It became a beehive of activity. She couldn't stop thinking about the child she was carrying.

Gates' child.

She hadn't wanted to think about him, but she hadn't been able to stop, especially after she'd practically thrown herself at him, after swearing not to let him touch her again.

So much for willpower, she told herself, feeling her heart rate dip. But when she had seen him standing in the door with nothing on but his underwear, her body had betrayed her, big time. Later, after she had awakened and found him gone, she'd blamed her weakness on the shock she'd received.

Liar.

Regardless of whether she'd been upset or not, she would have welcomed him into her bed.

He was like a drug that had gotten into her bloodstream, and once there, she couldn't do without it. And while she'd been off the drug for years, it had remained in her system.

Even though they had no future, her baby did. She wanted it desperately. Out of the numbness had come that certainty. But what about Gates? The thought of telling him was terrifying. Yet how could she *not* tell him?

The fact that this pregnancy came at the wrong time in her life didn't enter into it. And whether Gates wanted the baby or not didn't enter into it, either. Somehow she would keep the baby and work, too.

If and when she told him, how would he react? She couldn't help but ask herself that. Pausing in her thoughts, she smiled, then placed her hand over her stomach, where that tiny life existed.

She felt her pulse jump.

A sane relationship with Gates was still impossible. In her heart, she knew that. More than likely, he would be furious at the thought of replacing Patrick with another child.

And what about herself? She believed in going forward

and not looking back. Gates fit in the "looking back" category.

On the other side of that coin, this baby could heal Gates, help him forgive himself and her. Would he let that happen?

Although no clear-cut answers to those questions were forthcoming, one thing was clear. Though he had hurt her terribly with his guilt and mistrust, she still loved him; last night had proven that. She had ached for him in more ways than just the physical. Before Patrick's death, he had been her rock, her mainstay.

She longed for that again, despite all the seemingly insurmountable problems that went along with that admission.

Sighing, and with her thoughts still turbulent, Juliana got up and crossed to the fish tank. She removed the dead fish, then concentrated on the rocks, checking them for slime.

When she moved the biggest rock, she saw it.

"What on earth?" she muttered, her brow wrinkling into a frown as she removed what appeared to be a waterproof pouch of some sort. What was in it? And how had it gotten there?

Juliana returned to the couch and opened the bag. A small but thick spiral notebook winked up at her. Was this the infamous book? Was this what Margie's death had been about?

She leaned against the cushions and began reading. When she finished, Juliana sat as if in a stupor, knowing beyond a shadow of a doubt who had killed Margie.

Rusk O'Brien.

Thirty-Three

Gates felt as if a grenade had been dropped in the pit of his gut and detonated. He was in his office, but he wasn't getting much accomplished. Not only did he have the frustrations of dealing with the prison scandal, which was growing into some evil beast with tentacles reaching farther than he'd ever imagined, he had Juliana, as well.

What to do?

His job would go on. In the end, many of the contractors he'd been investigating would end up in criminal or civil court, maybe both. He was sure that Mason, with his well-padded checks and smooth bullshit, would be one of those, especially when it came to the millions in fencing that lay idle.

He just kept hoping that Rusk had been telling him the truth and that Margie's association with Carl Mason had nothing to do with him or his campaign. If Rusk was associated with Mason in any way, then his brother could kiss his political career goodbye. Mason would squeal on Rusk like a pig caught in a trap.

Gates had warned his brother, and that was all he could do. The rest was up to Rusk. He wanted to think his brother was telling the truth.

True, Rusk had lied about his affair with Margie. But that was different, Gates told himself. Being unfaithful to his wife, especially in the political arena, might or might not spell suicide. That depended on the press and whether or not they took a dislike to someone.

So far, Rusk had been the apple of the press's eye, and no hint of the affair had surfaced, although Rusk had been questioned in depth by Detective Bishop, which had been no secret.

Carl Mason, however, was another story. After following a long and exhausting paper trail, Gates was confident he would soon have enough evidence to nail Mason for his part in the prison corruption and for Margie's death, as well. His gut wouldn't let go of the fact that it was Mason who Margie had had by the short and curlies.

Detective Bishop, however, had come up empty-handed when he'd leaned on Mason.

"If he was screwing that woman, then they must have gone to another country," Bishop had told him just that morning when they had talked.

"Don't be too sure about that," Gates responded.

"I don't get it," Bishop said in a huff. "You know something I should know?"

"Not really," Gates hedged. "All I have is a hunch. If it proves to be more than that, you'll get a call."

Gates had toyed with telling Bishop about Margie's trysts with Rusk at the motel, but that would only have served to further incriminate his brother, who he knew hadn't killed her.

The other lover was a different matter. If that man turned out to be Mason, Gates would break both legs to get the information to Bishop. Until he had that proof, though, he'd decided to keep his mouth shut.

"How's Ms. Reed holding up?"

"All right, but then, she's a fighter."

Bishop grinned. "You're telling me."

"I won't stop worrying until the scumbag who's after her is in custody."

"We're doing everything we can to get the S.O.B."

Gates shoved his Stetson back and massaged his wrinkles deeper into his forehead. "If I ever get my hands on him…"

"We'll get him before you do."

"For his sake, I hope so."

"Do you still think there's a connection between that dead body in the channel and the shots fired at y'all?"

"Has to be, only I haven't found the thread that ties it all together."

"Neither have we."

"How 'bout the floater? Have you identified him yet?"

"Yep."

"Damn, I thought you'd call me."

"Sorry. I meant to. I'll get all the info on him and call you."

"I'd appreciate it," Gates said. "That should at least give us another needle to thread."

Bishop gave him a pointed look. "Our man's back on Ms. Reed during the day."

"I'm much obliged for that, too."

"How come you two split the sheets?" Bishop asked. Then, as if he realized he'd overstepped the boundaries, he turned red, then added, "Sorry. That was out of line."

"It's okay. We lost a child and—" Gates broke off with a painful shrug.

"You don't need to say any more. I understand and I'm sorry."

"Yeah, me, too."

"So back to Mason. Have you been able to link him directly to your investigation?"

"I'm working on it. I'm convinced he's up to his eyeballs in corruption, especially the acres of fencing. I think that screwup's his baby. He's one sleek bastard, though, more so than all the other contractors involved.''

"It seems to me you want to nail him awfully bad. Any particular reason why?"

"There's just something about that guy that jerks my chain. I suspect it's because he's pissing in my ear and telling me it's raining."

Bishop chuckled. "I hear you."

"Anyway, thanks again for letting me horn in on your investigation."

"Hell, man, any help we can get, we'll take. Besides, when family or even ex-family's involved…"

He let his voice trail off, and Gates was grateful. He didn't want to discuss Juliana with Bishop. Hell, he didn't even want to think about her himself.

Now, forcing his attention off the conversation with Bishop and back to the matter at hand, Gates peered at the papers strewn over his desk.

The person who was ultimately to blame for this prison mess was the executive director at Texas Department of Criminal Justice, who had given the contractors carte blanche with the taxpayers' money. He, along with all the company executives who'd had their hands in the till, ought to be strung up. Conflict of interest was just the beginning.

Gates shook his head. And to think Mason still hadn't been nixed from the list to build the new units. If he had anything to do with it, Mason wouldn't get another friggin' dime of the taxpayers' money.

He scrutinized the papers, and disgust formed a knot in the pit of his stomach. For one day, he'd plowed through as much of this carnage as he could endure. He would like nothing better than to arrest the entire gold-digging bunch. But he knew that wasn't likely to happen. Those sons of bitches were greasier than snake oil. They hadn't lined their pockets with Texas gold by being stupid.

He just had to be smarter.

At the moment, he had something else pressing on him, a decision he had to make before he could get back to his work and give it his undivided attention.

What was he going to do about Juliana?

He still loved her, had never stopped loving her. Last night, when he'd made love to her, that fact had slugged him upside the head with all the power of a heavyweight in the ring.

He'd as much as admitted that to Nicole when he'd stopped by her house and told her that he wouldn't be seeing her anymore except as a friend. She hadn't been surprised, nor had she ridiculed him or made a scene.

Still, he hadn't been in the best of moods last night when he'd walked into Juliana's room and heard her crying. When he'd figured out that no one had hurt her physically, he hadn't pressed the matter, though he suspected those tears had been triggered by him and the sequence of events.

At this moment, he was as worried about his own sanity as he was hers. Should he tell her that he loved her? If he did, what would that accomplish? Granted, their bodies were as compatible as ever, but their minds weren't, which was of equal importance, if not more so. When they had been young, it was all right to be in constant heat, but now they had to have more solid underpinnings.

Patrick's death had knocked those down.

And while his death had reared its ugly head, it hadn't been brought out in the open and discussed. He couldn't do that. An old, biting fear forced him into doing something he hadn't done in a long time.

He got up, walked to the file cabinet, opened it and pulled out a framed picture of his son, a duplicate of the one Juliana had in her condo.

The impact of staring into that innocent, grinning face almost knocked him to his knees. He literally clung to the drawer as the old loathing for himself welled up.

Turning the picture facedown once again, Gates slammed the drawer shut, strode back to his desk, then slammed his fist down.

His negligence had killed his son.

He leaned over and sucked air into his lungs, trying to hang on to his sanity. When no relief was imminent, he thought he might pass out. Yet at the height of that dizziness, in his soul, he was aware of the harsh reality. There was a question he had to answer before he could take another breath.

What gave him the right to think he could start over with Juliana?

He had told her that he would take his guilt to the grave with him, and he'd meant every word he'd said. Even now, that blame formed a steel circle around him from which there was no escape.

In that moment, Gates knew what he had to do.

Juliana heard him come in the front door. She sat straighter on the couch, and her heart skipped a beat. She turned to the lamp beside her and upped its power a notch. That was when he reached the entrance to the living room.

As if startled by her appearance, Gates stopped abruptly. For the longest time neither one said a word. The weariness mirrored in his face and eyes robbed her of speech.

"Waiting for me?" he asked.

She knew he was trying to be humorous with his cryptic remark, but that humor fell flat.

"As a matter of fact, I was," she said. Hearing the husky note in her voice, she cleared it.

"Look, if it's about last night—" Gates broke off, his eyes narrowing to slits.

Juliana wet her bottom lip and watched as his eyes darkened. Suddenly a hot silence invaded the room as the erotic events of last night flared between them.

"What about last night?" Juliana heard her voice ask the question she'd had no intention of asking. To make matters worse, it seemed to have come from somewhere outside herself.

"It was a mistake."

She reeled against the shock that hit her. She didn't know what she had expected him to say, but it wasn't that.

"And so were all the other nights," he added in a raw voice.

The second hit packed more punch than the first. She winced, then stared into his gaunt face until she found her voice. "Gates...I don't understand."

"Yes, you do."

Juliana suddenly laughed a cold, mirthless laugh. "Why don't you just cut to the chase, here?"

"I thought that was what I just did."

Red-hot fury suddenly replaced her shock. How dare he take this insulting, contemptuous attitude toward her? "What's going on, Gates?"

"Us. This. All a mistake. We've been living in fairyland."

Juliana wanted to grab her stomach, but she didn't dare. Instead, she placed her hand on the arm of the couch to hold herself steady.

"Then get out," she snapped. "I'm certainly not stopping you."

He looked ill. "I will, but not until Margie's killer is in custody." He paused. "Until then, I promise I won't touch you."

She nearly choked on the bile that rose to the back of her throat. "You're damn right you won't."

"Once you're safe, you won't see me again."

"Don't put yourself out on my account." Her voice caught, but then she went on with bitter sarcasm, "In fact—"

"It's not your fault," Gates interrupted in a dead voice. "I'm no good for you. You deserve better than me."

"God, you do flatter yourself," she spat to mask her pain.

This time he staggered. "Maybe. But I can never give you my whole heart again. The majority of it died with Patrick."

"You're a fool for continuing to live in the past," she lashed back. "But you've finally convinced me that you should have taken a gun and blown your brains out. Then I could have buried you both at the same time."

"I wished I had."

A scream stuck in her throat.

"Now that you mention it, maybe it's not too late."

Having heard enough, Juliana headed toward the hall that led to the bedrooms. She stopped and turned around. "I want you out of here," she said through white lips. "Now!"

Ignoring the desolate look on Gates' face, she reached into the pocket of her robe and flung the book at him.

It landed at his feet. He glanced down, then back up. "What's that?"

"Evidence."

"Juliana…"

She stared at him with all the contempt she could muster. "Your brother's going to look great in prison stripes!"

Thirty-Four

The show must go on.

Juliana kept repeating those words to herself. She couldn't have made it otherwise, especially since the show had been hands-on, dealing with diet and physical fitness.

Two health experts had been the guests. The audience had been rigorously entertained as some had participated in the exercises. A good time was had by all, with the exception of Juliana, the reason being her condition.

When she'd gotten pregnant with Patrick, the first trimester had been tough. Crackers by the side of her bed were what allowed her to get up every morning without retching.

With this second child, it appeared she was going to be plagued by the same malady. But she wasn't complaining, despite the way things had fallen apart with Gates.

Juliana bit down on her lip, unable to think about that conversation without crumbling inside. At dawn, she still hadn't closed her eyes. She had spent the night battling panic brought on by a renewed sense of helplessness.

At daybreak, she'd walked out to her deck and breathed in the fresh air and the smell of flowers, and that helplessness had dissipated like a dark cloud.

She had lived without Gates for eleven years, and she could do so again. And while she wouldn't deny he'd broken her heart again, she would rebound. Again. For her baby's sake. She refused to wallow in a pit of self-pity.

Besides, Gates would do enough of that for both of them.

Though he was over six feet, when she'd walked out, he'd looked like a mere shell of himself, shrunken in misery.

She wondered what he thought about his brother now. Recalling the contents of the book, another bout of queasiness hit her, though for a different reason. She expected Rusk to be arrested for murder. Margie's murder.

Just desserts.

So why didn't she feel jubilant? The entire fiasco left a terrible taste in her mouth. Rusk had had so much potential, only to throw it away for sex, greed and power.

She should have reveled in the fact that she'd been the one who had kicked Gates in the rear with the indisputable evidence, but satisfaction had escaped her. She'd just wanted him out of her sight.

Now, as she made her way off the set, she figured he'd gone straight to Nicole, which was fine with her. Nicole could have him with her blessings. Her biggest regret was that she had let him touch her again. But then, without that she wouldn't have this promise of a precious new beginning.

Reaching her office, Juliana went straight to the bathroom, where she sponged off, then changed her clothes. She would take a bath later. Now she had another interview to do, if she could hold herself intact.

Nausea toyed with her stomach, forcing her to sit on the commode seat. Bending over, she took deep, gulping breaths. Minutes passed before she was able to get to her desk.

Benson was waiting for her. Her hand flew to her chest. "Gosh, you frightened me. I wasn't expecting you."

"A doctor, maybe?"

"Excuse me?"

Her response was taut, she knew very well what he meant. She looked god-awful, and Benson hadn't missed that fact.

"You look like you did after that guy used your throat to test his knife."

"I feel that way, too."

"Are you sick? There's a virus going around, you know."

"That's probably what I have," she said.

She didn't intend to share her secret with anyone, not until she'd made some decisions concerning the baby and her career. Secrets shared with a dear friend, which she considered Benson to be, oftentimes had a way of leaking out. She couldn't take a chance on that happening.

There was always the possibility that she was wrong about Gates. Even though he didn't want her, he might want the baby, especially after he got over the shock of finding out that he had fathered another child.

And Lord knows his family had the money to take her to court on that very issue. She had lost one child; she wasn't going to lose another one.

This baby was *hers*, and no one was going to take it from her.

"Go home and get some rest," Benson was saying.

"I need—"

"No, you don't. Just do as you're told."

She gave him a weak smile. "Thanks."

"If you feel better, come over. A friend made me a pot of chicken and rice soup. Just what you need." He looked her up and down. "If you get any thinner, I'm going to have to look hard to find you."

"You're certainly good for the ego," Juliana said drolly. "But thanks for the invite. I just might take you up on it."

"I'm expecting you to. We can have a heart-to-heart, though I might have to leave."

"Oh?"

"My wife's running a low-grade fever." He shrugged. "I never know when I'll have to go to the home. But then, I don't have to tell you that."

"Right. So no apology necessary," she said softly with a smile.

The moment Benson left, her smile disappeared at the same time that her phone buzzed.

"You have a call from New York on line one," her secretary said.

"Who is it?"

There was a momentary pause, then Gwyn added, "Would you believe Sam Wiesman?"

Juliana's jaw sagged. "You're kidding?"

"Would I kid about *that?*"

"Oh, Lord, what will I say to him?"

Gwyn chuckled. "You'll think of something."

She wasn't so sure. Sam Wiesman was one of the biggest and most respected names in daytime television. He'd given many of the top talk-show hosts their start. The idea that he was calling her made Juliana giddy. God, she was nervous.

"Okay, put him through."

"Ms. Reed, it's a pleasure." His voice was deep and strong, a lot like Gates'.

She cleared her throat. "Same here, Mr. Wiesman."

"I think you and I can do some business," he said bluntly.

"When can you fly to New York?"

Gates' head felt like a bowling ball sitting on his shoulders, while his stomach burned like something had set it on fire. It had. Booze.

When he'd left Juliana's, he'd called in a favor from a cop who was off duty, asking him to keep an eye on her place for the remainder of the night.

Then he'd headed for home, all the while trying to dodge the pain knifing through his body. When he'd walked inside, he'd gotten a glimpse of himself in the foyer mirror. Then he'd crashed on the couch, taking that image with him.

It hadn't been a pretty sight.

His face had been white and distorted. His eyes had been black pits in that white face. And nothing inside him had worked. No saliva in his mouth, no feeling in his limbs.

He'd been one miserable son of a bitch. Juliana's pale, hurt eyes had never left his vision. Desperate for relief from his sorrow and fear of tomorrow, he'd jumped up, grabbing the infamous black book along with a bottle.

He hadn't wanted to believe that the book belonged to Rusk. Instead he'd wanted to think that Juliana had merely been angry and had played a cruel joke on him.

But once he'd opened it and begun reading, his disbelief had turned into rage, then full-blown panic.

Dates and amounts of money that Rusk had illegally received for his campaign were carefully documented. While Gates had choked on that flagrant breaking of the law, it was the person in cahoots with Rusk, the person who had made those contributions, that delivered the lethal blow.

Carl Mason.

In exchange for filling Rusk's campaign coffers with money and promises of enough votes to assure him of winning the governorship, Rusk had given his word that Mason's company could build as many prisons as they wanted to, lining his pocketbook with millions of dollars.

"Rusk, you stupid son of a bitch," he'd muttered, throwing the book across the room.

He'd picked up the bottle of liquor then and started drinking in earnest. He had indulged himself all night and into the day, before he finally passed out and slept.

Now, sober, he had to confront his brother.

Maybe he could talk him into turning state's evidence, which would hopefully keep him out of prison. There was no way to save his political career. It was circling the toilet and when Gates shoved down the handle, it would be flushed.

The hair stood up on the back of his neck. Before any kind of deal could be struck, he had to find the answer to another brutal question.

Had Rusk poisoned Margie Bowers?

Without warning, the room seemed to sway. His body was bathed in sweat. Two karate chops in one day was too much. He was so busy trying to regain his equilibrium that he didn't realize the phone was ringing.

On feet feeling too large for his body, he lumbered to the phone. "Gates," he snapped.

It was Detective Bishop. "The floater's name is Harold Lacy."

"Got an address?"

"Yep. He lived with his parents."

"Thanks, Bishop. I owe you."

Since the floater had specifically mentioned Rusk's name, Gates decided to check Harold Lacy out before he faced down his brother. The thought that Rusk might somehow be involved in that murder, too, didn't bear thinking about.

An hour later Gates knocked on the door of a rather run-down house in a run-down neighborhood. He was about to give up on anyone being at home when the door opened.

A tired-looking elderly woman with graying red hair and thick bifocals gave him a hostile stare. "We don't want none of what you're selling, mister."

Gates tipped his Stetson. "I'm a Texas Ranger, ma'am."

She gulped, and her eyes widened. "What do you want?"

"Are you Mrs. Lacy?"

She nodded.

"Is Mr. Lacy here, as well?"

She nodded again, then stepped aside, indicating that he could come in.

The instant he crossed the threshold, the odor of stale food filled his nostrils. Gates held his breath for a moment, then let it out. He fared no better the second time.

"Gabe, git in here," Mrs. Lacy yelled. "There's a Ranger here."

Gates waited in silence in the middle of the dark, dank living room and watched as a stooped, bald-headed man shuffled up to him.

Following the introduction, Gates didn't mince words. "I'm sorry to intrude on you like this, but I need to ask some questions about your son, Harold."

"He's dead," the woman said, tears filling her eyes. "Someone shot him."

"I'm sorry for your loss, but that's why I'm here."

"We tried to tell the cops that something had happened o our boy when he first come up missing."

"Again, I'm sorry to intrude on your grief—"

"We've already told the police everything we know," Gabe said, his voice wobbly. "We...we just got back rom identifying the body."

Gates' heart wrenched, knowing how they felt. Losing a child, even a grown one, wasn't supposed to happen. Children were supposed to outlive their parents.

Jerking his mind back to his job, he said, "If you wouldn't mind, please tell me what you told the other officers."

"Ain't nothing much to tell." Gabe scratched his bald head. "Harold pretty much kept to himself when he was here, which wasn't much."

Gates inquired about his work, his friends, his hobbies. For all of his delicate probing and handling of the matter, he came up empty-handed. Curbing his frustration as best he could, he tried another tactic.

"Mind if I take a look at your son's room?"

They both looked at one another, then simultaneously shook their heads, indicating that they didn't care. Seconds later, Gates was alone in another offensive room.

What could this young man have known that cost him his life?

He had told Juliana on the phone that he had additional information about the boating accident and Rusk, which just could not be so.

There were no secrets associated with that incident. Because of his family and their prominence, the media had created that tragedy as a feeding frenzy and delved into every aspect of it. To this day, that use and subsequent abuse of their heartbreak made him despise the media.

Rusk and his parents hadn't felt that way. Not about the media, anyway. Rusk had come out a hero for his valiant efforts to save Patrick, a feat that had catapulted his political career to new heights and put him on the road to the governor's mansion.

So if Lacy had been blowing smoke up Juliana's skirt, then what had gotten him killed? *Who had killed him?* Ignoring the tightness in his chest, Gates set about finding the answers to those questions.

He had about given up hope of finding anything when he came across the diary. It was stuffed in the back of the bottom drawer of a chest otherwise crammed with junk. A smirk touched Gates' lips as the adage jumped to mind: One man's trash, another man's treasure.

In this case, Gates was banking on the treasure. Standing in the middle of the room, he opened the diary and was about to start reading when the door opened.

Mr. and Mrs. Lacy stared at him, their eyes red and swollen from crying. Gates silently cursed his job.

"What's that?" Mrs. Lacy asked, a catch in her voice.

"Your son's diary."

"Oh," she muttered, wringing her hands.

"Do you mind if I borrow it?"

He didn't have to ask. Since it was possible evidence, he could take it without permission or explanation.

"I don't—"

"It might help us find out who killed your son," he said gently, not wanting to come on to them like gangbusters.

"Go on, take it," the old man said. "Won't do him or us no good now."

"I'll see that you get it back."

"Find out who…who…"

"I'll do my best," Gates cut in, then tipped his hat. "Meanwhile, take care."

A few minutes later, after he'd gotten out of sight of the house, he whipped his truck over to the curb and shoved it into park.

Even though evening was approaching, there remained enough light for him to see. With the air conditioner blasting on his face, Gates thumbed through the diary. Halfway through, a particular page caught his attention.

As he read it, the blood in his veins iced over.

Thirty-Five

"Hey, come on in."

Juliana forced a smile and walked into the foyer of Benson's garden home. She'd only been there a couple of times, once with Margie for a private production meeting and once when he'd had a party for the staff.

Since then, Benson had made some decorative changes, making his home appear warmer than it had before. When they were in the kitchen area, she made that comment.

"I like the changes you've made."

"I don't," he replied in a sharp tone. "In fact, I was thinking about redoing the entire house again."

Juliana's eyes widened. "Whoa, sounds like I hit a sore spot."

"You did, but that's all right."

"What did the decorator do to make you so unhappy? Charge you an arm and a leg?"

Benson averted his gaze, and when he spoke, it was in a low mumble. "It's not worth discussing. Anyway, it's too late now."

Juliana frowned. "You're not making a bit of sense. Why are you so bent out of shape about something so trivial? That's not like you. Besides, I think whoever decorated it did a bang-up job."

He didn't respond, so she switched the subject, suddenly feeling tired of it herself. Tired period.

"I'm surprised you showed up," Benson was saying, gesturing toward the couch. "But I'm glad you did. Have a seat."

"Thanks. The thought of spending the evening in my own company was awful."

Benson gave her a keen glance. "Taking the afternoon off didn't seem to work. You still look washed out."

"That's an understatement."

"What's going on, Juliana?"

"Like you, I'm just out of sorts."

"Nah, you're holding out on me."

"It's something I can't talk about right now." Juliana toyed with a strand of her hair. "Just bear with me, okay?"

"It has to do with Gates, doesn't it?"

"Please, Benson, don't ask any more questions."

"All right, you win for now. Are you hungry?"

"Sort of yes and sort of no."

"Well, why don't we just sort of eat?"

In spite of herself, Juliana smiled. "Let's go."

However, when they got into the kitchen and she smelled the chicken soup warming, her stomach revolted. Feeling weak-kneed, she sat in the nearest chair.

"Are you going to—"

Juliana shook her head, breathing deeply. "I need a minute, that's all."

"Do you have a virus?"

Rather than keep lying, she maintained her silence.

"Look, why don't we forget eating for now and go back into the living room? I'll fix you some peppermint tea, which is guaranteed to settle the old tummy."

"That sounds good," Juliana responded, her queasiness abating somewhat.

A few minutes later, Benson returned carrying two

cups. She took hers, blew on the red liquid, then took a sip. Almost immediately, she felt a sense of relief.

"I do have something to tell you," she said, staring across at him.

"Oh?"

"New York called."

He cursed.

"Hey, don't take it like that."

"Don't mind me." Benson sighed. "So when do you leave?"

"Whoa, you're putting the cart before the horse. I told Mr. Wiesman—"

"Sam Wiesman?"

"The one and only."

"If he called, then you've hit the big time."

"He didn't offer me a job, Benson. He just wants me to fly to New York to talk."

"So when do you leave?" he asked again, sounding sad but resigned.

"Not right away, even to talk." And maybe not ever, Juliana thought. She had more than herself to think about now. She had the baby, which put a different perspective on things.

"Oh?" Benson said again, perking up.

"Until Margie's killer is behind bars, I don't want to think about changing jobs."

"Anything new to report on that front?"

"Yes, something important." Benson looked stunned but waited for her to continue.

"I found the book Margie stole," Juliana added.

"And you're just now telling me?" To say the least, Benson sounded perturbed.

"I was getting around to it."

"So, go on," he urged in a calmer tone.

"After reading its contents, I know why Margie was killed."

"Obviously because she knew too much." Benson made a blunt statement of fact.

"Exactly."

"I can't believe you found the infamous book. Where was it?"

She told him.

He whistled. "*Whose* is it?"

Juliana didn't hesitate. "Rusk O'Brien's."

"Well, I'll be damned."

"It has to do with a deal he struck with Carl Mason, the contractor, who's already built several prisons." Juliana paused. "Margie was apparently sleeping with Rusk *and* Mason."

Benson looked disgusted.

"I'm betting she wanted to marry Rusk because of who he is, and that's why she took the book. It was her insurance."

"Blackmail."

"That's my guess."

"Appears our Margie was playing a dangerous game. Either Mason or O'Brien could have killed her. They both had a lot to lose if that book got into the wrong hands."

"I'm betting on Rusk," Juliana said.

"Does your ex-husband know?"

"I gave him the book," she said flatly.

"Bet that made his day."

"I didn't stick around to find out."

A tic in Benson's right cheek went into action. "Now that the book's surfaced, you won't be in any more danger."

"I'm counting on that. After all, their goons can't knock off everyone involved in Margie's game."

Before Benson could reply, the phone rang. Excusing himself, he crossed to the desk and answered it.

Juliana watched his face change yet again, this time turning a sickly gray. His wife. He was indeed going to have to leave.

"It's the home. As I predicted, she's worse."

"I'm sorry. Is there anything I can do?"

"Just don't leave. I shouldn't be long. Maybe by the time I get back, we'll both feel like having some soup."

"Maybe so."

After he left, Juliana wandered around the strange room, feeling lost and thinking she should be home. Running away from her problems was not going to help her. She had to accept the truth and face it. Gates didn't want her back in his life. She and the baby would have to go it alone. They didn't need him, anyway.

Juliana had her purse on her shoulder and was about to leave Benson a note telling him that she'd decided to go back home when her stomach heaved. She barely made it to the guest bath before she threw up.

After wiping her face with a cold cloth, she went back to the sofa and lay down. Moments later, she eyed the TV, then clicked on the remote. It didn't matter what she watched. Anything would do as long as it diverted her attention from her heartache.

At first she thought her eyes were deceiving her, that she had gone mad. She blinked several times, sat up, then peered more closely at the screen. No mistake.

"Oh, my God, no," she whispered, feeling the room spinning.

Gates' jaws were clenched so tightly he feared they might snap. Still, he kept the pressure on. He had given up trying to put a lid on his temper.

When he reached his brother's house, he wheeled into the drive and braked next to his parents' car. Too bad they had to be there, but maybe it was for the best. Sooner or later they would have to know the truth. It might as well be sooner.

Gates jerked open the door and bounded out. Not bothering to knock, he strode past the astonished housekeeper, straight into the dining room. He paused in the doorway.

All eyes swung to him.

"Why, Gates," his mother said, laying her fork down and smiling at him. "What a lovely surprise."

Gates' eyes went straight to Rusk and clung.

"Hey, bro, pull up a chair and join us," Rusk said, smiling. "The prime rib's excellent."

"That it is," Norman added, also smiling and sticking his chest out as if he was bursting with pride.

"I'll pass. I'm afraid I'd puke."

Tamara gave Gates a cold, astonished look. "I find that—"

Ignoring her, Gates crossed to Rusk, reached down, grabbed him by his tie and jerked him to his feet. "You know what? You're a sorry piece of shit!"

For a moment following his outburst, the room fell into a stunned silence.

"Listen here, Gates!" Norman thundered, shoving back his chair and rising. "I've had it with your grandstanding nonsense. This is the second time you've attacked your brother."

Gates saw him out of the corner of his eye. "Sit down, Daddy. For now, this is between Rusk and me."

"You're...you're choking me!" Rusk cried.

Gates continued to stare into his brother's bulging eyes, not easing his grip one iota. "Confession's good for the soul, or so they tell me."

"Have you lost your mind?" Tamara's voice shook with rage. "Turn him loose. This second!"

Gates gave another twist to Rusk's tie. Only when Rusk started turning blue did he let him go. Rusk fell back into the chair, where he went into a fit of coughing.

Afterward, he peered up at Gates, hate glittering in his eyes. "You'll pay for this!"

"I take it that means you're not going to come clean?"

"What are you talking about?" Opal asked in a teary voice. "You're behaving like a wild man."

Gates swung around and glared at his parents before switching his gaze back to Rusk. "Okay, we'll play it your way."

He reached into his pocket, pulled out a ratty-looking spiral notebook and dangled it in front of his brother's face.

"What…what is that?" Rusk whispered.

"Harold Lacy's diary." Gates watched Rusk's stomach muscles visibly contract before hammering on. "That name ring any bells?"

"Damn you to hell, Gates!"

"Shut up and listen." Gates began reading from the tattered pages.

I played hooky today. Man, what a day it was, too. I didn't catch no fish, but it was still exciting. While I was snacking on my crackers, a boat came flying around the corner. I didn't think nothin' about that until it slammed into a stump.

Bam! You could hear the noise for miles, only there wasn't no one around but me or at least I didn't see no one. A kid flew out of the back seat of that boat and landed in the water.

There was two men with him. The driver finally

jumped in to rescue the kid. First though, he did something real weird.

He pulled the guy sittin' in the passenger seat under the wheel of the boat. By the time he got to the kid, it was done too late. Even from where I sat, I knew the boy was a goner.

Too bad. But watching that was sure better than sittin' in some boring math class.

When Gates finished, a pin could have dropped on the plush carpet and everyone in the room would have heard it.

Then, without taking his eyes off Gates, Rusk scrambled out of the chair, falling to his knees in front of his brother.

"Oh, God, Gates, I'm so sorry," he sobbed, tears flooding his cheeks. "I didn't want to do it."

Gates' lips twisted in a snarl. "Get up!"

"I had to do it. Don't you see?" Rusk blubbered, struggling upright before continuing in a frantic tone. "I'd been drinking, and if I'd been caught driving the boat, my political career would have been over."

"Now, let me get this straight," Gates said in a tone that was so low it was barely audible. "All these years, you've let me think I was responsible for my son's death in order to save your political ass!"

"I had no choice," Rusk wailed, dropping to his knees again, then crawling toward Gates' feet.

Gates kicked him in the face. "Get away from me!"

Thirty-Six

"Stop it!" Norman said, his booming voice shaking. "Both of you!"

Opal stood and went to Rusk, who was still on the floor. As she placed a hand on his shoulder, her eyes darted from one son to the other. "Your father's right. Please, for God's sake, let's be civilized."

Gates' features contorted. "Civilized! Is that all that matters to you?"

"Don't you talk to your mother in that tone," Norman put in, charging from his spot at the head of the table and positioning himself on the other side of Rusk.

Gates almost choked on the anger that for a moment seemed to have a lock on his throat.

"It's all right, Norman," Opal said, staring at Gates. "This is a terrible blow, and I know how you must be feeling, but—"

"But what, Mother?" Scorn punctuated Gates' words. "Are you excusing Rusk, saying what he did was right?"

"Of course not!" High color settled in Opal's cheeks. "But we're a family. We can work this out if we stick together."

"Even if there's a Judas among us?"

Her color deepened. "Rusk was...drinking. He didn't know what he was doing. He—"

"That's no excuse for what he did, Opal," Tamara

said, giving her husband a loathing look. Then, transferring her gaze to Gates, she added, "But having said that, what's done is done. There's no going back."

"She's right," Norman chimed in, his tone less unsteady than a few moments ago, as though he'd collected himself.

Gates looked at his family and fought down the urge to say "screw you," walk out and never look back. But he couldn't. That would be the easy way out. While it was indeed too late for past sins to be undone, the present and future remained a minefield.

Regardless of what Rusk and his family thought, his brother was not about to escape this "come-to-Jesus" meeting.

"So what you're all suggesting is that I should just forgive big brother for betraying me and pretend the accident never happened?"

Another profound silence followed Gates' words while the other members of the family looked at one another before their eyes settled back on him.

Opal broke that silence. "I certainly don't condone what Rusk did." She broke off and looked at her eldest son, a pained expression on her face. "It was inexcusable. But what good will it do to beat him up?" She paused again, reached over and placed her hand on Gates' arm. "Nothing you do will…bring Patrick back."

An animal-like groan sprang from deep inside Gates. Ignoring his mother and focusing on Rusk again, he reached down and jerked him up.

"Gates!" Norman bellowed. "I said, enough!"

"Stay out of this, Daddy. If you think I'm going to let Rusk get by with murdering my son and blaming it on me, think again."

"Gates, please," Rusk wheezed. "Don't do this."

"Don't do what? Don't take your head off for betraying your own flesh and blood?"

"I'm sorry, so sorry." Rusk's eyes were wild, and his cheeks were drenched with tears.

Gates wasn't moved. "Save the crocodile tears. They won't work on me."

In one quick move, he yanked Rusk closer until their noses were almost touching. Fear had turned Rusk's breath foul.

"Please," Rusk whimpered.

"Please what?" Gates taunted. "Please let you off the hook? Or better yet, please forgive you?"

Rusk's lower lip trembled as he tried to lick off the tears. "Yes!" he cried. "I...I told you I was sorry."

"And you think that's good enough for forcing me to live with a lie all these years?" Gates' voice was filled with venom. "For letting me think I was responsible for killing my own son when all the time, it was you, huh?" Gates shook him.

Rusk began sobbing.

"Shut the fuck up, you coward!"

"Gates, don't," Opal pleaded. "I beg you."

Without taking his eyes off Rusk or loosening his hold, he addressed his mother. "Beg all you want, Mother. It won't do any good."

"What do you propose to do?" Tamara asked. "Expose what he did to his constituency? It might make you feel better, but as Opal said, it won't bring Patrick back."

Gates let go of Rusk so unexpectedly and quickly that his sniveling brother lost his balance and once again landed on the floor. Then, turning, Gates glared at them. "Rusk's career, that's the bloody bottom line here, isn't it?"

"Rusk made a terrible mistake," Norman said. "We

don't condone that, but that one mistake shouldn't cost him the governor's mansion.''

In an emotional rush, Gates responded. ''God, I can't believe I'm hearing this, not from my own father, who supposedly adored his grandson.''

Norman flushed at the unmasked contempt in Gates' voice, yet he held his head high. ''Rusk will make a good governor. Somehow, I'll see that he makes it up to you.''

''I'll do whatever it takes.'' Rusk scrambled to his feet, wiping the tears off his face. ''I'll do whatever it takes, if you'll just forgive me.''

''No can do,'' Gates said, once again closing the distance between him and Rusk.

Rusk backed up, terror leaping into his eyes.

''Gates,'' Norman thundered. ''I forbid you to touch him again.''

''That's not your call.'' Gates crossed his arms over his chest and smiled. ''Actually, we're just getting started.''

''What do you mean?'' Tamara asked, fear lacing her voice.

Ignoring Tamara, Gates reached into his other pocket and pulled out another book, this one black. ''I bet you recognize this one, big brother, right?''

Rusk literally recoiled as if Gates had put a gun to his head. ''Where…where—'' He couldn't finished the sentence; his petrified voice seemed to have run out of energy.

''Where did I get this?'' Gates laughed an ugly laugh. ''Is that what you were about to ask?''

Norman stepped forward. ''What the hell's going on, now?''

''You'll find out soon enough, Dad,'' Gates said, keeping his eyes locked on Rusk. ''Why don't you do the honors, big brother?'' Gates demanded. ''This is your show. This is your meeting, up front and center stage.''

''I...don't know what you're talking about,'' Rusk whined.

Gates pitched his head back and laughed. ''Man, that's choice. That's really choice.''

''Gates...''

''Tell 'em, you sniveling bastard.''

Rusk opened his mouth, but before he could say anything, Gates raised the book and used it to slap Rusk on both cheeks.

''You're the bastard!'' Rusk cried, shuffling back from Gates.

''Gates, whose book is that?'' Opal asked in a weary tone. ''And what's in it?''

''Trust me, Rusk will explain.'' Gates faced his parents and Tamara. ''But I'll tell you this. Not only is his political career over, but his life may be, as well.''

Another stunned silence greeted his declaration.

''Because of what's in this book, which by the way belongs to Rusk here, it's a good chance he'll be charged with the murder of Margie Bowers.''

''Oh, my God,'' Opal gasped, then crumpled to the floor.

Tamara raced to her side, but not before glaring at Gates.

Rusk, looking a sickly yellow, fell into the nearest chair, lowered his head in his hands and sobbed louder than before.

Gates stared at his daddy, who suddenly seemed old and broken. ''He's all yours.''

''Then leave us alone,'' Norman said, his lusterless eyes back on Rusk.

Gates tipped his hat. ''With pleasure.''

* * *

Gates didn't know how long he stood beside his car after stumbling into the night and gulping the air into his lungs as though he were starving.

He couldn't believe the fiasco he'd just endured. Yet the feelings churning through him were bittersweet. For sure, nothing would ever bring his son back to this earth. But knowing that he wasn't directly responsible for his death might make it possible for him to stop using himself as a whipping post, to get past the tragedy and get on with his life.

Was that possible?

He hadn't thought that day would ever come. Still, he had trouble grasping that it had. Suddenly his thoughts turned to Juliana, sending an ache so intense shooting through him that his knees buckled.

He had to see her, had to tell her the news. But more than that, he had to tell her that he still loved her, that he always had and always would.

If he could indeed put the past behind him, could they perhaps start over? Would she give him another chance? Before he could test those waters, there was something else he had to do.

He had to turn over the incriminating evidence, knowing that Rusk's arrest would soon follow. Carl Mason would likely be next. Only time would tell which one had poisoned Margie Bowers.

It was with mixed emotions that Gates got into his truck and drove off.

Lovers! Benson and Margie?

Hours later, at her condo, Juliana remained in a frozen state of shock. Nothing could erase from her mind the homemade porn movie that had showed Benson and Margie abusing the lovemaking process in every conceivable way.

When she'd flicked on the remote and the sex film had filled the screen, she hadn't realized right off who the two people were, nor had she cared. She'd been merely disappointed and repulsed that Benson indulged in that kind of filth.

It was while she had scrambled to turn the TV off that she'd recognized her friends.

A few minutes of the tape had been all she could watch. She'd lunged off the sofa, grabbed her purse and dashed out the door.

Now, after having had a bath and brewing herself a cup of tea, she sat on the couch with her legs folded under her. Questions with no logical answers whirled through her brain.

Should she tell Gates? Should she…?

The doorbell rang, shutting down her thoughts. It occurred to her not to answer it, especially since it was so late. Nonetheless, she made her way toward the door, her heart laboring inside her chest. Her visitor was more than likely Gates or Benson, neither one of whom she wanted to see.

Pausing at the door, she asked, "Who is it?"

"Benson."

"It's late. I'm about to go to bed."

"Let me in, please. We need to talk."

"We can talk tomorrow."

"Please. What I have to say can't wait."

I just bet it can't. She heard the pleading note in his voice, and a mind-war pitted their good friendship against her sound judgment.

"I can explain, if only you'll let me."

If only she hadn't left the TV blaring, but in her haste to get away, she'd done just that. "Benson…"

"I promise I won't stay but a minute."

Any explanation she was interested in would take more than a minute after what she'd seen, but she didn't tell him that. But then, who was she to set herself up as judge and jury over his sexual behavior? She didn't care.

Still, Margie *had* been murdered, and no one had been charged. God, she couldn't believe her mind had veered in that direction. Rusk O'Brien had killed her friend. She had no doubt about that.

"Juliana!"

She opened the door, then stepped aside for him to walk past her. Once she closed the door, she followed him into the living room. "You don't owe me an explanation, you know."

"Yes, I do."

She remained silent, tightening the sash on her robe.

"I'm sorry you saw that tape."

"I'm sorry, too," she said in an embarrassed tone.

"Margie had this thing about sex," he said, shifting his gaze.

Juliana felt queasy again, then spoke before she thought. "How…how could you, the two of you, do those things? I mean—" She couldn't go on. The entire conversation, the entire scenario, was too disgusting.

"I loved Margie."

Juliana gasped. "*You* loved Margie?"

"I wanted to marry her. In fact, she promised she'd marry me. Only—" Benson broke off.

"Only what?" Juliana pressed, then wished she hadn't. Something about him had changed so suddenly that she was barely aware of it. But the change was there, nonetheless. A strange light appeared in his eyes.

"Only I was just her sexual toy." He laughed, a harsh, bitter laugh.

Juliana felt a pinch of uneasiness. "Look, Benson, if it's all the same to you, I'd rather not hear about your and Margie's sex life. I've already *seen* enough to last a lifetime."

"Yeah, the bitch refused to marry me," he said as if she hadn't spoken, a feverish quality in his voice. "She was hell-bent on marrying Rusk O'Brien."

Juliana choked. "Rusk marry Margie? Surely she didn't think—"

"Oh, but she did. The bitch actually thought he would leave his wife and marry her. Ain't that some shit?"

Without answering him, Juliana inched back toward the door. He followed her, step by step, staring at her, but not seeing her, she knew. His eyes were too glazed-over.

"Go home, Benson."

"I warned her. I sure did." He snickered, looking maniacal. "But she wouldn't listen to me. That's when I knew I had to do something."

Juliana pulled up short, an alarm clanging loud and clear inside her head. "It was you," she whispered. "*You* killed Margie!"

Thirty-Seven

"It was all Margie's fault."

The light in Benson's eyes had brightened, making him appear more insane than ever.

"Benson, you—"

Again he interrupted, continuing his babbling. "She made me do it, you know. I didn't want to hurt her, just like I don't want to hurt you."

Terror suddenly paralyzed Juliana's limbs. Yet her mind was clicking. How could she have been so blind when it came to Benson? How could she have missed this side of him? In defense of herself, how could she have known?

It was as though he had suddenly been possessed by a demon or developed a Dr. Jekyll and Mr. Hyde personality. Had there been signs? Had she been so wrapped up in her own problems and miseries that she'd missed them? But even if she had been aware that something was awry in his personality, would she have recognized this crazed instability?

No.

Benson had been her friend and her boss, but they hadn't been bosom buddies. And to know another's deepest and most intimate thoughts, one had to be just that.

"You've been my friend," Benson said, jolting her

back to the moment at hand. "I really do hate to hurt you."

"Then...don't."

"You've left me no choice."

"We can work this out."

"It's too late for that."

Just so it wasn't too late for her. She *had* to get to a door. The front one was locked, but not bolted. The French door, however, was not locked, which would give her a chance to open it and run like hell—if she could ever reach it. At the moment that looked doubtful.

"You really shouldn't have turned on the TV. I never intended for you to see that video."

Oh, God, she wished she hadn't seen it, either. But it was too late to backtrack. She had to get out of this harrowing situation with her life and that of her baby.

Another shiver of fear coursed through her. *Her baby.* She couldn't lose this child. She would do whatever it took to protect them both.

"As your friend, I can help you."

"Help me? It's too late for that, my dear. As long as you thought Rusk was the killer, then everything was fine."

Gates had tried to tell her that Rusk wasn't the killer, but she hadn't believed him. Another mistake.

If only Gates were here. He would know what to do. But he wasn't here. He didn't want her anymore. She couldn't count on him. She had to count on herself, which meant she had to keep Benson talking until she could make her move.

But only a coffee table separated them.

"Rusk certainly turned out to be your saving grace, didn't he?" she asked, trying to keep his mind occupied and her desperation at bay.

Benson smiled again. "Yup. But I have Margie to thank for that."

"You're right. If she hadn't stolen that book, which threw suspicion on Rusk, then your real relationship with her might have come to light."

"Absolutely."

He sounded so rational, so much like the old Benson, who she'd always thought was so sweet, so low-key, so together, that she couldn't believe he was a cold-blooded killer. But he was. Juliana shuddered with renewed fear.

As if he could read her mind, Benson made a diabolical effort to console her. "Don't worry. Because you're my friend, I'll make sure you don't suffer."

"Don't do this, Benson," Juliana pleaded, licking her lips again, struggling to fight off her burgeoning panic.

"You've left me no choice."

"No. There are always choices. Don't you see?"

He gave her that sick smile again, then reached in his pocket and pulled out a large pocketknife.

"No, Benson, no!" Juliana cried, all the while shaking her head.

He moved to one side of the table. She moved to the other. A cat toying with a mouse, she thought, hysterics building inside her.

"You won't get away with this."

"We'll see."

Without taking his eyes off her, Benson flipped out the blade.

Gates pulled up in front of Juliana's house, but he didn't get out of the truck. He noticed a car parked just beyond her drive. Did she have company? Nah. If so, whoever it was would have parked in her driveway proper.

Yet something about the vehicle looked familiar. Then, brushing that thought aside as a lawman's nosy nature, Gates slumped down in the seat, shoving back his Stetson. A sudden numbness seemed to have invaded his system and robbed him of the ability to function.

Good. He need to calm down. He couldn't go in there half-cocked. He had to think, to organize his thoughts. He would have no interruptions, that was for sure. The neighborhood was as quiet as a mausoleum. Probably because it was too damn hot to do anything except stay inside under the air-conditioning.

Sultry.

That was the word that came to mind as he pushed the automatic-window buttons, hoping to get a cross breeze. None was forthcoming. By the time he got up the gumption to go inside, he would be sweating like a man with a gun pointed at his crotch. Nervous sweat. Not only did he have to tell her the truth about the accident, but he had to confess he'd never stopped loving her. If she threw that love back in his face, he wouldn't blame her.

Still, he had to try. The thought of her disappearing from his life a second time was no longer an option. But he wouldn't blame her if she refused to listen and told him to take a permanent hike.

After all, he was the one who had fucked up.

He thought of just how much he had to tell her, though he didn't relish repeating what he'd been through with his brother and his family. That fiasco was only the beginning of a long siege of nightmares.

Once he'd left Rusk's house, he'd called Ferguson on his cell phone and they had met. When Ferguson had seen his grim face, he'd said, "You look like shit."

"Shit's good compared to what I feel."

"That bad."

"Worse."

"Lay it on me."

Gates tossed the black spiral book and the diary on Ferguson's desk. While the older man perused their contents, Gates fell into the nearest chair and stared at the ceiling.

Ferguson cursed, drawing Gates' eyes back on him. Even then, neither one said a word.

"This is a bit much to digest at one time," Ferguson commented at last, his thin face as grim as Gates'

"You got that right."

"At least you know the truth about the accident that killed your son."

"Too bad that truth won't bring him back."

Silence.

"I'm sorry about your brother."

"Not half as sorry as I am."

"You think he…he killed the Bowers woman and Harold Lacy to keep them quiet?"

"That's a good possibility. As you can see from those books, he'll stop at nothing to get what he wants."

"What about Carl Mason? What's your gut telling you about him?"

"Hell, they both had a lot to lose. As a murder suspect, I'd say Mason's running neck and neck with my brother."

"We'll bring 'em both in and see how things shake down."

Gates stood, his eyes hard. "That's my recommendation."

"I'll call Bishop." Ferguson paused. "You okay with this?"

"I have to be."

"You want to make the arrests?"

"Thanks, Cap, but no thanks. If I had to look at either

of those sons of bitches right now, I'd be tempted to save the taxpayers the expense of a long trial.''

God help him, he'd meant that.

Now, shoving that conversation aside and forcing his attention back to the matter at hand, Gates peered at Juliana's house, then opened the truck's door.

He might as well stop procrastinating. He needed to hold Juliana more than he'd needed anything in a long time. But there were no guarantees that would happen. He would simply take his best shot. The rest was up to fate.

Still, when he reached the porch, he froze. He couldn't even push the friggin' doorbell. There was so much at stake, and he didn't want to blow it.

A harsh breath kicked out of his lungs as he put his finger on the bell. That was when he heard the god-awful noise. Gates tensed, unable to identify the sound *or* the voice that followed the noise. But it was a man who had spoken, a voice he recognized, yet didn't.

What the hell was going on?

His internal radar took over. Something was wrong. "Juliana?"

Silence answered his call.

"Hey, I know you're in there." Gates yanked on the doorknob; it was locked. "Please, let me in. I have to talk to you."

Silence.

"Shit!" Gates muttered, a badass feeling washing through him. Drawing his gun, he darted around the side of the house. He stopped at the nearest window, praying that he would be able to see inside. Luck was with him; the blind was open.

He peered inside and took in the scene playing out before him. The big, round coffee table in the living room was turned on end, its contents on the floor, which had accounted for the loud noise.

However, it wasn't the piece of furniture that made every nerve in Gates' body jump to attention, but rather Juliana cringing against the wall while a man inched toward her.

At first Gates didn't recognize the man, then it hit him.

Benson Garner. Juliana's boss and friend. But he wasn't in a friendly mood now, Gates noted, not with that knife in his hand and that crazed expression on his face.

What the hell?

The answer to that question didn't matter. What mattered was getting this lunatic away from Juliana before he used that knife.

Without further hesitation, Gates bent over, then ran to the back. He tiptoed onto the deck just as Benson raised the knife, poised to strike.

With the strength of a madman, Gates jerked open the door. "Freeze, you bastard!"

His unexpected appearance stunned Garner, all right; the lethal weapon flew from his hand. But before Gates could get control of the situation, Benson grabbed Juliana with a hammerlock across her throat.

"Gates." His name came out a squeak.

Benson hissed, "Shut up!"

"Let her go, Garner." Gates held the gun steady, aimed at the middle of Benson's forehead. "Whatever's going on here, we can talk about it. No one needs to get hurt."

"I'm through talking," Benson spat. "Go away."

Gates shook his head. "I can't do that, Garner."

"I'm calling the shots here, not you!" Benson's voice shook.

Gates' gaze shifted briefly to Juliana. Tears now clung

to her thick lashes. But he saw something else mirrored in those lovely eyes: trust.

If this scumbag so much as put a scratch on her, Garner was another one who wouldn't ever make it to trial. He would kill the bastard on the spot with his bare hands. But now he had to ignore his emotions and think with a clear head.

"What's going on here?" Gates asked, buying time. "I thought Juliana was your friend."

"She...she was. She is."

"Then why are you doing this to her?"

Before Benson could answer, Juliana whispered, "He...he killed Margie."

Benson tightened his grip on her. "I told you to shut up."

Juliana's words not only stunned Gates but chilled him to the bone. If what Juliana said was true, then Benson didn't have anything to lose.

"If you don't leave, I'm going to break her neck," Benson declared. "One quick jerk is all it'll take."

"I don't believe you really want to hurt Juliana," Gates said in a low, unhurried tone while he eased forward.

"Stop!" Benson yelled.

Gates stopped and stared at Juliana. He knew exactly what was going through her mind—the same thing going through his. Benson had gone around the bend. He was becoming more unpredictable and lethal by the minute.

"Juliana, are you all right?" Gates asked.

"I told you—"

Benson didn't get any further. Juliana suddenly gasped, then went limp, her head dangling forward.

"What—"

Again Benson's sentence was cut off, this time by

Gates. In the split second that was his, he lifted his gun, aimed and pulled the trigger.

Juliana screamed and fell to the floor.

Thirty-Eight

He hadn't expected to find her there. He didn't know why he was so surprised. For all he knew, she came here often.

In the years since Patrick had died, he'd visited his grave all of two times—the day of Margie's funeral and today. He'd never felt he had a right to be anywhere near his son, even in the grave.

Shame had kept him away; it had become a scabbed-over sore inside him, and every time he thought of Patrick, it would knock that scab off and new poison would flood through him.

Now, however, a week after the terrible showdown at Juliana's, Gates felt he had the right to grieve. No more hammering himself with old pains and regrets.

Oh, he would never get over the loss of his child, and to some extent he would also always feel responsible, but at least he wasn't the murderer he'd secretly labeled himself.

As he watched Juliana, his fingers tightened on the stems of the spring flowers he held in his hand. She was dressed in shorts and a tank top that showed off her breasts to their utmost perfection. Her tanned, slender legs were partially curved under her buttocks as she sat at the foot of the grave.

The gentle breeze teased her hair.

While desire certainly swept through him, his feelings ran much deeper than that. He wanted ownership of her soul once again. To counteract that ache, he closed his weary eyes.

When he reopened them, his attention settled on her face.

She had been crying. Her face bore the ravages of anguish. But there was tenderness there, as well. She had always told him she held no bitterness toward God or him for the loss of her child, though she would miss Patrick until the day she died.

He knew in that moment, despite the sadness permanently etched in her features, that she had meant what she said. If only he'd known the truth when Patrick died. He groaned inwardly at all the wasted years. If only...

No. He wouldn't go down that road, not ever again. It was a dead end, anyway.

The scent of the roses in the bouquet teased his nose. He breathed deeply, but continued to stand and watch. Should he leave? Should he come back another time to make his peace with his son?

He hated to intrude on Juliana, though he yearned to share his thoughts with her. Good thoughts, the kind he hadn't known in years. They were crowded together in his brain, just waiting to spill from his lips.

Before, they had each grieved alone, which was his fault. He'd rejected her efforts to comfort him and in doing so had refused to comfort her. Now, the need to do just that was like a painful throb inside him. He hadn't seen her for several days, not since that night he'd shot Benson Garner.

Seemingly within minutes after she'd crumpled to the floor, the cops were called and the place surrounded. He had remained with her throughout the ordeal, cradling her trembling body until the doctor had come and given her something to counteract the shock. Even then, he hadn't left. Till daybreak, they had clung together in darkness and their common pain.

The following morning, when she'd rallied somewhat, he had wanted to tell her that he loved her, that he was sorry for everything, then tell her about the diary. But his instincts told him the timing was off. She was too vulnerable, too shaky. What she needed was time alone, time to mend.

After all, another maniac had tried to kill her.

"If I leave, will you be all right?" he had asked, his voice raspy and filled with uncertainty.

"I'll...be fine."

"Juliana..."

"Not now, Gates, please," she had whispered. "I need some space."

He'd nodded. "All right. I'll...talk to you later."

Although her eyes had followed him to the door, she hadn't tried to stop him, much to his heartbreak.

Even though the heat index was nearly a hundred, Gates felt cold. What if he had waited too long to try to make amends? What if she had no feelings left for him? What if he'd already killed them?

He knew he still had the power to take her to sexual heights, but he wanted more. The thought of a final rejection was more than he could handle, especially here at the cemetery.

Maybe he would see her later, at her house. Panicked, he turned. That was when he heard her voice.

"Gates."

He turned and held her gaze while she scrambled to her feet. They stared at one another, tongue-tied, like strangers meeting for the first time, as though they didn't know what to say.

Gates cleared his throat. "I...was about to leave."

"I figured as much."

There was no bitterness in her tone, only a note of resignation.

"I didn't want to intrude."

"I wouldn't have minded."

He closed the distance between them, stopping just short of touching her. Her eyes dropped to the flowers, then moved back up.

"They're lovely," she whispered.

Unable to respond, he nodded, then knelt and placed the bouquet on the grave. Fighting off the raw, aching need that filled him, he stood and clenched his empty fists at his sides. "How are you doing?" Even to his own ears, his voice sounded strained.

"Pretty okay, considering."

"I was worried about you." Again that strain on his vocal cords. God, he wanted to hold her and cushion her sorrow with his own. But she was so standoffish, so suddenly unapproachable.

He'd blown it, he told himself. He didn't have a snowball's chance in hell of patching things up between them.

"I had a lot to think about," she said.

He tried to downplay his sudden burst of hope. But as long as she hadn't told him to go away, he still had a chance, still had one foot on the bottom rung of the confession ladder. Too bad it was such a long climb to the top.

"Are you all right?" she asked at length, an odd note in her voice.

"I've been better."

"That's understandable. We've both been through the wringer and back."

He smiled. "Is that your way of saying we've earned the right to teeter on the edge?"

She smiled in return, which made him catch his breath. "Maybe I am. Only you'll never do that. You've got nerves of steel."

"Yeah, right." Too bad she couldn't see his insides; they were a mass of putty.

Another awkward silence ensued, during which Gates was aware of the grave beside them, which would link them—or separate them—forever.

He wouldn't allow the latter to happen. In reality, this unplanned meeting was a godsend. He wouldn't let the opportunity slip through his fingers. He would say those words that begged to be said. Perfect words. The kind that were the hardest.

"I'm sorry about…Rusk," she said.

She took him by surprise. "Are you?" he asked in a low, shaky tone.

"Yes. He's to be pitied."

"Pity's the last thing I feel for him."

"I've spoken to Detective Bishop briefly."

"I figured he'd keep you informed."

"So far he's told me very little. I'm assuming Rusk is out of jail on bail."

"No, he isn't, and neither is Mason."

"Have you and Bishop made it all the way to the bottom of that sordid mess?"

"We're working on it."

"Do you know who attacked me?"

"Rusk hired a detective to get the book back, telling him to do whatever it took."

"God, Gates."

"I know."

"What about Harold Lacy? Who...killed him?"

"Like Rusk, Mason hired some lackey to do *his* dirty work, as well."

Gates figured she would ask for more details, and when she didn't, he was glad. He planned to share what he knew with her, only the timing wasn't right.

"Are you aware that Benson's going to pull through?"

"That's what I heard," Juliana said in a faraway voice. "He's also to be pitied."

"That son of a bitch is lucky to be alive."

"It's a miracle you didn't kill him."

"It's no miracle." Gates could feel his rage recharging. "If I'd wanted the son of a bitch dead, he would have been."

She shivered, as though she could feel that rage.

"Juliana..."

She looked up at him, and for a moment he couldn't say anything personal. Like a lovesick idiot, he stood there, drowning in her deep brown eyes, shadowed by that ever-present sadness.

"I'm thinking about looking for a job in New York."

He tried not to react physically to her words. But they hit him like a blow below the belt. He almost bent double. "So is a move to New York a done deal?"

"No."

"I see."

She stared at him for a long minute, then asked, "Why are you here, Gates, at...Patrick's grave? It's not something you do on a regular basis, I know."

"Actually, this is only the second time I've been here."

Juliana turned and faced the headstone, her eyes focusing on the picture. "I come here when I need to sort through things."

"That pretty much sums up why I'm here."

She swung back around. "Oh?"

"I have a lot I want to say, but first you need to see this."

He handed her the diary. She took it, but with a confused look on her face. "What's this?"

"Can we sit down?"

She barely hesitated. "All right."

They sat on the grass, facing one another. "Read the pages I've marked."

Following a sigh, Juliana lowered her head. A few minutes later, she looked back up at him, her face tissue-paper white. "What kind of monster would do a thing like that? I—" She seemed to struggle for more words, words she couldn't find.

"Someone who's so damn ambitious that he loses his soul in the bargain."

"Do your parents know?"

"They know, and so will everyone else. This is one time Rusk has fallen in shit and won't get up smelling like a rose."

"How could he have done such a thing to you? To me?"

"Because he's a sorry piece of shit, like I told him." He paused. "But I don't want to talk about Rusk anymore, at least, not right now."

"What do you want to talk about?"

"Us."

"Gates…"

"Please, hear me out, okay?"

She nodded.

"I love you, Juliana."

A flush bathed her cheeks. "You…you love me?"

"I never stopped."

"Even after you thought I'd...slept with your best friend?"

His green eyes went dark with unbearable pain. "I knew better. But at the time I wanted to believe it, thinking it would appease some of my own guilt."

"Only it backfired," Juliana said without rancor.

"In the worst possible way. When you left, I wanted to die."

"Oh, Gates."

"Even before I read the diary," he went on in a strangled voice, "I knew I still loved you and wanted you back. But you know why I couldn't tell you that." He paused and looked at Patrick's grave.

"I don't know what to say."

Gates' heart was cracking. "The truth. That's all I'm asking. That's all I can expect."

Juliana reached up and captured his face in her hands. For the longest time they were silent while the tears that were gathered on his lashes turned loose.

"Oh, my darling," she whispered, tears streaming down her face, as well.

"Hey, don't cry. It's okay if you no longer love me. It's okay for you to go to New York. I'm glad for you. Hell, you'll give them all a run for their money and then some."

"You still don't get it, do you?"

"I guess I don't."

"I've never stopped loving you, either, you big jerk."

Before Gates could respond, she took his hand and placed it on her stomach, then smiled, the loveliest smile he'd ever seen.

"What...what are you saying?" he stammered.

"You know."

"Are you...?"

"Yes. Yes!"

He grabbed her then and held her, his body shaking and his breathing hard. Then he began to sob.

Her tears mingled with his.

After a moment she pulled back and gently wiped his tears. "I'm going to have a baby. *Our* baby."

Epilogue

Sunlight filtered through the blinds. Juliana blinked, stretched, then frowned. Her body felt like one big ouch. It also felt different in another way. Would today be the day she had their child? Feeling her heart race, she turned toward Gates, who was still asleep.

Her husband.

Juliana smiled a contented smile, still unable to believe they had reconciled and were actually living together as man and wife. Again.

Even more unbelievable was that she would soon have their *son*. She hadn't wanted to know the sex of the baby, but Gates had, insisting it was a girl and insisting that was what he wanted. Juliana didn't doubt him for a moment. A girl was what they both wanted.

But a girl wasn't what they were getting. When the doctor had done the sonogram, leaving no doubt as to the sex, they were both stunned.

The doctor, having noticed their expression, chuckled. "Sorry, you're stuck with the little fellow, folks. This is one item you can't exchange for something else."

Gates' lips twitched, and he'd said, "You're right, Doc. And I wouldn't if I could. Another boy's just fine with me. This time we'll—" He stopped and looked away.

Juliana reached over and squeezed his thigh, tears well-ing up in her eyes. "Love him as much as we loved Patrick."

He swallowed, then nodded.

Now, recalling that scene in the doctor's office, Juliana felt a lump rise in her throat. But she wouldn't cry, not today, not ever again, except maybe from pure happiness.

In fact, she hadn't thought it was possible to be this happy. During the nearly nine months they had been married, she was certain she'd been given a glimpse into heaven, even though they had been through some tough times as well as some great ones. But they were together, and *sharing,* which made it all okay.

Deciding he'd slept long enough, even though this was his day off, she snuggled closer to his side and dipped her tongue in his ear.

He groaned but didn't open his eyes.

"Wake up, sleepyhead," she whispered, outlining his entire ear.

Suddenly he rolled over and pinned her on her back, gazing deeply into her lovely eyes. "Uh-huh, now look who's in the compromising position."

Juliana grinned. "I'm not complaining."

"I am. Thanks to him, my erection's the size of your belly."

Her eyes went to her swollen stomach, then back up to meet his. "In your dreams," she quipped.

"You'll pay for that, woman!"

They both laughed; then Gates turned serious, his voice becoming anxious. "Are you okay?"

She caressed the dark stubble on one side of his cheek. "Uncomfortable is what I am, but that comes with the territory."

"I don't remember your tummy sticking out this much with Patrick."

Though there was a somber note in his voice, he no longer stumbled over Patrick's name. They had even pulled his baby pictures out not long after they remarried. By the time they had finished going through them, they were laughing and crying from so many precious memories.

"Actually, I didn't get this big with him."

"Why not?"

"Age, darling."

He snorted. "It's because you're still working like a field hand."

She pinched him on the chest. "So are you. And speaking of work, don't forget we still have to celebrate your promotion."

Three weeks ago, following Ferguson's official retirement, Gates had achieved his goal; he'd made captain of the Texas Rangers.

"Don't count on it anytime soon, sweetheart, not with all the work I have on my desk."

"Do you think you'll ever see the end of the prison investigation?" When she mentioned that subject, it never failed to send her heart to her toes and bring to mind the family tragedy that stemmed from that scandal.

"Not as long as contractors like Carl Mason and his cronies, who'll do anything for money and power, stay in business."

"I still can't believe Mason hired someone to kill Harold Lacy just so Rusk would remain in the clear and get elected."

"That's how those guys work. If Lacy had exposed Rusk on national TV, he would have gotten drummed in the polls. No way was Mason going to let that happen. He was determined that my brother was going to be his yes-man."

"If it hadn't been for you fitting all the pieces of this bizarre puzzle together, they might have pulled it off."

"But they didn't. Actually, Margie was the one who put the stopper in the bottle by stealing Rusk's book with all that incriminating evidence against them both."

"Only to have a jealous lover poison her to death." Juliana shook her head. "Unbelievable."

"More unbelievable is that he tried to kill you. When I think of that day, I wish I had shot the bastard to death."

"No, you don't."

Gates grinned. "You're right, especially since he's in a padded cell in the same institution as his wife." Gates' grin widened. "That's poetic justice, if ever there was any."

"Do you think Rusk will serve time?"

"No, especially since he's turning state's evidence against Mason and his partners. Of course, Mason's facing an accessory-to-murder charge."

Juliana was quiet for a time before saying, "I don't think your parents will ever get over all this."

"Maybe another grandson will help dilute the pain." He paused. "You still don't have any problems with that? I mean—"

"Of course I want them to share our baby. Now that know you love me, I can forgive. Your mother wants to come and help after the baby comes."

Gates lifted his eyebrows. "What did you tell her?"

"Yes. But I'll have to admit it'll take time for *all* th wounds to heal."

"On everyone's part," Gates added. "They've alway been partial to Rusk, and I know that. But that's the problem to deal with, not mine. As long as I have you, don't need anyone else." He paused. "Even if you decid to go to New York."

Juliana was stunned. "New York? What on earth possessed you to mention that?"

"I don't want you to think you have to give up your dream because of me."

"Hey, for a smart man, you can be kind of dense."

"Oh, really?"

She grinned. "Really. I'll admit that at one time going to New York and competing with the biggies was my only goal. But once you told me you still loved me, my priorities changed. I'm perfectly content to stay syndicated and concentrate on blowing away my competition there.

"Another thing that changed me was staring death in the face." Juliana shuddered. "That tends to make you look at things differently."

"I know about that."

Her eyes shadowed. "Speaking of death, promise me you'll be careful."

He kissed her then, long and hard, and his hand roamed her burgeoning stomach.

"Are you crazy? I wouldn't do anything to jeopardize my second chance with you. Not many people are so blessed."

She trapped his hands against her hard belly. "And we're doubly blessed. We're getting another baby."

He stared at her with his heart in his eyes. Then he asked, "Speaking of our baby, if we hadn't accidentally met at the cemetery that day, would you have told me about him?"

He didn't bother to mask the pain. It was in his face and in his voice. "Yes," she said in a whisper. "Even though you had hurt me by rejecting me again, eventually I would have had to tell you, even though I was scared."

He kissed her again and only pulled back when she

started to struggle. "What's wrong?" he asked. "Did I hurt you?"

Juliana managed a smile through her grimace. "My water just broke."

He leapt off the bed, then stared down at her. "Oh, my God! I love you. I love you. I love you!"

She laughed, then said calmly, "That's wonderful, and I love you, too. But right now I think we should be on our way to the hospital. Your son is about to make his grand entrance."

Take 3 of "The Best of the Best™" Novels FREE
Plus get a FREE surprise gift!

Special Limited-time Offer

Mail to The Best of the Best™

3010 Walden Avenue
P.O. Box 1867
Buffalo, N.Y. 14240-1867

YES! Please send me 3 free novels and my free surprise gift. Then send me 3 of "The Best of the Best™" novels each month. I'll receive the best books by the world's hottest romance authors. Bill me at the low price of $3.99 each plus 25¢ delivery per book and applicable sales tax, if any.* That's the complete price and a savings of over 20% off the cover prices—quite a bargain! I understand that accepting the books and gift places me under no obligation ever to buy any books. I can always return a shipment and cancel at any time. Even if I never buy another book, the 3 free books and the surprise gift are mine to keep forever.

183 BPA A4V9

Name	(PLEASE PRINT)	
Address	Apt. No.	
City	State	Zip

This offer is limited to one order per household and not valid to current subscribers.
*Terms and prices are subject to change without notice. Sales tax applicable in N.Y.
All orders subject to approval.

UBOB-197

©1996 MIRA BOOKS

They called her the

Champagne Girl

Catherine: Underneath the effervescent, carefree and bubbly facade there was a depth to which few had access.

Matt: The older stepbrother she inherited with her mother's second marriage, Matt continually complicated things. It seemed to Catherine that she would make plans only to have Matt foul them up.

With the perfect job waiting in New York City, only one thing would be able to keep her on a dusty cattle ranch: something she thought she could never have—the love of the sexiest cowboy in the Lone Star state.

by bestselling author

DIANA PALMER

Available in September 1997 at your favorite retail outlet.

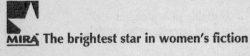

She was innocent...of everything but love

PRESUMED GUILTY

Someone was sleeping in Miranda Wood's bed. But he wasn't really sleeping—he was dead. There was no one who would believe she hadn't murdered her former lover, least of all the dead man's brother. But Chase Tremain couldn't help but fall for her—even when it was clear that someone wanted to keep them apart...forever.

TESS GERRITSEN

Available October 1997 at your favorite retail outlet.

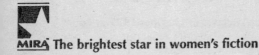

MIRA The brightest star in women's fiction   MTG2

Look us up on-line at: http://www.romance.net

The SECRETS WITHIN

The most unforgettable Australian saga since Colleen McCullough's *The Thorn Birds*

Eleanor—with invincible strength and ruthless determination she built Australia's Hunter Valley vineyards into an empire.

Tamara—the unloved child of ambition, a catalyst in a plan to destroy her own mother.

Rory—driven by shattered illusions and desires, he becomes a willing conspirator.

Louise—married to Rory, she will bargain with the devil for a chance at ultimate power.

Irene—dark and deadly, she turns fanatical dreams into reality.

Now Eleanor is dying, and in one final, vengeful act she wages a war on a battlefield she created— and with a family she was driven to control....

EMMA DARCY

Available in October 1997 at your favorite retail outlet.